SMALL TOWN *Harmony*

MILLA HOLT

Published by Reinbok Limited, 111 Wolsey Drive, Kingston Upon Thames, Greater London, KT2 5DR

Publisher's Note: This is a work of fiction. Names, characters, places, and incidents are a product of the author's imagination. Locales and public names are sometimes used for atmospheric purposes. Any resemblance to actual people, living or dead, or to businesses, companies, events, institutions, or locales is completely coincidental.

Cover by Willette Cruz

Editing by Sara Turnquist

Small Town Harmony / Milla Holt. -- 1st ed.

ISBN 978-1-913416-28-7 Print ISBN 978-1-913416-29-4

Small Town Harmony

**A WHOLESOME CHRISTIAN ROMANCE
RHAPSODY OF GRACE BOOK 2**

Milla Holt

REINBOK LIMITED
United Kingdom

Welcome to the Mosaic Collection

WE ARE SISTERS, A beautiful mosaic united by the love of God through the blood of Christ.

Each month The Mosaic Collection releases one or more faith-based novels or anthologies exploring our theme, Family by His Design, and sharing stories that feature diverse, God-designed families. Stories range from mystery and women's fiction to comedic and literary fiction. We hope you'll join our Mosaic family as we explore together what truly defines a family.

If you're like us, loneliness and suffering have touched your life in ways you never imagined; but Dear One, while you may feel alone in your suffering—whatever it is—you are never alone!

Learn more about The Mosaic Collection at

www.mosaiccollectionbooks.com

Join our Reader Community, too!

www.facebook.com/groups/TheMosaicCollection

Mosaic Collection Books

MID-YEAR ANTHOLOGIES
Before Summer's End: Stories to Touch the Soul
Song of Grace: Stories to Amaze the Soul
All Things New: Stories to Refresh the Soul
Dancing in the Rain: Stories to Shelter the Soul
Sounds Like a Plan: Stories of Change and the God
Who Doesn't

CHRISTMAS ANTHOLOGIES
Hope is Born
A Star Will Rise
The Heart of Christmas
A Whisper of Peace
A Thrill in the Air
A Weary World Rejoices

JOHNNIE ALEXANDER
The Mischief Thief (Rose & Thorne #1)
When Memory Whispers (Echoes of War #2)

BRENDA S. ANDERSON
A Beautiful Mess
Pieces of Granite (Coming Home Series Prequel)
Broken Together (written with Sarah S. Anderson)
Chain of Mercy (Coming Home #1)

ELEANOR BERTIN
Unbound (The Ties that Bind #1)
Tethered (The Ties that Bind #2)
Lifelines (The Ties that Bind #3)
Flame of Mercy (Burning Bright #1)
Flicker of Trust (Burning Bright #2)

SARA DAVISON
Lost Down Deep (The Rose Tattoo Trilogy #1)
Written in Ink (The Rose Tattoo Trilogy #2)
Every Star in the Sky (two sparrows for a penny #1)
Every Flower of the Field (two sparrows for a penny #2)
The Color of Sky and Stone (In the Shadows #1)

JANICE L. DICK
The Road to Happenstance (Happenstance Chronicles #1)
Crazy About Maisie (Happenstance Chronicles #2)
Calm Before the Storm (The Storm Series #1)
Eye of the Storm (The Storm Series #2)
Out of the Storm (The Storm Series #3)

DEB ELKINK
The Red Journal
The Third Grace
Vagabond Come Home

CHAUTONA HAVIG
Spines & Leaves (Bookstrings introduction)
Hart of Noel (Bookstrings "Noella")
Twice Sold Tales (Bookstrings #1)
Clock Tower Bound (Bookstrings #2)

MILLA HOLT
Into the Flood (Seasons of Faith # 1)
Through the Blaze (Seasons of Faith # 2)
Within the Storm (Seasons of Faith # 3)
Amid the Ashes (Seasons of Faith # 4)
After the Frost (Seasons of Faith # 5)
Home Town Melody (Rhapsody of Grace #1)
Small Town Harmony (Rhapsody of Grace #2)

ANGELA D. MEYER
This Side of Yesterday
Where Hope Starts (Applewood Hill #1)
Where Healing Starts (Applewood Hill #2)
Where Joy Starts (Applewood Hill #3)

STACY MONSON
When Mountains Sing (My Father's House #1)
Open Circle

LORNA SEILSTAD
More Than Enough
Watercolors

CANDACE WEST
Through the Lettered Veil (Windy Hollow #1)
Among the Kindled Embers (Windy Hollow #2)

OTHER
Totally Booked: A Book Lover's Companion

To my husband, who is my biggest cheerleader. Special thanks to my beta readers: Emily, Joanna, Rebekah, Dalyn, Kathy, Carmen, Rose, and the HG Two, I owe you so much. This story wouldn't be what it is without your tough love.

Chapter One

EVERY WORD OF EZRA Falconer's best man speech was a masterclass in hypocrisy. But he needed to sell this nonsense, starting with "true love" and ending with "happily ever after". The groom, his younger brother Levi, was counting on him.

So, Ezra pasted on a smile and forced himself to maintain eye contact with the wedding guests gathered on the grounds of Falconhurst, the family estate in Surrey. "Ladies and gentlemen, today we celebrate a journey of love that began in the most unexpected way."

The marquee tent overflowed with cream roses and baby's breath, their perfume competing with the scent of lavender that drifted in from the gardens. Every lungful of that familiar fragrance—his wife Martha's favorite—twisted the knife deeper, underscoring the sham of him standing here, saying these empty words.

"Marriage often begins like a sailing trip into calm seas."

His rehearsed speech felt stale and lifeless on his tongue. Here he was, the supposed family expert on marriage, dispensing wisdom while his own wife was goodness knew where.

He'd told her it was a mistake to squeeze in that last concert appearance. Known that it would make it tricky for her to get back to England in time for Levi's wedding. But Martha—or Morgan, as she called herself now—always gave her best to her fans. Her husband was left to pick up whatever crumbs he could scavenge.

"In marriage, we commit to supporting each other's dreams, cheering each other on, whether you're home or traveling the world. It's about love that stretches across continents and comes back stronger." Had he actually written this drivel? He gave his phone a double take. What on earth had he been thinking?

His wife, England's fastest-rising music sensation, was following her dreams. Her extended tour had lasted close to three years now, leading to a patchwork marriage made up of her occasional month-long visits home, his trips abroad when their schedules allowed, and stolen weekends between shows. But even those precious moments together couldn't prevent the gradual toll of separation.

And now, they'd been apart for their longest stretch yet. Nine months. Nine months of screens, strained conversations, and silences that stretched across continents. Nine months of explaining her absence to family and friends. Nine months of telling himself that this was just a rough patch... and not the new normal.

He glanced at his brother Levi, who beamed at his beautiful new bride, Adria. Their three-year-old son wriggled happily beside Ezra's mother at the head table. Their journey might have begun in an unorthodox way, but they looked like the perfect family now—everything Ezra's own marriage failed to be.

"What starts as smooth sailing can turn stormy before you know it."

Wait, what?

Ezra paused, catching himself. He'd gone off script. Time to reel it back in.

"The key is weathering those storms together."

He wasn't even halfway through his prepared speech, but he needed to wind it up before any more of his bitter thoughts could leak out of his mouth.

He stuck his phone into his pocket and raised a glass of sparkling grape juice. "To Levi and Adria."

The guests echoed his toast, and Ezra sank into his chair. Maintaining this everything's-fine mask was exhausting.

Mum squeezed his arm. "Lovely speech, dear. It's such a shame Martha couldn't make it. It's been a fairy-tale wedding."

"I'm sure she really wanted to be here." His words were so practiced they'd lost all meaning. Like bubblegum chewed over until it was completely flavorless. "You know what it's like being on tour."

The master of ceremonies announced the bride's speech and Ezra forced his attention back to the present as Adria stood, microphone trembling in her hand. So, she'd held her nerve and decided to give a speech after all. Good on her for getting past her fear of speaking in public.

"Hi, everyone," she said, a tremor in her soft voice. "Thanks so much for coming here today to celebrate with Levi and me. When I—"

A commotion at the back of the tent dragged Ezra's gaze away from his sister-in-law.

Two men wearing designer suits, who looked as if they bench-pressed cars for fun, cleared a path between the guests with practiced efficiency.

Ezra's heart stuttered. He knew those movements—personal protection officers.

Then she appeared.

Martha glided through the parted crowd. She wore an exquisite lilac dress that barely reached mid-thigh, her new body lean and elegant where soft curves used to be. Nine months had transformed the pleasantly fluffy woman who lived in turtlenecks and floor-length skirts into this elegant lissome vision who commanded attention with every step.

Blood rushed to Ezra's face, roared in his ears.

Gasps rippled through the guests as phones appeared like magic, lifting to capture England's newest star.

At the microphone, the bride's voice faltered. "Um—thank you." She put the mic down and shuffled back to her seat.

Her speech hadn't even lasted twenty words.

A smattering of applause spread across the few guests who weren't staring at Martha.

She drew attention like a magnet in a field of iron filings, pulling every gaze irresistibly toward herself.

Ezra rose, his feet carrying him forward before his brain could catch up.

When he was a few steps away, her gaze swept upward and met his.

Her brown eyes were still the same. So was her dewy skin, the color of burnished mahogany, and her exquisite, generous lips. But the soft, abundant curves that used to fill his arms were gone. Her new body was lean and supple, dwarfed by the hulking frames of the PPOs who sat on either side of her. What would it be like to hold her now?

As Ezra drew closer, one arm half stretched out, the bodyguards jumped to their feet, their bulk forming a barrier between him and his wife.

The man on the right, a mountain with a shaved head and a square jaw, held up a ham-sized hand. "Sir, kindly don't come any closer."

Martha stood, glancing at the PPO. "It's okay, Ray. This is my husband."

Ray looked Ezra up and down, as though weighing whether to obey Martha or snap Ezra like a twig.

Martha spoke again. "Actually, guys, why don't you take a break? Grab some food. This place is safe. I'm sure no one's going to bother me here."

Ezra stepped closer as the PPOs left. "You made it. I thought you weren't coming."

"It's Levi's wedding. Of course I'd do everything I could to come," she said, her voice steady but her gaze searching his face for something—he didn't know what. She hesitated, her poise momentarily faltering. "You look well."

"Thanks. So do you." She looked more than well. She looked stunning. The kind of beauty that caused men to rubberneck and trip over their own feet. Especially with a dress which exposed her long, toned legs.

A guest approached, phone extended. "Excuse me, Morgan? Could I get a picture?"

Just like that, Martha's expression shifted into her public persona, bright and magnetic. She stepped around Ezra to pose for photos, and the crowd around her swelled.

By the cake, the bride and groom stood forgotten by half their guests.

Ezra watched as Martha raised a hand to brush a lock of black hair off her face, the gesture drawing his gaze to her bare ring finger. When had she stopped wearing her wedding band? Before or after their last fight, when she'd hung up on him?

Chapter Two

ARTHA HAD STOPPED KEEPING track of numbers after the tenth wedding guest asked her for a selfie. It was all very polite and civilized. Not like the chaotic scenes after some of her shows.

At some point—she didn't notice when—Ezra slipped away. Through gaps in the mingling guests, she saw him at a table at the far end of the marquee, staring into a glass. She'd done her best to steel herself for seeing him again, but clearly her preparations hadn't been enough.

Had he wanted to hug her just before Ray stopped him? She'd sensed it. Braced herself for it. Wanted it. But the moment was gone. Is this what their marriage had come to? When after nine months apart, they couldn't even greet each other with an embrace? Part of her wanted him to hold her. But another part was relieved that he hadn't tried.

Were the whispers she'd heard true? Her fingers curled into a fist. No. She would not let her mind go there. Listening to rumors never ended well. Especially when they were about her husband.

Still, through long-ingrained habit, she scanned the crowd, dreading the sight of an all-too-familiar figure—the tall, elegant, aristocratic woman who used to be ever-present wherever Ezra was, whose very existence was a shadow over Martha's marriage. She let out a slow breath. Good. *She* wasn't here.

Her throat ached as her gaze went back to her husband. There were few gatherings where Ezra Falconer would not be the best-looking man in the room. As always, his dark brown hair and designer beard were impeccably groomed. His thick eyebrows framed the deep-set blue eyes that had first drawn her in. She'd always been afraid he was too handsome for her, certain that people looked at them together and wondered why a man like him was with someone like her.

Now those old insecurities crept back, sharper than ever. Every conversation they'd attempted over the past few months seemed to be laced with barbs. And, despite wanting desperately to fix things, she couldn't figure out how to break the cycle. The last time they'd talked, she'd hung up on him—a childish reaction she regretted the moment she did it. No wonder he kept his distance now.

"Martha, sweetheart, it's so good to see you!"

She spun to face Beth, her mother-in-law. The older woman's blonde hair had more silver in it than Martha remembered, and her kind face was lovelier than ever, even with its new laugh lines. A little curly-haired boy stood at her side.

Beth pulled her into a long, tight hug.

Martha leaned into it, surprised by the sudden sting of tears. She should have made more of an effort to be in touch, especially since everything the family had been through with Beth's now-incarcerated husband. But her mother-in-law's embrace held no reproach, only welcome.

"I thought you weren't going to make it," Beth said. "I guess Ezra was tamping down our expectations so we wouldn't be disappointed. And you're so tiny! Aren't they feeding you out on tour? Oh! I'd better introduce my date."

She beamed at the little tawny-skinned boy. "Owen, this is your Aunt Martha. Will you say hi?"

The child raised a solemn, brown-eyed gaze to Martha's face. "Hi, Auntie Martha."

He pronounced it "Marfa." Her heart squeezed.

This must be Levi's son. Levi had asked her to come for his second birthday party last year, but she'd canceled at the last minute when she'd agreed to extend her southeast Asia tour. Ezra had not been happy about that.

She crouched to Owen's level. He'd grown so much from the last photos she'd seen. "Hi, Owen."

His serious little face and big brown eyes made her chest ache over all the milestones and little moments she'd missed and how she was a complete stranger to her nephew. Beth's texts were full of this adorable boy—his new words and toddler chatter, trips they'd taken together—messages Martha read between concerts, meaning to respond but somehow never finding the right moment.

Owen shuffled closer to Beth's legs, but kept watching with the frank curiosity only a child could get away with. For a fleeting moment, Martha imagined a little boy with Ezra's eyes looking at her that way, with skin the perfect blend between her complexion and his. The image pinched her heart.

"I like your bow tie," she said. "It makes you look like a very big boy." That earned her a tiny, shy smile, and oh—there was Levi in that expression.

She glanced up at Beth. "He looks like his mum, but that smile is pure Levi."

Beth laughed. "You see it too? So, how are you? It's been way too long."

Martha's conscience clobbered her again as she stood, reproaching her for how she'd let communication lapse with Beth. "You know how it is. It's been pretty crazy."

"I can imagine. I hope you're going to stay for a while this time. We have so much catching up to do."

"I'll need to talk to my manager, but we agreed that the team is overdue for an extended break."

"And I'm sure you need one, too." Beth squeezed Martha's arm. "I've been following your career. You've done so well. But it must be hard to keep up that pace of back-to-back performances."

It was. Not to mention recording and releasing an album every year for the past three years. She was physically drained—she hadn't realized just how much until the flight home. But even though her body cried out for rest, her heart knew that rest was far away. Not with things the way they were with Ezra.

Her gaze homed in on him. He was talking with Zach, his elder brother. Both of them wore dove gray suits, identical to Levi's. Of course, they were their little brother's groomsmen.

Eden Chaplin approached with a slice of wedding cake. As the pastor's wife at Grace Community Church, Hatbrook, where all the Falconers worshiped, she'd always been close to the family. She was stunning in a floor-length teal dress, her long, dark hair cascading over one shoulder. A warm smile lit up her face.

Balancing the plate with one hand, she hugged Martha with her free arm. "It's so good to see you. You look amazing!"

Martha smiled back. Here was another friend with whom she'd lost touch. Although, to be fair, Eden did try her best to send texts on messenger apps. Martha was the one who was rubbish at staying in contact.

Eden still emailed Bible verses and weekly devotions from the church women's group. But Martha quickly scrolled past them these days, not wanting to examine too closely why they made her uncomfortable. Her life nowadays looked nothing like when she was a model member of the women's fellowship.

She pushed the thought away, keeping her voice light. "You look wonderful as well. Maid of honor, right?"

"Yes. You haven't met Adria yet, have you?"

Martha shook her head. Another sign of the growing disconnect between her and her family. During the time she'd been away, Levi had fathered a child, fallen in love, and gotten married. Apparently, in that order. She made one brief visit back to England about a year ago, but Levi and his now-bride had been abroad at the time.

She felt like an outsider, and it was nobody's fault but hers.

Eden said, "She's such a lovely girl. I think you'll like her. Will you be able to stay awhile, or do you have another trip planned soon?"

Martha repeated the answer she'd just given Beth. "Nothing immediately planned, but I don't expect my manager to allow me to get too idle. He has a few irons in the fire he wants to talk through within the next couple of days. But the tour crew needed some time off."

"And I'm sure Ezra will be glad you've got time off as well," Eden said.

Her words hung in the air a fraction of a second too long, before Martha said, "Yes, of course."

Again, her gaze sought him out. Did Eden think it was weird that Ezra chatted with his brother instead of being glued to her side? If she did, her face didn't show it.

Eden and her husband, Pastor Noah, weren't much older than Ezra and Martha. Seen from the outside, Eden and Noah's marriage looked perfect. Together, they were the heartbeat of Grace Community Church. Did that golden couple ever have doubts? Quiet moments of despair about their relationship? Cracks that they hid from a watching world?

Martha changed the subject to Eden herself, her little girl, and the latest happenings in the church.

Soon, Eden left to resume her maid of honor duties, and Martha carried on with surface chatter with a group of people she knew slightly from church.

The party wound down and Martha's face was as sore from all the polite smiling as her feet were from her Louboutins.

Ezra appeared at her side, towering over her despite her four-inch heels. "I'm thinking of going home soon." His voice sounded uncertain. "I'm not sure whether... are you coming home?" The question seemed to cost him something—his shoulders tensed, as if bracing for a response he didn't want to hear.

It stung that he even thought he had to ask that question. "Of course I'm coming home. Why would you ask that?"

His jaw stiffened. "I didn't want to assume anything about your plans, since I usually get it wrong. I don't even know when you arrived in the country."

Martha's manicured nails bit into her palms. How had they ended up here? She and her husband had spent the entire evening at this reception in the same space for once, after months apart, yet somehow avoided any real conversation.

For the second time that evening, tears stung her eyes. This was their reality now—this careful dancing around each other, failing in even the most basic communication. When had they stopped being the couple who shared everything? Who couldn't wait to tell each other about their day?

She took a deep breath, willing her lips to stop trembling. "I changed my schedule so I could make it back for Levi's wedding. My flight landed at Gatwick this afternoon. My PA went home with my luggage while I came straight here. She's probably still there unpacking and sorting out other things. I tried to let you know I was coming. Jane said she'd email my itinerary to you."

His expression softened. "Maybe she did. It's been a busy day, and I haven't checked my messages." He reached for the knot in his tie, loosening it with a finger.

"I'll head back home, then. Will you come with me? Or maybe you already have a ride arranged?"

She glanced at her PPOs, Ray and Marcus. Ray doubled as her chauffeur, and the original plan had been for him to drive her home. But something in Ezra's face made her know she had to change the plan.

"I'll come with you. Could you give me a couple of minutes?"

"Sure."

Ray and Marcus walked to her at her signal, and she spoke to them both. "Guys, I'll be going home with my husband."

She caught the appraising glances that passed between her bodyguards and Ezra.

Ray said, "Okay, Mrs. Falconer. We'll follow you if you'll let us know which vehicle you'll be riding in."

"A silver Audi. I don't remember the license plate." She turned toward Ezra.

"Actually, I have a black Tesla now. Number plate is SNGWRTR1."

Martha's face burned. She hadn't even known that her husband had a new car.

Ezra said, "I'm parked at the front of the house, so it should be easy to spot when we leave."

"Yes, sir," Ray said, and the PPOs headed across the wide green space.

Ezra turned toward her. "Do you need to say bye to anyone?"

Before she could answer, Beth came up to them. "I'm so sorry I disappeared. I've been putting Owen down. He'll stay with me while Adria and Levi are on their honeymoon. Are you two leaving already?"

Ezra nodded. "Yes, we were on our way out."

"Oh. Well, Martha, I hope we'll have a proper catching up soon."

"Me, too," Martha said.

"Don't worry, I won't call too soon. I know you'll need some time and space." Beth reached out and hugged Martha, whispering into her ear. "He's missed you a lot. Been going around lately like a bear with a sore head."

The blood rushed to Martha's face as she fumbled for an answer. None came to her, so she stepped back, fidgeting with her purse.

Ezra hugged his mother. "Talk to you soon."

He fell into step beside Martha as they walked in the direction of the circular driveway. His tall frame had once made her feel safe and protected—like nothing could harm her when he was near. Now that same presence only reminded her of the space between them, heavy with words they couldn't seem to voice.

She crossed her arms tightly, nodding a greeting toward some guests as she and Ezra walked in silence.

"I'm glad for Levi," she said, finally. "He and Adria seemed really happy."

"I'm sure they are. They've been through a lot."

The lights of a black Tesla Model S flashed on, and Ezra opened the door on the passenger side.

Martha slid inside, the tension in her body defying the luxurious seats.

Ezra started the engine. Glancing at her, he said, "I noticed you're not wearing your wedding ring. Am I supposed to read anything into that?" His voice was carefully controlled, but he held the steering wheel in a white-knuckled grip.

Martha stared at her bare ring finger. "What? No, of course not. There's nothing to read into. Why would you think that? I lost it and haven't had a chance to replace it yet."

The car glided down the long driveway, slowing as the gates swung open.

Ezra shrugged. "Why would I think that? Maybe because we've not seen each other in months, and communication hasn't exactly been great." His tone, although quiet, hinted at things she'd rather not grapple with right now.

Anger flashed within her. He was the one who'd refused to travel and meet her on tour since her record label started leaning heavily into her new branding. Over the last year, Harmony Records had reinvented her from a soulful singer of emotional ballads into a sultry, chart-topping pop sensation. But as the label rolled out the provocative photoshoots, the revealing outfits, and the carefully crafted "Morgan" persona, Ezra had made his disapproval clear without saying a word.

She wasn't ready to have that talk, though. She was too tired. The elephant in the room could loom, ignored, for another day.

She glanced at his smooth, manicured hand as it rested on the steering wheel. He still wore his flat court platinum wedding band, the counterpart to her missing one. She could explain more about how she'd lost the ring. But his deeper question—the one that demanded more complex and painful answers—would have to wait.

She said, "After I lost all this weight, my ring got very loose. It must have slipped off during one of my shows in Seoul. I wanted to replace it but thought I'd better wait until I got back home and could get one from the same jewelers."

His shoulders relaxed. "Your shows are pretty high energy."

"I'm surprised you know that. You've never actually been to one." The words were out of her mouth before she could stop them, like soda spraying out of a shaken can. She hadn't meant to get into this tonight.

He shot a glance at her. "We've already been over this. You know how I feel about some of the companies backing your tour."

Okay, so they were going to talk about it. She rolled her eyes. "Because energy drinks are so sinful and

Christians never need a boost when they're studying or working late. Got it."

"It's not that simple. 'Unleash Your Wild Side'—isn't that Blitz Energy's latest slogan? You've seen how they brand themselves and who they're trying to sell drinks to. They're targeting people who are into a party life-style." He was on the same old well-trodden ground.

"It's just a drink," she said. "People can use them responsibly."

"You know that's not the message they're pushing, Martha. And what about Moonshine Spirits? Yes, Jesus might have turned water into wine, but I doubt He'd be okay with the binge drinking culture Moonshine feeds into. I want to support you, but I have to think about the message I'm sending to my own audience if it looks like I'm endorsing those sponsors."

Martha crossed her arms tightly across her chest. It was a convenient excuse for him not to come to the places where she was performing. His stated reason for staying away for the past nine months. But who knew what he'd really been up to here at home? Quite a lot, if the rumors were to be believed.

"I guess that means you can't be seen associating with me, either." Her voice was tight.

He sighed. "That's not what I meant. You know what? Let's just drop this. We're both tired."

They were already pulling up to the gates of their home, which was only a few minutes' drive from Falconhurst.

Glancing over her shoulder, she glimpsed the headlights of her PPOs' car following them.

Ezra punched the button on the remote control and the gates slid open. "Whose cars are these? And why's the house lit up? I left it locked."

"I told you, my PA came here to help me unpack. She's also setting things up with my security team. The other car is probably the guard who's on evening duty."

"I wanted to ask you about that," Ezra said, steering to a stop in front of the house as Ray and Marcus pulled up beside his car. "What's with all the PPOs? It really disrupted the reception when you came in and they were shooing everyone away. Poor Adria lost her nerve and abandoned her speech. Was all that necessary?"

She bristled at his tone. "I didn't know Adria would be speaking. I'm really sorry about that. I didn't want to ruin her speech. But, yes, I need my PPOs. The label started providing security after I got mobbed at a show in Sydney and someone broke into my villa."

It was the ugly side of fame, something she'd only come to know when her popularity blew up over the past year. Being clawed and groped by baying fans who acted like animals, she'd never felt so frightened... or so alone.

Ezra went still, the color draining from his face. "I—I'm sorry. I didn't know that."

Lifting her chin, she met his gaze. "You would have known how things were if you'd come to see me."

He flinched. "Martha, I..." He pushed his hand through his hair. "I don't know what to say. You must have been terrified. Why didn't you tell me? I would have dropped everything and come right away."

His fingers brushed against hers and she glanced down at their hands, almost touching, but not quite.

A lump formed in her throat. "That's just it, Ezra. I needed you long before it happened, but that wasn't enough reason for you. You were more concerned about Blitz Energy and Moonshine Spirits. I didn't want you to come just because of some incident. Why didn't I matter enough before you knew about it?"

She could tell that her words crushed him.

Before he could respond, Jane, her PA, walked toward the car, tablet in hand.

Martha opened the door and stepped out, blinking quickly.

"Good evening, Martha," Jane said, adjusting her glasses. "I was just about to text you to let you know we're all set up. The nighttime guard will use the guest house. He's done a sweep of the property. And cameras and motion sensors have been installed at key points around the perimeter."

Martha nodded wearily, barely registering the details. She sensed Ezra standing beside her.

Jane turned to face him. "Mr. Falconer, I presume? I'm Jane. Nice to meet you in person instead of just over email."

"Hi. Lovely to meet you." Ezra shook Jane's hand, his voice tight. "Could you let me know more about this security setup? What's been put in place to keep Martha safe?"

As Jane began explaining the details of the security measures, including mention of panic buttons installed throughout the house, Martha's shoulders sagged.

She tried to grasp Jane's words, but they scattered from her mind like beads rolling away from a broken string. The day's events and emotions had left her drained.

She broke into Jane's explanation. "Sorry. I'm too tired to listen to all of this."

"Okay, I get that you're tired," Jane said, frowning. "But could I just explain the panic button system? It's important for you to understand that at least. We can go over the rest another time."

Ezra's hands rested on Martha's shoulders, radiating warmth. "Why don't you go inside and rest? I'll get up to speed on all this and fill you in later."

She leaned into him instinctively, her body responding to his touch before her mind could intervene. It was such a sweet relief to have him here, stepping in to take care of her.

His arms circled around her and his voice, pitched only for her ears, whispered, "I'm sorry."

She hugged him back, gulping back a sob.

His embrace felt so good, and she wanted to lose herself in his arms. But why hadn't he been there for her before things got bad enough for her to need bodyguards and panic buttons? Where was his concern when she'd been four thousand miles away from home, amid a sea of strangers, desperate for his arms around her?

She loved how protective and caring he was. But his attentiveness now only seemed to highlight how absent he'd been for all those months, when she needed him most.

Still... he wasn't a mind-reader. How would he have known unless she told him?

"I'm sorry, too," she whispered.

She pulled out of his embrace and headed toward the house.

Chapter Three

As THE MORNING SUNLIGHT streamed through the kitchen windows, Ezra nudged a vase of fresh-cut flowers one inch to the right. Martha would be walking in any second—he'd heard the shower going. Everything was perfect, from the exquisite china Martha loved to the linen napkins he'd folded beside each plate.

He'd made her favorite breakfast treat, a platter of fluffy, golden Belgian waffles, their deep pockets perfect for holding pools of maple syrup. Beside the waffles sat a bowl of whipped cream and another filled with plump strawberries. The rich aroma of freshly brewed coffee filled the air and a carafe of fresh-squeezed orange juice stood ready.

Maybe these waffles would make up for last night's disastrous homecoming. In the early days of their marriage, this was what he made on her birthday and Christmas morning, using his grandmother's recipe, which called for buttermilk and a touch of vanilla. Crisp on the outside and tender on the inside, they were absolutely decadent when topped with syrup, cream, and fruit.

Every tiny detail reflected his heart. Hopefully, this breakfast would let his wife know that her being home with him was worth a celebration. The waffles, the berries, and whipped cream—it was all a peace offering served up on Wedgwood Wild Strawberry china on the altar of their kitchen table, a desperate attempt to bridge the disconnect between them.

Blended with the smell of coffee, the subtle scent of lavender lingered in the air. He smiled. It was another sign that she was home. That, and the pair of stilettos kicked off near the door. He'd missed her so much.

She had been sound asleep when he'd slipped into bed last night, so there'd been no opportunity to talk. But maybe today they'd have a chance to reconnect and figure some things out.

Some of her corporate sponsorships made him want to hold his nose. He cringed every time he saw her face plastered across those drink billboards. And although her voice could bring tears to a stone statue, her label seemed more interested in showcasing her sex appeal.

But now that she was home, they could work out their differences face to face instead of through screens. In real time, rather than tag-teaming emails and messaging apps. And, more importantly, get their marriage back on track.

He stood straighter at the sound of footsteps coming down the hallway. Martha entered the kitchen dressed in a dark blue denim jumpsuit that emphasized her trim new physique, still jarring to him. He watched her features, hoping to see a flicker of the joy she used to express at the sight of his homemade waffles.

Her eyes widened as her gaze fell on the table. "Oh, Ezra, you've gone to so much trouble. This looks wonderful."

He moved forward, pulling a chair out for her. "It's been a while since I made you breakfast."

She sat slowly, running her finger along the edge of a napkin.

He settled into his seat. "Shall we give thanks? Lord, we're grateful for this meal and for Martha's safe arrival home. Bless this food before us. May it be for our strength and health. Amen."

He nudged the platter of waffles toward her. "Go on. Help yourself. I managed to get real maple syrup from Waitrose. They didn't have it in Hatbrook, so I had to go all the way to Dorking."

She looked up at him, biting her lip. "I'm really sorry, but I can't eat this."

"What? Why not?" Wasn't she feeling well?

She gestured over the table. "It looks and smells wonderful. And I can see how much of an effort you've put into all this. But..." She twisted the napkin. "It's just that I have to keep my weight under control. I know how good this is, and if I have even one bite, I'll scarf the whole pile—you know what I'm like. I really appreciate you making all of it, though."

He read the plea in her eyes and struggled to keep the disappointment out of his voice. "Right. Okay." So much for his peace offering and attempt to recreate the special mornings of the past. Her new image mattered more. "What do you have for breakfast these days? Maybe I could make you that?"

"I don't really have breakfast anymore. Sometimes I have a smoothie. Or a glass of warm water with a slice of lemon."

He got to his feet. "I can get you that."

Maybe the security guard out in the guest house would like some waffles. Ezra had lost his appetite, too. He knew next to nothing about Martha's daily life anymore.

He flicked the switch on the kettle, then grabbed a lemon from the fridge.

"Ezra... I'm sorry." Her voice was soft.

"It's okay," he said, slicing into the sour fruit. "People and tastes change, right?"

"That reminds me." She got up from the table. "I bought something for you."

As she went upstairs, he filled a glass with lukewarm water and dropped a couple of lemon slices inside. Setting the glass next to Martha's empty plate, he sighed as he looked at the breakfast he'd made.

He grabbed the platter of waffles and put them on the counter, then covered them with aluminum foil.

Martha came back into the kitchen, holding a small, beautifully wrapped package.

Her brown eyes glowed as she held it out. "I know it's not your birthday for a couple of months, but when I saw this, I thought of you."

"You didn't have to get me anything." He took it from her.

"I wanted to. Go on, open it. I've been dying to see your face when you see what it is."

Her excitement warmed him as he unwrapped the package, revealing a sleek, dark blue box with a logo embossed in silver.

His heartbeat quickened as he recognized the luxury watch brand. Surely she hadn't... Fingers trembling, he opened the box.

She had.

Nestled on a bed of plush cream-colored velvet was an IWC Portugieser Automatic. Holding his breath, he lifted the watch from its cushion. He'd seen pictures of this model, but it was even more stunning than he had imagined.

The stainless steel case gleamed, its polished finish catching the morning light. Its face was the color of a clear summer sky, and the numerals and sleek hands stood out in silver against the blue background.

He brushed his fingers against its blue leather strap.

Bouncing on her toes, Martha clasped her hands under her chin. "Do you like it?"

"Like it?" he breathed. "It's... It's absolutely exquisite. I can't believe you got this for me."

"You used to say you wanted one someday. So, when I was on tour in the south of France, I took a weekend break in Switzerland and I picked it up for you. It was supposed to be a birthday gift, but I didn't want to wait any longer."

"It's perfect. I love it." Seeing her face bloom with delight, he almost held back from saying anything else. "But Martha, this is so expensive. We always said it was too extravagant. I almost feel guilty for even wanting it." With prices of this model running to well over twenty thousand pounds, he'd never been able to justify getting something like this for himself.

Martha's smile dimmed. "I know, but... well, we can afford it now. I wanted you to have something special. Look, I had them inscribe something on the back."

He turned the watch over, his throat tightening as he read the fine, flowing script.

Yours always. Martha.

Was she still his? Changed as she was?

"Go on." She touched his hand. "Put it on."

He slipped on the watch, adjusting it to fit his wrist. Man, the thing was beyond perfection. He made a very good living, but he'd never thought he'd own an IWC. He'd never imagined his wife giving him a gift he couldn't afford. And she'd bought it in Switzerland. One of the bucket list destinations he'd always hoped they'd experience together.

His heart ached as he looked at her face. Why was he being ungrateful and letting his ego get in the way? She just wanted to give him something nice. That was all that should matter.

He held out his arms, and she stepped into them, her head resting on his chest. "Thank you," he said, his voice thick.

The doorbell chimed, and Martha pulled away. "It must be Jane."

Ezra glanced at his shiny new watch. "This early? It's Saturday."

"She said she'd be in to touch base," Martha said, heading for the door.

Ezra busied himself clearing the uneaten breakfast, listening to the muffled voices from the entrance hall.

A few moments later, Martha's voice grew clearer with her approach. "...and Ezra's just made some coffee if you'd like a cup."

Martha reappeared in the kitchen, Jane following close behind, holding several garment bags over her arm.

"Good morning, Mr. Falconer," Jane said with a polite nod.

"Morning, Jane. And, please, it's just Ezra." He reached for the coffeepot. "Coffee?"

"That would be lovely, thank you. Just black, please." Jane turned to Martha. "There's been an urgent change of plan. Libertine Lingerie called while I was on my way here. They want to do the shoot today. They've got Andre Bishop, but he's leaving for Milan tonight and won't be back in England for another eight weeks. So, they need a response from you."

Ezra filled the coffee cup. Surely no one could expect Martha to work the day after she'd just landed home after months away. Worse still, Libertine Lingerie? As in underwear? What kind of shoot did they want with Martha?

Martha's shoulders slumped. "Today? I was hoping to spend the day at home."

Ezra brought Jane her coffee. "Here you go. Strong and black."

"Thanks," Jane said. Shrugging, she spoke to Martha. "It's Andre Bishop. And this is when he's available."

"They're putting me in a real bind, then. I wouldn't want to do this with anyone else." Martha sighed. "Okay, fine. Tell them I'll do it. When and where?"

"Lumière Collective Studios in Shoreditch. They want you to head there immediately if you can, and be prepared to work all day."

Ezra couldn't believe what he was hearing. There were so many things wrong with this.

"All right," Martha said. "Is Ray here? I'll ask him to take me there. And could you come, too? I need to go over some things with you."

Jane held up the garment bags. "Sure. I'll just put these in your closet and let Libertine know you're on your way."

Ezra waited until Jane had left the room, then turned to Martha. "What is this? You're modeling lingerie?"

She crossed her arms. "Yes, I signed a contract with Libertine to promote their new line."

"But lingerie? Is it really appropriate? They're going to take pictures of... of you in your underwear?"

"They do sleepwear as well. It'll be professional and tasteful. Andre Bishop is very well-respected in the industry. It's not like I'm shooting porn."

He winced at the word. "Of course not. But I'm just not comfortable with the thought of you being exposed like that. Those kinds of ads can be pretty risqué. I don't like it, Martha."

She glanced away for a moment, chewing her lower lip. "I know it's hard for you, but it's important for me to do this. It just..." She faced him again. "It seems to me you don't like a lot of what I do lately."

True words. And he was getting nowhere with this line of argument. He tried another tack. "I was talking with Ray last night about the kind of attention he's seen some of his female clients get—the sickos who he needs to protect people from. Wouldn't this just encourage that sort of thing?"

Jane came back into the kitchen, phone in hand. "Everything's a go with Libertine. Ready to leave when you are, Martha."

"Go ahead and let Ray know I'm coming," Martha said.

Ezra's heart sank. She really was going to do this.

As Jane headed for the door, Martha turned back to Ezra. "I don't want to fight about this. This is a great opportunity."

Ezra threaded a hand through his hair. "I don't want to fight, either. It's just hard for me. The Martha I knew would never want the whole world to see her in lingerie."

"The Martha you knew hated her body and wanted to disappear." She brushed her fingers against his arm. "Is it such a bad thing that I'm more confident now? That I'm proud of who I've become?"

How was he supposed to argue with that?

She glanced at the door, then back into his face. "Listen, I've got to go. Can we just agree to disagree for now?" Her fingers squeezed his arm.

He sighed and shrugged as she walked to the front door. It wasn't like he had a choice. Glancing at the kitchen table, he scanned what was left of the breakfast she hadn't eaten, and the box that contained the watch she'd gotten for him.

His wife was back home, but she wasn't the woman he married anymore. A chill struck his core. He loved Martha. But would loving her be enough to mend the widening chasm between them?

Chapter Four

IDMORNING LIGHT SPILLED INTO Ezra's home studio, casting shadows among the scattered musical scores and half-finished lyric sheets. On the monitor to his left, a silent video looped a slide show of children and families in rural Uganda.

He wanted to give these images a voice, create a stirring song of hope that would inspire the supporters of the freshwater charity that had commissioned him. His hand hovered over the keyboard of his Roland Fanton 8. Playing a few notes, he tried to capture the elusive melody he needed for the bridge of his song.

But the tune escaped him.

He paused, rubbing his temples as the morning's non-breakfast with Martha invaded his thoughts. Right now, she was in some London studio, posing in lingerie. Was he the one who was so off base? How was it that she couldn't see anything wrong in being the poster girl for Libertine Lingerie?

He sighed, looking around the studio filled with mementos of his past successes and the early promise of his career. This place used to inspire him.

Taking a deep breath, he played the bridge again, seeking to channel his emotions into the music. He needed this composition to resonate with compassion, to echo far beyond the confines of his personal world. The problem was, he felt the wrong emotions. Each note clashed with the next, much like the unresolved tension between him and Martha.

Pushing back from the keyboard, Ezra stood and paced. He stopped by the window, looking out at the backyard. One of Martha's PPOs walked across the lawn. She had grown so successful that she needed round-the-clock protection.

"Focus, Ezra," he muttered, returning to his seat and staring at his slideshow. "This is bigger than you."

Putting on his headphones again, he closed his eyes and did his best to envision the faces from the screen. With each deep, intentional breath, he fought to steady his racing thoughts, allowing the music to flow through him. This time, his fingers found a tentative melody, a fragile thread of sound he could work with.

His phone buzzed like a hive of angry bees, pulling him out of his hard-won concentration.

How had he forgotten to put it on silent? He moved to reject the call, then changed his mind. Maybe it was Martha.

It was his manager, Fiona Blackwell. Calling on a Saturday. Anxiety stabbed at his gut as he answered the call, setting it on speaker mode.

"Hi, Fiona. What's up?"

"Hey. Congratulations on Levi's wedding. I'm sorry I couldn't make it."

"That's all right. He knows you'd have been there if you could. How's the grandbaby doing?"

"Mother and baby are doing really well. And I heard Martha's back in town. You must be thrilled to have her home again."

Ezra shifted in his seat. "Yes, she got back last night. She's great, too."

Fiona was stalling. Small talk wasn't her thing. She didn't call him on a Saturday just to chat about his family.

After a foray into a discussion about the weather, his manager cleared her throat. "Ezra, I just got off the phone with the folks at Silvertone Records. You heard about the takeover, right?"

"Yeah," Ezra drew out the word. "What about it?"

"There's been a big shake-up. The new owners are an investment group, which means their priority is profit and ROI, and they want to shift the label's focus. They're overhauling the artist roster, focusing more on... let's say, more mainstream, chart-friendly acts. They want to chase the pop market, aiming for high streaming numbers. They're not renewing contracts for several artists, Ezra. I'm sorry, but that includes yours. They cited the sales figures from your last two albums and the overall shift in market demands."

Ezra's mouth went dry. No wonder Fiona had stalled so long. The news was as brutal as the slice of a guillotine. When he finally spoke, his voice was raspy. "So, that's it? After all these years, just cut loose?"

"It's harsh, I know," Fiona said. "And, frankly, it's their loss. But listen, Ezra, even without a record deal, your songwriting is still on fire. Several of your tracks are charting."

Ezra clenched a fist. "Yeah, but only the ones covered by other artists."

Another bitter truth. His last two solo albums, though critically acclaimed, had met only lukewarm sales. "The writing has been on the wall for a long time, hasn't it?"

Fiona's silence lasted a beat too long, confirming that she couldn't contradict Ezra's point. "It's a merciless industry. But you've got a lot more going for you than most. Your skills as a songwriter aren't going anywhere. I'm getting calls pretty much every day from people who want you to write for them. In fact, there's one I'd like to run by you now."

Ezra stood and walked to the window. "Songwriting pays the bills, sure, but it's not the same as performing my own work. Feels like I'm just ghostwriting my career away."

"I get that, but it's not the end of the road. Think about it, Ezra. You've got a name, and respect in the industry. I don't want to rush you, especially after dumping this news, but I think you ought to consider the call I got last night."

Ezra sighed. "Sure. What is it? Some hot new reality show winner who wants me to write their debut album?"

"Not exactly. Have you heard about the *Promise Ridge* book series, written by W. M. Baxter?"

"Yeah, my mum loves them. Why?"

"Well, they're being made into a TV series by Light Haven Productions. Yesterday the executive producer called to say they want you to write the theme song and episode score for the first series."

"Really? They asked for me by name?"

"Yes. James Warner, Light Haven's Head of Drama, specifically requested you. He brought up that indie film you scored last year—*The Winter House*. Said your score was exactly the kind of emotional storytelling they need for *Promise Ridge*. Light Haven's putting serious money behind this. They're positioning it as their next big prestige drama."

Fiona's words were like a balm to the sting of Silvertone's rejection. Having someone at Warner's level champion his work meant something. Even if his own albums weren't selling, he could still create music that moved people who mattered in the industry.

"I'm surprised anyone even saw *The Winter House*," Ezra said. "How about that?"

"Warner did. And *Promise Ridge* is yours to refuse. Only, they want to move quickly. They need a theme song by the end of the month so they can start promotion, and the score for the pilot episode by mid-July."

Ezra glanced at his calendar. "That gives me just over two weeks to write the theme song."

"Yes. Are you in?"

"You bet." The world didn't look so bleak anymore.

"Excellent. And remember what I told you last week? About Threads of Hope looking for someone to write the jingle and background music for their Christmas campaign?"

"I remember," Ezra said. He'd turned down the offer because he thought he'd be working on an album for a record deal that no longer existed. "Are they still looking?"

"I just need to make the call."

"Go ahead. Fiona, sorry if I'm sounding rather bummed, but I really appreciate all you're doing for me. I'm not ungrateful. You're right—I'm a lot luckier than a lot of guys out there."

"No need to apologize. I'll make those calls and get things going. You'll definitely not be out of work anytime soon with your songwriting chops. And don't give up on your dream of being a recording artist, either. It's not the end of the road. I can still pitch your new material to some other projects, maybe look into independent labels, or even self-producing."

Her enthusiasm cheered his heart. "You're the best, Fiona. My brother's got a charity album project he wants me to help with, so there's no rush to find me anything else. Let's see how things go with *Promise Ridge*."

"Of course. Say hi to Martha for me."

"Will do."

Ezra ended the call and sank into the chair in front of his keyboard. Swiveling slowly around, he stared at the framed certifications that decorated his walls—gold and platinum records marking streaming and sales milestones.

He was grateful for the career heights he'd reached, which were nothing to sneeze at. But his biggest commercial success was a song he hadn't even performed. Another artist had recorded "Whispers of You" and taken it multi-platinum, with streaming numbers north of eight hundred million. Twenty-three weeks in Billboard's Top 10, peaking at number two.

He could write songs that lit up the charts like fireworks—as long as someone else performed them. His own albums? They barely made a spark.

He sighed. There was no point in throwing a pity party. At least he still had a career, and plenty of work to do. And his music did connect with people, if in a more roundabout way than he'd like. He needed to wrap up this song so he could have time to concentrate on that TV series music Fiona was sending his way.

He bowed his head and prayed out loud. "Lord, it hurts that my label has dropped me. I'm not going to lie. But thank You for opening other doors."

As he reached for his headphones, his expensive new watch caught the light. The cynical thought rose before he could stop it—his wife's face on billboards probably earned more in a week than he made in a full month of work. No wonder she could afford to get him gifts like this. But that was unfair. Martha was a star because her voice had something special. Something that touched people deep inside.

He just wished her success didn't remind him of his failure. And he hated himself for even thinking that way.

Chapter Five

"THERE YOU GO, MADAME. What do you think?" Celine, the hairstylist for the Libertine Lingerie photo shoot, stepped back from Martha's chair.

Wrapped in a soft terrycloth robe, Martha stared into the dressing room mirror. Her natural hair had been expertly blended with extensions, creating a voluminous, slightly messy hairstyle that exuded an effortless sensuality.

Admiring her handiwork, Celine gently tousled Martha's hair and spoke in her French accent. "I was going for a Black Brigitte Bardot look. An undone updo, as if you had it perfect for the red carpet last night, but you've just rolled out of bed this morning."

"I love it. I wish I looked like this when I've just woken up," Martha said, chuckling.

The style captured the essence of Bardot's iconic bedhead, with soft tendrils framing Martha's face, while the bulk of her hair was piled high on her head in a series of seemingly careless twists and tucks. The overall effect was both elegant and slightly disheveled, as if

Martha had just emerged from bed looking impossibly chic.

"I'm glad you like it," the stylist said. "I'll see you on the set."

As Celine left, a young woman walked into the room carrying several garment bags.

"Hi, Morgan," she said brightly. "I'm Zoe, the wardrobe stylist. I've got your looks for today's shoot. And can I just say how excited I am to be working with you? I'm a huge fan."

"Aw, thanks," Martha said. When she was working, she seldom bothered telling people her real name. It helped her get into the zone, especially when "Morgan" was going to do something that "Martha" never would. Like pose in lingerie.

The Martha who'd been in church every time the doors opened would be horrified by what she was about to do. But that Martha felt like a completely different person.

Zoe hung the bags on a nearby rack and started unzipping them. "So, for the first set, we're thinking of starting with this piece." She pulled out a delicate lace bra in a deep midnight blue, paired with high-waisted briefs.

Martha blinked. The panties were more revealing than she had expected. "Oh. Okay," she said, trying to keep her voice neutral.

"It'll look amazing on you. I've got a couple of sizing options here. From the measurements your PA sent, I'm thinking either an XS or XXS should be perfect. We'll make sure everything fits just right."

As Martha stared at the tiny scraps of fabric, Ezra's voice rang in the back of her mind. *I'm just not comfortable with the thought of you being exposed like that. Those kinds of ads can be pretty risqué.*

She pulled her dressing gown closer around her neck. "Will there, um... will there be a robe or a wrap to go with these?"

Zoe's mouth fell open. "Well, um, I don't think this set comes with one, but I can certainly go back and check."

She returned the lingerie to the rack. "Andre's vision for this shoot is all about confidence and artistic expression. We're calling it 'Intimate Harmonies.'"

As if on cue, the door opened again, and a slender man with wavy salt-and-pepper hair strode in. "Morgan, darling! So glad you could make it on such short notice. I'm Andre Bishop."

Leaning forward, he kissed her on both cheeks.

He stood back, his eyes lighting up as he took in her hair. "I love what we've done here. Your face is perfection. And those curls are going to photograph like a dream."

Martha smiled. "Thank you. It's a pleasure to meet you, Andre."

"Now," he said, pulling up a chair, "let me walk you through what we're envisioning for today. We've created a luxurious, bohemian-chic lounge setting. Picture plush velvet sofas in deep jewel tones, vintage musical instruments scattered artfully about—an antique guitar or two, a classic record player. We've added lush green plants for an organic feel, and the lighting... oh, the lighting is pure magic. Soft, warm, intimate."

He waved his hands in front of him. "This is about music and intimacy. A perfect blend of elegance, sensuality, and charisma. You are not just a model for the shoot. You embody the spirit of intimate harmony. I'm looking for spontaneity, complete ease in your own skin. This is the energy that will flow between you and Ricardo, our male model. A creative connection that is ethereal, almost spiritual, while still completely sensual."

Martha's heart pounded in her ears. A male model? "Oh. Um... No one mentioned there would be anyone in the shoot with me."

"Yes, for some of the shots. Nothing too suggestive, darling, just intimate artistic chemistry. He'll play the role of a fellow artist or perhaps a muse. It's up to you how you'll interpret it. The interaction between you two will be subtle yet impactful—shared moments in space that hint at a deeper connection."

He stood. "I'll let you get changed, and we'll see you out on the set soon. It will be magical, I promise."

With a wave and a grin, he headed out of the room.

Martha sat still, trying to process Andre's words. Why hadn't she considered that she might be expected to pose with a man? What would Ezra think about this?

She took a deep breath. This was just a job. The male model would be a professional. They'd just be acting a role, and she was nothing more than a mannequin that moved its limbs and struck the correct pose.

She grabbed the lingerie set Zoe had selected for the first shoot and changed quickly into the padded lace-trimmed bra and high cut briefs.

She pulled her robe back on as a knock sounded at the door. "Come in."

Zoe walked in with the makeup artist behind her.

Zoe's face scrunched up apologetically. "I checked, but there's no appropriate robe for this first shoot. They just want to highlight the set. But there's a silk robe for the next one."

Martha bit her lip. She'd just have to grit her teeth and do her best to sell this outfit. If panties and a bra qualified as an outfit.

The makeup artist approached with a bottle in hand. "Last thing before you go to the set. This is a light-weight, illuminating body oil. It'll give your skin a beautiful, healthy glow under the lights. If you don't mind, please remove that robe."

With swift, smooth strokes, the artist began to apply the product, starting at Martha's shoulders. She chatted as she worked, as though she sensed Martha's nervousness. "It's got tiny, light-reflecting particles which will catch the light beautifully in the photos without looking greasy. Plus, it'll leave a subtle shimmer that complements your skin tone perfectly."

Martha stared at her reflection. The oil left behind a soft, dewy sheen that made her dark brown skin look radiant and moisturized. Closing her eyes, she took a deep breath, inhaling the subtle scent of coconut and vanilla. She would need to pull on every ounce of "Morgan" energy she possessed in order to get through this shoot.

Martha sank into the chair in her dressing room, her body still tingling from the adrenaline of the modeling shoot. She glanced at the clock—just past five in the afternoon. They'd wrapped up much earlier than expected.

She couldn't wait to get out of this lingerie and go home. She'd been back in England for twenty-four hours, but she'd hardly spent any time with Ezra.

A loud knock on her door made her pull her robe around her tighter. "Come in."

Her manager, Alex Thompson, burst through the door, his face split with a wide grin. Even on a Saturday evening, he still wore a beautifully tailored Saville Row suit. His presence here at today's shoot showed how important he thought it was.

He waved his phone at her. "Morgan, darling, you've absolutely nailed it! Andre is raving about the shots he got, and Libertine is over the moon. They've already teased the collaboration on social media, and it's blowing up!"

Martha's stomach churned as Alex thrust the phone in front of her. Her cheeks burned as she read the comments flooding into Libertine's social media account.

"Morgan in lingerie? I'm SO here for it!"

"Get your extinguishers ready, because this is going to be fire!"

"C'mon, Libertine! Don't leave a guy hanging like that. Pix, please!"

"Can't wait to see more!"

Alex pocketed his phone, still beaming. "This new direction for your image is pure gold. Thanks to your weight loss story, you're hitting that sweet spot—aspirational and accessible to women, desirable to men. It's a delicate balance, but you're walking it perfectly."

Martha shifted uneasily. She knew that's what "Morgan's" carefully curated image was meant to be, but hearing it in those words didn't sit well. Since taking this new direction leading up to the launch of her latest album, her sales had skyrocketed. It was hard not to conclude that her meteoric rise was because of Morgan's edgy, more provocative image.

"Oh, and I've got more great news," Alex continued. "We've received invitations for a round of TV appearances in Sweden and Norway. Friendly sit-downs, perform a couple of songs from the new album. It's perfect timing with the buzz this lingerie campaign is creating."

Martha's heart sank. "How soon?"

"Next week. We'd be gone for about ten days."

She bit her lip. "I don't know, Alex. I've only just got home after months away. I've barely spent any time with Ezra."

Alex stroked his chin. "This is a crucial time for your career. Ezra's been in the business a long time, and he knows how important it is to capitalize on the kind of momentum you've got right now." Alex paused, tilting his head, his eyes widening. "If he really wants the best for your career, which I know he does, he'll understand that you need to grab opportunities like this. He wouldn't hold you back. Would he?"

Martha frowned. "No, of course he wouldn't. But I'm making the decision here. I've been away from home for over a year and the last thing I want to do right now is travel straight away."

"If you say so." Alex sighed. "It's a real missed opportunity. When do you think you'll be ready to travel again?"

Martha shrugged. "I don't know. Not for at least a month. But let's not talk about it now."

Jane poked her head into the room. "Sorry to interrupt, Martha, but we need to get going if you're going to make it to the video premiere on time. I've told Kelsey and C.J. to meet you at home in an hour to put your look together."

Martha nodded, grateful for the interruption. "Right, of course. Let's go."

Alex headed for the door. "Will you bring your husband with you for the premiere? It's been ages since I saw Ezra."

Martha winced. The music video for her latest single, "Resonance," would be screened to a select audience for the first time tonight. Jane had only reminded her of the premiere on the way here this morning. Ezra didn't know about it yet.

He was probably hoping for a quiet evening at home, especially since tomorrow was Sunday and he'd be wanting to go to church. Once, she'd have been just as eager as he was to attend the service, her faith as steady as his. Now, though, God seemed so far away.

"Actually, I haven't had a chance to ask him yet," she said. "But I'll see if he can make it."

She stared at her reflection. Hopefully, he'd agree to come with her.

Chapter Six

ARTHA WALKED INTO THE house. Ezra's Tesla was in the garage, so he must be home. But all was quiet. Was he in his studio?

Her video premiere started in about two and a half hours, which didn't leave her much time to get ready. Her glam team would arrive any minute, but she had to talk to Ezra first.

She could have just called and told him she was going out again tonight, but after how tense things were this morning, a phone call just wouldn't cut it. This conversation needed to happen face-to-face, no matter how rushed she might be.

Walking down to the lower level of the house, she heard the whirring of the treadmill. Ezra must be in the gym.

She pushed the door open. The scent of rubber mats and metal hit her nostrils, mingling with a hint of crisp cologne and clean sweat. The rhythmic thud of feet on a treadmill filled the room, punctuated by deep, controlled breathing.

Ezra, shirtless, was running hard, his muscled torso glistening with perspiration as his feet pounded against the moving belt. Exertion strained his features as he stared straight ahead, lost in whatever was playing through his earbuds.

Martha paused where she stood, her gaze tracing the familiar lines of his body.

As if sensing her presence, Ezra turned his head toward the door. His face relaxed as he reached out and jabbed at a button on the treadmill's console. The whir of the machine decreased as it slowed to a walking pace.

Chest heaving, he pulled out one earbud. "I didn't hear you come home. Have you been here long?" He grabbed a towel from the handrail and wiped his face and neck.

"No, I just got back." She stepped closer. "You don't normally run that hard unless you're working through something. Everything okay?"

Still walking briskly, he took a long swig from his water bottle. "I just got word today that Silvertone's cut me loose."

Martha's gut twisted. "Oh, no, I'm so sorry to hear that. Did you... did you have any warning?" Alex had said something about Silvertone's new direction, mentioning rumors that heads might roll. But she'd not expected Ezra's would be one of them.

"The writing was on the wall if I'd been smart enough to read it." He ran a hand through his sweat-dampened hair, his breath still coming quickly. "New management, changing focus, the usual spiel. Plus, my last album tanked. So, no, it shouldn't have been a surprise, and I'm probably the only one who didn't see it coming."

He must be taking this hard. He only got this cynical and down on himself when he was really hurting. What could she do to help? Martha reached for his hand as it rested on the treadmill bar, her fingers brushing against his. "That really stinks."

"Yeah." He took another sip of water. "But Fiona set up a contract for me to write a theme song and music for a new TV show, so it's not all bad news. I still have a healthy career as long as other people perform my stuff." His mouth twisted in an imitation of a smile.

"That sounds hopeful." She stroked his hand. "Fiona always comes through for you."

"She does. The show's great, and I have a couple of other writing jobs lined up. But losing the contract is a pretty big blow." He draped the towel over his shoulders. "Good thing the royalty checks for 'Whispers of You' and the other songs are still coming in."

Martha hesitated, weighing her words. "Actually, I've been thinking about our finances. It's been a really good year for me. With what I've made, we could pay off the mortgage. It would give us more financial freedom, especially now."

His hand tightened under hers. "What? No, we're managing fine. I've always handled the mortgage. That won't change because I've hit a bump in the road."

"I know, but things are different now. I'm contributing, too. Why carry a mortgage if we don't have to?"

He stabbed a finger at the treadmill console and stepped down, pulling his hand away from hers. "I'm not struggling to carry it. Is that what you think? That I can't provide for us anymore?"

"No, that's not... Look, you just said your contract wasn't renewed, and I thought—"

"You thought you'd swoop in and save the day?" Ezra spun around to face her, gripping the ends of the towel in his fists. "I don't need saving, Martha. I've been taking care of us for years."

"I know you have. But now that our financial situation has changed, it's okay to do things a bit differently, isn't it?"

"You mean *your* financial situation has changed." He sat down heavily on a workout bench and grabbed a free weight, lifting it in a slow bicep curl. Through gritted teeth, straining at the effort, he said, "Mine's the same as it's always been."

"Ezra, please. We're in this together. Your career has ups and downs, just like mine will. I just want us to make the most of this opportunity while we have it."

He barked out a sharp laugh and set the weight down with a clang. "Great. So, on top of losing my record deal, my wife wants to support me. This day keeps getting better."

"That's not what I meant, and you know it. Why are you making this so difficult?"

"I'm making it difficult?" Ezra picked up the weight again, his grip tightening as he resumed his curls. "You're the one trying to change everything. Our home, our finances..."

"That's not fair, Ezra." Tears stung her eyes.

He'd never spoken to her like this. But this was his pain talking, she reminded herself. Instead of reacting to his harsh words and letting them sink in, she would speak to the man she knew him to be, the one who was so clearly hurting.

She forced herself to take a breath and let it out slowly before she spoke again. "Do you remember what Pastor Phillip told us during our premarital counseling? He said it wouldn't be your money or my money, but *our* money. He said how we handle our finances would say a lot about the state of our relationship."

Ezra set the dumbbell down, a flush spreading across his face.

"When we met, I had nothing," she said. "You gave me a life and a lifestyle better than I could have ever dreamed. You got us this beautiful home. And you've never, ever made me feel like it's your money or like I'm living off you."

Breathing heavily, he rested his elbows on his knees. He was listening.

"Now that I've had some luck, it's not about me supporting you," she said. "I want to help us. I'm not trying to take over or push you out."

He pushed both hands through his hair, exhaling sharply. "I know. I'm sorry for sounding like a jerk. I know you're not..." He paused, blinking rapidly. "I'm not handling this well. It's just a lot to take in."

She sat next to him, wrapping an arm around his waist. "I understand. It's been a whirlwind for me too."

Ezra sighed, then looked at Martha with a rueful smile. "I think I need to play my jerk card here."

A smile tugged at her lips. "Your jerk card? Are you sure? You know you only get one of those a year."

"I'm pretty sure my behavior qualifies right now," Ezra said, his tone softening. "I was being an insensitive idiot, and I said stupid things. Will you accept my jerk card for one instance of dumb behavior, and can we rewind this conversation to before I started being a numpty?"

Martha's smile widened. "Jerk card accepted. But use it wisely, mister. You've got a long way to go before your next one."

He took her hand, his face growing serious. "Please forgive me. I was completely out of line to talk to you like that."

"Of course." She reached up and brushed a lock of hair off his forehead, letting her hand linger on his face.

"Thank you," he whispered.

Suddenly, she was aware of the heat radiating from his bare skin, of his body so close to hers. Her heart stuttered at his proximity, at the familiar scent of his cologne mingled with clean, manly sweat.

Ezra cupped her cheek, his thumb brushing across her skin. His gaze dropped to her lips, and time stood still as he leaned forward, stealing her breath with a scorching kiss.

He gasped as her hands slid up his back, her fingers tracing the solid strength of him, the tremor in his muscles. His other hand settled at her waist, drawing her closer.

The kiss deepened naturally, as though their bodies knew what to say where words had stumbled.

The doorbell chimed loudly, echoing through the house.

They both jumped, Martha's heart jolting at the sudden interruption.

She groaned. "Oh no, that must be Kelsey and C.J. I completely forgot—"

"Kelsey and C.J.?" Ezra's brow furrowed.

"My glam team," she explained hurriedly, standing up. "I got caught up in our conversation and didn't tell you—there's a premiere tonight for my new music video. It's at that fancy cinema in Soho. They've come to help me get ready."

Ezra blinked. "A premiere? Tonight? But you just got home."

"I know, I know. I'd completely forgotten about it, but my manager says it's important. I wanted to ask if you'd come with me, actually." She bit her lip, suddenly uncertain. "Would you? Come with me, I mean?"

The doorbell chimed again, more insistently this time.

"I should get that," Martha said, glancing toward the door. "But please, think about it? I know it's short notice, but it would mean a lot to me to have you there."

Ezra stood. "I'll come," he said with a wink, "as long as when we get back, we can continue our—what did you call it?" He gestured toward the bench. "Continue our conversation where we left off."

Martha's face warmed. "It's a deal," she said, hurrying toward the door with a smile on her face.

Chapter Seven

*E*ZRA SAT NEXT TO Martha in the back of the limo, his fingers intertwined with hers. He couldn't get over how stunning she looked, although he wished her blush pink off-the-shoulder gown wasn't quite so... off-the-shoulder.

The luxurious fabric left her shoulders, arms, and much of her back bare, its color a striking contrast against her glowing brown skin. Her hair was swept up in a twist, the style emphasizing the graceful line of her neck.

Martha's face was flawless, her eyes dramatically enhanced with smoky makeup that made them seem even more captivating than usual. Her full lips, painted a deep, rich nude shade, reminded him of the kiss they'd shared at home and the promise of more to come.

But she wasn't just his Martha anymore. She was Morgan, the star, ready to dazzle her legions of adoring fans. This was her world now, and he would find a way to support her.

Ornate gold earrings caught the light as she shifted in her seat and turned toward him. "I think we're almost there," she said, smiling and squeezing his hand. "I'm excited to see the video, too. I've not had a chance to see the whole thing yet."

Raising her hand to his lips, he kissed her fingertips. "I'm sure it will be amazing. But I hope it won't run too late. I'm on the roster to lead worship tomorrow."

"Alex said there's a cocktail party after the screening, but I'm sure we can leave when we've done the rounds."

He stroked her hand. "Everyone at church is really looking forward to seeing you again."

Martha's smile faltered for just a moment. "Mm hm." She looked down, smoothing her dress.

It would be wonderful to worship with her by his side again. They would figure out how to do life together, even with everything that had changed.

The limousine glided to a stop in front of The Velvet, Soho's most exclusive private cinema. Even through the tinted windows, Ezra could see the chaos outside—a sea of flashing cameras and excited fans waving behind metal barriers.

His heart quickened. All of these people had come just for a glimpse of his wife.

Her PPO opened the car door. A wall of sound shattered their quiet cocoon. Shouting paparazzi, screaming fans, and the steady thrum of dance music pumping from hidden speakers. The soundtrack of Martha's new world.

Martha squeezed Ezra's hand one last time, flashed him a reassuring smile, then stepped out of the car.

He could pinpoint the moment her blush pink gown came into view from the way the crowd erupted.

"Morgan! Morgan! Over here!"

"We love you, Morgan!"

Camera flashes exploded in a dizzying rhythm, temporarily blinding Ezra as he stepped out behind her. He blinked rapidly, trying to adjust to the onslaught of light and noise.

Martha—no, he corrected himself, this was definitely Morgan now—stood poised at the edge of the red carpet. Her smile was dazzling, her posture perfect as she struck a pose for the wall of photographers. She turned slowly, giving them shots from every angle, her bare back now fully on display to the ravenous lenses.

A tall, slender man in an elegant suit appeared by Martha's side. He placed a hand on her bare back, his grin exposing a mouthful of expensive veneers.

Bristling, Ezra stepped forward, then he recognized who it was—Martha's manager, Alex.

"Morgan, darling, they're ready for you inside," Alex said. He began guiding Martha toward the cinema's ornate entrance.

As the sea of photographers called out for "Morgan" to turn this way and that, Alex leaned in close to Martha's ear, whispering something that made her laugh.

Ezra hung back, unsure whether he should follow.

Martha turned around, her gaze landing on Ezra. She reached for his hand. "Come on. Let's go find our seats."

Alex's smile grew rigid. "Ah, you're here, too, Ezra. I hadn't noticed you back there. Nice to see you again. I'm sure we can squeeze you in."

Martha elbowed Alex. "He'll sit next to me, of course." Her fingers tightened around Ezra's hand.

Alex bowed. "Right this way."

He ushered them both toward the entrance of the cinema.

They stepped into the already crowded lobby of The Velvet. The air buzzed with excitement and the clinking of champagne glasses.

Martha's fingers trembled on his arm, the only sign that she might be nervous.

After years in the music industry and countless events like this, Ezra could tell at a glance whether or not a party was a big deal. The caliber of guests who had come for this premiere made it immediately apparent that Morgan was a very big deal. If the mayhem outside wasn't proof enough, the people in this room showed Ezra beyond any doubt just how bright Martha's star was shining right now.

He spotted Claire Peterson, the head of A&R at Harmony Records, chatting animatedly with Daniel Foster, the influential music critic from *Soundwave* Magazine. Sipping from a champagne flute near the bar, Leo

Chang, CEO of StreamTune, was deep in conversation with Mia Winters, the hotshot music video director known for her boundary-pushing visuals. No way. Was she the one who'd directed Martha's video?

Even more telling was the presence of Olivia Thornton, the notoriously picky editor-in-chief of *Tempo* Magazine. She rarely graced events like these unless she sensed a major story in the making.

Ezra recognized more faces from music award shows and industry events he'd attended over the years, each one a power player in their own right. And they were all here for Martha.

A woman with a sharp angular bob bore down on Martha, calling out, "Morgan, darling!"

It was Sophia Reynolds, the sharp-tongued host of America's top-rated music talk show, "The Beat." Had she come all the way to London for this?

Sophia air-kissed Martha's cheeks. "We're all dying to see this video. I hear it's absolutely scandalous!"

Martha laughed, a throaty chuckle that must be part of the "Morgan" playbook. Martha's genuine laugh sounded nothing like that. "Well, you'll just have to wait and see, won't you?"

Sophia turned toward Ezra. "And who's this divinely gorgeous hunk of manhood with you, darling? You must introduce us."

"This is my husband Ezra."

Sophia leaned forward, kissing the air around Ezra's head. "Some girls have all the luck. Ezra, do you mind if I steal your wife for a minute? There's someone I want her to meet."

Before Ezra could respond, Alex appeared, deftly commandeering the conversation. "Lovely to see you, Sophia. I'm so glad you made the trip across the pond. I promise it'll absolutely be worth your while. But I'm afraid your chat with Morgan will have to wait. We're starting soon."

Martha's hand was still firmly on Ezra's arm, so he walked on her other side while Alex guided them through the crowd.

Ezra couldn't help but marvel at how effortlessly Martha—Morgan—navigated this world. She smiled at just the right moments, laughed the Morgan laugh at all the right jokes, her hand never leaving his arm even as she worked the room. Everyone here saw her as an equal, a star in her own right, an outsized presence with a gravitational pull that belied her petite frame. He was just Morgan's arm candy—her tall, silent shadow.

When Alex had apparently decided Martha had schmoozed enough, he took a step back and spoke loudly, his voice ringing out over the crowd. "Ladies and gentlemen, if you'll please make your way into the screening room through the doors on the left, we're about to begin."

The crowd filtered into the adjoining room, a plush, state-of-the-art mini theater. Red-jacketed ushers guided Ezra and Martha to the roped-off front-row seats.

As they sat down, Martha leaned close to him, her breath warm on his ear. "You okay?" she whispered.

Before Ezra could respond, Alex stepped to the front of the room, microphone in hand. The chatter in the room died down as he began to speak.

"Good evening, everyone. Thank you all for coming out tonight for this exclusive premiere of 'Resonance,' the latest video from the incomparable Morgan."

He paused as a smattering of applause rippled through the room. "This video, much like Morgan herself, pushes boundaries and challenges expectations. I think you'll all agree it's her most provocative work yet."

Ezra felt Martha tense beside him.

"So without further ado," Alex continued, "please enjoy the world premiere of 'Resonance'!"

The lights dimmed, and a hush fell over the audience. Martha's fingers trembled as they rested on Ezra's arm, and he covered her hand with his.

The screen flickered to life, and the opening notes of "Resonance" began to play. A pulsing beat filled the room, and Ezra's chest tightened as the opening shot appeared.

Martha—no, Morgan—writhed on a bed of silk sheets, the camera panning slowly over her body. Her costume, if it could be called that, was little more than strategically placed scraps of shimmering fabric.

Ezra's jaw clenched as he watched his wife arch her back, lips parted in a sensual pout.

The music swelled, a far cry from the soulful melodies Martha used to love, which were about touching hearts rather than inflaming desires. This was pure pop—auto-tuned and over-produced. The lyrics were shallow, filled with double entendres and not-so-subtle innuendos.

As the chorus hit, the scene shifted. Morgan was now dancing in a rain of glitter, surrounded by a troupe of scantily clad male dancers. As she gyrated from one man to another, her movements exuded a sinuous and provocative allure.

Ezra's face grew hot. Why had she brought him here to see this? How could she possibly think this was okay?

He glanced around the darkened room. Everyone, *everyone* was watching his wife writhe and undulate on the massive screen. This wasn't art. This wasn't the music they'd dreamed of making together. This was... this was something else entirely.

The video rolled on, each scene more provocative than the last. Morgan in a steamy shower. Morgan, wearing thigh-high boots and hot pants, straddling a motorcycle. Morgan dancing in a cage.

With each new image, Ezra felt a piece of his heart crack.

Where was the woman who used to sing about faith and love, who wanted to glorify God with her gift? Where were the lyrics that touched people's souls? This glossy, hyper-sexualized persona on the screen was a stranger to him.

As the final notes of the disgusting spectacle faded, the theater ignited into thunderous applause. Cheers and whistles filled the air as the lights slowly came up.

Ezra blinked, stunned by the enthusiastic response around him. These industry elite weren't just accepting what he found shameful—they were praising it, rewarding it. And Martha was learning to see through their eyes. This was Martha's world now. These were the people shaping her values.

She turned, searching his face, a question in her gaze.

Alex's voice boomed through the speakers. "Ladies and gentlemen, wasn't that absolutely incredible?" The applause surged again. "And now, please welcome to the stage, the woman of the hour, the sensational Morgan!"

Martha squeezed Ezra's hand briefly before she rose. As she made her way to the stage, the entire audience leaped to their feet. The standing ovation was deafening, a sea of clapping hands and beaming faces.

Ezra stood too, clapping mechanically.

Martha ascended the steps to the stage, her blush pink gown shimmering under the lights, floating around her body with a sensual grace. She was radiant as she basked in the crowd's adoration.

As she took her place next to Alex, flashing her megawatt smile, Ezra wondered how the modest, shy woman he'd married had turned into the seductive vixen he'd seen on the screen.

Alex raised a hand, and gradually the applause died down. "Morgan, that was sick," he gushed. "Everyone with eyes in their head was simply blown away. Am I right?"

Loud whistles from the audience answered his question.

Grinning, Alex spoke again. "Now, I'm sure our guests have plenty of questions. Shall we open the floor?"

As hands shot up across the auditorium, Ezra sank back into his seat. Martha wanted his support. But how could he support her when everything about her new music and her new image was abhorrent to him?

Chapter Eight

THE LIMOUSINE'S DOOR CLOSED with a soft thud, sealing Martha and Ezra into a sanctuary of quiet after the whirlwind of the premiere.

She sank into the plush leather seat, exhaling slowly. The energy that had carried her through the evening was quickly evaporating, leaving her feeling drained but still wired. Tonight had been a complete triumph. A glimpse at Alex's phone showed that her video was blowing up on social media. And everyone at the premiere had raved about it. Everyone except Ezra.

She glanced at her husband, who stared out the window. The passing streetlights illuminated his profile at rhythmic intervals. He'd been strangely quiet after the showing, standing in the corner at the post-premiere cocktail party nursing a glass of soda water until she'd come to him, ready to leave.

His silence unnerved her. Usually, after events, he'd be full of observations and gentle teasing about the quirks of industry folks. Tonight, his lips were pressed into a thin line, his shoulders tense.

She pushed a button and the privacy partition hummed as it rose, cutting them off from Ray.

"So," Martha began, her voice sounding too loud in the quiet car, "what did you think? Everyone seemed to love the video, but I want to know what you thought about it."

He turned to face her; his expression unreadable in the dim light. He opened his mouth, then closed it again, as if weighing his words carefully.

Martha's heart raced. She knew some parts of the video were risqué, given Ezra's conservative tastes. Having not seen the full video until tonight, Martha was surprised and, if she was honest with herself, a little shocked at just how sensual the camera work made it all look, with all those angles and shots trailing over her body.

But surely Ezra could see past that and appreciate how incredible it was, how it showcased her growth as a performer. Couldn't he? Everyone, all the industry heavyweights and her fans, absolutely loved it.

"Ezra," she prompted gently, reaching for his hand. "Please. Be honest with me."

"You want me to be honest?"

"Yes." Her stomach churned.

He glanced at her face, then sighed. "I hated it."

His blunt words were a punch to the gut. She swallowed, struggling to keep a handle on her emotions. "Wow. Okay. I know you're not a fan of the song."

He squeezed her hand, which still lay in his. "You know what? I'm sorry I said anything. Maybe it's better to talk about this another time, when I've had a chance to think and have a filter in place. I don't want to hurt your feelings."

She shook her head. "No, I want to know how you feel now. You clearly have strong opinions about it. You actually *hate* it? That's a strong word."

"Okay, if you really want to talk about it... It's not just the song, although you don't need that auto-tune stuff. Your voice is incredible already, without all the electronic manipulation. It's... it's the video. The way you were dressed, the dancing, the overt sexuality of it all. It made me feel very uncomfortable. You have this amazing God-given talent. And what I saw tonight, just... just cheapened it."

She pulled her hand away. "Go on, tell me how you really feel."

"This is why I didn't want to talk about this now. I knew you'd get upset."

"Of course I'm upset. You just called what I did cheap."

"That isn't what I meant," he said. "I meant you've got so much more to offer. You're so much better than what I saw today. You don't need to titillate people. You don't need to perform like an exotic dancer."

"I'm cheapening my talent and performing like a stripper. Got it."

Ezra threw his hands up. "You asked for my opinion and insisted that I tell you what I thought. And now you won't even listen."

"Okay, fine, I did ask." She clenched her fists. "I made the mistake of thinking that maybe, just maybe, my husband might give me a tiny pat on the back."

"Haven't you heard a word I said?" Frustration edged his voice. "Martha, look at me."

He covered her fists with his hands and held her gaze.

"I think you're amazing. You have an insane gift. The way you sing? You give me goosebumps every single time. I wish I had half your talent. But it's just this whole Morgan image that bothers me. I can't pretend to like or encourage the direction Alex is leading you in, with all that overt sexuality."

Was it pathetic that she drank in his praise like a parched wanderer falling upon an oasis? Why couldn't he appreciate what she could do?

"But everyone else absolutely loved it, and they're some of the biggest names in the industry," she said. "They got it. Maybe you're the one who's not seeing the entire picture. This video isn't just about shock value or sex appeal. Mia Winters meant it to be a powerful artistic statement about female empowerment and owning my strength as a woman. The choreography tells a story of breaking free. And did you even notice the symbolism in the set design? The cage scene represents the music industry's attempts to box me in, while the motorcycle symbolizes my journey to freedom and self-expression."

Even as she spoke the words, a small voice inside questioned whether these artistic justifications really made the video's overt sensuality okay. She shut the voice down, talking over it. "Mia and I worked closely together to ensure every frame, every movement, had purpose. It's a visual poem, a declaration of artistic freedom."

Ezra frowned. "Maybe that's how you see it, but I don't think any red-blooded male saw any poetry in that. All they saw was you moaning on a bed, writhing in the shower, and straddling a motorbike."

She yanked her hands away. Anger washed over her, and it was almost a relief—an excuse to face his righteous indignation with some of her own. "Well, at least they noticed me. At least I'm not invisible anymore."

His eyes widened. "You were never invisible, Martha."

"Really? I was. Even to you. Why didn't you ever notice I could be a recording artist? Why didn't you see anything in me beyond the fat, frumpy wife in the background? Do you remember who first discovered what I could do? Alex. Not you. Alex."

He stared at her, shock written all over his face. "I never knew you wanted to perform until that open mic night."

"No, it never occurred to you because I was a hundred pounds too heavy and dressed like a bag lady. And now, for the first time in my life when I feel beautiful, seen, and valued, it seems like everyone in the whole world is happy for me about it, except you."

"Martha, I—I don't even know what to say." He shook his head. "You're wrong. I've always thought you were beautiful. How could you even believe I didn't?"

"Have you? Because I don't remember ever feeling that way. Not until now."

"Martha, please—"

"No." She held up a hand, cutting him off.

"How can you say all this stuff and not even give me a chance to respond?"

She shook her head. "I can't do this right now. I just... I can't."

She hadn't meant to say all that to him. All that stuff about feeling invisible. She hadn't even realized she'd thought it.

Martha stared out the window, her body shaking, blinking back tears, while Ezra sat rigid beside her, the weight of unspoken words hanging heavy between them.

This wasn't just about the music video anymore. It had gone way beyond that. The argument had ripped open a well of intense resentment she hadn't even known existed within her. Resentment toward her own husband. The depth of these feelings frightened her. What else might spill out if they kept talking?

The rest of the ride passed in suffocating silence. When the limo finally pulled up to their house, Martha was out the door before Ray left the driver's seat. She hurried inside without a backward glance, running straight upstairs.

In their bedroom, Martha changed quickly into her pajamas and scrubbed off her makeup with shaking hands.

She clicked off the lights and slipped into bed in the dark, turning her back to Ezra's side. Her body was tense, waiting. She heard his footsteps come up the stairs, then pause just outside their room.

The door opened, spilling light in from the hallway.

"Martha?" His voice was soft, hesitant. "Are you awake? I... I don't want us to go to bed angry."

Martha squeezed her eyes shut, forcing her breathing to remain slow and steady. She couldn't face him right now. Her emotions were too raw.

"Martha?" His voice was closer.

Biting her lip, she lay still.

After a long moment, he stepped away.

From the en-suite bathroom, Martha heard the muffled sounds of his bedtime routine. The soft click of the bathroom door. The faint rush of water from the faucet. The barely audible hum of his electric toothbrush. Then silence, broken only by the quiet pad of his feet on the plush carpet. The whisper of fabric as he changed into his pajamas. The subtle creak of his bedside drawer opening and closing.

The bed dipped when Ezra got in and she felt him hesitate, as if debating whether or not to reach out to her.

Finally, he settled on his own side.

As she lay there, feigning sleep, part of her yearned for Ezra's approval, longed to turn over and seek comfort in his arms. Then his words in the limo came back to her like a slap in the face.

I don't think any red-blooded male saw any poetry in that. All they saw was you moaning on a bed, writhing in the shower, and straddling a motorbike.

She clenched her fists. Then, unbidden, darker thoughts crept in. When had everything shifted? When had being seen become more important to her than what she was showing? What if Ezra was right? If that video were shown in front of the people at Grace Community Church, could she so easily justify her choices? What about God? Would He—

No. She wouldn't go there. She tried to push the questions away, but they lingered at the edges of her consciousness.

His breathing was now slow and even. He was asleep.

She'd always envied his ability to drop off as soon as his head hit the pillow. While she lay here and stewed.

He was only inches away, but she felt farther away from him than when she'd been halfway around the world. And even further from the woman she used to be.

Chapter Nine

*E*ZRA BURST THROUGH THE doors of Grace Community Church, his hair still damp from his rushed shower.

"I'm so sorry I'm late," he called out to the worship team already assembled on the stage.

As he hurried down the aisle, fumbling with his guitar case, he couldn't shake the gnawing worry in his gut. In his rush to get here, he hadn't had a chance to see if Martha was awake, let alone speak to her. This was the worst possible start to the morning after a miserable night.

He felt sick after the shock of Martha's video and their fight. And now he was supposed to somehow pull himself together and lead the congregation in worship.

Nathan Lang, who played drums, waved away Ezra's apology with a chuckle. "Don't sweat it, Ez. You're always here for us. We can cut you some slack once in a blue moon." In his early forties, the balding ex-soldier was like a second big brother to Ezra.

The whole team felt like family.

Ezra unclipped his guitar case and lifted out his cherished Martin D-28. He ran his fingers along the smooth, sunburst-finished spruce top and cradled the mahogany neck. The rich, warm color of the wood matched the shade of Martha's skin.

Martha. A pang went through his chest. Would she come to church today? Those things she'd said to him last night—did she really believe them? Had he made her feel so invisible and undervalued that she was seeking validation from the admiring gazes of other men?

Maybe it was a mistake to come today. He could have called someone—his brother Zach, perhaps—to fill in for him while he stayed home and sorted through this thing with Martha. But he was here now, and he had to somehow hold it together and minister to the church.

As he slung the leather guitar strap over his shoulder, Mike, the bassist, walked past and squeezed his shoulder. Leaning in, Mike whispered with a knowing smile. "I hear Martha's back in town. I get it, mate. No one's going to blame a husband for oversleeping under those circumstances."

Ezra forced a smile, his chest tightening as he plugged his guitar into his pedalboard. If only they knew the actual circumstances. His bed last night was as frosty as a glacier.

He stepped on his tuner pedal, muting his signal. The digital display lit up with a soft glow. As he plucked each string from the low E to the high E, adjusting the tuning pegs, Nathan's voice broke his concentration.

"Hey Ez, will Martha be joining us this morning? It's been ages since we've seen her."

Ezra's fingers fumbled, and he strummed a dissonant G chord. Wincing at the sound, he cleared his throat. "She... she might." The way they'd left things last night, he doubted it.

He bent his head over the guitar, pretending to focus on the tuner's display, but really using the moment to compose himself.

He'd been over and over his words last night, and he still felt he was right about her music video. Fine, he'd been rather blunt with his opinion, and he regretted that. Maybe if he'd expressed himself more tactfully, she wouldn't have felt so hurt and defensive. But it hadn't taken her long to go into attack mode, switching the topic on him so they were talking about something else entirely and she was lobbing those rapid-fire accusations at him.

And the things she'd said. Where was all that coming from? And how long had she felt like that? A tendril of fear snaked around his gut. There was a lot more going on with her than he knew.

He swallowed hard, grateful for the familiar routine of prepping his guitar. This was something he could understand. Unlike the weird alien landscape his marriage had become.

Strumming a G chord, he frowned at a slight dissonance in the B string. With a quick twist of the peg, the string sang in harmony with the others. If only fixing things with Martha was so simple.

He ran through a quick series of chords and a scale, the practiced movements grounding him.

"Guys, let's warm up with 'How Great is Our God,'" he called out. "One, two. One, two, three, four."

As the band launched into the familiar worship song, Ezra stepped on his volume pedal, gradually swelling the sound into the amp. He reached down to tweak the EQ settings directly on his amplifier. Adjusting the low, mid, and high frequencies, he fine-tuned the tone to sit perfectly in the mix with the other instruments.

A final strum confirmed everything was set just right, the rich, warm tone of the Martin filling the church sanctuary. Here, in this moment, one thing in his life was in tune. And God was still on His throne, still in control. He needed to get his mind and his heart away from his troubles and focus on worship.

Ezra took a deep breath. "Let's pray before we start. Nathan, could you lead us?"

The team gathered around him, heads bowed. As Nathan led them in a quick prayer, asking for guidance and that their music would truly glorify God and touch hearts, Ezra added his own private plea.

Lord, things are so strange with Martha now, and I don't know what to do. Forgive me if I did or said anything wrong last night. Help me this morning. Use me to serve Your people despite my weaknesses.

The team members chorused, "Amen," and dispersed back to their instruments.

"All right," Ezra said, pulling out the set list. "Let's run through the intros for these songs. I want to try something different with 'Amazing Grace.' Let's start a capella for the first verse. We'll repeat verse one, with guitar only. Nathan, you'll come in with soft brush strokes on the snare as we start the second verse. Mike, bring in the bass halfway through that verse. Sarah, join in for the last verse. Can we run through that quickly?"

The church began to fill up as the band finished their rehearsal. Ezra spotted his brother, Zach. And there was Mum, with little Owen.

Pastor Noah Chaplin announced the first hymn and Ezra stepped up to the mic, guitar in hand. He strummed a single D chord, letting it resonate for a moment.

"Amazing grace, how sweet the sound." His voice was clear and strong in the hushed sanctuary. "That saved a wretch like me."

As he started the third line, movement at the back of the church snagged his gaze. A petite, dark-skinned woman slipped in through the doors, and Ezra's heart bounded.

Martha?

His voice caught in his throat, the words of the hymn dying on his lips. He stood frozen, staring at the back of the church as his band members picked up the hymn, their voices blending in to cover his silence.

Ezra realized his mistake. It wasn't Martha. He closed his eyes, forcing himself to focus, and joined back in for the last line of the verse.

"Was blind, but now I see."

The service went on with its familiar rhythm, and Ezra tried his best to keep his mind and heart centered on the worship and teaching. But it was difficult when his wife constantly intruded into his mind.

Their story had started here, at Grace Community Church. This was where they first met and fell in love, when they were both active members of the youth group. He could almost see her sitting in the front row, her eyes shining with love and pride as he led worship.

It was a universe away from the glittering world she now inhabited. His shy, modest Martha didn't exist anymore. In her place, Morgan was cavorting in skimpy attire, drinking in the adulation of rabid fans.

Pastor Noah announced the final hymn, "In Your Presence," a song Ezra had composed five years ago. Based on Psalm 16, It was now a favorite of this congregation, also sung in churches across the UK, United States, and Australia.

Martha had once loved it, too.

Tears pricked his eyes as the song ended. He gathered himself as Pastor Noah prayed the closing prayer. What would he find when he went back home?

As Ezra packed up his guitar, he sensed someone approach.

"Hey," his brother Zach said, including the team in his greeting. "Excellent service today, guys."

Stepping closer to Ezra, he spoke in a low voice. "Everything okay? Didn't see Martha today."

Ezra swallowed hard. "She's resting. It's been a busy time for her."

"I can imagine. Being on tour can be brutal, and she's had a really long one. Not to mention back-to-back album releases." Zach's brow furrowed. "I've felt a burden to pray for you lately. Is everything all right?"

Zach's words caught Ezra off guard. For a millisecond, he considered unburdening himself about the fight with Martha, but the words wouldn't come. Instead, he shrugged. "I lost my recording contract with Silvertone."

Zach's eyes widened. "What? When did this happen?"

"Yesterday." The half-truth was bitter on Ezra's tongue. He hadn't thought about Silvertone since Martha's video premiere. His recording contract was the last thing on his mind, but it was a convenient excuse to give to his brother. Easier to tell him about his career failures than to voice his worries about his wife and his marriage.

"Man, I'm sorry." Zach squeezed Ezra's shoulder. "Did they tell you why?"

Ezra snapped the latches shut on his guitar case, giving his brother the summary of his contract termination and the news of his newer projects.

"Listen," Zach said, "I know this feels like a major setback, but God's got a plan here. Maybe this is Him clearing the way for something better." He paused, studying Ezra's face. "I meant what I said about praying for you. There's something... I don't know. Let me know if you need anything. And say hi to Martha. Maybe we can hang out sometime soon? Mum was talking about doing something when Levi and Adria get back from their honeymoon."

Ezra picked up his guitar case, avoiding his brother's searching gaze. "Sounds good. And thanks for the prayers."

If his brother knew how much he needed them, Zach would be on his knees beseeching heaven right now.

Chapter Ten

ARTHA SIPPED A GLASS of lemon-flavored water at the kitchen counter, fighting an impulse to bolt to the spa and hide there for the rest of the day.

Ezra had left without speaking to her. After oversleeping and missing church, her stomach churned at the thought of facing him.

The things she'd said to him last night... Where had that even come from? That bitter accusation about him never seeing her potential. She hadn't known those feelings ran so deep, and that scared her.

Her phone buzzed with a message from Alex. He was ecstatic about how her music video had gone viral overnight, trending across all the social platforms. Two major labels had already reached out, interested in poaching her from Harmony Records when her current contract was up for renewal. Alex said this kind of buzz could spark a bidding war.

The news left her feeling strangely empty, and she couldn't muster a reply. She sent him a single thumbs-up emoji, then silenced her phone. It seemed as though the happier Alex was with her career, the more tense things were with Ezra.

Morning sunlight streamed through the windows, casting long shadows over the granite countertops. Martha looked around their beautiful open-plan kitchen and living room. Not even this lovely house brought her pleasure. The colors, the textures and furnishings, the artwork—every hand-picked detail reflected another woman's vision for Ezra's home.

Her hand tightened around her glass. Even after all these years, she sometimes felt like a visitor in these perfectly curated rooms, with their constant reminders of a woman who'd understood Ezra's taste better than his own wife had.

She tensed at the sound of his key in the front door.

His quick footsteps echoed as he approached through the entryway, and he stopped short in the kitchen doorway, his gaze landing on Martha.

She burst straight out with her apology as he walked into the kitchen. "I'm sorry I missed church. I overslept."

"It's okay," he said, his voice gentle. "I overslept, too, and had to rush straight out because I was late for the worship team setup. I didn't plan to leave without talking to you."

He came closer to her. "Martha, we need to talk. I couldn't stop thinking about last night. The things you said."

Martha's heart kicked into a higher tempo. She wasn't ready for this conversation. Not when she'd barely processed things herself. "Ezra—"

"Please." He pulled out the stool next to her at the counter. "I need you to know that I've always thought you were beautiful. And I support your career, I do. But what you said about feeling invisible..." His gaze searched her face. "Have I really made you feel that way?"

The genuine pain in his voice brought tears to her eyes. "I shouldn't have said those things."

"But you did say them. And you meant them. They came from somewhere." He reached for her hand. "Talk to me, Martha. Please."

A lump filled her throat. She sensed his deep love for her. It washed over her like a warm, tender embrace. What could she say to him? There was so much he didn't see, didn't understand. How could she make him understand without destroying everything they had?

For a moment, looking into his earnest face, she wanted to tell him everything. About how alone she'd felt, about all those times when he had... But no. It was too dangerous.

She'd made discreet enquiries, and it seemed Ivy had moved out of town. Ezra no longer talked about her. Maybe she was gone for good, and it was all over. And if it was, why bring it up? If Martha tugged at that thread, her entire marriage might unravel.

"I was just tired," she said finally. "Overtired. You know how I get when I'm exhausted."

"Martha." His voice was so gentle it made her chest ache. "You're always tired lately. And I get it—your schedule is brutal. Maybe that's part of what's wrong."

"Nothing's wrong." The words came out too quickly.

"Let me make you some lunch." He squeezed her hand before letting go. "I haven't seen you have a proper meal since you got home. And you've had back-to-back events going on." He moved to the fridge and pulled out a bag of pre-washed salad greens. "And all these late nights, early mornings. It's not sustainable."

Martha watched him preparing lunch, her throat tight. He was trying so hard to understand, to help. Classic Ezra, in full fix-it mode. Like that character in the cartoon who bashed broken things with his magic hammer and made them instantly all right. She loved that about him—his immediate impulse to take care of her, to jump in and do something.

But, as always, he was focusing on surface things— her diet, her schedule—when the reality was so much more complicated.

"Mum asked about you this morning," Ezra said, popping open a can of sweetcorn. "Zach, too. Actually, everyone did."

"Really? How's Beth?" A pang of guilt shot through Martha. Her mother-in-law had a heart as vast and deep as the ocean. Beth had been like a true mother to her ever since she first started dating Ezra. Yet, as the distance between her and Ezra grew, Martha found herself pulling away from Beth as well.

It wasn't anything Beth had done—rather, Martha feared that being close to Beth would inevitably lead to sharing the troubles brewing between herself and Ezra. And she didn't want to put Beth in the awkward position of being caught between Martha and her son.

"She's loving being a grandma. Having a blast babysitting Owen." He glanced over his shoulder at her. "Zach talked about us all getting together soon."

"I'd like that."

Ezra smiled as he tossed a salad in a large bowl. "Great. Maybe we can set something up next week. If your schedule allows for it, I mean."

He served a plate for Martha and set it in front of her, then settled on the adjacent stool with a plate for himself. He reached for her hand and closed his eyes. "Thank You, Lord, for this meal," he prayed. "Please bless it for our health and strength. Amen."

"Amen. Thanks." She picked up a fork and pierced a cherry tomato.

"You know, Eden asked about you, too. She said she'd call you later."

"Ezra," she started, trying to keep her voice even, "have you been talking to people about us? About me?"

Ezra stared at her, brows drawn together. "No, of course not. Everyone's just noticed you've been... well, absent more than usual. They're worried, that's all. They miss you at church," he added carefully. "Have you been... attending anywhere while you're on tour?"

"When I can." She had caught a couple of online mega-church sermons months ago. That counted as 'when I can,' right? Life was just so busy, her schedule so packed. She relished the chance to sleep in on Sundays. And while moving from city to city, it was hard to find a congregation to attend.

His shoulders relaxed. "I'm glad you've still had some sort of fellowship."

His gentle acceptance made her stomach twist.

"Maybe we should talk to someone," he said. "Get some counseling, or at least some outside perspective. Pastor Noah would—"

"No." Martha pushed the plate away. "We don't need counseling, Ezra. I don't need fixing."

"That's not what I—" He broke off with a sigh. "I just want to help. Last night, you said things that... I hate thinking I made you feel invisible. I'm just trying to find a way to help us through this. If not counseling, then what do you suggest? We can't keep going like this. If there are things we need to work through—"

"There aren't." Her voice came out sharper than she intended. She wanted to keep on believing her words were true. Maybe they would be if she said them to herself often enough. She spoke in a softer tone. "I just need some space. Some time to think."

"Space? We haven't seen each other in nine months. You need even more space?"

"I—" She groped for words that made sense, even to her. "Maybe we just need to get used to being together again. Some time to adjust."

"Okay," he said slowly. "How can I help do that?"

Dear Ezra. He was trying so hard. She had to figure out how to get herself under control, so she didn't ruin everything. Her fingers curled around his hand. "We're doing it now. Just having a normal meal together like this."

Silence fell between them as she poked at her salad. Would time really help? It had to. If she let him keep probing, if she started talking about why she'd felt so invisible... other things might come spilling out. Things she wasn't ready to face. Maybe she never would be. It was better to put it all behind her and let sleeping dogs lie.

Chapter Eleven

HE HOUSE FELT DIFFERENT at night. Bigger. Emptier. Ezra moved through the ground floor, checking the windows and doors.

Through the kitchen window, he caught a glimpse of Marcus, the PPO on night duty today, patrolling the grounds. Beside him trotted a Belgian Malinois, its coat gleaming under the moonlight, ears perked and alert.

The dog moved with trained precision, a silent yet formidable guardian. While Ezra was sure his wife was physically safe with such vigilance, the health of their relationship was a different question entirely.

Today hadn't been too bad, though. Sharing lunch and a quiet dinner together felt like a tiny step forward.

In the living room, he found Martha's phone on the coffee table, its battery almost dead. Smiling, he plugged it into her charger. She always forgot to charge it before bed. Some things hadn't changed, at least.

Switching off the last light, he paused at the foot of the stairs. The security panel showed all green. Safe and secure.

He climbed the stairs quietly, then paused in their bedroom doorway.

Martha sat up in bed, propped against a pile of pillows, reading a glossy magazine. The soft glow of her bedside lamp cast shadows that highlighted the contours of her face. All her makeup, the gloss and glamor of "Morgan," was stripped away.

Her bare face, so open and unguarded, tugged at his heart. This was the Martha he cherished, the one beneath the megastar's facade, the woman whose inner radiance and unadorned grace had first captured his love all those years ago. Seeing her like this, so vulnerable yet serene, reignited a flicker of hope that perhaps the girl he once knew was still there, waiting to reconnect.

What could he do to make things right between them?

He sighed, and she glanced up. Was he imagining it, or did some sort of shutters close behind her eyes?

She put her magazine on the table. "Ready for bed?"

"Almost."

She clicked off her lamp and settled down, curling onto her side with her back to him.

He moved quietly around the room in his regular nighttime routine, changing into his pajamas and cleaning his teeth.

Finally, he slipped under the covers. For a moment, he lay still, listening to Martha's breathing. Then he moved closer, sliding an arm around her waist, his fingers resting on the silky fabric of her nightdress, relishing the warmth of her body.

He leaned closer, breathing in her distinctive scent of lavender mingled with sandalwood as his lips caressed the tender skin in the hollow of her neck.

"Not tonight, Ezra. Please."

Her quiet words packed the force of a gut punch. He withdrew his arm and rolled onto his back, staring up into the darkness. She'd asked for space earlier. He should have respected that instead of pushing.

"I'm sorry," he whispered. "I just... I miss you."

Martha didn't respond. His words were so quiet, he wasn't even sure she'd heard him.

Minutes, or maybe hours, later, her breathing settled into the rhythm of sleep, but his own mind raced. When was the last time they'd made love? That weekend in Amsterdam last year? It was depressing to even try to calculate.

Don't take it personally, he told himself. She was exhausted. She'd only just arrived from a grueling tour, going straight from the airport to Levi's wedding. Then she spent the day at her modeling shoot, immediately followed by the video premiere. Their fight and today's talk must have taken an emotional toll as well. She needed time to adjust to being home, just like she'd said. To adjust to being with him.

She wanted space. But had distance ever actually healed a marriage? In his experience, 'space' was just another word for growing apart. The thought terrified him.

What if those things she'd said about feeling invisible went deeper than he realized?

Every fiber of his being longed to reach for her, to bridge the physical gap between them, but he kept his hands at his sides.

Instead, he closed his eyes and prayed silently for wisdom, for patience, for whatever it would take to heal what was broken between them.

Chapter Twelve

ZRA STOOD AT ONE of the ornate bars scattered throughout Thornfield Manor's grand ballroom, waiting for the bartender to make Martha's virgin mojito. His mind kept drifting to the half-finished *Promise Ridge* theme song.

It was Friday night, and the producers wanted the final mix by Monday. But he was still wrestling with the bridge and the last verse. The bridge needed something to lift it, make it less forgettable, and the lyrics were an embarrassing mishmash of overused cliches that did nothing to capture the show's essence.

He'd been pulling fourteen-hour days in his studio all week, but tonight he'd torn himself away to escort Martha to this charity gala thing. The invitation had come in "Morgan's" name, of course, and he was her plus one among the entertainment industry movers and shakers schmoozing and making deals under the guise of supporting good causes.

They'd hardly seen each other all week, with Martha flying from one engagement to another, in between the time-consuming beauty appointments and rigorous training schedule that maintained her glamorous new image. He'd agreed to come tonight, hoping they might finally spend some time together.

So much for that idea. She'd been networking since they arrived, while he hovered on the periphery. All around him, industry players worked the room, their laughter a touch too loud, their smiles not quite reaching their eyes.

Martha—no, Morgan—was in deep conversation with some executives from StreamTune. Even from across the room, he could see how the men leaned in, caught in her orbit. She was dazzling tonight in a burgundy gown that draped her figure like liquid silk. The strapless bodice wrapped asymmetrically across her body, gathering at her waist and flowing into an elegant skirt with a daring side slit.

What was the point of him coming at all if the evening was turning out like this? If he couldn't enjoy her company here, he'd rather be working on *Promise Ridge*.

At least they'd be going home soon. The plan was to spend two hours here, then have a late dinner. The first time they'd be sharing a meal all week.

The bartender slid the mojito across the polished mahogany. "There you go, sir."

As Ezra reached for it, a familiar voice spoke close to his ear. "Well, if it isn't Ezra Falconer."

Ezra's fingers jostled the frosted highball glass, slopping half of the drink onto the polished counter.

He turned, slowly. Here was the perfect ingredient to sour an already unpalatable evening.

Ivy Willis stood there in an emerald green dress, her lips stretched wide in a smile she couldn't possibly feel. She'd cut her chestnut brown hair since he'd last seen her—it now fell in a sleek bob that framed her delicate china-doll features.

After what had happened the last time they met, how could she be so poised and unruffled?

"Ivy." He managed to keep his voice neutral. "I didn't know you'd be here."

"I'm surprised to see you here, too. This isn't exactly your scene. Though I suppose you're here because of Martha. Or perhaps I should say Morgan?" Her smile widened. "This must be quite a change for you both. Martha coming to industry events now instead of staying quietly at home. It's so nice to see her coming out of her shell. She looks absolutely fabulous tonight. What a transformation."

"I should get this drink to Martha," he said, grabbing the glass with what was left of the virgin mojito.

"Yes, of course. You mustn't keep your wife waiting. It must be quite an adjustment for you being married to the UK's hottest rising artist. Who would have thought shy little Martha would end up being the real star in the family? And so sexy, too." She leaned toward him, her lips drooping into a pout. "I was really sorry to hear about Silvertone, by the way."

He froze. "You know about that?"

"Of course. Old friends keep tabs on each other." She touched his arm lightly. "I've just been hired as a songwriter for Harmony Records. Maybe I could put in a good word for you. Oh, and give Martha my best."

Ezra glanced across the room, seeking Martha. She was staring right at him.

He threaded his way through the crowd, but by the time he got to where she stood with a group of executives, her back was to him.

He waited for a moment, but she was absorbed in some anecdote the short, heavyset man opposite her was telling. When the punchline came, her laugh was a shade too bright.

"Your virgin mojito," he said quietly, touching her elbow.

She accepted it, taking a sip before speaking as the loud conversation swirled around them. "I saw you talking to Ivy."

"Oh. Yeah." He shifted his weight. "Haven't seen her in a while."

She shot him a glance. "Really? That surprises me."

"We haven't been... uh..." His face burned. Should he tell Martha about what had happened with Ivy? But where would he even start? The words stuck in his throat. No. It was finished—a complete non-issue.

He cleared his voice. "Ready to head home soon?"

She studied her glass. "Actually, I think I'll stay for the after party."

He stared at her. "We said we'd be here for only a couple of hours. I've already wasted an evening here instead of working on *Promise Ridge*."

"Seems the evening wasn't entirely wasted since you could catch up with Ivy." She looked up at him, a hard glitter in her eyes. "You know what? Why don't you go on home if you're really done talking with your friend. I'll have Ray drive me back later."

"You're changing our plans just like that?"

"I'm not ready to leave yet. There are some people I still need to talk to."

As if on cue, the dark-haired executive waved a hand animatedly, capturing Martha's attention. "Come on, Morgan, what do you think? You've got to tell this Yankee friend of mine how wrong he is."

Martha's face transformed into bright animation. "Sorry, I didn't hear that. What do you want me to decide?"

"We're debating who's going to steal the show at the Brit Awards next year. What's your take? Who are you backing for Best Album? We've got a friendly wager going and could use your expert opinion to settle it."

Martha stepped forward. "That's a tough one, but I have a few thoughts."

As she joined the banter, the executives nodded eagerly and drew in closer to catch every word, edging Ezra out of the circle.

He clenched his jaw. Another evening alone, another chance to connect slipping away. He headed in the direction of the door, pausing briefly to cast one last glance over his shoulder.

Martha was laughing now, her attention fully absorbed by her companions. She'd probably not even noticed he'd left.

Chapter Thirteen

ARTHA STEPPED THROUGH THE front door of her home and slipped off her heels, the cool marble floor a relief to her bare feet. The impromptu jam session at Jared King's home studio should have been exhilarating, with some of the industry's most innovative artists dropping by, everyone feeding off each other's creative energy.

But she hadn't been able to focus. Her mind kept drifting back to the gala, to Ezra and Ivy having that intimate chat at the bar.

Ezra had been so patient and attentive this week, giving her the space she thought she'd needed to bury some of the whispers that haunted her. But the sight of Ivy touching his arm in that familiar way raised all the painful memories... and questions she didn't want to ask. She was terrified of what he might say—or not say—if she confronted him.

The house was silent and dark as she made her way toward the stairs, her strappy Jimmy Choos dangling from her fingers.

"Martha."

She startled at Ezra's quiet voice coming from the living room. As her eyes adjusted to the darkness, she made out his figure in the armchair. He was still wearing his dress shirt and suit pants from the gala, though he'd loosened his tie.

"You're still up?" Why wasn't he already asleep? Had he been waiting for her? She wasn't ready to talk to him yet. There was too much churning in her brain that she needed to process.

He stood and walked toward her. The dim light from outside traced the planes of his face, deepening the shadows under his eyes and highlighting the tension in his jaw. "We need to talk."

"Right now? It's late. I'm tired—"

"That's been your answer all week." His voice was subdued, but she heard the hurt in it. "Whenever I try to spend time with you, you're tired. Or busy. Or have another event to go to."

Martha shifted her weight. "We've both been working. You've been in your studio all week with *Promise Ridge*—"

"Martha, tell me the truth. Is there someone else?"

"What?" His question knocked the breath from her.

"Are you seeing someone else?" he repeated quietly, his gaze boring into her face.

"How dare you even ask me that." Her voice shook as anger swelled within her. After everything—after she'd seen him so cozy with Ivy tonight—he had the gall to accuse her of this? To even consider it?

"What else am I supposed to think? You've been in the country only a few days after months away, but you're hardly ever home. And when you are home, you can barely stand to be in the same room with me. You're happy to flaunt yourself for the whole world, but you flinch if I touch you."

Her hands tightened into fists. "If you think I could ever be unfaithful to you, you don't know me at all."

"You're right." Although his voice was quiet, his words lashed her like a bullwhip. "I don't know you anymore. The woman I married valued modesty and treasured our intimacy. Now you're doing lingerie shoots and strutting your stuff in music videos, but you can't bear for your own husband to touch you. This woman who avoids her husband, who would rather spend time with strangers than come home? I don't know her at all."

His words cut so deep, lacerated her so painfully, that all she wanted to do was lash out, to hurt him as deeply as he was hurting her. "Maybe you can't handle the fact that I'm not just your quiet, little, anonymous wife anymore." She clenched her fists. "Maybe you liked me better when I depended on you for everything. Maybe you're just threatened that my career is doing better than yours."

His face paled.

She had gone too far, said too much. Horror flooded through her as her words hung in the air.

"Wow." His voice was icy. "Is that really what you think of me? That I'm some controlling, insecure has-been sulking because he can't handle his wife's success?"

"Ezra—" His name froze on her lips.

He stared at her. "You wanted space, *Morgan*?" The name sliced through the air like a dagger. "You've got it. I'll give you all the space you want."

He brushed past her and went upstairs, two stairs at a time.

Martha stood alone in the darkened entryway, her shoes still dangling from nerveless fingers. What had she just done to her marriage? She was terrified of losing him, but she'd just pushed him away. Perhaps over the edge.

Chapter Fourteen

ORNING SUNLIGHT FLOODED THE kitchen as Martha hesitated in the doorway, her hand on the door frame.

Ezra stood at the counter, his back to her as he made coffee. He was already dressed in dark jeans and a T-shirt. Where had he spent what was left of their night? Not in their bed.

The cruel words she'd flung at him last night echoed in her head. She'd wanted to hurt him, and she had. What had possessed her to say those things? She took a deep breath, tightening her grip on the door frame to steel her nerves.

"Ezra—"

"Coffee's ready if you want some." His shoulders were rigid, his movements precise and controlled as he poured a cup for himself. He didn't look at her.

As she moved to the coffeepot, he stepped away, creating distance between them.

Filling up her mug, more because she needed something to do than because she wanted coffee, she tried again. "About last night—"

"Are you coming to Levi's today?" He cut her off. "Or do you have somewhere more important to be?"

The razor-sharp edge in his voice made her flinch. "Of course I'm coming."

"Good. I'm leaving in an hour."

She wrapped her fingers around her coffee mug, as though its warmth could shield against the icy chill radiating from her husband. "Ezra, please. I said some horrible things yesterday. I didn't mean—"

"Don't." He turned to face her, and the naked pain in his eyes froze her heart. "You wouldn't have said that if you didn't believe it at some level. Can you deny that's how you feel? The rising star and the has-been husband? Is that how you see us now?"

"No, that's not how I feel."

His jaw tightened. "Even if it's not how you feel, you knew exactly what I've been dealing with. And you weaponized that."

"No, I..." But what could she say? That she'd lashed out because seeing him with Ivy had reopened old wounds? That she was terrified of confronting what lay beneath their problems? That she'd rather push him away than have him choose to leave her?

He was right. She knew where he hurt. And she had attacked him with words calculated to inflict maximum damage. Her throat closed up as she stared up at him, tears filling her eyes. "I'm sorry, Ezra."

"I'll be in my studio until we leave." He walked out, leaving his coffee untouched on the counter.

She pressed a hand to her mouth as tears spilled down her cheeks. His cold fury was a palpable thing, a wave of ice that crashed into her, leaving her numb and shaken. The way he'd looked at her... How had they gotten here?

She dumped her coffee into the sink, leaning over it, her tears blending with the swirling brown liquid.

Straightening, she forced herself to draw a deep breath. She didn't have the luxury of falling apart. Not today. Somehow, she had to keep it together for Levi's sake. Wear a mask. Pretend everything was okay. She could do that.

But first, she had to know where Ezra had slept last night.

She headed upstairs. The first guest suite was untouched, everything still in its pristine state. But when she opened the door to the second bedroom, her heart clenched. The navy and gray suite still held traces of his presence from the night before—the faint imprint of his body on the plush quilted duvet, his running shoes placed neatly by the door, the lingering scent of his cologne in the air.

She moved closer, drawn by the evidence of his departure from their marriage bed. A half-empty glass of water stood on a coaster on the bedside table, next to his leather-bound Bible. His phone charger snaked across the surface, and in the bathroom, his electric toothbrush hummed quietly in its charging stand.

The closet door was slightly ajar. She pulled it open to find several of his shirts hanging in regimented array, enough for a few days. A couple of pairs of jeans lay folded on the shelves. A garment bag swung at the end of the rail.

He must have gotten his things while she was still asleep—come into their room, gathered what he needed, and moved out.

His last words from last night echoed in her mind. *You wanted space, Morgan? You've got it. I'll give you all the space you want.*

Regret, thick as a smothering fog, threatened to choke her. She spun around, hurrying to their bedroom.

Stuff down the pain. Push it aside. Focus on Beth. On Levi. She wouldn't let this overshadow Levi's homecoming. There would be time to go to pieces later.

But as she stepped through their bedroom door, her gaze fell on Ezra's dresser. The surface was stripped almost bare. His wallet, his cologne bottles, every item of his daily life was gone—except for one thing. The IWC watch sat in its case, her early birthday gift to him from just last week.

His message couldn't be clearer. She'd flung her success in his face, mocked his career, hacked at his self-worth with calculated cruelty. And now he had rejected her gift—the expensive watch bought with her new wealth, a symbol of the very success she'd used to wound him.

She sank onto the edge of their bed, her legs suddenly weak. What was that verse Eden liked to quote? Proverbs 14:1. *Every wise woman buildeth her house: but the foolish plucketh it down with her hands.* Martha was tearing down her home, her marriage... with her own actions.

She buried her face in her hands, letting the tears fall. Three minutes. She would allow herself three minutes to fall apart, to let the grief and regret overwhelm her. Then it would be showtime.

When the minutes were up, she dragged herself to the bathroom mirror. The woman who stared back at her was a mess—swollen, red-rimmed eyes, blotchy skin. Nobody could see her like this. Not even Ezra.

She could do this. She'd learned from the best makeup artists in the business how to hide anything—dark circles, blemishes, a broken heart. Time to put those skills to use.

First, eye drops to take away the redness. Then a cold compress to reduce the puffiness. She went through the familiar steps mechanically, watching as each product, each careful brush stroke, transformed her tear-stained face into a blank canvas.

Now she had just twenty-five minutes left until Ezra wanted to set off.

Walking into her closet, she faced the meticulously organized racks. Her stylist Kelsey had selected most of her wardrobe. She understood the intricacies of fashion far better than Martha ever could and had created a detailed and comprehensive catalog and reference guide to ensure "Morgan" was always perfectly dressed when she stepped out into the public eye.

In this world, with mobile phones everywhere, "Morgan" had to be camera ready at all times. She never knew when someone might snap a picture of her and publish it to the world. Her image was her brand. And her brand was her career.

Each section in the huge closet was clearly labeled—"Industry Events," "Performance," "Media Appearances." Attached to each item of clothing were detailed notes advising on appropriate occasions, combinations, and even the mood each outfit conveyed. It was like a roadmap to a world Martha admired but found perpetually confusing.

Martha found the section marked "Casual Family Events" and pulled out one of the recommended outfits—a pale yellow silk blouse and white palazzo pants. A clear plastic sleeve attached to the hanger held Kelsey's styling card and a photo of the complete look on a mannequin.

Martha glanced at Kelsey's notecard: "Effortlessly casual, photographs well in natural light. Appropriate for daytime family gatherings. Pair with minimal gold jewelry."

Time to become Morgan—although "Morgan" would be performing only for the family today. She dressed quickly, twisting her hair into a bun and applying light makeup, then headed down to the front door.

At precisely the hour he'd mentioned, Ezra's footsteps sounded on the stairs as he came up from the lower level.

His face showed no emotion. "I spoke to Ray. Since Falconhurst has its own security and it's only ten minutes away, he thinks you'll be fine just riding with me. But he can follow if you'd prefer."

She forced her fingers to still at her sides. "No, that's fine." She watched him check the house alarm. Hurt and angry as he was, he was still thinking of her safety.

He held the door for her—not out of warmth, but from the same courtesy he'd show to a stranger—then followed her to his Tesla. Even with all her careful preparation, one look from him—or rather, his refusal to really look at her at all—was enough to make her feel like she was coming apart at the seams. But she could hold it together. She had to.

The silence hung heavy between them as Ezra navigated the winding country lanes. The familiar ride seemed to take hours rather than minutes, and Martha exhaled in relief when the gates of Falconhurst appeared.

When she'd first met Ezra and he invited her home for Sunday lunch, Martha had been mortified to learn that this vast country estate was where he and his family lived. But Beth hadn't cared that Ezra's new girlfriend was a poor Black girl who grew up on a notorious council estate.

Her only concern was that Martha was a committed Christian, and that she made her son happy. Guilt gnawed at Martha's gut. Were either of those things still true? Ezra wasn't happy, and it was her fault. As for her faith, when was the last time she'd read her Bible? Or prayed? Or been to church? Or let what she believed influence her choices?

As they pulled up to the grand house, Beth was already hurrying down the front steps to meet them, her face wreathed in a smile, just like on that day ten years ago when Ezra first brought her to Falconhurst.

"Martha, darling! We've missed you so much." Beth enveloped Martha in a warm hug that brought unexpected tears.

"I've missed you, too." It was wonderful to soak in her mother-in-law's love. But would Beth be hugging her so warmly if she knew what Martha had said to Ezra last night? If she knew just how bad things were between them?

His footsteps crunched on the gravel behind her as he made his way to where Levi and Adria stood in the doorway. The young couple and their son now lived in the main house, while Beth had moved into the guest house on the property.

Ezra grasped Levi's hand and gave him a side hug. "So, this is what married life looks like on you, little brother?"

"Looks like I'm finally getting a taste of all those perks you've been hoarding to yourself, huh?" Levi shot back, grinning.

Martha watched Ezra's smile freeze, but he hid it quickly as he leaned in to kiss Adria's cheek. "Welcome to the family."

"Thank you." Adria smiled. She turned to Martha. "I'm so glad you could come. I know how busy you are."

A flicker of unease unsettled Martha's gut. Had Ezra said anything about her schedule? "I wouldn't have missed it for anything. Hello, Owen."

The little boy clung to his mother's sundress, peeking out at his new aunt.

"Come in, come in," Beth urged, linking her arm through Martha's.

They found Zach in the family room, manning an elaborate drinks station set up on the sideboard. His face lit up when he saw Martha. "Hey, Martha! It's great to see you." He came around to give her a quick hug. "Can I interest you in one of my world famous mocktails?"

"Yup. He's a drink mixing legend in his own mind," Levi said.

"And soon in yours, too, once you try one of these. Levi's just jealous he hasn't figured out my secret recipe yet. Let me guess—a virgin mojito, Martha?"

She smiled back. "Yes, please. You know me too well." How had she stayed away from her family for so long? She missed all the Falconers.

Zach went back to the drinks station, where he grabbed a bottle of chilled ginger ale from an ice bucket. "And for you, Ezra, I have perfected the Virgin Moscow Mule. It's got all the zing without the sting."

Martha walked to a plush armchair near the open French windows. The warm summer breeze brushed against her skin as she settled down. Why did this space have a warmth and comfort that was lacking in her own home?

Across the room, Ezra leaned against a wall near the drinks station, occasionally glancing through the open window, his mocktail untasted in his hand. Despite the casual facade and the occasional chuckle shared with Levi and Adria, there was a deliberate distance in his positioning, an invisible barrier he had erected between himself and Martha. Did anyone else notice?

Levi settled onto the side of Adria's armchair. "I wanted to talk about the charity album, Ez. Now that we're back, I'm hoping we can really get moving on it ASAP."

Beth shook her head. "Can't it wait until after lunch? Ezra and Martha just got here."

"I know what Ezra's like," Levi said. "The minute he sits down, he'll get so distracted by Adria's cooking that we won't get any sense out of him for at least half an hour."

"What charity album is this?" Martha asked.

From the shifting eyes and the silence that fell, Martha wondered whether she'd just asked an awkward question. Perhaps this was something that everyone expected her to already know about. Which she would have known about if she and Ezra were talking.

Ezra shifted his weight, but Levi jumped in smoothly.

"Sweetheart," he said, touching Adria's shoulder, "why don't you tell Martha about the project?"

Adria glanced up at her husband with a sweet, loving look that tore at Martha's heart. "Well, um, it's for my charity, New Beginnings Outreach. We work with young people aging out of the care system." Her voice grew steadier as she continued. "We've purchased some land, and we want to build transitional housing—apartments where care leavers can live while they find their feet. It's not just about providing an affordable roof over their heads. We want to offer psychological support, life skills training, everything I wish I'd had when I aged out of foster care."

Martha's throat tightened as memories of her own teenage years surfaced. If it hadn't been for the Falconers' kindness when her mother was more focused on keeping her latest boyfriend happy than parenting...

She sensed a kindred spirit, a shared hurt that drew her to Adria, and wanted to get to know her new sister-in-law better. "Sounds like you'll be doing some amazing work."

"The album will help fund Phase One," Levi explained, his hand still resting on Adria's shoulder. "Ezra, Zach, and I are working on it together. Ezra's writing all the songs and..." His face lit up. "Wait a minute. Martha, I know it's a lot to ask, but you should join us!"

Before Martha could react, Ezra spoke from his position at the window. "I'm not sure Martha will have the time. Her schedule's quite full."

Levi shrugged. "Oh. Well, never mind. It was just a thought."

"I'd like to help." Despite Ezra's implied refusal, the offer escaped before Martha thought better of it. She couldn't bear the thought of being excluded, of watching from the sidelines while the Falconers worked together on this family project.

"The cause is important, and..." She glanced at Adria, willing her new sister-in-law to understand. "I'd really love to be involved."

From his position by the window, Ezra went very still. His fingers tightened around his mocktail, though his expression remained neutral.

Martha's stomach clenched, but she couldn't take the words back now. And she didn't want to.

Chapter Fifteen

ZRA SAT SILENT AS the rest of his family burst out in ecstatic chorus. His fingers were tight around his glass as their excitement washed over him. Was Martha serious about joining in on this charity album project?

Levi's face blazed with enthusiasm. "Really, Martha? Are you sure?"

Martha smiled back at him. "I'll need to check with my manager, but I'm sure I can make him understand that this is something important to me."

Her words stung Ezra. So, she could squeeze in things that mattered to her. What did that say when time with him never seemed to make her priority list?

Adria's soft voice broke into his thoughts. "That would be wonderful, Martha. I thought about asking whether you could be involved, but didn't think it would be possible. The young ladies we work with love you."

"I got a lot more respect when our teens figured out that you're married to my brother," Levi told Martha with a grin. "With you on board, we'd be able to reach so many more listeners."

He glanced around at his brothers. "Am I right? Martha is on fire lately. She's got more pull than the three of us combined, and that's what we need to move sales and get streaming downloads."

Martha ducked her head. "Aw, come on, you're giving me way too much credit."

"He's right," Zach said. "Thanks for even considering joining in."

Ezra's jaw tightened. Had everyone forgotten the image "Morgan" projected these days? He glanced at Adria. Surely the young women in her program needed role models they could look up to, not the brand of female "empowerment" Martha portrayed in her "Resonance" music video.

But, no, every member of his family, including Mum, was delighted about Martha's involvement in this project. They clearly thought she was still the Martha they knew, with the values they all cherished. Values she appeared to have forgotten.

Levi had his phone up and was swiping at the screen. "The timing works perfectly. I've already blocked out studio time for next month, and I can coordinate everything around your schedule, Martha."

There was no avoiding it, then. This was happening.

Ezra stood and set down his glass, interrupting Levi mid-flow. "Sorry, I need some air." He walked to the French doors and stepped out into the garden.

The summer breeze did little to cool his temper. He heard footsteps behind him and turned to find Zach following him out.

"You okay?"

"Fine." Ezra leaned against the stone balustrade, staring out at the familiar landscape of his childhood home.

"Fine? Really? Then why did you look like you'd been called in for a root canal when Levi asked Martha to join the project?"

Ezra's fingers tightened on the weathered stone. "It's just... Look, the songs I've been working on for the project are not exactly 'Morgan's' style." He made air quotes with his fingers as he mentioned his wife's stage name. "My songs are explicitly Christian, deeply rooted in scripture. Her fans—"

"Will hear truth wrapped in beautiful melodies," Zach said, moving to stand beside him. "What better way to reach her audience? These young people who might never set foot in a church could encounter God through music they're willing to listen to."

Ezra lowered his voice. "Have you seen Martha's latest video?"

"No, I haven't. But does it matter? This is Martha. We know her heart, and she's already said she wants to do this." He paused, studying Ezra's face. "Is everything all right with you two, bro?"

Why was his brother so annoyingly perceptive? Ezra pulled off what he hoped was a nonchalant shrug. "Of course. It's just... her sound is so different. All that synthetic production, those manufactured beats—"

"Is that all?" Zach cut in. "Martha's voice is insane. You know that better than anyone. She could sing the telephone book and make it sound amazing."

"Yes, Martha could. But to get the real Morgan sound, I'll have to learn how to work with auto-tune."

A movement by the French doors caught his eye.

Martha stood there, her lips pressed tightly together. "Adria asked me to let you know lunch is ready."

"Thank you," Zach said quickly. "We're coming."

Martha turned and walked back inside.

Ezra's stomach dropped. How much had she heard? From the set of her shoulders, more than enough.

"Ez..." Zach's voice was quiet. "You might want to work on your timing. And your attitude."

Ezra didn't respond. He brushed past his brother, following Martha back into the house.

Chapter Sixteen

On Monday morning, the glass doors of Harmony Records swept open at Martha's approach. With her marriage feeling like an Arctic wasteland, home was the last place she wanted to be right now. "Morgan" was a tremendous success. "Martha," not so much.

The security guard's face lit up in recognition. "Good morning, Ms. Morgan."

"Morning," she said, smiling at the blushing young man. He must be new. The regular staff were used to seeing all the stars in Harmony Records' galaxy stopping by. The rookies knew not to ask for autographs or selfies, but they often couldn't avoid staring. Or turning red.

A larger-than-life image of "Morgan" dominated the wall of the atrium. It showed her on stage at Wembley, head thrown back, sequins catching the light. Images of the label's other top artists were placed around her in the promotional display, but judging by size and central placement, it was clear who Harmony Records counted as its most bankable star right now.

Today's packed schedule would allow her to spend most of the day in the "Morgan" bubble, in places where she could feel celebrated. Valued. Adored. Her first appointment was a meeting with her manager Alex, followed by a long list of commitments that would keep her away from home until this afternoon's charity album discussion with Levi, Ezra, and Zach.

Two days after she'd overheard it, Ezra's comment to Zach about auto-tune still lodged in her mind like a barbed hook. It just sank in deeper the harder she tried to shake it off. But what hurt even more than the words was knowing he was talking to other people about her in such a way. As though he despised her.

She'd made it through the family lunch, even managing to smile and laugh with everyone. It was easy as the rest of the Falconers were still so warm and welcoming.

But when going back home, there was nothing but silence between her and Ezra, a silence that stretched through the rest of Saturday evening. The size of their house meant they didn't have to cross each other's paths.

She'd skipped going to church with him yesterday, choosing to spend the morning at the spa instead. It was becoming far too easy to avoid church. And that scared her.

People were noticing her absence now. Eden, the pastor's wife, had left a message asking to meet for tea tomorrow. Unable to think of an excuse, Martha had agreed.

Here at Harmony Records, though, where "Morgan" reigned supreme, "Martha's" troubles were far away. Her Saint Laurent blazer dress was a subtle reminder of how far she'd come—the price tag alone would have made her younger self faint. And the buttons wouldn't have even closed over the heavier frame she'd had back then.

Staff members nodded respectfully or offered quiet greetings as she made her way to the executive elevator. A group of junior executives huddled by the coffee machine fell silent as she passed, then burst into excited whispers.

The elevator opened directly into the top floor's marble-floored corridor. Through the floor-to-ceiling windows, the iconic view from London's South Bank sprawled beneath a gray sky.

Martha's Christian Louboutin heels clicked against the polished floor as she made her way past the label head's office suite toward the main conference room.

Alex had commandeered the A&R department's prestigious space for their meeting. Two years ago, she'd have been lucky to even get a meeting room on one of the lower floors. His ability to get this space spoke volumes about his status as manager of Harmony's biggest star.

Through the glass walls, she saw him already seated at the head of the long table, phone pressed to his ear, his other hand making short, stabbing motions as he hectored the person at the other end of the line.

As she opened the door, his loud voice carried on.

"No, Morgan gets top billing. Her last three singles have topped the UK charts, and 'Resonance' is trending all over Europe. She doesn't do support slots anymore."

He winked at her as she settled into one of the leather chairs.

"Look, I've got to go. She's just arrived. Don't call me back unless it's to confirm that she's headlining that slot." He jabbed a button on his cellphone, then tossed it onto the glass-topped conference table. "Great to see you, Morgan. Have a good weekend?"

"It was fine." If she didn't count the frozen silence between herself and Ezra. Or the silence between her and God.

Alex rubbed his hands together. "Great, because we need to talk about Scandinavia. I've reworked those publicity dates for October, though I still think we're missing an opportunity here. Your streaming numbers are incredible in the Nordic countries, and those fans are not just loyal, they're also loaded. The kind who'll not just stream your music on a loop but buy physical albums and every piece of merch we put out. Let me show you the weekend sales figures." He grabbed his tablet and swiped the screen.

"Actually," Martha interrupted, "I need to talk to you about a different project I've agreed to work on."

Alex's fingers stilled on the screen. "What kind of project?"

"A charity album. My brother-in-law Levi is putting it together to raise money for young people leaving the care system. His wife has this amazing charity that's doing meaningful on-the-groundwork with former foster kids, and the album will help build accommodation for them as they transition into adult life."

"A charity album," Alex said slowly. "And who else is involved in this project? You mentioned Levi Falconer?"

"Yes. All three Falconer brothers are producing it." She hesitated, then added, "My husband is writing the music."

"Ezra?" Alex set down his tablet. "So, let me get this straight. Your latest music video has gone viral. Your fans in Scandinavia, who are among the most loyal, are desperate for you to go over there. And instead of making the most of that, you're talking about taking time out to work on a charity album?"

He leaned back in his chair and leveled his gaze at Martha. "Which charity are you helping, exactly? Is it the former foster kids? Or your husband's flagging career?"

A wave of heat flashed over Martha. Her marriage might be in trouble, but nobody got to throw shade on her husband. Not even her manager.

She clenched her fists. "I don't appreciate what you just implied about Ezra, Alex."

He raised his hands. "Sorry. It was meant to be a joke, but I admit it was in poor taste."

"Yes, it was." Her voice hardened. "Ezra has written some of the most beautiful songs I've ever heard. And he's a highly sought after composer. Do you know 'Whispers of You' just passed eight hundred million streams on StreamTune? Or that he's been hand-picked to score the *Promise Ridge* adaptation? His career is not flagging, and I won't sit here while you dismiss his talent."

"Whoa, whoa, whoa, Morgan. I'm sorry, okay? Please sit down. I know I was out of line."

He didn't look the least bit sorry. She'd always known that her husband and her manager would never be best buddies. But it bothered her that Alex felt bold enough to make such a comment about Ezra to her face. Almost as though he expected her to agree with him. Were the cracks in her marriage that visible?

She lowered herself back into her seat. "This project matters to me. These young people need support, and if I can help—"

"All right, all right." Alex drummed his fingers on the table. "I suppose it wouldn't be the worst thing, having you involved in a project like this. Shows your charitable side, and we could work with that to get some positive press coverage."

Martha bit back a retort. Of course, he'd find a way to spin it into something that benefited her career. And, by extension, himself.

"But," he said as he held up a finger, "if you're going to take time away from actively promoting 'Resonance,' you need to maintain visibility in other ways. Media appearances, industry events. Remember your new perfume launches in just a few days. And we should start working on material for your next release. Keep the momentum going, especially with how well the video's doing."

Martha nodded. She could work with that. "Levi's sending a production schedule sometime today, and I can plan my other engagements around that."

"Good. Speaking of new material..." Alex reached for his phone. "I've just negotiated a deal with a new lead songwriter for your next album. Someone who really understands where we want to take your sound."

Martha settled back into her chair. Good. She was keen to talk about her favorite part of being Morgan— the actual music. "What direction are you thinking?"

"We want to build on what worked with 'Resonance.' Keep that sensual energy, those catchy tunes, but add more emotional depth. Show your vulnerability while staying strong." He scrolled through something on his screen. "The label's very excited about this, and they gave us our pick of all their best talent. They think this songwriter can help craft the perfect balance—keep your existing fan base happy while pulling in new listeners. And I agree."

Martha shifted in her chair. Although Alex's instincts had been on point so far, steering her to a level of success she'd never dreamed of, he and the label had moved pretty far ahead without consulting her. "Don't you think it's time I got a say in who writes my music?"

"Of course, of course. You've earned that right. And you're free to ask for someone else if you don't like what your songwriter's come up with. But I think you'll be fine. You actually know her already. She tells me you go back a long way."

"She? Who is it?" Martha ran through her mental list of female songwriters.

"She's actually here in the building, meeting with the label head." Alex glanced at his watch. "Should finish up any minute. You'll love working with her—she's got an incredible track record. And I think—"

A knock at the door interrupted him.

"Come in," Alex called out.

Martha turned toward the door, and her heart froze. Ivy Willis stood in the doorway, elegant as ever, a portfolio tucked under her arm. She wore a red pants suit and a broad smile.

"Sorry to interrupt," Ivy said brightly. "Your assistant said you wanted me to join you?"

"Perfect timing." Alex stood. "I've just been breaking the news to Morgan. I don't believe introductions are necessary. Morgan, you already know Ivy?"

Martha's throat was too dry for speech. She forced herself to nod, her professional mask sliding into place even as her mind raced.

Ivy stepped into the room, her smile now on full blast. "I'm so excited, Martha! Sorry, I mean Morgan. When Alex approached me about working with you, I could hardly believe it. I mean, I knew you long before you were Morgan! And now look at you—it's just amazing how far you've come!"

"Ivy's track record made her an easy choice," Alex said. "Her collaborations with Ezra are pure gold. Between that and her own chart success, Harmony practically threw the contract at her."

Martha's stomach clenched. The studio time Ivy and Ezra spent together, under the guise of those "collaborations," had involved countless hours alone, shared jokes that excluded Martha, and a connection between the two of them that made her deeply uncomfortable.

"It feels like everything's come full circle," Ivy gushed, settling into a chair. "That 'Resonance' video? Absolutely iconic. The way you've transformed yourself..." She shook her head in admiration. "I just know we're going to create magic together."

"So, here's what I'm thinking..." Alex leaned forward. "Ivy will start working on some material to capitalize on your current momentum. We want songs that showcase everything that makes Morgan unique."

Martha nodded mechanically, her mind spinning. Ivy would be writing for her. The woman who used to spend those long nights closeted away in the studio with Ezra would now craft her songs.

"Your vocal style has evolved so beautifully," Ivy added. "I've already got some melodies that would really showcase your range."

Alex beamed. "Excellent. Why don't you tell us a bit about what you've been working on?"

"I'm sorry," Martha cut in, reaching for her bag. "I need to go. I have a session with my vocal coach." Escape. She had to get out of here.

"I understand." Ivy's smile never wavered. "No rush. Gotta take care of that golden voice. I'll send through some demos when they're ready. I think you'll love where we could take your sound."

"Perfect." Alex clapped his hands together. "This is exactly the fresh direction we need. Harmony is looking for great things from the two of you."

Martha stood, holding her bag like a shield. "Bye."

"See you soon. And give my regards to Ezra." Ivy's remark, delivered with a smile, sliced into Martha's heart. Of course, she would mention his name, making it the perfect parting thrust.

And Martha had no defense, no armor against this. She managed a professional response, but her heels couldn't carry her out of there fast enough—past her larger-than-life image on the wall, past the respectful nods of staff members. Only when Ray ushered her into the back of her waiting Range Rover did Martha finally let her composure slip, burying her face in her hands.

Work was supposed to be her refuge. The place where she could forget the troubles plaguing her marriage. But now the woman who'd shared so many private moments with her husband, the woman whose shadow loomed over her marriage, was going to write her songs. There would be no escape.

Chapter Seventeen

EZRA GLANCED AT HIS watch. Of course, Martha was late. His brothers and Adria sat around his living room, ready for their first meeting about the charity album, which should have started fifteen minutes ago. Was this how Martha was showing her commitment to the project?

On the sofa, Levi had his arm around Adria. He looked up at Ezra. "I wanted to wait until everyone was here, but maybe we should just go ahead so we can get through everything on time. Adria and I have to catch a flight to Brisbane tonight."

"You're going back to Australia?" Ezra's question came out in chorus with Zach's.

Levi nodded, drawing his wife closer. "Adria's grandfather had a fall Saturday night. He developed pneumonia from being bedridden, and with his heart condition. . ."

His voice softened as Adria tensed beside him, her lips trembling.

"The doctors are concerned about complications. We need to get there as soon as possible."

Ezra saw in an instant everything that Levi was leaving unsaid. Cedric was well into his eighties, and every year they had with him was a bonus. He was Adria's only living relative, apart from her and Levi's son, and Adria would want to be close by in case...

Ezra pushed the thought away. It was a no-brainer that Levi would drop everything and go to Australia to support his wife at a time like this.

Ezra stared at their joined hands, at how Levi's thumb stroked Adria's knuckles in silent comfort. No, he wasn't envious at all about the bond they shared.

"I'm really sorry to hear that," Zach said. "Of course you need to be with Cedric. I'll keep all of you in our prayers. Do you need a ride to the airport?"

Levi's lips stretched in a smile. "Mum is taking us, but I appreciate the offer." He cleared his throat. "We're not sure how long we'll be gone, but we'd like the album project to go ahead."

Adria nodded. "If possible. We're hoping to break ground early next year. But I understand if this changes things too much for you to keep the album going."

They all turned at the sound of Martha's heels hurrying through the entryway. She emerged into the living room, looking every inch the glamorous star she was. Her salmon-pink blazer dress landed several inches above her knees, and those high-heeled Louboutin pumps emphasized the length of her well-toned legs.

Her makeup was perfect—smoky eyes paired with glossy nude lips.

But although she had the looks and charisma to command any room she walked into, why did Ezra feel Levi was the luckier man, because of the sweet, gentle woman who sat close to him, her fingers entwined with his?

Martha lowered her Birkin bag. "I'm so sorry I'm late. There was an incident on the M25. Snarled up traffic for miles."

And, of course, phones don't exist to give us a heads-up, Ezra thought. Because that would have meant she'd have to text him.

"We'd only just started," Levi said. "I was telling everyone there's been a change of plan."

Ezra watched as Martha crossed the room and sat on an armchair as far away from him as it was possible to get while still remaining in the living room. Her gaze was fixed on Levi while he filled her in on Cedric's health and his and Adria's decision to go to Australia for an indeterminate length of time.

The concern on Martha's face looked real. She could show tender feelings to everyone else apart from him, apparently.

Levi concluded his recap. "Anyway, Adria and I hope the album project can still go ahead even though we're away, because we'd like to break ground on the building project early next year."

"I'm happy to go ahead," Martha said. "I met with my manager this morning and I've told him I'm committed to this for the next few weeks. I can fit my schedule around whatever the project needs."

"Are you sure about that? Zach's got his hands full with this super-secret project of his that he's not telling any of us about—" Levi shot a glance at his eldest brother. "So he won't actually have any musical contribution to the album. He'll handle formalizing intellectual property rights, production and distribution contracts, and all the other boring stuff involved in the project. You and Ezra will be in charge of the music."

Ezra didn't miss how Martha stiffened. He didn't like this change much either.

Zach nodded. "I can only give occasional support when needed. So, yeah, this will fall on you two."

Levi turned to look at Ezra. "Is it too much to ask?"

Yes, it was. Ezra had been counting on having Levi to act as a buffer. How was he supposed to record an entire album with Martha when the two of them were barely speaking? Not to mention his deadlines with *Promise Ridge*. He'd just about managed to deliver the theme song today, and they expected him to score the first three episodes within the next couple of weeks.

Everyone was looking at him. "I'll do what I can."

He had over a dozen songs already written that could be a good fit for the project. Maybe they could get through this quickly. Several of his songs would work well with the project's message, songs about hope and new beginnings. If they could settle on the track list today—

"Before we go," Levi said, "I think we should spend some time discussing the album's vision. Now that Martha's on board, we have an incredible opportunity to reach beyond the usual Falconer brothers' audience."

Ezra's jaw tightened. Of course. Now that "Morgan" was involved, everything had to change.

"The songs need to maintain their spiritual depth," Levi continued, "but we should think about arrangement and production choices that would appeal to Martha's fanbase. What do you think, Martha?"

She leaned forward. "I think we could find a balance. My audience responds to—"

"To whatever's trending?" Ezra cut in. "Whatever will keep them streaming?"

Zach shot Ezra a warning look.

Martha's tone remained steady, though her fingers curled around the arm of her chair. "Actually, my audience connects deeply with emotional truth."

"Assuming they can hear it through all the production," Ezra muttered. "And when the songs are radio-friendly enough to keep their attention for more than thirty seconds."

Martha bristled. "My fans are not all looking for auto-tuned dance tracks all the time."

Levi raised a finger. "Exactly what I was thinking. We need to find that sweet spot between—"

"Between scripture and secular appeal?" Ezra interrupted. "Between worship and commercial success?"

"Between different ways of reaching people's hearts." Zach stood and turned to Levi and Adria. "Look, you two shouldn't worry about this right now. Cedric is your priority. You should probably start getting ready for your flight. Good thing it takes off at night. Owen will be asleep for the first leg."

Ezra didn't miss the hard look Zach gave him as he added, "I'm sure between the three of us, we can keep the project moving forward."

The warning in his brother's eyes was clear—*watch your mouth.*

"Are you sure?" Adria asked. Her gaze flickered between Ezra and Martha. "We really don't want to create problems."

"Absolutely." Zach was fully embracing his role as the older brother. "Go take care of your grandfather."

As everyone stood and said their goodbyes, Levi's arm slipped naturally around Adria's waist, and she leaned into him.

The easy intimacy made Ezra's chest ache. He and Martha used to be like that. But now they stood apart, the space between them wider than the physical distance.

"I'll call when we land," Levi said, then he and Adria left.

Ezra stopped Zach as he moved toward the door. "Before I forget. You still want my old MacBook? The one from before I upgraded last month?"

"Another hand-me-down?"

"Yes. I've got it in my studio." Ezra headed down the stairs.

Zach followed him, leaving Martha in the living room. "You know, some of us manage just fine without upgrading every time Apple sneezes."

"Says the guy who's still using my four-year-old model." Ezra retrieved the laptop from a cabinet. "This one's barely eighteen months old. Still perfectly good."

"Unlike your attitude today." Zach's voice dropped as he took the computer. "Seriously, Ez. What's going on with you and Martha? I've never seen you sniping at each other like that. And after what I saw on Saturday... I'm worried about you."

Ezra busied himself with the charging cable. He would not get into this with Zach. "The usual ups and downs. You can't be married for eight years without having them."

Zach stared at him as though he wasn't convinced.

Ezra handed over the power adapter. "Want me to show you where the 'on' switch is? I know how these things confuse you."

"Funny." Zach rolled his eyes. "Just because some of us don't need the latest tech to make music—"

"No, you just need your little brother's old laptops." Ezra managed a small smile. "How many is this now? Four?"

"Five, if you count that ancient MacBook Air." Zach tucked the laptop under his arm. "But back to what matters. I hope you'll manage to record this album despite your, um... ups and downs."

Ezra faced him, arms crossed. "We're professionals. We'll manage."

They returned to the living room where Martha stood by the window, her back to them. She had slipped her pumps off and her bare toes dug into the plush rug.

She turned to face them as Zach approached.

"I'll be off, then. See you later."

She raised a hand in a half wave. "Take care. See you soon."

When Ezra came back into the living room after seeing Zach off, Martha was still there, sitting on the sofa with her feet tucked under her.

She was absorbed with her phone screen, but at least she hadn't retreated to her bedroom. Was he really so used to this coldness between them that he thought in terms of her and his bedrooms? How long would this last?

He stood in front of her, hands stuffed in his pockets. He'd just assured Zach he could be professional about working with her. Time to prove it.

"Martha, since this project has been left in our hands, we should start the song selection process as soon as possible. Do you have time tomorrow?"

She looked up from her phone. "It depends. What time do you want to start?"

"Nine? Unless that's too early with your schedule."

"Nine is fine." She hesitated, then added, "I could make coffee. Honey cinnamon latte. You still like those, right?" Her gaze searched his face.

His fingers itched to reach for her, to bridge this gulf between them. But the echo of her words came back to him. *Maybe you can't handle the fact that I'm not just your quiet little anonymous wife anymore. Maybe you're just threatened that my career is doing better than yours.*

His hands clenched. He wasn't ready. Not yet. The wound was still too raw. "No need. I'll have been up for hours by then."

Pressing her lips tightly together, she nodded, then dropped her gaze. She stood and gathered her things, her face averted. Without another word, she walked quickly past him and headed upstairs.

Chapter Eighteen

EZRA GLANCED UP AS Martha walked into his studio at nine on the dot. Her hair was pulled back in a loose bun, and she wore leggings and an oversized button-down cotton shirt. She held one of those vomit green smoothies that she counted as breakfast in one hand, and her iPad in the other.

Her sweet lavender scent teased his senses, and he ached to pull her into his arms. But what if she pushed him away?

How had this become their new normal—sleeping in separate rooms like strangers in their own home?

He'd heard her moving around early this morning, had listened to her work out with her trainer in the garden while he sorted through demos in his studio. Now here they were, pretending to be any two professionals about to discuss a project, ignoring the whopping great elephant stomping all over their marriage.

He handed her a printout of song lyrics. "I've put together some songs I think would work well for the project."

Taking the paper from him, she settled into the chair next to his desk. "Thanks."

His finger hovered over the spacebar. "We'll start with 'Shelter', which is first on the list." There was a time when she would have perched on his knee while she listened to a demo of a new song, her head tucked against his shoulder. But he had to stop thinking about things like that if he was going to get through today's session.

He pressed play, and the studio filled with the sound of his own gentle fingerpicking on his Martin D-28. He'd kept the arrangement simple, and the introduction stripped back, letting the words carry their full weight. His voice came in, soft but intense.

Empty rooms and empty spaces
Footsteps echo down these halls
But even in the darkest places,
I hear the Father's call

As the chorus began, a second guitar wove melodic lines through the chord progression, and a subtle synthesizer pad added warmth, like sunlight through stained glass.

In the shelter of Your grace,
I found a place where every broken piece is seen.
Here in Your light, each shard You reunite,
Making beauty from what has been.

His gaze strayed to Martha's face.

She leaned forward, her eyes closed as she listened, her body swaying.

His heart stuttered. She liked it!

Fragments of a life once shattered
Scattered pieces on the floor
By Your hands, what truly mattered
Pieced together, whole once more

He hit pause as the song faded out.

Martha opened her eyes. "The lyrics are beautiful. And the melody..." She laid her hand over her heart. "It gets you right here."

Her words loosened something inside his chest, made him dare to hope. "Thank you."

Martha shifted in her seat. "It's a wonderful start, but the arrangement needs work if we want to reach a younger audience."

The hope died. "What do you mean?"

She held up a hand. "Don't get me wrong—I love it. It's just very... traditional. And I thought we were trying to reach a wider audience with this album. What if we added some contemporary elements? Maybe layer in some atmospheric synths, give it a more current sound."

Martha used to be his biggest cheerleader. Now it sounded like she, too, thought he belonged on the scrapheap. Just like Silvertone.

He tried to keep his voice calm. "The simplicity is the point. It needs to be raw and authentic. Drowning it under all that production would just distract from the message."

"I'm not talking about drowning it in anything." Martha held up the lyric sheet. "But this song could reach so many more people if—"

"If we strip away everything that makes it genuine? Turn it into another disposable pop track?"

She pressed her lips tightly together. "That isn't what I'm saying."

He knew it wasn't, and he hated how defensive he sounded. But it felt as if she was picking apart not just his song, but him. As though he wasn't good enough. Once again, she was throwing his failing career into his face.

He took a deep breath. He could keep it together. Be professional. "Okay. What are you saying?"

"Production value doesn't automatically compromise integrity." She held up the lyrics. "The message matters, yes, but so does making sure people actually hear it."

Ouch.

Martha put down her smoothie. "I just think that we need to reach the audience where they are. Give them the kind of sound we know they respond to. I know you don't think much of my music, but there's a reason young people connect with it. This song is beautiful. I think it's beautiful. But the way it is now, I worry that a lot of young people won't even give it a chance."

He couldn't do this anymore. In his mind, he knew he should separate himself from his music and not take her criticism personally. But it felt like she was ripping him open and finding fault with his still-beating heart.

He stood. "Maybe we should take a break."

She stared at him for a long moment. Then she looked away, worrying her lower lip. "Would it be easier if I listened to the songs on my own first? It's just... I mean, it's tense when you're watching my reaction to every note."

And it would also give her time to work out how to tell him in the most diplomatic way that she found his music boring and old-fashioned.

She'd once adored everything he'd created. Or was that a lie? Perhaps, as she'd evolved into Morgan, she'd simply moved beyond the things—and the husband—she used to love.

His voice was tight as he answered her. "I'll send you the SoundCloud links."

"Thanks." She stood, gathering her drink, her iPad, and the song lyrics.

Standing at the door, she hesitated for a moment, as though she wanted to say something else. Then, without another word, she walked out, leaving nothing but the lingering scent of lavender and a hollow space inside him.

Chapter Nineteen

ATER THAT AFTERNOON, MARTHA leaned back in her chair beside the sprawling mixing console in Studio A at Harmony Records, trying to shake off the hollow ache that had followed her from Ezra's studio. Lately, everything she said to him seemed to come out wrong.

It was so hard to talk to him about his music—or anything, really—without him twisting her words and going on the defensive. But Adria and Levi were counting on them to make this charity album work, so she had to try, no matter how much she'd rather drop everything and retreat from these painful interactions with Ezra.

She forced her thoughts to focus on the throbbing electronic beat that pumped through the monitors. This remixed version of "Shelter" would grab young listeners—if only Ezra would give it a chance. Her chest tightened. If she could just show him how his beautiful song could reach more people, maybe he'd understand what she'd tried so clumsily to explain earlier. Perhaps music could reach him when her words couldn't.

Communicating with him used to be so easy, a single look conveying paragraphs of meaning between them.

But it hadn't been like that for a long time. Not since she'd started touring.

Jim Chen, the label's twenty-two-year-old producing prodigy, had been thrilled when she'd asked him to help remix Ezra's song. He'd been even more excited when she'd suggested that he lend his voice for their little experiment, his dark eyes sparking under his peacock-blue hair. The live room where they'd re-recorded the vocals was empty now, the microphones standing like silent sentinels.

From his position at the center of the console, his fingers dancing over the faders, Jim had kept the bones of Ezra's song intact while adding layers that made it feel current—atmospheric synths that built tension in the verses, a driving beat that kicked in with the chorus, little electronic flourishes that made it sound fresh without overwhelming the message.

Jim's vocals were nowhere near as polished as Ezra's—no one's were, really. The warmth, depth, and authenticity of Ezra's voice had always touched something deep in Martha's soul. But Jim's track would serve for demo purposes.

She closed her eyes in the dimly lit control room, imagining teenagers connecting with these lyrics, finding hope in the message.

Hope. She needed some of that right now after another night in their too-big bed, aching for the closeness they used to share, seeing him so cold and distant this morning.

"Wow, is this what you're working on?"

Martha's eyes snapped open.

Ivy stood in the doorway in a floaty summer dress, her designer perfume overpowering the coffee-and-electronics scent of the control room.

As Ivy stepped inside, her sleek chestnut bob swung as if she was filming footage for a shampoo commercial. "That sounds amazing. Is this for your latest album?"

"It's just a demo," Martha said, suddenly aware of how small the space felt with Ivy in it. "We're playing around with some ideas."

Jim swiveled in his chair at the center of the console, grinning. "Want to hear it from the top?"

"I'd love to!" Ivy settled onto the leather sofa that ran along the back wall, her enthusiasm filling the intimate space. "Whose song is it? Wait no, don't tell me. Let me guess. Is it one of Ezra's?"

Martha stared at her across the dim control room. "How could you tell?" Jim's arrangement sounded nothing like a typical Ezra Falconer song.

Ivy leaned back into the sofa. "It's obvious, really. There's a lyrical depth and a melodic integrity that's unmistakably Ezra. His music has a certain... emotional resonance. An intimacy." She crossed her legs, settling in like she belonged here. "When you work with someone as closely as Ezra and I have, you learn how to recognize their musical signature." Her smile softened. "Working with him was always such an enriching experience."

Martha's stomach tightened. From her position by the console, she felt suddenly trapped between Jim's presence and Ivy's knowing gaze. "Was it?"

"Absolutely. He has this amazing way of getting to the heart of things." Ivy's hands gestured expressively in the soft light. "It was like we could read each other's minds sometimes."

Why had she started this conversation? A familiar pain twisted in her heart, like shrapnel embedded in an old wound. Ivy and Ezra had this easy, fulfilling collaboration, while Martha had been at odds with him over every aspect of the charity album. He hadn't even wanted her to be involved in it.

Ivy was still raving, her voice bouncing off the acoustic panels. "I always thought that's what made working with him so special—that connection, you know? And it shines through in his music. But I'm preaching to the choir. I'm sure you two have that same magic when you work together."

Martha answered with what she hoped was a convincing smile. She couldn't remember the last time making music with Ezra had felt magical. Unless it was the kind of magic that involved stabbing things with pins.

Ivy turned toward the mixing console. "And, Jim, I can see what all the hype over you is about. The production on this is fantastic. Very current. Very Morgan."

Jim blushed to the roots of his blue hair, his reflection visible in the glass wall. "Thanks."

Ivy shifted on the sofa to face Martha again, her perfume intensifying in the enclosed space. "It must be wonderful, being able to work so closely with your husband on a project like this. Having that natural connection, that effortless collaboration."

"Um, yeah. It's an interesting experience." Martha gripped the armrest.

"You're so lucky." Ivy's sigh floated across the control room. "Nathan and I never had that. We tried working together a few times, but..." She shrugged, the movement elegant in the soft lighting. "I guess some couples don't have that creative chemistry. You just can't force it. It was one of the many signs we weren't meant to be."

Martha's stomach clenched. "You and Nathan aren't together anymore?" In the early days, Nathan and Ivy had been couple friends with her and Ezra. But somewhere along the line, the dynamic had shifted, with Ezra and Ivy becoming besties while Martha and Nathan drifted to the sidelines of the little quartet.

"Oh, no. We split up last year." Ivy's voice echoed in the small space. "The divorce was finalized last month."

Martha gripped the arm of her chair harder. Why hadn't Ezra mentioned that Ivy and Nathan had split up? As close as he and Ivy were, he must have known. "I... I'm sorry."

"Thanks." Ivy smoothed her dress, the fabric rustling in the quiet studio. "But I'm glad it happened before we had children. Sometimes you have to admit when two people are pulling in different directions. When the connection just isn't there anymore."

Martha felt the blood drain from her face. Ivy's words hit too close to home—the disconnect, the pulling apart, the loss of that easy chemistry she and Ezra once had.

"But hey..." Ivy brightened, leaning forward on the sofa. "At least you and Ezra have that special bond. I mean, look at this." She gestured to the studio setup. "Taking his song and elevating it like this. He must love how you understand his vision."

Martha's throat closed up. She stared, wordless, at Ivy, who smiled back, head tilted.

Pushing her chair back, she stumbled to her feet. She needed to get out before the emotions roiling within her burst out in a howling scream.

Clutching her bag, she turned to Jim. "Could you send me the mix when it's ready?"

"Sure thing," Jim said, swiveling back to the console.

Ivy leaned forward. "Would you mind playing it for me again, Jim? See you later, Morgan. And give my regards to Ezra."

Martha hurried from the control room, gulping in air free from the cloying scent of Ivy's perfume.

Her phone buzzed.

Eden's name lit up the screen.

She answered just as she reached the elevator doors. "Hello?"

"Martha? I'm at your gate, but your security people won't let me in. Didn't we have an appointment today?"

Tea with Eden. It was today? She'd completely forgotten. "I'm so sorry—it slipped my mind. I'm in London."

"Oh. Well, do you want to reschedule for some other time? I really don't mind if you—"

"No!" Heads turned at Martha's raised voice, so she spoke more quietly. "No, I really need to talk to you. Can you wait? I'll be there in about forty minutes. I'll tell the security guys to let you in."

"Of course I can wait, sweetheart. See you soon."

Chapter Twenty

S RAY PULLED INTO Martha's driveway behind Eden's Ford Focus, Martha regretted begging the pastor's wife to stay. Her desperation to talk had ebbed with every mile of the drive home. Did she really want to dig into all of this? To admit how things really were between her and Ezra? Maybe she could come up with some kind of cover story and avoid spilling her guts.

She was going to Paris tonight for a quick business trip related to her perfume launch—a welcome escape from the tension at home. Perhaps she could use that as an excuse to cut the visit short.

But as she got out of the car, Eden was already walking toward her, arms stretched out.

Martha stepped into her friend's warm hug, and tears threatened afresh. Why hadn't Ezra told her that Ivy was divorced? Was it because it cleared the way for him and Ivy to...

She marshaled every ounce of willpower into keeping her voice steady. "I'm so sorry about the security mess. I forgot to tell them you were coming."

Eden chuckled. "No worries. Though I have to say, this is quite different from the days when I could just pop by for coffee."

"I know." Martha sighed as she led the way inside. "I can't even go out for a walk anymore without it being a whole production. So, I just don't bother now. And forget about running to the grocery store."

"I can't even imagine," Eden said.

"Yeah, it's insane. Let's sit down."

They walked into the living room, where sunlight streamed in through the French doors. "This house is just stunning," Eden said. "Like it came straight out of a magazine spread. You must be glad to be—"

"I hate it." Martha's voice was raw, harsh, foreign to her own ears. "I hate every perfect, coordinated inch of this house." Confessing the truth felt like releasing a pent-up flood.

Her heart thundered, echoing the shock on Eden's face.

Stepping toward her, Eden took hold of her hands.

Her gentle concern and quiet strength broke the last taut string that had been holding Martha together.

Wracking sobs burst out from somewhere deep inside her, with such force that she gasped for breath as she cried.

"Oh, sweetheart." Eden guided her to the sofa, rubbing circles on her back.

When Martha gained a measure of control, Eden went to the kitchen and returned with a glass of water, which Martha accepted with trembling hands.

She gulped down a sip, then set the glass down. "I'm sorry. You must think I'm completely unhinged."

Eden handed her a tissue and stroked her arm. "I think you've been holding onto something for a very long time. And I'm here to listen whenever you're ready to talk about it."

That almost set Martha off again, but she kept a tight grip. The question of whether to confide in Eden was moot now, after this display.

She took a shaky breath. "I just had a nightmare of a talk with Ivy and then what you said about this house just brought everything back. All the stuff I've been trying not to think about. Because she was Ezra's best friend, and—" She broke off, twisting the tissue in her hands. "I'm not making any sense. I should probably start at the beginning."

"That would help." Eden's voice was gentle. "Ivy is who, again? The name rings a bell, but I'm not sure I know her."

"She's a songwriter and she and Ezra did a lot of work together at his old label. Back then, when Ezra was the successful one, and I was just his plain, overweight, nobody of a wife, Ivy was..." Martha twisted her tissue tighter. "She was everything I wasn't."

Eden stroked her arm. "What do you mean?"

"She has this upper-class background, and she was sophisticated and talented and understood the music industry. She and her husband Nathan were couple friends with Ezra and me at first, but somehow..." Martha stood abruptly, pacing the room. "Somehow it became the Ezra and Ivy show."

She hugged herself as she walked.

"They'd spend hours in the studio together, working on songs. Or, at least, that's what he told me they were doing. Sometimes all night."

Eden's eyebrows rose. "All night? Ezra and this Ivy?"

Martha's voice trembled. "Yes. Several times a month. They'd go to all the industry events and parties. He did ask me to come at first, and I tried, but I felt so out of place and awkward that I went less and less. And then he stopped asking me. And I..." She stopped at the window, staring out. "I was just the fat, frumpy, embarrassing wife."

"Oh, Martha."

Martha swiped at her eyes with the crumpled tissue. "I tried not to be jealous. I mean, they were just friends, right? And their collaboration was so successful."

She resumed her pacing. "When Ezra wrote 'Whispers of You' and Dylan Marrow recorded it for that movie *Twice in a Lifetime*, everything changed. The film became this phenomenon, and suddenly the song was everywhere. It broke streaming records, won awards. Ezra could afford to buy us this beautiful house, but..."

Martha gestured at their surroundings. "You know where I come from. What kind of home I grew up in. I had no idea how to decorate a place like this. And, of course, Ivy stepped in and offered to help. Because she had such amazing taste."

"He asked her to decorate your home?" Eden hit her face with her palm. "Why are men sometimes so clueless? Even the smart ones? Martha, that's—that's not okay. No wonder you said you hate this place."

Martha wrapped her arms around herself. "That wasn't even the worst of it. They had all these inside jokes. She knew things about his career before I did. Like when and where he was going on tour. Or when he sold a new song. I think they even discussed my weight issues—yes, really. She'd make these little comments to me about how I ought to lose weight because Ezra was surrounded by all these beautiful women. And I just... I took it. Because I was afraid of losing him."

"Did you ever tell Ezra how you felt?"

"How could I? What was I supposed to say? 'Hey, honey, are you having an affair with Ivy?'" Martha's voice cracked. "I still don't know how far things went between them. And that's the worst part—not knowing. Then when Alex started working with me and got me my record deal, when I got the chance to go on tour, I grabbed it. It was easier to leave than to face what was happening to us. I told myself I was focusing on my career, but really... I was running away."

She sank back onto the sofa. "They were still close when I left. But I had my own work to think about, and I poured myself into that. The label made it clear that having a good singing voice wasn't enough. They needed the complete package. Something Ivy said, too, and she was right."

"Is that why you lost so much weight?"

Martha nodded, sucking in a deep gulp of air. "Yes. And I wanted to. I didn't want to be plain, boring Martha anymore. I didn't want Ivy to be able to sneer at my shape or my clothes. And when I started getting smaller, the label decided to lean into this whole Morgan image." She gestured vaguely at herself. "Goodbye, frumpy Martha. Hello, sexy Morgan."

She let out a bitter laugh. "The irony is, Ezra hates it. He says I've changed so much that he doesn't know who I am. The label says this image is working—the sales, the streaming numbers, the sponsors... everything depends on me being Morgan."

"And how do you feel about it?" Eden asked.

"I feel... trapped." Martha's voice trembled. "I was invisible before. I felt like Ezra only saw Ivy. And now that people finally notice me, I feel like Ezra can't even bear to look at me anymore. He says I've cheapened my talent." She drew a shaky breath. "Sometimes I'm so angry with him. I was the perfect little wife at home, but that wasn't enough for him. I know it's sick, but I feel like that's one way I can let him know that other people see me."

"Martha, hurting him back isn't the answer. That's just pushing him further away."

"I know." Martha's voice caught. "I've said some horrible things to him. And now we're barely speaking. When we do speak, we end up arguing. We're sleeping in separate bedrooms."

Eden leaned forward, gripping both Martha's hands. "You need to talk to him about this. All of it. Before it costs you your marriage."

"How?" Martha's voice was small. "How do I even start that conversation?"

Eden stroked her hand. "The same way you just told me. Honestly. From your heart."

"It's not that simple." The tears were threatening again. "What if... what if I find out there was more between them than I want to know? I heard rumors they had some kind of falling out, but I don't know what happened. I'm afraid to ask."

"What's worse? Finding out the truth, or letting these fears and resentment poison what's left of your marriage? Because no matter what happened between them, there are things he's done that aren't okay. At the very least, it sounds like their friendship was inappropriately close, and you need to talk about that with him."

Martha's eyes were leaking again. She dabbed at them with her tissue. "Did I tell you she's working at my record label?"

Eden's eyes widened. "No way."

"I know, right?" Martha gave a bitter laugh. "You couldn't make this up. Of all the labels in London. And she's been assigned to work with me on my next album. So I have to see her all the time. I actually saw her just before I came here. She told me she and Nathan got divorced. Which I didn't know, because my husband—who used to tell her everything—never mentioned it to me. He must have known."

Eden, wordless, just stroked her arm.

Martha stared out at the garden, at the climbing roses Ivy had suggested would look so lovely from the French doors. "You should have seen them together. The way they connected over music. Even today at the studio, she was going on about their amazing creative partnership, how they could read each other's minds..." She swallowed hard. "And Ezra and I can't even agree on a single song arrangement without fighting."

"That's because you're carrying all this hurt and suspicion into every interaction with him. Of course, you can't connect—you're both walking on eggshells." Eden paused. "And Martha? I'm not going to excuse Ezra for the things he needs to answer for. But it sounds like Ivy knew exactly what she was doing, both then and now."

"What do you mean?"

"Just because someone's actions look natural doesn't mean they're innocent. Making suggestions about your weight? Knowing your husband's schedule before you did? That's not normal friend behavior."

"I never thought of it that way." Martha's voice was quiet. "I just felt... inferior. Like I wasn't good enough for him. We started dating when we were just seventeen and got married at nineteen. I began to wonder whether he regretted that. Whether he couldn't have done better."

"Which was probably exactly what she wanted you to feel." Eden's tone hardened. "And now she's at your label, talking about her 'connection' with your husband? Martha, that's not a coincidence."

Martha sat straighter. "You think she's trying to—"

"I think she's trying to get in your head. And from what you've told me, she's pretty good at it." Eden leaned forward. "But here's what matters, sweetheart— Ezra chose you. He married *you*. And whatever happened or didn't happen with Ivy, you need to know the truth so you can either deal with it or put it behind you."

"I just... it's just... I'm afraid to find out."

"You need to talk to him, Martha." Eden's voice was gentle but firm. "All of this—the suspicion, the hurt, the distance between you... it will not get better on its own." She hesitated. "Have you thought about talking to someone professionally? A counselor? Even without Ivy in the picture, your life has changed so dramatically in such a short time since your career took off. It's a lot to process on your own."

Martha twisted the tissue in her hands. "Funny enough, Ezra said I should see a counselor. I got so angry with him because I thought—never mind what I thought. I wouldn't even know where to find one I could trust."

"I know someone." Eden reached for her bag and pulled out a business card. "Clara Mitchell. She's excellent, and she understands both faith and marriage issues."

"Thanks." Martha took the card, running her thumb over the embossed lettering. "I'll think about it." She took a sip of water. "Part of me just wants to go back on tour. My manager's been pushing for a trip to Scandinavia. It would be so much easier to throw myself into work again, into being Morgan..." She met Eden's gaze. "But I can't keep running away, can I?"

"No, sweetheart. It's time to stay put and deal with this. But please don't feel you have to go through this alone. Clara can help in some ways I can't, but I'm your friend and my door is always open. And, of course, Noah and I are here for you if you decide you want marriage counseling, which I strongly advise you to start. You can come with or without Ezra. Hopefully, with him."

Martha nodded, her throat tightening.

"Let's pray about all this," Eden said.

Martha's eyes filled with fresh tears. "That's another thing. God feels so far away. I can't remember the last time I properly prayed, or read my Bible, or..." She gestured helplessly. "Everything feels disconnected. My marriage, my faith, my sense of who I am..."

"He may feel far away," Eden said, "but He's still close to you and He loves you. You're His beloved daughter, Martha. He wants you to bring all these fears and worries to Him. He'll give you wisdom about what to do."

Martha wiped her eyes with a fresh tissue. "I don't even know where to start."

"Then let me pray with you now."

Eden squeezed her hand, and Martha nodded, letting out a shaky breath as her friend began to pray.

Chapter Twenty-One

"HAVE YOU GOT A minute?" Ezra hovered in Pastor Noah Chaplin's office doorway. "Gladys said I could come straight in."

He should have been working on the *Promise Ridge* score. But after this morning's disastrous meeting with Martha, the melodies wouldn't come. It was a waste of time sitting in his silent studio when his guitar felt dead in his hands. He needed to talk to someone who might help him make sense of what was happening to his marriage. And he couldn't think of anyone better to talk to than his friend and pastor.

"Of course." Noah gestured to the chair opposite his desk. "Coffee? Tea?"

Ezra shook his head, settling into the chair. "No, thanks."

"What's on your mind?"

"It's about Martha."

"I see." Noah stood and crossed to the door. He closed it gently and returned to his seat. "Go on."

"I think I'm losing her." Ezra's throat thickened, and he drew a deep breath.

Noah's brows pulled together. "I'm sorry to hear that. Tell me what's been happening."

"She's changed so much." He ran a hand through his hair. "I don't just mean the obvious things—her appearance, her image. It's like she's becoming this whole other person."

"What makes you say that?"

"Her values, her priorities—everything's shifted. She made this music video. It was—" He broke off and Noah waited, letting him find the words.

"It was so... provocative. So different from anything I'd ever associate with her. I know that's the industry standard, but this is Martha. I couldn't believe she'd even want to expose her body like that, perform in such a way. I felt sick. And when I told her what I thought, she—" He broke off, remembering the hurt and anger in her eyes. "She said at least she didn't feel invisible anymore. That I'd never seen her or recognized her talent."

"Is that true?"

"I—" Ezra stopped, caught off guard by Noah's quiet question. "No. I mean... I always knew she had a beautiful voice. But after that solo went wrong—you might remember, it was years ago, here in church—at the Christmas gala. She had such terrible stage fright she completely froze up and then ran off the stage. She was so adamant she'd never sing in public again. She couldn't even handle the thought of doing backup vocals."

He rubbed the back of his neck. "I tried to encourage her at first, but she shut down every time I brought it up. So I stopped asking." He paused, a memory coming to him. "That's actually how we started dating. When she bolted off the stage, I went after her to talk to her, and I asked her to have a coffee with me. She was always so quiet, and it was the first time we really talked."

He stared at the floor. "Maybe when we got closer, I should have seen that she still wanted to try. To perform, I mean. That she just needed to build her confidence. Instead, I just accepted what she said and focused on my own music. Then one day, years later, we'd gone to support a colleague of mine who ran a jazz club. It was an open mic night. Martha and I were in the VIP room, along with some friends of ours who were also married. I don't know what made her do it, but she went on the stage and belted out 'Summertime' from Porgy and Bess. Brought the whole house down. Turns out there was an agent there that night, and he signed her on the spot."

Ezra pressed his fingers against his eyes. "All this time, I thought I was being supportive by not pushing her to pursue her music. I was making a name for myself in the industry, but I never thought of encouraging her gift. What if that's why she resents me now?"

"What makes you think she resents you?"

"She said—" His voice caught. "During our last big fight, she said I couldn't handle her success. That I preferred her when she was insecure and dependent on me." He looked up at Noah. "And I've been telling myself that's not true. That I'm just struggling with how much she's changed, with the values she's throwing away. But maybe..."

He swallowed hard. "Maybe there's some truth to what she said. My career's tanking while hers is soaring, and I'd be lying if I said that wasn't hard to accept. But it's more than that. Sometimes when I look at her now, I barely recognize her. And I'm starting to wonder if that's because I never really saw her at all."

Tears stung his eyes. As one spilled onto his cheek, he brushed it away with a fist.

"I love her so much, Noah," he said, his voice rough. "But I don't know what to do anymore. How to reach her when every conversation turns into a fight. When everything I say seems to come out wrong."

He drew a ragged breath. "This morning, she tried to give me feedback on a song, and I just... shut down. She was being professional, trying to help, but all I could hear was criticism. Like she was saying I wasn't good enough."

He pressed his fingers against his eyes. "And I know I'm making it worse. Every time she reaches out—whether it's offering to make coffee or trying to find common ground in our work—I react like she's attacking me. I can see myself doing it, but I can't seem to stop."

Silence hung between them for a moment before Noah spoke. "When you feel yourself getting defensive—which is natural—take a breath. Ask questions instead of reacting. If she critiques your music, for instance, instead of withdrawing, try asking her to explain her thoughts more fully. Show her you value her perspective, even if it's hard to hear."

"That's... not easy."

"I know. Marriage is hard. You have two sinners, imperfect people with sharp edges, rubbing against each other, trying to make a life together. We're bound to wound each other." He leaned forward. "The thing is, though, although you see her faults, you can't change her. All you can do is work on yourself. From what you've said, you're both carrying a lot of hurt and assumptions about what the other is thinking. Maybe instead of focusing on how she's changed, you need to look at what you might have missed. Listen to understand her, not to respond."

"And what about the things she says that really are an attack? Like what she said about me making her feel invisible?"

"That's when you really need to listen. Often when people lash out, they're really expressing pain," Noah said. "When she says she felt invisible, that's not about your career success or hers. That's about feeling unseen in your marriage. Look, I'm not saying Martha isn't at fault for some things. Like what you've said about that music video and everything around that. But it's so easy to focus on your spouse's faults when you feel they're doing something wrong. To build a case against them in your mind."

Ezra winced. He'd been doing exactly that. Like that fight they had after the gala. When he'd moved out of their bedroom.

Noah's lips curved upward. "Did I hit a nerve? You know, when I counsel couples, I always remind them that a husband's primary call is to love his wife as Jesus loves His church. That's a stubborn, unrelenting love. A love that pursues her, serves her, forgives her, provides for her needs—and not just material needs. It goes far deeper than that. It's not our job to fix our wives or change them, but to love them sacrificially, holding nothing back. To seek to understand them."

"How do I do that when it feels like she's pulling away?"

"With perseverance and humility. So much humility. And with God's strength. It may not be easy—in fact, it probably won't—but He'll help you. Remember what I said about how spouses hurt each other with our sharp edges? Through His Spirit, God can heal those wounds and give us the grace and patience to keep going, to love well, even when it's hard. And all the while, He's transforming us and making us more like Him. Plus, don't forget that marriage is God's idea. That always encourages me—this was His plan, and He can help us grow together in selfless unity." Noah stood. "Why don't we pray about this?"

Ezra nodded. For the first time in weeks—months, really—he dared to hope that maybe the best days of his marriage weren't behind him.

Coming around the desk to where Ezra sat, Noah placed a hand on his shoulder. "Father, we come to You with Ezra and Martha's marriage. Lord, You see their hurt, their struggles to connect, their difficulty understanding each other. Give Ezra wisdom and patience as he seeks to love Martha the way You love Your church. Help him to see her through Your eyes. Show him how to reach her heart. And Lord, we ask that You would begin a work of healing in their marriage, that You would help them find their way back to each other. In Jesus' name, amen."

"Amen," Ezra said through tears. "Thanks, Noah."

"Any time, brother. My door's always open."

Chapter Twenty-Two

ZRA CHECKED THE TIME again. Martha's producer friend would be here soon.

He'd come home from his talk with Pastor Noah last night, hoping for a chance to talk with Martha, forgetting that she'd flown to Paris for final meetings with executives from the perfume house, Maison Duval, about the launch of her new fragrance.

She'd sent him an email, suggesting they meet with a producer she'd been working with, someone who could help them find common ground on the song arrangements for the charity album. Bridge the gap between emotional resonance and contemporary sound, as she put it.

After his talk with Noah, Ezra was determined to be more understanding, to really listen to Martha's perspective.

He'd replied, agreeing to the meeting, suggesting they invite Zach. His brother's steady presence would have been welcome, but Zach had a prior commitment he couldn't get out of. Still, maybe a neutral third party would help him and Martha find a way forward they could both be happy with, for the song and the whole album.

Martha's answer had given him some hope. She'd signed off her email with, **"I have a few other things going on today. But maybe we could have dinner tonight? I'd like to talk."**

The spark ignited from those short lines warmed his heart as he went to answer the doorbell. It would be the producer, of course. Martha's flight was slightly delayed, and she was still on her way from Gatwick Airport.

Drawing a deep breath, he put his hand on the door handle. Time to put those good intentions into practice.

He opened the door to find not just a tall, thin young man with striking blue hair, but Alex Thompson as well.

Martha's manager flashed a smile and held out his hand. "Lovely to see you again."

"Alex." Ezra shook the other man's hand. "I wasn't expecting you."

"I know. I need to tie up some loose ends with Morgan after her Paris trip. Since Jim was headed this way, I gave him a lift." Alex swept past him into the house. "Beautiful home, by the way."

"Thanks." He turned to the young man. "Jim, I presume? I'm Ezra."

Jim returned a firm handshake. "Yes, I'm Jim Chen. Great to meet you."

"Please come in." Ezra stepped aside. "Martha said she admires your work."

Jim blinked at him. "Martha?"

"Oh, sorry. Morgan."

"Oh," Jim said. "Thank you. That means a lot, coming from her."

"The studio's this way," Ezra said, leading them toward the stairs to the lower level. "Martha's on her way from the airport, but she said we could go ahead and start."

The young producer stopped short as they entered the studio, his gaze landing on the platinum records mounted on the wall. "'Whispers of You'... Wait. You're *that* Ezra? Ezra Falconer?"

"The one and only," Alex said before Ezra could respond. "Though that was quite a while ago now, wasn't it?" He winked at Ezra. "We're not here to recall the glory days, though. Jim, why don't you set up your laptop and play the arrangement for Ezra?"

"Play the arrangement?" Ezra addressed his question to Jim, grateful for something to distract him from Alex's punchable smirk and condescending tone. "I thought you were here to listen to some of my songs. To discuss direction for the charity album."

"Um, I—" Jim began.

But Alex inserted himself into the conversation again with a chuckle. "Discuss direction? No, no, no.

We're here so you can hear Jim's arrangement of your song. Morgan's already approved the demo."

What? Martha had shared his song without telling him? And asked this Jim guy to make a demo? Ezra drew a deep breath, remembering Noah's words about understanding and listening. He could do this. He could be open-minded. "I see. Let's hear it, then. Jim, I'll show you where to hook that up."

Jim glanced between them, clearly uncomfortable, then began setting up his laptop and audio interface.

Alex invited himself into a seat and examined his manicured nails.

When Jim pressed play, synthetic beats commandeered the air, pulsating beneath the melody of Ezra's song.

Electronic elements replaced the delicate strands of his simple guitar line. Booming basslines and slick electronic gloss obliterated the intimate nuance of his song. As the chorus swelled, layers of production surged, transforming his introspective ballad into a jarring club track. It was commercial, all right, but at the cost of stripping away its sincerity and depth.

As the song ended, Jim turned toward Ezra, his eyes bright with anticipation. "What do you think?"

Ezra picked through a minefield of words. What was the most tactful way to tell this keen, enthusiastic kid that he'd butchered Ezra's song? He spoke slowly. "On a technical level, I understand what you've done here. I totally get why Martha's such a fan, and it's interesting to hear where you took the song."

Jim's smile widened. "So, you like it?"

"Well... it's certainly... different from what I had in mind. This song is about God's gentle healing and finding shelter in His presence. I didn't want to overwhelm the message, which is why I went for a stripped back approach. And I still think, for this particular song, that's the way to go. Although I'm very impressed by the vibrancy and freshness of your arrangement."

Jim's smile faded, but he nodded. "Okay, I respect that. Great song to work with. I had a lot of fun trying some things I'd had in mind for a while. The melody was so clean and strong that it inspired one of the quickest arrangements I've ever done. It just flowed naturally."

"Are you kidding me?"

Ezra turned as Alex's strident voice clanged like a cowbell in a string quartet.

"Let's think about this practically. The market data is clear." The agent swept a hand toward Jim's laptop. "This sound is what sells. If you want this charity album to succeed, to actually help those kids you're trying to reach, you need to think about what appeals to younger listeners."

"With all due respect, Alex, not everything is about market appeal."

Alex stared at Ezra, head tilted as though he were speaking to a cognitively challenged toddler. "But that's exactly why Morgan wanted to try this approach. She felt that by making it more accessible to younger listeners, we could preserve the heart of the song while reaching a broader audience. Morgan knew this, so she asked Jim to bring your song into the twenty-first century. And I think he's done an excellent job. He's produced three top-forty albums already since January. And you've had—how many again this year?"

Ezra's nails dug into his palms. "Zero. Okay, Alex? I've had zero hits this year. But that doesn't affect my opinion about preserving my song's message and integrity as I envisioned it."

Face flushed, Jim stepped away from the console as he fidgeted with the edge of his shirt. The poor kid must wish he was anywhere but here, caught in the crossfire between two grown men.

Alex jabbed a finger into Ezra's face. "That. That right there? That attitude is exactly why your recording career has stalled. Have you ever thought about why the only real hits you've had are when other people record your songs?"

Ezra's hands curled into fists. How dare this man stand in his home, in his studio—his sacred space—and insult him to his face? "This meeting is over, Alex. Please leave."

Jim snapped his laptop shut and pulled his cables off the console.

"And this is what you call professional behavior?" Alex sneered. "Thanks for proving my point."

Face flaming, Ezra held Alex's gaze. "I *am* being professional. That's why I'm letting you leave on your own two feet instead of kicking you out."

"My, my. Is this how a Christian behaves? What would your congregation think?"

"Ezra?"

He whirled toward the door.

Martha stood in the doorway, her gaze fixed on his face. "What's going on?"

"Perfect timing, darling." Alex's tone turned smooth, as though by the flip of a switch. "We were just wrapping up here. Jim, you'll need a ride back to the studio?"

"I—" Jim's gaze darted between everyone's faces as he shouldered his laptop bag. "Okay. Thanks."

"I can take him," Martha said, still looking at Ezra.

How much of this debacle had she heard? Ezra took a step toward her. "Listen, I—"

Breaking eye contact, she raised a hand, palm outward. "We'll talk later."

Turning to her manager, she said, "Alex, Maison Duval says there's been a shipping delay, so they have fewer than expected perfume samples for the launch. We need to decide which influencers get them."

"Of course, darling. Not a problem. After you."

Martha followed Jim out of the studio.

Alex threw Ezra a smirk over his shoulder as he stepped into the hallway.

Ezra clenched his fists. He had never come so close to rearranging Alex's veneers.

He sank into his chair. Given his recent behavior, Martha probably thought he was being too precious about his music. No doubt, Alex would work hard to spin it that way. His carefully laid plans for understanding and patience had just gone up in flames.

Chapter Twenty-Three

ARTHA SETTLED INTO THE back seat of her Range Rover, her cheeks still flaming from what she'd walked into.

After her talk with Eden yesterday, she'd been so excited to get home, to have dinner with Ezra, to bridge the gap between them. Instead, she'd arrived to find her husband throwing Jim and Alex out of his house while literally threatening violence. And now here she was, leaving again barely five minutes after arriving from the airport.

Mortification twisted her stomach into knots as Ezra's words echoed in her mind.

I am being professional. That's why I'm letting you leave on your own two feet instead of kicking you out.

What could have made him so angry? His email about meeting Jim had been so positive.

The demo. Her chest tightened. He must have heard it before she had the chance to explain to him why she'd had Jim work on a new arrangement for "Shelter". Was he that angry because she hadn't asked him first? What must Jim think of both of them now?

Jim slid into the car beside her, not meeting her eye. Poor kid. It was her fault he was in this position. He'd remixed "Shelter" as a favor to her. He never asked for this.

She opened her mouth, then closed it again. What could she possibly say?

Ray pulled away from the house and drove down the long driveway.

She had to say something to Jim. Anything. She turned toward him. "Um, listen. I don't know what happened in there, but—"

The opening riffs of "Whispers of You" cut through the air. It was the song she'd assigned as Ezra's ringtone. Her stomach clenched as her phone rumbled. What did he want to say?

She pulled the phone out of her purse, her thumb hovering over the "call reject" button. No, that would make her a coward. She swiped to answer. "Hello?"

"Hi, Martha." His voice was quiet. "Is Jim with you?"

"Yes." She glanced at the young man. "Why?"

"Could I speak to him, please?"

"Um... of course." She held the phone out to Jim. "It's Ezra. He'd like to talk to you."

Paling, Jim eyed the phone as though it would sprout teeth and bite him. Then he took it and pressed it to his ear. "Hello?"

Martha stared out the window, trying to look as though she wasn't eavesdropping, but tracking every word of the side of the conversation she could hear.

"Yeah. No, man, seriously, no worries... I get it, tensions were running high..." Jim's shoulders lowered, and his voice relaxed. "Really cool of you to clear the air, man. Appreciate that."

Forget pretending not to eavesdrop. Martha turned to stare at Jim. What was Ezra saying?

Jim chuckled. "No, honestly, it's cool. I've seen way worse in this industry, believe me... You mean that? Wow, yeah. Sure, I'd still love to be involved, if you're willing. Thanks, man. I appreciate that... Yeah, we'll figure something out... Take care."

Jim handed her phone back. "He wants to talk to you."

Fingers numb, she took the phone. "Hello?"

"Hi. It's probably not the right time to have a proper conversation, but I just wanted you to know I'm sorry, and I've told Jim that. I'll make it right."

"Okay."

He hesitated, then said, "Bye."

Jim smiled as she put her phone away. "Your husband's a class act, you know that?"

Martha's hand twisted around her purse strap. "Thanks. But he shouldn't have thrown you out."

"But he called to own it and apologize. And to be honest, Alex was being a grade A jerk. I was embarrassed to be there."

Martha stared at him. "Alex was being a jerk? Is that what happened?"

"Yeah. He was in Ezra's face the second we got in there. Just kept throwing shade every chance he got. I could tell it was getting to Ezra, but he held it together. Even when he wasn't feeling what I did with his song, we were still cool. Then when Alex started saying stuff about how long it's been since Ezra's had a hit? Bruh, I began packing up my laptop and marking the exits."

Martha let out a long breath. So, that's what happened. Ezra wasn't being overly touchy about his song. "I'm sorry you had to be there for that."

"Look, I know I'm just the new kid on the block here, but Ezra's arrangement was solid. Different from what I did with it, sure, but it had heart. He told me he's happy to try to find a middle ground. Learn something from *me*. Can you believe that?"

Martha stared at him. "You'd still want to work with us after what happened?"

"Are you kidding? The chance to collaborate with Morgan *and* Ezra Falconer? It's like hitting the jackpot." He laughed. "Man, 'Whispers of You' was literally the soundtrack of my entire senior year. My girlfriend played it non-stop—all the girls were obsessed with that movie. I used to act all annoyed but, honestly?" He grinned. "I knew every word. Still do." He began to sing. "In the quiet of the morning, when the world's still asleep."

Martha chuckled and joined in the song. "I hear whispers of you in the dreams that I keep."

Sometimes she forgot how young Jim was, that he'd been in high school when Ezra's career was at its peak.

The thought stilled her laughter. Maybe she was part of the problem if she, like Alex, believed Ezra's career was past its peak.

Ezra wasn't the only one who needed to make things right. She just needed to figure out how.

Chapter Twenty-Four

As Martha walked into the glass and marble lobby of Harmony Records, she wished she could turn straight round and go back home. She should be talking to Ezra now. Figuring things out.

After what had happened, how did it look to him that she'd gone off to meet with Alex?

And now, here she was, heading for a meeting about some blasted perfume samples. Alex could figure it out himself—it's what she paid him to do. She needed to go home and sort out this mess with her husband. A mess Alex might have stirred up, but which she had started by getting the demo made.

"Morgan! There you are!"

Martha's stomach dropped. Ivy Willis was the last person she wanted to talk to right now.

Ivy strode toward her, glamorous in skinny jeans and a tailored linen blazer, her sharp-eyed gaze trained on Martha.

For a fleeting moment, Martha felt like the overweight, dowdy, forgettable woman whose dress sense Ivy once mocked. Then she lifted her chin. She wasn't that woman anymore. She stood her ground. Might as well get this conversation over with so she could get on with the rest of her day.

Ivy stopped in front of her. "I wasn't expecting to see you. Not after I heard about Ezra's meltdown." As she spoke, she leaned into Martha's space with a stage whisper that half the lobby could probably hear. "Imagine throwing Alex and Jim out of your home."

A chill swept over Martha. How on earth had Ivy already heard about that?

Ivy giggled. "Everyone's talking about it. Crazy how fast news travels. I'm not surprised he had trouble with Jim's input. He's always been... particular about creative control."

Martha crossed her arms. "I don't know who you've been talking to. Actually, Ezra was perfectly professional about the arrangement. Until Alex started deliberately provoking him."

"Oh?" Ivy giggled again, raising her eyebrows. "I saw it so often when we worked together. Not denying he's insanely gifted at what he does, but it was always his way or the highway. You know, I was probably the only songwriter who could really collaborate with him. We just... understood each other's process."

Martha knew she shouldn't take the bait. But the question slipped out. "What do you mean, the only one who could collaborate with him?"

"Ezra and I just had a special... connection when it came to music." She brushed a strand of silky hair behind her ear. "I saw how protective and touchy he could be about his work. But I knew how to... handle him." She waggled her eyebrows.

Martha stepped back, something clicking into place. If she hadn't known for sure what went on between Ezra, Jim, and Alex, if she hadn't witnessed for herself Ezra's grace, maturity, and restraint, she might have bought the line Ivy was spinning.

Eden's words came back to her. *I think she's trying to get in your head. And from what you've told me, she's pretty good at it.*

Well, Martha was not falling for Ivy's mind games. Not this time. She glanced at her watch. "You know, Ivy, it's been nice chatting, but I've wasted enough time today. I've got some meetings to deal with, and then I need to get home to my husband." She adjusted her bag on her shoulder. "Bye, now."

Ivy's perfectly shaped mouth formed a small 'o' of surprise. For a moment, she looked almost comical, like a cat that had pounced and found its prey suddenly wasn't there. Then her features settled back into a smile.

"Of course," Ivy said. Her voice was honey-sweet, but something in her eyes made Martha's skin crawl. "Give Ezra my best."

Chapter Twenty-Five

E ZRA PULLED OFF HIS headphones and listened to the cue again through the studio monitors. The *Promise Ridge* pilot episode filled his screens—the lead character Emily's face crumpling as she left the courthouse, rain streaming down her face, mixing with tears she finally let fall.

He'd layered the strings just right—cellos carrying the weight of her fear of losing custody of her best friend's children, while violins hinted at her determination to fight for them. Dan, the musical supervisor on *Promise Ridge*, had suggested Ezra tone down the violins to enhance the raw emotion of the scene without overpowering it. Listening to the result, Ezra agreed that Dan's suggestion was spot on.

He smiled at the irony of being the one told to strip back his arrangement. He had more in common with Jim than he thought. Thank God the young man had accepted his apology after this morning's fiasco of a meeting.

He adjusted the EQ on the violin track, then added the subtle piano motif that would be Emily's theme throughout the TV series. Using his DAW, Logic Pro, he automated the volume levels to gradually increase during the transition, enhancing the emotional impact. Create, layer, adjust. Delete, try again. If he'd done his job right, viewers would be in tears right along with Emily.

He'd already finished the opening sequence where David returns to Promise Ridge to claim custody of his late sister's children, threatening to rip them away from Emily, their small-town community, and the only home they'd ever known.

Ezra had gone with sparse orchestration to emphasize the male lead's isolation. Stupid David. Couldn't he see that Emily was the best thing to happen to those children and, possibly, to him? But no, he was too wrapped up in his success as a New York hedge fund manager to recognize what was right in front of him.

Ezra's fingers stilled on the keyboard. Was he any better than the clueless David? How long had he been blind to what his wife needed from him? Going along on his merry way while never grasping just how far apart they'd grown?

The scene played on. David watching from his silver Lexus as Emily hugged the children goodbye after her supervised visit with them.

Ezra had scored that moment with a single, haunting oboe line. All that pride and stubbornness, keeping people apart who should be together.

He rubbed his eyes. What could he possibly say to Martha to get them back on track? After the way he'd behaved this morning—even if Alex deserved it...

Focus. Just this final courthouse cue to polish, and he could upload the pilot score to the *Promise Ridge* production team's server.

A movement caught his eye.

His heart stumbled.

Martha stood in the doorway, fingertips resting on her throat, as though unsure of her welcome. She still wore her travel clothes—a smart-casual ensemble that accentuated her slender figure. The tailored black blazer cinched slightly at her waist, layered over a soft white blouse and dark blue jeans that hugged her curves. Her figure was conventionally beautiful now, after her dramatic weight loss and punishing training regime. But her fluffy body of two years ago had been just as lovely to him.

"Hi," she said. "Are you busy?"

His pulse thudded. Half an hour. He just needed half an hour to wrap this up, but if she walked away now... "Kind of. But I'm glad you're home."

"Me too." She shifted her bag on her shoulder. "I thought maybe we could talk?"

"Yes. Please. I mean, that is, I've still got to—" He gestured at his screens. "It's *Promise Ridge*. I just need to finish this cue and upload the pilot score. Thirty minutes? Unless—" He couldn't read her expression. "Unless you'd rather talk now?"

Her shoulders relaxed. "No, that's fine. I should shower anyway. Get the airport off me."

And now the image of Martha in the shower was in his head. How was he supposed to get any work done? "Um, okay."

"Dinner after?"

"I'd like that," he said. "I'll do something quick. Salmon and asparagus okay?"

"Sounds good." She gave him a small smile and turned to go.

"Martha?"

She looked back.

"I'm sorry," he said. "About this morning. About a lot of things."

"Me too." Her gaze met his for a moment. "Thirty minutes."

As her footsteps faded up the stairs, Ezra turned back to his screens with renewed focus. On the other side of this pilot episode stood a dinner date with Martha.

The courthouse cue. Right. He adjusted the violin track's reverb, building the tension as Emily faced David across the courtroom. He added a subtle countermelody that would weave through future episodes, hinting at their eventual connection. Would anyone notice it?

He was so close now. Just one final listen through. He closed his eyes, listening to the story his music told. Yes. There. Perfect.

His fingers flew across the keyboard, rendering the final mix. While the file processed, he pulled out his phone and texted Noah.

Talking to Martha in 10 mins. Pray for me!

Noah responded immediately with a praying hands emoji.

The render completed. Ezra logged into the *Promise Ridge* production team's secure server, uploaded the pilot score, and fired off a quick email to the music supervisor. Everything was tagged and labeled according to their specifications—full score, individual cues, stems, alternate versions.

He glanced at the time. Eight minutes. Just enough time to save everything and back it up.

And after that... Martha. After this morning's disaster, after everything that had happened these past months, they had to get this conversation right.

The salmon was perfectly cooked, the asparagus tender-crisp. But they could have been eating cardboard for all Ezra tasted it. The silence stretched between them, broken only by the soft clink of silver cutlery against Wedgwood china.

Martha had come down later than expected, having to take a few phone calls to deal with some last-minute crisis with her perfume launch. She'd changed into soft loungewear and her lush, ebony curls framed her face in an untamed halo. Tomorrow, her hairstylist would probably subdue it into something sleek and sophisticated, but he loved how it spilled freely over her shoulders now.

His heart was full to bursting with things he wanted to say. But now that she was in front of him, so close that he could touch her, the words couldn't find a way out. In the space and time they'd created to talk, it was as though they'd forgotten how to connect, even as the pent-up feelings inside him pushed for an outlet, a way to make his heart known.

"This is good," she said, again, as she sliced into her salmon. "The dill is nice."

"Thanks." He pushed an asparagus spear around his plate. When had small talk become so hard? He used to be able to tell her anything.

The thought sparked a memory.

"Do you remember song swap night?"

Her fork paused halfway to her mouth. "I remember. It's been a while."

"Sometimes..." he met her gaze. "Sometimes it's easier to say things through music."

"It is, sometimes." She set down her fork. "Are you suggesting we should do a song swap now?"

"If you want to." His heart hammered. "There's a lot I want to say, but I'm not sure how to start."

Her lips twisted. "I'm not doing so hot, either. I've complimented your salmon four times in the last five minutes. It's delicious, by the way."

He laughed. "Let's do it. When you're done with my delicious salmon, I mean."

"Okay." She put another bite in her mouth, then dabbed her lips with a napkin. "I'm done now."

He stood. They'd deal with the dishes later. "You take the piano and I'll go outside with my guitar." He hesitated. "One hour? Will that give you enough time?"

She nodded, and something eased in his chest. At least they still had this—this way of speaking to each other through music.

He grabbed his Taylor GS Mini—lighter than the Martin, perfect for using outdoors—and walked outside through the French doors.

The evening air was mild, heavy with the scent of lavender beds that lined the stone path. Behind them, climbing roses rambled over the pergola, their blooms catching the last of the sunset. These lavender beds were the only thing about this house that Martha had insisted on having, letting their decorator choose every other detail.

Ezra settled into one of the Adirondack chairs, angling away from the window where soft lamplight spilled from the living room. Martha was in there now, writing a new song to share with him in an hour. And he would write his now.

He turned his gaze away from the house and looked toward the town of Hatbrook. In the distance, he could just make out the silhouette of the church spire where Martha's Christmas solo had gone wrong, and he'd followed her outside into the street. She'd been so upset, so sure she'd never sing in public again. But something in her voice had called to him, even then.

Noah's words came back to him. "Listen to understand her, not to respond."

His fingers found the strings, picking out a gentle pattern. He hummed a few notes, tried a different chord progression. No. Not quite right. He closed his eyes, letting the memories flow. Martha's shy smile when he'd asked her out for coffee. Long walks through Hatbrook's quiet lanes under the glow of the streetlights. Falling in love with the sweet, shy girl he'd never noticed before. The starlit picnic on the hill when he asked her to marry him. The distance of the recent years. The hope of his heart that he could find her again. When had he stopped seeing her?

The melody came to him then, soft and wistful, wrapping around the words forming in his mind.

Martha stared at her notebook, the hour nearly up. The words she'd written were too raw, too honest. Like opening a vein onto the page. She touched the piano keys, not pressing them, just feeling their cool smoothness beneath her fingertips.

Could she really sing this to him? Did she dare to be so open, so naked? That was the whole point of song swap night—to share what was in their hearts with a new song. But this—this song—

The French doors opened, and Ezra came in from the garden, his Taylor in one hand. The evening air drifted in with him, carrying the scent of lavender. "Time's up. You done?"

She nodded, closing her notebook. "Yes, but... would you sing yours first?"

"Sure." He settled onto the couch, adjusting the guitar in his lap. His gaze was bright, intense. "I've been thinking about when we first started dating. About that Christmas gala, and coffee afterwards."

Her heart squeezed. Of course he had. She'd been thinking about that too, lately.

He began to play, his long, sensitive fingers moving over the strings in that way that had always mesmerized her. When he started to sing, his pure tenor filled the room.

"In this small town where every road leads back, I find my footsteps tracing the memories we left..."

His voice caught slightly on the next lines, raw emotion bleeding through. "How did we drift so far apart, silence in our melody? How can we blend in harmony when we're singing in different keys?"

Martha's eyes filled with tears. He was right—they'd lost their harmony somewhere along the way.

His voice broke into a heart-rending falsetto as he sang the chorus. "Can we find the rhythm lost in time? Can forgiveness speak? Turn the discord into rhyme, in your arms I find my peace. Back to where our song began in our small town's streets, let's find the harmony again, just you and me."

She pressed her fingers against her lips. She wanted that. With all her heart. That pure, innocent love wrapped up in hope, that started when the town's biggest teen heartthrob took the time to chase after her and make sure she was okay on the worst, most humiliating night of her life.

She'd accused him a few days ago of treating her like she was invisible. But he'd been the first one to really see her. To love her just like she was.

"Thank you," she whispered when the last note faded. "I... I wasn't sure I wanted to share what I wrote. But I will now."

She turned to the piano, her fingers hovering over the keys.

Chapter Twenty-Six

Ezra put his guitar aside, watching Martha's fingers tremble as they touched the piano keys.

She went straight into the song without an intro, her rich, warm voice flooding his senses like a mighty wave.

This wasn't Morgan's overproduced performance style. It was Martha, raw and real, filling the room with a power that came from deep inside her. She sang with her eyes closed, as though she were pulling the words out of her very soul.

"Words we never said linger between us, echoes of doubt that we can't just ignore. I'm reaching for your hand across this cold distance, searching for a way to you and me once more."

He gripped the arm of the couch, knuckles white, forcing himself to stay seated and listen when every instinct screamed for him to go to her.

His chest felt too tight to breathe.

Her voice cracked as she started the second verse. "Angry words we said, daggers between us. Find someone to blame, go slam the door. Mistakes we both made, regrets we carry. I'm wounded but wiser, longing for more."

Tears burned in his eyes, his throat aching as she laid her heart bare through the song.

"Can you see me? I'm lost behind these walls. Do you hear me crying out in the silence? Will you love me though our past is broken? Can we find our path back to who we are? I still love you, though our past is broken. Can we find our path back to who we are?"

When the last note faded, her hands fell from the keys into her lap. Her face was angled away, but he could see tears sliding down her cheeks, could hear her ragged breathing. Did she want to hide from him again?

"I see you, Martha," he whispered. "I love you. Please... let me love you."

A sob escaped her.

He crossed to the piano bench, sitting next to her. She turned to him, fingers clutching his shirt as though she might drown if she let go. He wrapped his arms around her, feeling her whole body shake as she cried. His own tears fell, unchecked, into her hair as he held her tightly against himself. All their years of hurt and disconnection spilled out in a flood that was first painful, then warm and healing.

"I'm sorry," Martha whispered against his chest. "For shutting you out. I was trying to protect myself because... because I've been so scared of losing you."

Was that what she thought? The ridiculous irony. He drew in a ragged breath. "I thought I was losing *you*." His voice was rough. "That you didn't love me anymore. That you'd... outgrown me."

She pulled back, placing her hands on his cheeks, her thumbs brushing away his tears. She gazed into his eyes for a long, aching moment. Then she leaned in, pressing her soft lips to his with exquisite tenderness.

Her kiss was like her song—a confession soaked in tears, a tender heart laid bare and open before him. She spoke to him without words, and he answered, their hands and lips eloquent in a language that belonged only to them. Tentative at first, questioning, exploring, then deeper, pouring all their love and longing into this one moment.

"I love you," she breathed against his lips, her fingers resting where the pulse throbbed on his neck. "I've never stopped loving you."

"Martha." Her name was a prayer on his tongue.

His hands tangled in her hair as he drew her toward himself, then slid gently down to cradle her neck and caress her back, pulling her into a deeper embrace.

The last walls between them crumbled. Her fingers traced his jaw, his neck, his shoulders, as their kisses grew more urgent.

The evening air stilled around them, the rest of the world fading away until there was only this—only them.

Chapter Twenty-Seven

MOONLIGHT SILVERED THE GARDEN below as Martha stood on the balcony, drawing her silk robe closer against the cool night air. Her lips felt tender, slightly swollen from Ezra's sweet, passionate kisses. Behind her, he lay asleep in their bed—their shared bed.

Joy bubbled up inside her. They'd found their way back to each other, shared their hearts through music, then made love with an intensity that left her breathless. Tonight was a beautiful answer to her prayers for her marriage. And yet...

Her gaze drifted to the artfully arranged throw pillows on the window seat, the carefully curated artwork on the walls. Even here, in their most intimate space, Ivy's touch lingered. It reminded Martha of the other ways that woman had intruded on the sanctity of her marriage. Just how far had that intrusion gone?

Eden's words echoed in her mind, a warning klaxon that would not be silenced. *You need to talk to him about this. All of it. Before it costs you your marriage.*

She knew she ought to speak to Ezra about his friendship with Ivy, tell him how their closeness had made her feel, learn the truth.

But what they'd rebuilt tonight felt so delicate, like a soap bubble that might burst at the slightest touch. The way Ezra had held her, kissed her, touched her—that was real. She believed in his love for her. Wasn't it enough to build from here? To leave the past where it belonged and move forward?

She gripped the balcony railing, the wrought iron cold under her fingers. She would redecorate. They could afford it now. Bring in a professional interior decorator and obliterate every mark of Ivy's hand from her home. Every rug, every piece of art, every stick of furniture, every—

"Martha?" Ezra's voice was raspy with sleep. "You okay?"

She turned, looking back through the French doors. He'd propped himself up on one elbow, his hair adorably mussed.

"I'm fine," she said. "Just getting some air."

Sliding back into bed, she nestled against him, his chest warm against her back. His arm draped over her waist, drawing her closer to him. Exactly where she belonged.

"I love you," he whispered into her hair.

The words sent warmth radiating through her chest. Tonight, they had been so vulnerable and open with each other. They were closer than ever before.

But she'd kept a corner of her heart locked away. She recoiled from bringing up Ivy. That was the past. It was better to leave it shrouded in shadow. She knew now that Ivy twisted things to suit herself. Maybe all those hints Ivy had dropped about her "close bond" with Ezra were lies, too.

This—her husband's arms around her, his love surrounding her—this was true. This was now. This was what mattered.

His breathing deepened again, but sleep eluded her as the moonlight painted silver patterns on the wallpaper Ivy had chosen.

Chapter Twenty-Eight

EZRA WOKE SLOWLY, AWARENESS filtering in. Sunlight filled the bedroom, and Martha was curled up next to him, her breath slow and even. Forget dreams—this reality was far better.

He raised himself onto one elbow and watched her sleep, memorizing the gentle curve of her cheek, the sweep of her eyelashes, the way her hand rested near her face, next to her full lips. He longed to touch her but held back. He should let her rest.

Last night was beyond any answer to prayer he could have conceived. Their songs that laid bare their hearts, tears and forgiveness flowing between them, discovering each other all over again as they made love.

What could he do to nurture this reconnection, to make sure he never gave her a reason to pull away from him again?

She sighed in her sleep, her warm breath tickling his arm. This wouldn't do. If he didn't get up now, he'd forget his resolution to let her rest.

He slipped out of bed and took a quick shower, then headed down to the kitchen.

The dinner dishes were still on the table, something which never happened, but they'd had better things to do last night than load the dishwasher and clean the cast-iron skillet. He smiled as he set everything in order.

Once that was done, he pulled out ingredients for breakfast. That failed meal of waffles the morning after Martha's arrival home felt like a lifetime ago. This time would be different. For one thing, he now knew what she'd eat. He got to work on the stove, and the coffee was just finishing when he heard her footsteps.

"Morning." She came up behind him, sliding her arms around his waist. His heart swelled at the effort-less intimacy.

"Morning." He turned in her embrace, circling his arms around her. "Sleep well?"

"Mm." She raised herself up on her toes to meet his kiss. "Something smells good."

"I've made breakfast."

"I wasn't talking about that." She pulled his face toward hers and this time, their kiss was deep and slow. He lost himself in the taste of her, in her shower-fresh fragrance, in the velvety softness of her skin.

A soft sigh escaped her lips as her hands slid up his chest.

"Breakfast will get cold," he murmured against her mouth.

"Better be worth breaking this kiss for, Chef." She smiled up at him, a playful light in her eyes, and moved over to the table.

He put a plate in front of her, a fluffy egg white omelet speckled with spinach and crumbled feta, with berries on the side. "I aim to please. Shall we give thanks?"

His heart overflowed with gratitude as she bowed her head.

He prayed, "Thank You, Lord, for this beautiful morning, for this meal, and for all Your good gifts to us. Amen."

"Amen." She took a bite. "Mm. You're almost forgiven for stopping that kiss."

"Only almost?" He reached for her free hand. "I'll have to work on earning a full and free pardon."

She grinned. "I'm counting on it."

The doorbell rang.

"Oh." Her smile faded. "That'll be Jane. The perfume launch is today, and my schedule is crazy."

He'd totally forgotten. There would be no lazy, peaceful morning lingering in the glow of their magical night. "In that case, you'd better finish your breakfast. I'll get the door."

Martha's PA stood there, perfectly put together despite the early hour, her tablet in one hand and a thick folder tucked under her arm. "Good morning, Ezra."

"Morning. Come in." He stepped aside.

Jane walked to the kitchen and set her things on the counter. "Good morning, Martha."

"Hi. Want some coffee?"

"No, thanks." Jane checked her watch. "We need to leave in twenty minutes. You have a full schedule today."

Martha popped a blueberry into her mouth. "Run it down for me?"

Ezra moved behind Martha's chair, his hands settling on her shoulders. His thumbs brushed the nape of her neck in a gentle caress, and she relaxed into his touch.

Jane pulled out her tablet. "First, we have a brief rehearsal at the Lumen Gallery at 9:00 AM to go through your setlist and hosting script. We've scheduled a sound check immediately afterward. 12:30 to 1:30 you'll meet with the event organizers. We'll go over the final details of the event flow, check the guest list, and confirm the setup for the VIP area."

Martha nodded, taking another bite of her omelet while Jane continued.

"At 1:30 PM is your briefing with the Brand Manager and the Marketing Specialist from Maison Duval."

"Again?" Martha's shoulders tensed beneath Ezra's fingers. "We had a three-hour briefing in Paris yesterday. What else do they want?"

"I know, but they insisted. They want to prep you on sensitive questions you might get from the press and the overall narrative they wish to present during the event. After that, we'll bring you back home by 3:00 PM at the absolute latest to get ready for tonight. Your glam team will meet you here at half-past three. Kelsey's already sent your options for what to wear tonight. They're in your wardrobe, labeled and cataloged. And that's it for before the event. Let's talk about this evening's schedule," Jane added, checking her tablet.

Ezra watched as Jane went through the timeline she'd sketched out for the perfume launch. His wife was transforming before his eyes—the relaxed intimacy of their morning was giving way to Morgan's world.

The girl who was too timid to sing a solo in a village church was now commanding the VIP launch of her own signature perfume. His heart swelled. She had come so far. But where did he fit in all this?

"Okay, that's finally it." Jane swiped her tablet screen. "I've got some dry cleaning in my car, which I'll grab and put into your wardrobe. Will you be ready to go soon?"

"I will. Just give me a couple of minutes," Martha said. As Jane headed for the door, Martha turned to face Ezra, slipping her hands into his. "Will you... will you come tonight? To the launch?"

His chest tightened at the hint of uncertainty in her voice. The events he'd attended with her lately hadn't gone very well—not for him. He was an outsider in Morgan's world. The music video premiere where he'd sat in silence, hating every frame. That industry gala where he'd felt like a discarded relic.

But she still wanted him there. And that was what mattered. He stared into the depths of her eyes. From now on, his place in Morgan's world would be whatever Martha needed it to be. He cradled her hands against his chest. "Of course I'll come."

Her face lit up. "Thank you." She stood, taking a step closer. "Ezra, last night meant everything to me. It's so dumb that today's the launch and my day is so crazy. I don't... I don't want to lose us again."

His heart squeezed. So, she felt it, too. "I don't, either. And we won't."

"I'll ask Jane to put you on the list and coordinate timing for the Lumen Gallery." She stretched up to kiss him, her lips lingering on his despite Jane's approaching footsteps in the hallway. "I love you."

"Love you too."

Jane appeared in the doorway. "Martha, we really need to go."

Martha squeezed his hands one last time before letting go. "I'll be back at three to get ready."

"I'll be here."

Martha grabbed her bag while Jane gathered her things.

"The teleprompter's been loaded with my welcome speech?" Martha slid the strap of her bag over her shoulder.

"Yes, and I've got printouts just in case. Your performance will be after the brand presentation."

"And we're sure about the timing?" Martha asked. "I don't want to keep people standing too long."

"All mapped out. Whoops, I almost forgot my folder." Jane turned back to the counter.

As she picked up the thick folder, a glossy magazine slipped out and slid to the floor. She followed Martha toward the door.

Ezra bent to retrieve the magazine, about to call out to Jane—but the words died in his throat.

Martha was on the cover, wearing a slinky negligee that suggested more than it revealed as she pouted at the camera over her bare shoulder, her eyes smoky and seductive. The headline screamed: "MORGAN BARES ALL!" and below it: "8-Page Exclusive: England's Hottest Music Star Models Libertine's Steamy New Collection."

His throat tightened. He wanted to support Martha's work, wanted to fight for their reconnection, but seeing his wife displayed as a seductress for the world's hungry eyes, when just hours ago she'd been so tenderly vulnerable with him alone—how could he reconcile this?

"Lord," he whispered, "how?"

He set the magazine face down, his fingers lingering on the edge as if touching a wound.

Chapter Twenty-Nine

ARTHA SLIPPED HER KEY into the front door. It would be good to have a couple of hours at home before the perfume launch, even though most of it would be spent getting ready.

Despite having barely any time to breathe between this morning's rehearsals, meetings, sound checks, and stage blocking, she was half an hour ahead of schedule, which meant a tiny reprieve before the real work tonight.

Was Ezra here? He'd said he would be.

He wasn't in the kitchen or living room. She headed toward the lower stairs. He was probably working in his studio.

She found him staring at his monitors, headphones on, his fingers moving in time to music only he could hear. On the screens, a rain-soaked woman trudged away from a building, her shoulders slumped.

Swiveling his chair around, he looked up as Martha walked in. Her heart skipped at the warmth in his smile.

"Hi." She went straight into his arms, perching on his knee.

He pulled his headphones off and pressed a kiss to her temple. "Hi yourself. Good rehearsal?"

"Mm. But I missed you." She breathed in his familiar scent, her head resting on his shoulder. "Is that *Promise Ridge* you're working on?"

"Yeah. I got the green light to score the rest of the series."

She sat up. "Ezra, that's wonderful! Thank God."

"Amen." He smiled back. "What's next on your schedule?"

"I've got about forty-five minutes before the glam squad arrives. Enough time for a quick catch-up with you. I mean, if you're not too busy."

"No, I planned on a break when you got back," he said, drawing her closer. "So, tell me about your perfume."

Of course—he probably didn't know about it. Another reminder of how new their togetherness was. There was so much about her working life he didn't know about.

"It's called Serenade." She traced a pattern on his shirt with her finger. "The launch has been in the works for months."

"Serenade?" His voice held a smile. "That's fitting."

"I wanted something that connected to music." She lifted her head to look at him. "The perfumers at Maison

Duval were amazing. We went through dozens of combinations before we found the right notes."

"Notes?" His eyebrows lifted. "Are we talking musical notes or perfume notes?"

She chuckled. "Both, actually. They developed this whole concept around musical layers. The top notes are bright and sparkling, like the opening of a song. Then it settles into something warmer, deeper." Like us, she thought, nestling against his chest. Last night's intimacy still hummed between them, new and familiar all at once.

"Sounds complicated."

"It is, but it's really fascinating. There's this whole science behind fragrances. They call them notes because of how they unfold over time, like a piece of music."

His fingers stroked her arm. "What does it smell like?"

"You'll find out tonight." She smiled against his shoulder. "But I hope you'll like it. I thought about you when we were creating it."

His hand stilled. "You did?"

"Mm hm. I wanted something that felt... authentic. Pure." She hesitated. "Something that would make you proud."

He kissed her hair. "I am proud of you. Even when I don't show it very well."

Her throat tightened at his simple words. They sat in comfortable silence for a long moment, his thumb drawing circles on her shoulder, before she stirred.

The clock was relentless, and she had no more time. "I should go up and look through the outfits Kelsey picked out."

"Okay. I'll be up in a minute with something to eat. When Jane called me about my ticket, she mentioned you missed lunch."

"You're so good to me, Ezra." Her voice caught. Whenever he saw a need, he moved straight to provide for it. Even during their worst moments, he'd never stopped taking care of her. How could she have ever let things get so bad between them? She blinked quickly, pressing her face into his shoulder for a moment longer.

He gathered her closer, turning his face into her hair. "I love you."

Finally, she made herself stand. "See you in a bit."

Her heart full, she went up to her walk-in wardrobe. The three options for tonight's event were clearly marked, thanks to Kelsey's efficiency. Each hanger bore a detailed styling card with suggestions for hair, makeup, and accessories.

The first was a black column dress with a plunging neckline and a thigh-high slit. "Sleek, sophisticated, commands attention," according to Kelsey's note. The second, in emerald green, had strategic cut-outs that would showcase her toned abs—"fresh, youthful, emphasizes fitness journey." The third was a deep scarlet mini dress with an entirely open back. "Bold, sexy, memorable."

But something felt off about all of them. All of them aligned perfectly with the Morgan aesthetic Kelsey worked so hard to curate. But after last night, she wanted to be more Martha.

"Here you go." Ezra's voice behind her made her turn. He held out a green smoothie and an energy bar.

"Thanks." She accepted both items gratefully. "I needed this."

Her eyes widened as a jolt of heat danced on her tongue, cutting through the sweet, creamy drink. "Mm... What did you put in this?"

He smiled. "Spinach, yogurt, banana, and fresh ginger."

"Ginger—that must be what I'm tasting. It's delicious."

"And it should give you an energy boost." He glanced at the rack of dresses in front of her. "Having trouble deciding?"

"A bit. What do you think?" She gestured at Kelsey's selections.

Tapping his finger on his chin, he studied the options. Then his gaze shifted to another section of the wardrobe. He walked past the designated choices and pulled out a pale yellow evening gown with elegant draping. "What about this one?"

Martha touched the silk georgette. She'd bought it in Milan on a whim, drawn to its timeless grace. Her fashion sense was hopeless, hence her dependence on Kelsey, but the dress reminded her of ancient Greece with its flowing lines and artful gathering at the shoulders. It was one of the few garments in her wardrobe that Kelsey hadn't picked.

"You like this one?" she asked Ezra.

"It reminds me of what you wore that night at the jazz club." His voice softened. "When you got up and sang 'Summertime.' You looked radiant. Like the sun bursting out of a veil of clouds."

Heat rose to her cheeks. "That was years ago." She'd been bursting, all right, carrying a hundred extra pounds and looking like a shapeless sack of potatoes.

When she came off the stage, while everyone was raving about her song, Ivy had smiled sweetly and murmured into her ear, "Brave of you to wear something so. .. fitted. Though you might want to check that seam before it gives way completely."

Ezra's fingers brushed the fabric. "I remember every detail. This is the kind of dress that makes people notice the woman wearing it, not just the dress itself. It's elegant. Sophisticated. You."

She studied the dress with new eyes. "You really think I should wear this?"

"I think you'd look beautiful in it." He squeezed her hand. "But it's your choice."

"Okay, I'll wear it since you like it so much."

His face lit up. "Thank you for asking what I think. That... that means a lot."

"Of course I'd ask you." She put the dress on the rack, then stretched up to kiss him. "What time is your haircut?"

"In twenty minutes. I'd better go." He touched her cheek. "I'll see you on the red carpet?"

"Can't wait."

The doorbell chimed just as Ezra reached the bedroom door. "That'll be your glam team. I'll let them in on my way out."

Martha heard the murmur of voices downstairs, then the click of heels on the stairs.

Kelsey burst in first, her trademark red bob swinging, chunky designer jewelry catching the light. As always, she looked both effortlessly chic and slightly intimidating—the kind of woman who could spot a fashion *faux pas* at fifty paces, arrest it in its tracks, and make it plead for mercy.

She carried an armload of garment bags while the hair and makeup team followed with their cases.

"Morgan, darling!" Kelsey's eyes sparkled. "After checking out the event space, I brought a few more last-minute options for tonight. The space is absolutely spectacular—the lighting alone is going to be incredible. I wanted to make sure we have something that will photograph beautifully."

Martha gestured at the yellow gown. "Actually, I've already decided to go with this one."

Kelsey stared at the dress, her perfectly shaped brows drawing together. "That's not one of my selections. Where did that even come from? The retirement home?"

Heat crept up the back of Martha's neck. Even after two years of working with Kelsey, she still felt like that awkward teenager who used to shop at Goodwill. "I bought it in Milan. It's a Luca Romano."

Kelsey's perfectly lined eyes widened. "Oh, honey, Romano designs for grandmothers. And even his current collection is more modern than this. The cut, the fabric—it's all wrong for the venue. Especially in the main gallery with those crystal chandeliers. You'll be making your big entrance through there, and that lighting will wash this color out completely." She pulled out a dress from her garment bag. The light danced off the shimmering gold fabric, scattering in a hundred directions.

Martha's breath caught. The dress was stunning.

"This will be sensational in the photos," Kelsey gushed. "The way it catches the light and contrasts with your skin tone—you'll literally glow. Plus, the way your body is now? The cut is perfect to show off all that hard work."

Martha glanced at the yellow gown, her fingers tightening on the cream silk. She didn't trust her own taste.

Ezra had liked this one, had been so happy she'd asked his opinion. But he hadn't been thinking about the lighting at the venue or the need for the dress to photograph well. Neither had she. There was a reason she relied on Kelsey's expertise for everything she wore in public.

"Look, honey, I know you like it, but the yellow dress is lovely for a different occasion," Kelsey added more gently. "For tonight's venue, with those crystal chandeliers and all that strategic lighting... trust me on this one."

"Okay, then." The words felt like little betrayals in Martha's mouth. "The gold one it is."

"Perfect!" Kelsey clapped her hands. "Now, let's get started on your transformation. C.J., she's all yours for makeup."

Chapter Thirty

THE LUMEN GALLERY ROSE before Ezra like a glass and steel cathedral, its modern lines softened by the glow of hundreds of lanterns strung throughout the private courtyard. The normally austere space had been transformed into something magical. Elegant flower arrangements perfumed the evening air.

The media pack lined the red carpet with military precision—camera crews at the front, photographers on raised platforms behind them.

He adjusted his slate gray tie. He'd chosen his charcoal suit carefully, knowing the dark gray would complement Martha's pale yellow gown without overwhelming it. All around him, the energy crackled with anticipation. Photographers jostled for position behind the velvet ropes, their cameras raised like weapons.

Ezra recognized the larger networks' logos—SoundByte, Fashion Now, StyleLife. Even Bloomberg had sent someone, suggesting this was more than just another celebrity perfume launch.

A woman with a headset was directing traffic, her sharp gestures positioning crews like chess pieces.

"Two minutes," she called out, sending a fresh wave of energy through the assembled press.

"Morgan's stylist just posted," someone called out. The announcement rippled through the crowd, cameras lifting in anticipation.

Entertainment reporters clutched microphones, their voices carrying across the courtyard as they delivered live updates about Morgan's imminent arrival.

Morgan. Even in his head, the name felt strange. Somewhere inside the gallery, Martha was putting final touches on tonight's arrangements. She'd actually arrived here hours ago. Her red-carpet entrance was just theater, he reminded himself—a carefully choreographed moment for the cameras. He should know. He'd attended enough of these events over the years.

But this was different. This was Martha's night. Her own fragrance launch, the culmination of months of work.

Enormous silk banners draped the gallery's glass walls, showcasing the Serenade campaign images. In each one, Morgan held the violin-shaped perfume bottle like a precious instrument, her pose both elegant and intimate. The translucent gold glass caught the light differently in each shot, sometimes highlighting the delicate fretwork texture around the bottle's neck, other times emphasizing its sensual curves. The deep gold gemstone cap gleamed like a crown.

The artistic direction was undeniably beautiful. Even the typography had a musical quality—the word "Serenade" flowing across the images like a melody, with "by Morgan" in smaller, elegant script beneath.

Behind him, an ornate digital display cycled through close-up shots of the bottle alone, each angle revealing new details that transformed it from a mere perfume bottle to a sculptural art piece. No wonder the fashion press called it the luxury launch of the season.

"Mr. Falconer?"

He froze. Someone actually knew his name? He was getting used to being invisible—just another face in the crowd watching Morgan shine. He turned toward the sound of the voice.

A young woman with a press lanyard around her neck broke away from the media pack and walked toward him. "Mr. Falconer? I'm Katie Wu from SoundByte. I was hoping to get a quick word?"

"Of course." He gave her a polite smile.

She gestured to her cameraman, who stepped up beside her. Her microphone appeared in front of him, the SoundByte logo clearly visible. "You must be proud of your wife. A signature fragrance is a huge milestone. And the buzz around Serenade has been incredible."

"Martha's worked very hard on this." The name slipped out before he could catch himself. "Morgan, I mean."

Katie's eyes lit up. "That's right—you knew her before she was Morgan. You were actually the one who discovered her talent, weren't you? At that jazz club in Hatbrook?"

"No, actually." Ezra smiled. "She already had the talent. I was just lucky enough to be there the night she decided to share it."

"And what's it been like watching her transformation into one of music's biggest rising stars?"

"I'm just as much in awe as anyone else. Her raw talent, her musicality, is phenomenal. Her vocal ability is as good as anyone out there. Better than most, if I'm honest. I don't think she gets enough credit for that. And she works incredibly hard." The words came easily—this much was always true.

Katie's head bobbed up and down. "And now she's become such a fashion icon, too. Her red carpet looks are always stunning." She gave him a conspiratorial grin. "Any hints about what she's wearing tonight?"

Ezra smiled. "Actually, for once I—"

A sleek black limousine pulled up, and Katie's attention snapped away while Ezra was still mid-sentence. The entire press pack surged forward as one ravenous entity, camera flashes popping.

Ezra was left speaking to air where the microphone had been. He turned toward the car, his pulse quickening.

The door opened, and Ezra's world tilted sideways.

Martha emerged in a sweep of gold sequins, each tiny disc catching and throwing back the light like stars. His wife was breathtaking—but this wasn't the elegant yellow gown they'd chosen together.

Her dress was a masterpiece, creating the illusion that light itself was flowing over her body, sparkling gold against her mahogany complexion. The halter neckline drew attention to her graceful neck and shoulders, while the fitted bodice emphasized the lissome contours she'd worked so hard to achieve. As she turned to acknowledge the cameras, the entire length of her back was exposed, an expanse of velvet-smooth skin that disappeared just above her waist. A thigh-high slit in the skirt revealed her long sculpted legs, elongated even further by strappy gold stilettos.

The crowd's reaction was instantaneous and deafening, a roar that made the ground tremble. Camera flashes exploded in a constant stream of light, each burst creating a new constellation of sparkles across the dress.

Martha looked incredible. But his chest ached as he watched her work the carpet with practiced ease, each pose calculated to show off another aspect of the dress, and more bare skin. This was Morgan in her element, glowing under the attention. But where was the Martha who'd stood in their closet just hours ago, who'd smiled so sweetly when he chose that other dress—the elegant, demure yellow gown?

What had been the point of asking his opinion on what to wear if she'd already known she'd wear whatever Kelsey chose?

She turned, and for a moment their eyes met across the carpet. Something flickered across her face that he couldn't quite read—uncertainty? Apology? But then a reporter called her name, and she was Morgan again, dazzling the cameras with her smile.

Martha—Morgan—extended her hand to him, and Ezra moved forward, muscle memory from countless industry events taking over. He knew the drill. As he stepped beside her, he slipped his arm around her waist, his palm meeting bare skin where the dress dipped low in the back. She leaned into him with practiced grace, her hand resting lightly on his chest, both of them automatically arranging themselves into poses that would photograph well.

"Morgan! Over here!"

"This way, please!"

"Give us a smile!"

She shifted closer to him, practiced and graceful in her sky-high heels. The sequins of her dress scraped softly against his suit—the suit he'd chosen specifically to complement a yellow gown that now hung forgotten in her closet. Her hand settled at his waist as cameras clicked frantically.

"Who's this, Morgan?"

"Your date for tonight?"

"My husband, Ezra Falconer," she said, her voice carrying clearly over the chaos.

More questions flew at them, but Ezra barely heard them. She stood next to him, her hand resting on his chest, declaring "my husband" with such pride and certainty while wearing a dress that felt like a denial of everything they'd shared this afternoon.

He smiled for the cameras, playing his part.

Beneath a sophisticated new fragrance—Serenade?—he caught the familiar scent of lavender. His Martha was still there, though she was wrapped in Morgan's sparkle and glamor. The woman who'd shared her heart with him last night and joined her soul with his.

Pastor Noah's words came back to him. A husband's primary call was to love his wife as Jesus loves His church. His role wasn't to fix her or change her—that was up to God—but to love her sacrificially, holding nothing back. Even when that love felt like a cross to bear. Even when every instinct told him to pull her away from these lights, these cameras, this world that seemed to demand more of her with each passing day, swallowing up the girl he fell in love with.

He drew her closer, feeling her respond to his touch. Whatever came next, this much he knew—he would keep choosing her. Every day. Both sides of her. Even when it hurt.

Chapter Thirty-One

ARTHA MOVED DOWN THE red carpet, Ezra's hand warm at her waist as they stopped to pose for photos. He was quiet, silent beyond telling her she was beautiful. But his steady presence beside her meant everything.

The next cluster of reporters lowered their cameras, and Sharon from her fan engagement team stepped forward. "Morgan, these are our contest winners—the ones who made that TikTok tribute to 'Resonance.'"

Two little girls stood waiting at the end of the red carpet. They bounced on their toes, dressed in miniature versions of an outfit she'd worn in her latest music video—crop tops, micro-mini skirts, and makeup that belonged on someone three times their age.

"Morgan! Morgan!" A woman—their mother?—pushed forward, designer handbag swinging. "My girls are your biggest fans. They absolutely worship you."

The children couldn't have been older than eight or nine. Martha's stomach clenched as she took in their carefully straightened hair, their attempts at smoky eye makeup, the way they posed with hands on hips, mimicking her photo shoots.

Ezra's hand tensed against her back.

Martha raised a hand. "Hi."

The little girls squealed, dissolving into giggles as they stared at her.

"They watch all your videos," the mother gushed. "Show Morgan your dance moves, girls! The ones from 'Resonance.'"

Martha's throat went dry as the girls started to gyrate in unison, imitating moves that had seemed artistic and empowering in her video, but now—watching these children—felt wrong on a visceral level.

Ezra's hand dropped away from her waist.

"Could we have your autograph?" The older girl thrust a glossy photo forward, an image from the Libertine Lingerie campaign.

Martha's hand shook as she reached for the ballpoint pen. What was she supposed to write? "Keep being sexy"? "Work it, girl"? These children should still be cuddling teddy bears and watching princess movies. Not dressing like pole dancers. Dressing like... her.

"What are your names?" she asked, buying time, trying to keep her voice steady.

"Amber and Jasmine," their mother answered for them. "They're eight and ten."

Martha forced a smile as she bent to sign the photo, trying not to focus on how much skin she was showing in the image. "To Amber and Jasmine," she wrote, then paused. What message could she possibly write that wouldn't encourage... this?

"Morgan is our role model," the mother continued. "The girls are learning that confidence is beautiful. They're already taking dance classes."

Behind Martha, Ezra shifted his weight, and she knew exactly what he was thinking. Dance classes were one thing. Bump and grind routines from "Resonance" were something else entirely.

"It's wonderful that you're dancing," Martha said to the girls. "Do you take ballet?"

"Ballet's boring," Amber, the younger one, declared. "We want to dance like you do in your videos."

"Like this!" Jasmine demonstrated another move, one that made Martha's cheeks burn. Had she really...? Yes, she had.

Her pen hovered over the photo. Finally, she wrote, "Chase your dreams through hard work and practice. Music is a wonderful gift."

It felt inadequate, but what else could she say while they were all watching her—the mother, Sharon, the hovering photographers eager to capture Morgan with her young fans, and Ezra, whose silence spoke volumes.

She smiled for a selfie with the children as Sharon announced, "And that's a wrap on the red carpet."

The coordinator stepped forward, steering Martha and Ezra toward the gallery entrance. Inside, the crystal chandeliers scattered prismatic light across the marble floors of the grand entrance hall.

An event coordinator stepped forward. "I'll show Mr. Falconer to the VIP area. Morgan, we need you backstage for final touches."

"I'll see you inside." Ezra's voice was quiet, meant only for her. He pressed a kiss to her forehead. "You look beautiful." The words were the same as earlier, but now they felt weighted with everything they'd just witnessed.

Martha caught his hand. "Ezra—" But what could she say about those little girls, about their dance moves, about all of it?

He squeezed her fingers, his gaze meeting hers. "We'll talk later. You go knock 'em dead." He turned to follow the coordinator.

In the makeshift prep room, Martha sank into the makeup chair. Her mind kept returning to those little girls, to their carefully copied poses and practiced moves.

"Tilt your chin up for me?" The makeup artist—Bella, according to her lanyard—leaned in with a powder brush. "Wow, your bone structure is absolutely insane. No wonder you broke the internet with that Libertine campaign."

Martha managed a weak smile as Bella worked.

"I was today years old when I found out you're married to Ezra Falconer!" Bella said, switching brushes. "No shade, but like, my mum has all his albums, and the Falconer Brothers stuff, too. She's really religious—actually dragged me to one of his worship concerts back in the day. I mean, the music wasn't bad, but it just wasn't my scene." She stepped back, examining her work. "You guys just seem so... different, you know? Like, he's all Jesus and modest living, and you're out here living your best life, being sexy and empowered. Breaking all the rules."

The words hit Martha like a slap. Is that how people saw them? More importantly, is that how they saw her? So incompatible with what Ezra stood for?

"It's... more complicated than that," Martha said, but had to stop as Bella started touching up her lipstick.

She stared at her reflection—perfect makeup, perfect hair, perfect image. Morgan stared back at her, confident and bold. What did those little girls see? What did everyone see?

What did Ezra see?

A coordinator appeared in the doorway. "They're ready for you, Morgan."

It was time. So much work had gone into putting this event together. So many people were depending on her. Falling apart wasn't an option. She was a lifetime away from that village church in Hatbrook.

Martha straightened her shoulders, feeling the weight of Morgan's persona settle around her like a mantle. With one last glance in the mirror, she stepped out of the dressing room and into the role she knew all too well.

The crystal chandeliers cast a warm glow over the gallery space as Martha stepped onto the small stage. The guests, a carefully curated list of fashion editors, beauty influencers and industry leaders, mingled between the perfume installations, signature cocktails sparkling rose-gold in their hands.

The meticulous planning of her team showed in every detail, from the floral arrangements that hinted at Serenade's notes to the way the lighting created intimate pools of warmth throughout the vast room.

"Welcome to the launch of Serenade." Her voice carried clearly through the space, practiced and professional.

The crowd nodded and chuckled in all the right places as she delivered her speech about blending music and fragrance.

She introduced the brand representatives, catching her own reflection in the polished surface of the nearby installation. Her smile looked real, and she held it steady through the presentations about market research and projected sales. All the while, her mind kept drifting to those little girls mimicking her dance moves.

The speeches concluded right on schedule. It was time for her performance.

The opening beats of "Resonance" filled the gallery space, bouncing off the stark white walls. As Martha moved into her first choreographed sequence, she saw them.

Amber and Jasmine had pushed their way to the front of the gathered crowd, mirroring her every move.

Their mother held up her phone, recording their routine as their little bodies gyrated.

Hours of grueling rehearsals kicked in as Martha sang every precise note and nailed her choreography, her body on autopilot, while her mind screamed.

The girls' lips mouthed her own lyrics back at her. *Dancing wild on liberation's beat. Tell me to be quiet, to behave, but I'm no puppet—my body won't be enslaved.*

What had seemed empowering in the studio and on the video set now felt hollow as she watched these children embody her words.

Her gaze found Ezra across the room, standing near one of the perfume installations. His face was carefully neutral, but she knew that look. He was praying. And for the first time, she wondered if he was praying for her rather than about her.

Chapter Thirty-Two

EZRA'S GAZE FOLLOWED HIS wife as the crystal chandeliers cast a golden light across her bare shoulders, her dress throwing sparkles onto the white wall. Poised and confident, she guided a fashion editor through Serenade's story.

She'd been at this for over an hour now—gliding between perfume stations, explaining the creative process to journalists, posing for photos with influencers. The moment one conversation ended, another guest would appear at her elbow. Through it all, she maintained that megawatt smile, that easy laugh, that unwavering grace.

Morgan was in her element. But Ezra knew Martha's tells.

The way her fingers kept returning to touch her bare collarbone. Her media training broke her habit of crossing her arms when she was nervous, but hadn't cured her of that unconscious gesture. The subtle shift of weight between feet that meant her heels were killing her. The almost imperceptible pause before each new smile, as though gathering strength.

He hadn't missed her reaction to those little girls on the red carpet. The shake in her hand as she'd signed that lingerie campaign photo, the careful way she'd redirected their conversation to ballet. How her gaze kept going back to them as they gyrated to "Resonance." His own gut had twisted seeing children that young mimicking Morgan's moves.

When had he learned to read her so well? Or maybe the better question was when had she learned to hide herself so completely from everyone else?

The crowd thinned, guests drifting toward the exits with gift bags and business cards. The air remained fragrant with bergamot, cedarwood, and Martha's signature lavender. Judging by their lingering smiles and their repeated gestures to sniff at their pulse points, Serenade was a success.

Martha finished her last interview, then made her way to where Ezra stood. Up close, he could see the strain around her eyes, the tremor in her practiced smile.

He touched her arm. "You okay?"

She moved closer, and her whispered words carried a note he'd never heard from her before. "Can we leave? Now?"

"Of course." He squeezed her shoulder. "Let me find Sharon."

The event organizer appeared as if summoned, efficiently steering them to a staff exit. "Ray's waiting with the Range Rover," she said, tapping her earpiece. "I'll have security clear a path."

Minutes later, they were enclosed in the quiet luxury of Martha's customized Range Rover, the tinted glass of the privacy partition rising between them and Ray.

Martha sagged against the leather seat, slipping off her heels with a quiet groan. The sequins of her dress caught the passing streetlights, throwing tiny fragments of light around the cabin.

Ezra found her hand in the darkness, lacing his fingers through hers. He waited, giving her space to gather herself.

"The dress," she said finally.

Ezra frowned. What was she talking about?

Her fingers twisted. "I owe you an explanation about the dress. I was going to wear the yellow one you liked, but Kelsey said it would wash out under the lighting, that it wouldn't photograph well." The words came faster now. "I should have explained, but everything was so rushed, and—" She broke off, pressing her free hand to her temple. "I know it probably seemed like I didn't value your opinion."

He let out a breath. So, that's what she meant. He was quiet for a moment, stroking the back of her hand with his thumb. "I was hurt," he admitted softly. "Confused. Especially after this afternoon, when you'd asked what I thought. But I understand now. Thank you for explaining."

Her fingers tightened around his, but she stayed silent. The streetlights played across her troubled face in strobe-like pulses as she stared into her lap.

He waited.

"Did you see those little girls?" she whispered finally. "The way they were dressed? And when they started dancing..." Her voice caught. "They were copying my moves from the video. Those sweet, innocent children, looking so... so..." She turned to him, eyes bright with tears. "That's why you hate all this Morgan branding."

Ezra chose his words carefully. "It's not that I hate it. It's just... the image disturbs me. Those sexually charged performances... it's celebrating exposure rather than the intimacy we share. I know it may sound old-fashioned, or even restrictive, but I cherish the parts of you that are meant just for us—sacred and private within our marriage. When you share that with the world... it wrenches my heart." He stroked her hand. "That's why it's so hard for me to see you like that."

His phone buzzed in his pocket. He ignored it.

Watching his face, she spoke slowly, as though wading through her words. "So, you feel like when I show off my body, I'm taking something that belongs to us, to our intimacy, and showing it to the whole world? And it's not just the clothes—it's also how I carry myself—how I play up my... my sensuality?"

"Yes." His throat tightened at her understanding. "It's not about wanting to control you or dictate how you dress or what you do. I love you no matter what. It's just... our physical intimacy is a gift we share only with each other. Seeing it packaged and sold as entertainment—"

He heard her sharp intake of breath. "Then I..." Her lips trembled. "I've been hurting you over and over. The shows, the video, the lingerie shoot..."

His phone buzzed again, insistent, intruding. He squeezed her hand, focusing on this moment of truth between them, this first real acknowledgment of what had been tearing at his heart.

"I didn't see it." Her voice cracked. "Ezra, I'm so sorry."

His phone buzzed yet again. He pulled it out, glanced at Fiona's name on the screen, and switched it off. Whatever she wanted could wait. This moment with Martha couldn't.

"Come here," he said softly, drawing his wife into his arms. She came willingly, curling against him like she used to, before Morgan and fame and everything else had crowded into their marriage. He breathed in the familiar scent of lavender beneath Serenade's sophisticated notes as he held her close.

"Today, one of my makeup artists was shocked that I'm married to you," she whispered against his shoulder. "Because she knows your music is about glorifying Jesus. But my entire career is wrapped up in how I look. My sex appeal. The way I present myself. I've made a name for myself by becoming someone who violates everything that's sacred to you—to us."

"No." He drew back slightly, needing her to see his face in the dim light. "I know that you love God. And your gift is your voice, Martha. The way you connect with people through music."

How could he make her understand?

"I just watched you host a VIP launch of your perfume as though you were born to do it. You were poised, polished, and confident... and you owned that stage. You had all your guests eating out of your hand. You're smart, you're funny, you work so, so hard and yet make it all look so easy. I'm in awe of you." He touched her cheek. "That's what makes you shine—that's what should be center stage, not... all of this." His hand dropped to indicate her dress, the whole Morgan package. "We just need to find a different way."

In the passing streetlights, he caught the shimmer of tears in her eyes. In that moment, he saw both versions of his wife—Martha's vulnerability and Morgan's glamor—and loved them both, knowing they were the same person who just needed to find her true path.

"We *will* find a different way," he whispered, drawing her back against his chest. "Together."

"I want that." Her voice was small against his shirt. "I'm so sorry, Ezra."

"Shh... I know." His fingers traced gentle patterns on her back. "I love you—all of you. Every version. I just want us to find a path that's true to who you really are."

"Thank you," she whispered. She relaxed fully against him, the last of her tension leaving her body.

Only now, feeling her go slack against his chest like a released bowstring, did he realize just how tightly stretched she'd been all evening and how much strain maintaining Morgan's perfect facade had cost her. Every bowstring had a breaking point. How close to hers had Martha come? The thought unsettled him. But for now, she was just Martha, soft and real in his arms.

He held her close as the car wound through the sleeping country roads. The weight that had been crushing his heart these past months lifted, allowing him to breathe again. This was an answer to prayer—not just Martha's understanding of his pain, but her willingness to change things, to find a path that honored her gift, their faith, and their marriage.

God was showing him how to love his wife—not by demanding change, but by helping Martha see her true worth beyond Morgan's carefully curated image. They were finding their way back to each other, facing the hard things together instead of alone.

The car pulled into their driveway. Ezra's hand found the small of Martha's back as they walked into the house through the darkened entryway.

She carried her shoes in one hand while the other held up the trailing hem of her dress. Without her heels, she was tiny beside him, the top of her head barely clearing his shoulder.

When they reached the kitchen, she turned into his arms, pressing her face into his chest, her arms sliding around his waist.

He could feel how exhausted she was, wrung out both physically and emotionally from the evening. He held her close, savoring her warmth against him, the way she fit so perfectly in his arms, tucked next to his heart, no matter what size she was.

Finally, looking down at her dress, she sighed. "I need to get out of this."

"Go ahead," he said, brushing a kiss against her temple. "I'll make you some chamomile tea."

Sometimes, the more tired she was, the harder she found it to sleep. And she needed to rest tonight. He watched her head upstairs, his gaze trailing her until she went into their room, then moved to fill the kettle and get their mugs ready.

While the water heated, his thoughts turned to Levi. With everything that had happened tonight, he hadn't had a chance to check how things were in Australia. He should at least send a quick text asking about Cedric's health.

He glanced at his watch. Half past midnight, which meant it must be nine thirty in the morning in Brisbane. He pulled out his phone and switched it on.

The phone erupted with notifications. Missed calls. Voicemails. Text messages. Fiona, his agent, had been blowing his phone up.

Heart pounding, he opened the most recent text.

URGENT!!! Ezra, where are you? You need to call me right now. You're being accused of plagiarism for "Whispers of You."

Chapter Thirty-Three

EZRA'S FINGERS TREMBLED AS he called Fiona. She answered on the first ring.

"Ezra? It's about time. Where have you been? Never mind—we need to deal with this now." Her voice was tight with tension. "SoundScene just published a piece about half an hour ago. Ivy Willis is claiming co-authorship of 'Whispers of You.'"

The kitchen counter pressed cold against his palm as he leaned heavily against it. "What?"

"She says you wrote it together, that you've collaborated on several songs, but you kept her name off this one. They've got extensive quotes from her about the writing process, about working with you on the melody—" Fiona broke off for a moment. "The piece says they reached out to me for a comment, but I only got their email an hour ago. I was still trying to reach you. They didn't wait for our response before running with the story."

Ezra's mind raced back through those writing sessions as he wrote "Whispers of You". Yes, Ivy had been there, offering suggestions, but the song—his song—had come from his own experience, his own heart. It was about his love for Martha.

"This is insane." His voice sounded strange in his ears. "I wrote that song. She knows full well that I did. Every word, every note—"

"I know." Fiona cut him off. "But right now, we need to craft a response. This is spreading like wildfire. The piece quotes her saying she was there for every session, that she helped develop the hook that made it such a hit. She's even describing specific moments—saying you were stuck on the bridge until she suggested nixing it."

The room tilted. Ezra gripped the counter harder, his knuckles white. Those sessions were years ago, but he remembered the exact moment he'd decided the bridge disrupted the song, overcomplicating the simplicity of its flow. Ivy had been there, had offered input like she always did, but—

"She's lying." The words came out raw. "That song came to me when... I'd been working all night and I came home at daybreak and saw Martha asleep. The light of the dawn on her face—it was nothing to do with Ivy."

"I believe you. But SoundScene is running with her version. They're painting it as another case of a male songwriter taking credit for a woman's work."

"What's happening?"

Ezra spun around.

Martha stood in the kitchen doorway in blue silk pajamas. Her face was fresh and makeup-free, her hair loose around her shoulders. Searching his face, she stepped forward. "Ezra? What's wrong?"

"I have to go," he said into the phone. "But first—draft a denial immediately and send it to SoundScene. Something simple. That I categorically deny these allegations and will respond more fully in due course."

"Already on it," Fiona said. "I'll send you the draft before it goes out."

"Thanks." He ended the call and turned to face his wife.

How had this evening twisted into such a nightmare? "Ivy Willis is claiming she co-wrote 'Whispers of You.'" Even saying the words felt surreal.

Martha's face turned to stone. "Ivy?"

"Yes. She's telling music blogs that I stole credit from her." He ran a hand through his hair.

Martha swallowed. "Why would she say that?"

Why indeed? Ezra's gut churned. Revenge. Vindictiveness. To get back at him for—

His gaze caught Martha's. She was still rooted to the spot, her eyes wide as she searched his face. "Who knows what goes on in that woman's head?"

"You used to be close."

"We did collaborate a lot back then. But not on 'Whispers of You.' She was around for most of my writing sessions."

He paced the kitchen, trying to remember details that suddenly seemed crucial. "She critiqued some lyrics and structure and we discussed whether or not it needed a key change, but the song was completely mine. I remember finishing it during one of those all-night sessions at the studio. She was there, but she was working on something else entirely."

He turned to Martha. "You remember that time, don't you? I was writing intensely, staying late at the studio most nights. The song just poured out of me and I had to get it down."

She had gone very still. "It's going to be very hard for you to prove what happened in those sessions. When it was just the two of you alone together."

His phone lit up with Fiona's call.

"I've drafted a statement," Fiona said without preamble. "I'm sending it now. And Ezra, we need to talk about exactly what proof we have of your authorship. Early drafts, demo recordings, anything from that time period..."

As he answered Fiona's questions, he glanced up.

Martha hadn't moved. She was still watching him with that unreadable expression.

He held out his hand, and she came to lean against the counter beside him. When he slipped his arm around her waist, her body was rigid beneath his touch.

"I know I have the final demo somewhere," he told Fiona, acutely aware of the tension in Martha's frame. "And there should be documentation from when we registered the copyright—"

Martha moved away, heading toward the French doors.

"We need to nip this in the bud," Fiona's voice held a sharp edge of urgency. "I've seen claims like this destroy careers. Even when they're completely baseless, the mud tends to stick."

"What do you suggest?"

"First, we get that denial out. Then we need to contact everyone who was around during that period—the sound engineers, the studio staff—anyone who can verify your writing process."

"Right." His gaze found Martha. She stood in front of the French doors, her hand pressed against the glass.

He lingered at the edge of the kitchen, unable to tear his gaze from her rigid back. "What about the movie people? They must have documentation from when they licensed the song."

"Already on it. I'm pulling everything we have." Fiona hesitated. "Ezra, I know the answer, but I have to ask. You're absolutely sure there's no truth to what she's saying?"

"Of course there isn't." His voice echoed in the kitchen. "Ivy is lying for some twisted reason of her own."

Martha turned around, her gaze colliding with his.

"I'm going to grab a pen," he told Fiona. "Let's make a list of everyone we could contact about this."

"Take a look at that draft statement first, though, so I can send it off." She sighed. "It's going to be a long night."

"Okay. I'll look at it now. Talk to you soon." He ended the call and looked up at Martha. She stood in the middle of the living room.

He went to her and placed his hands on her shoulders. "I don't think I'm going to get much sleep tonight. But why don't you go up to bed? You look shattered."

She stood still under his touch. "I should stay up with you."

For a moment, he was tempted. Having her beside him while he dealt with this nightmare...

But he could see the exhaustion in her face, feel her body trembling under his fingers. She'd been on the go all day, with her launch preparations, had pushed through an emotionally draining evening, and now this. She was probably more tired than she realized.

"No point in both of us being exhausted tomorrow." He squeezed her shoulders gently. "I'll feel a lot better if I know you've had a rest. We'll sort this out soon enough—the truth will come out."

She looked at him for a long moment. "It always does, doesn't it?"

She drew a shaky breath, and for a moment he thought she might say something more. Instead, she touched his hand where it rested on her shoulder. "Wake me if you need me?"

The quiet plea in her voice made his chest tight. But she was already pulling away, wrapping her arms around herself as she climbed the stairs.

Chamomile tea. He'd promised to make her some chamomile tea. But it was probably better that she try to sleep without waiting for it. She needed rest more than anything right now.

Only when he heard their bedroom door close did he return to the kitchen to look at Fiona's draft. His phone was already lighting up with more messages.

Somewhere above him, Martha was alone with her thoughts. He hated sending her to bed with all this hanging over them, but she was at the end of her strength. Hopefully, this would all be cleared up by tomorrow and they could move forward with healing their marriage.

He picked up his phone, squaring his shoulders. Time to put an end to these lies. Whatever twisted game Ivy was playing, she'd picked the wrong song to lie about. This one had come straight from his heart, poured out during his quiet time with God. It was about his longing for his wife when they were going through a rough patch.

Ivy might have been there when he wrote it down, might have offered her thoughts like she always did, but "Whispers of You" was his, completely and utterly. He'd make sure everyone knew that.

Opening Fiona's message, he began to read.

Chapter Thirty-Four

ARTHA CLOSED THE BEDROOM door behind her and sagged against it, sliding down until she sat on the floor, her arms wrapped around her knees.

"Ezra!" His name burst out in a half-stifled sob. "Lord, help me. I don't know what to believe anymore. I don't know what he did, what happened between them. But I can't—" Her voice broke. "I can't bear this alone."

She'd thought she was past this—past the nights alone in her bed wondering what went on in that studio, past the gut-twisting pain of watching his growing intimacy with Ivy, past the desperate need to know if there had been more.

This should have been over. Just an hour ago, she'd been in Ezra's arms, in pieces about how she had violated their intimacy by sharing with the world what should be sacred between them.

But hadn't he done the same thing first? He'd let another woman into spaces that should have been just for them—bonding with Ivy over music on those all-night jamming and songwriting sessions, forging a deep emotional connection, sharing private inside jokes that shut Martha out.

And now Ivy was weaponizing that intimacy against Ezra. What happened between them that would make her attack him like this? That flicker in his eyes when she'd asked him point blank. His quick deflection. He knew something he wasn't saying.

With trembling hands, she pulled out her phone and opened the SoundScene blog. The article was front and center. She read, the words blurred before her eyes: "...late night writing sessions... unique creative partnership... deep personal and musical connection..."

Her throat closed up. Ivy's quotes painted such a vivid picture of those sessions—working side by side at the piano, sharing ideas deep into the night, developing the hook that made "Whispers of You" a hit. The same sessions Ezra had dismissed so casually. *She was there, but she was working on something else entirely.*

The article linked to Ivy's own social media account, where she talked about her bombshell allegations. "The hardest post I've ever had to make," she'd captioned her video reel. Staring into the camera, looking vulnerable and sincere, her voice breaking, Ivy said, "Sometimes you have to speak your truth, even when it means confronting someone you once trusted completely."

Martha's finger trembled as she scrolled through the responses. Industry heavyweights weighing in, sharing their own stories of stolen credit. Rising artists expressing their disappointment in Ezra. Even some of his self-proclaimed fans were beginning to question everything.

The comments were getting uglier.

"Another male songwriter stealing women's work. .."

"Always knew there was something off about him.. ."

"Hey, #EzraFalconer, doesn't your Bible say thou shalt not steal?"

Martha's chest tightened. This wasn't just Ivy meddling in their marriage anymore. She was systematically destroying Ezra's reputation. She knew how the industry worked, how quickly people could turn, how a whisper could become a roar that drowned out everything else. And Ivy had played this masterfully, dropping this bomb late at night when it could spread unchallenged through social media.

As she went down the endless Internet rabbit hole, Martha found Ezra's hastily penned statement—a complete denial of Ivy's claims. But although the blog articles tacked it on as a fig leaf in a pretense of fair reporting, social media had already decided Ezra was lying.

"Of course he denies it..."

"Men always do..."

"Notice how defensive he sounds?"

The social media mob was coming after Ezra, bearing torches and pitchforks.

She looked up from her phone. The bedroom was dark except from the glow of her screen. How was it three in the morning? Ezra hadn't come to bed—he was still downstairs trying to contain this nightmare.

She pushed herself up from the floor, legs shaky. Grief and anger still churned inside her, but beneath it all lay something deeper, something that had survived every night alone, every inside joke and shared look between Ezra and Ivy that excluded her, every doubt that plagued her marriage.

He was her husband. And she chose to cleave to him.

The decision steadied her. Yes, he was hiding something about Ivy. Yes, there were secrets between them that would have to be faced. But right now, her husband was fighting for his career, his reputation, everything he'd worked for. Whatever had happened with Ivy, whatever Ezra wasn't telling her, he wouldn't face this alone. Her place was with him.

Drawing a deep breath, she reached for the door. As her fingers brushed against the door handle, her phone lit up with Alex's name.

"Morgan? Did I wake you?" His voice was gentle but urgent. "I'm really sorry for calling at such a crazy time. You must have heard about what's going down. Are you okay?"

"Hi, Alex. I'm…" She trailed off. How was she? Not okay, that's for sure. "I'm hanging in there."

"Listen, I know this must be difficult, but we need to meet right away to discuss how to handle this. I wouldn't have bothered you at such an ungodly hour, but the situation is escalating faster than anyone expected."

"You mean faster than a growing Twitter mob?" Although that was distressing enough. Some of the things people were saying about Ezra…

"I wouldn't be calling if it was just social media chatter. Or if it was just about your husband, frankly. But I've had calls from the label and your sponsors. They're deeply concerned about how this might affect you. Your image is particularly important right now with the perfume launch. A lot of people have a lot of money riding on your success." He paused. "I wouldn't ask this if it wasn't serious. We need to get ahead of this."

She sighed. "I understand. But I need to be here for Ezra."

"I get it. He's your husband and you feel a need to stand by your man and all that. But we've got to get our messaging right. How about you come meet with me now, we'll sort out a strategy, and then you can go straight back to be with Ezra? I would have come over there, but considering what happened the last time I was under your roof, I think it's best I don't. But this meeting needs to happen, Morgan. The sooner the better."

She closed her eyes. Every muscle in her body ached with fatigue. The last thing she wanted to do was go out now.

But maybe that was one way she could help Ezra. Morgan could come out with a robust statement supporting him. She had some pull in the industry. Surely, if she was firm in her belief in him, it might influence some people not to be so quick to believe Ivy. Her sponsors might not like it, but that was too bad.

"Fine. I'll be there as soon as I can. But let's make it quick."

She ended the call and headed down the stairs.

Ezra sat at the kitchen counter, his laptop open, phone pressed to his ear. "What I need from you is to look up exactly what documentation you have from when we registered the copyright."

Her heart twisted seeing him like this, desperately trying to defend himself against Ivy's lies. Whatever had happened between them, he didn't deserve this systematic destruction of his career, his reputation.

He looked up as she entered, his face drawn with exhaustion. "Thanks. I'll wait for your email." He ended the call.

As she walked over to him, he turned in his seat to face her.

His arms went around her waist. "Hey. You're supposed to be getting some rest."

There he was, doing it again. Thinking about what she needed when his world was falling apart. Not just his world. Their world. How could this man, who was so considerate, so loving toward her, be the same one harboring secrets about Ivy?

Her heart ached with the contradiction of it all. But he needed her now. This crisis was bigger than her feelings, whatever he may have done. And... she loved him. She couldn't not love him.

She linked her hands behind his neck. "I couldn't sleep. How's it going?"

He shook his head. "I've hit a snag with Silvertone's archives. The label that originally released 'Whispers' got bought out by Meridian Group, who then merged with Atlantic Vista last year, who've now been taken over by Silvertone. No one seems to know where the documentation from that far back ended up. Half the people I worked with aren't even there anymore."

He gestured toward his laptop. "I've been trying to reach someone in their LA office who might know where to look, but apparently, they're on vacation."

"And the movie people?"

"Different takeover, same problem. Fiona's trying to track down the original music supervisor, but he's retired now. Moved to Florida or somewhere."

"So, it's just your word against Ivy's?"

"No, there are other avenues to try, thank God. Even if we can't get the original documentation, I can still prove the song came from me. Early drafts, demo recordings, people who knew about it before I even took it to the studio. We just need to piece it all together. And we will. It'll just take time."

And during that time, Ivy might run his reputation into the ground.

She could feel the tension in his neck. He must be worn out. Adrenaline would only take him so far. He hadn't even changed out of his suit from the perfume launch.

"Have you told your family?" She combed her fingers through his hair. "You shouldn't be dealing with this alone. You need your brothers."

"I'm not alone. You're here."

As he pulled her closer to himself, his simple words stabbed her with guilt. He didn't know the doubts she had about him, the feelings of betrayal she was fighting to keep at bay.

"Anyway, I've not had time to get in touch with them yet," he said against her shoulder. "And it's late."

"Let me text them. They should hear it from us before they see it online or find out from someone else. Even at this hour, they'd want to know."

He was silent for a moment. "Thanks." His voice was husky. "I didn't know how to tell them."

She tightened her embrace.

His body leaned into hers for an instant, then he straightened his shoulders as a ping came through his email software. "I need to answer this."

"Sure." Stepping away from him, she let her hand linger on the nape of his neck for a moment, then pulled out her phone.

She opened her messaging app and tapped out a text.

Please pray. Someone is claiming she co-wrote "Whispers of You" and that Ezra stole credit from her. It's all over social media. He needs us all right now.

She found Levi and Zach's contacts, then added Beth, Eden, and Pastor Noah to the group. Beth and Eden would want to pray. And they would need Pastor Noah's counsel through this.

The message sent, she went over to the kettle. He could do with a hot drink. Their favorite mugs still stood on the counter, tea bags inside. Chamomile for her, Earl Grey for him. The tea he'd planned on making hours ago before this storm broke.

As the kettle heated, a message came through on her phone. It was Zach.

No! I'm on my way. I won't call and tie up his phone. Praying hard.

Good. If Zach was coming, it made it easier to tell Ezra she had to go out.

She made his Earl Grey the way he liked it—steeped just long enough to be strong but not bitter, with a slice of lemon. No sugar. She brought the mug to him, the steam curling up between them as he stared at his screen.

He looked up at her. "Oh. Thank you. I needed that."

As he took a sip, she pulled out the bar stool next to him and sat on the edge. "Ezra, Alex called earlier. He needs to see me. The label and my sponsors are worried."

"What?" He put his mug down. "They're dragging you into this already? I'm so sorry. This is just ridiculous. Should I tell Fiona? Maybe she can coordinate with Alex."

Martha shook her head. "He says it can't wait. It won't take long, though. I just need to tell him I support you fully and work out how to make that clear to everyone—the label, my sponsors, the media. We need to get the messaging right, so there's no doubt where I stand. I'll come straight back."

"What, you're going now?"

"He says the sooner we deal with this..." She couldn't finish.

His hand found hers, squeezing gently. "I understand. Let me get Marcus—"

"No, I'll drive myself. Marcus is working with the new protection dog tonight. They're still in the bonding period. He can't leave her." She managed a small smile. "It's late. The streets will be quiet. And I'll be back before it gets busy."

Ezra frowned. "I don't like it. For one thing, you've hardly had a wink of sleep since yesterday."

"Alex is only twenty minutes away. I'll be fine. Before I forget, Zach texted back. He's on his way."

Relief flickered across his face. "Good. That's good." Then his brow furrowed again. "But maybe you could wait for Ray? His shift starts in just a few hours—"

"I'd rather go now." She touched his cheek. "The sooner I go, the sooner I can get back. I'll just go change into something more practical than pajamas." She needed space to think, too. Being alone would be a relief.

Sighing, he laid his hand over hers. "Okay. But please hurry back."

Chapter Thirty-Five

ARTHA PULLED INTO ALEX'S circular driveway, her hands trembling on the steering wheel, her heart racing as she gasped a prayer. She shouldn't have attempted this drive. Not in this state. Not at this hour.

Light spilled from her manager's front door as he stepped out onto the portico. "Morgan?" His eyebrows shot up. "You came here alone? Without Ray or Marcus?"

"Ray's off duty. And Marcus couldn't leave the new protection dog." Her hands still shook as she closed the car door. "Maybe driving myself wasn't such a great idea."

"You think?" He hurried down the steps to her, concern etched on his face. "You look exhausted."

"I know." She drew in a shaky breath, letting him guide her toward the door, his hand on her elbow. "I dozed off at the wheel. On that straight stretch past Westcott. The rumble strip woke me up before I went off the road."

"I didn't expect you to do that, you silly girl. That was completely reckless! Come inside before you fall down. When was the last time you slept properly?"

She tried to remember. The perfume launch felt like days ago, though it had been just hours.

He muttered an oath. "Never mind leaving home without your PPO—you could have been killed driving tired. Come on, let's get you inside and sort this mess out."

Alex led her into his living room. He'd redecorated again. The clean lines and chrome accents of the art déco pieces gleamed under carefully positioned lighting. A sweeping curved sofa in deep charcoal dominated one wall, while geometric patterns in silver and black repeated across the cushions and artwork.

"Sit." He gestured toward the sofa. "Before you collapse."

She sank into the plush upholstery, her bag sliding to the floor.

"I've been on damage control since this broke," he said, moving to the bar cart that matched the room's chrome detailing. "Water?"

She nodded, watching as he filled a crystal tumbler. "What are people saying?"

"*Entertainment Weekly* has already run a piece connecting you to the scandal. 'Morgan's Husband Accused of Song Theft.' They've got photos of the two of you from your perfume launch splashed across their website. Pretty unfortunate timing, that cozy red carpet moment with Ezra. It's made it super easy for everyone to make the connection between the two of you." He handed her the water. "The story's spreading fast. Your name is getting dragged into every headline. People who have no clue who Ezra is are interested in the story because of you."

Her fingers trembled around the glass. "But I had nothing to do with—"

"Doesn't matter. You're Morgan now. Everything you touch becomes news." He settled into a chrome and leather armchair. "And this is exactly the kind of news we don't need. Maison Duval called me an hour ago. They're concerned about the optics. A women's empowerment brand can't be associated with—" He broke off, watching her face. "Well, you understand their position."

"Entertainment outlets are having a field day," Alex continued. "And it's not just them. The fashion blogs are picking it up. Social media is exploding. #Morgan-DeservesBetter is already trending."

She took a sip of water, trying to steady herself and process the flow of words. "What does that mean?"

"It means your fans think you're being dragged down by association. Look..." He walked to his laptop, clicking over to one of the dozens of open browser tabs. "Here. 'How is #RealMorgan partnering with #Maison-

Duval to empower women while married to someone who steals from them?' That tweet's gone viral. The comments are brutal."

Martha closed her eyes. The room spun around her.

"The perfume launch was perfect. Your image was exactly where we needed it to be. But now..." He leaned forward. "That's why I needed to see you immediately. We have to get ahead of this. We're just a few hours into this story breaking, but Eclat's marketing team is already asking questions about the holiday promotion. There's an ominous email from Libertine. And I've had three other potential sponsors pull back from deals we were negotiating."

She massaged her temples. "What do they expect me to do? He's my husband."

"And that's exactly the problem. Your whole brand is about female empowerment, about women supporting women. But right now, you're being associated with a man who—" He broke off again. "The longer we wait to address this, the worse it's going to get."

He shot her a piercing gaze. "I'm going to be frank. You need to distance yourself from this. Now, before it does irreparable damage to your brand."

"What?" She stared at him. "I won't do that. Ezra's telling the truth. He wrote 'Whispers' on his own, and he'll find evidence to prove it."

"By then, it'll be too late. If he finds proof at all." Alex's voice gentled. "Morgan, you've worked so hard to get here. Your career is taking off in ways we never imagined. But something like this? It could destroy everything we've built."

It was so hard to think. It was like her mind was moving at the speed of treacle. But she was sure of one thing. "I believe Ezra. And any statement I make has to support my husband. Let's be absolutely a hundred percent clear on that. What we need to work on is finding the right words. Something that's respectful to Ivy while still—"

She broke off, rubbing her eyes. She was so, so tired. "We don't have to say Ivy is lying. We can say that she might have genuinely rismerembered—misreminded—I mean, misremembered."

"Sweetheart, you can barely string a sentence together." Alex stood. "And you definitely can't drive home like this. Why don't you take a nap in the guest room while I draft something? We can look at it with fresh eyes."

Sleep would be such sweet relief. She could just lie down for a short while, then get up and look at Alex's statement, make sure her voice went out in support of Ezra. "Okay. But I have to tell Ezra I'm staying a while longer. He's expecting me back soon."

She reached for her bag, fumbling through the compartments. Keys, wallet, lip balm...

Where was her phone?

She turned the bag upside down, contents spilling onto the sofa. "Oh no, I must have left my phone at home. Can I borrow yours?" She looked up at Alex. "Just to let Ezra know. He'll be worrying about me. He didn't want me to come on my own."

"Battery's dead." Alex showed her the black screen. "But I'll send him a message as soon as it charges. Come on, you can barely keep your eyes open."

He was already helping her up, guiding her down a hallway that seemed to stretch forever.

The guest room appeared through a haze of exhaustion, all cream and silver, the bed a beacon of promised relief.

The sheets welcomed her, cool against her skin as she sank onto the mattress. It was like floating on the softest of clouds.

"Please," she murmured as Alex pulled the duvet over her, "tell Ezra I'll be later than I planned."

"Of course." His voice came from somewhere far away. "Don't worry about it. I'll let him know you're safe. You just rest now."

The door clicked shut as she closed her eyes.

Chapter Thirty-Six

EZRA CHECKED HIS WATCH, gut clenching. Five hours. Martha had been gone for five hours.

Across the kitchen, Zach paced up and down, phone held against his ear. "I appreciate your getting back to me. Right. Yes. Another merger. Could you at least tell me whom I should be speaking to now?" He glanced at Ezra, rolling his eyes. "No problem. I'll hold."

From her perch on the sofa, his mother covered the mouthpiece of her own phone. She looked up at Ezra. "I've been transferred three times. No one seems to know where the old licensing records went after Atlantic Vista took over."

"No, don't transfer me again—" Zach's voice rose in frustration. He sighed, catching Ezra's expression. "Still nothing from Martha?"

Ezra shook his head. "I guess she's still hashing out a media response with Alex." He hoped that's all it was. The alternatives turned his stomach. Martha, out on her own without her bodyguard, driving while exhausted—

Why had he let her go? He should have taken her to Alex's place himself. Or convinced her to wait for Zach to take her.

"Hello?" Zach said into his phone. "Starlight Corporation. Thank you. Could you give me a name I can talk to? Or at least a phone number?" He grabbed a pen from the kitchen counter.

Mum sighed. "I got cut off." She put her phone down.

Ezra ran his hand through his hair. When would he wake up from this nightmare? At least if he could hear from Martha and know she was okay. Then he could chase down that lead about locating the music supervisor from *Twice in a Lifetime*, the movie that featured "Whispers of You" on its soundtrack.

He pulled out his phone. Five hours was plenty of time for a meeting with Alex. Surely it was reasonable to call her now, just to check she was okay.

As the call connected, music drifted from the kitchen counter. The familiar opening strains of "Whispers of You"—his song, the one causing all this trouble—filled the kitchen like a cruel joke.

"Oh!" Mum jumped up from the sofa, moving to the counter.

There, next to the kettle where Martha had made Ezra's mug of Earl Grey, lay her phone, pouring out his song. It was her ringtone for him.

Mum picked it up and brought it to him, still ringing.

Martha's phone screen displayed an incoming call from "My Heart ❤ ," with a goofy photo of him giving two thumbs up to the camera.

His blood froze. If her phone was here, his wife was out there, somewhere, unreachable.

He pressed the end call button, his heart tightening as he put his and Martha's phones on the counter.

Mum touched his shoulder, her gaze on his face. "Don't worry. I'm sure she's okay. She'll probably walk through that door before you know it."

He prayed she was right. Maybe the meeting with Alex had just run long.

He snatched up his phone as it rang. Was it Martha? No, Fiona.

He put her on speaker. "Hi, Fiona. You're on with me, Mum, and Zach."

"Good, because we need to talk strategy." Her voice was tight. "The story's everywhere now. Not just music blogs—mainstream media's picked it up. And Ivy's giving interviews."

Ezra sank onto a bar stool at the kitchen counter. "What's she saying?"

"More of the same, but with details that make her sound credible. Times, dates, specific conversations. We need to counter this fast. I've been talking to other artists you've worked with, trying to find if anyone has solid proof. Matt Hawker and Peter Griffin are willing to go on the record to say they know for a fact that Ivy had no involvement with 'Whispers'."

Ezra blew out a breath. "Thank God for those guys."

"Yeah," Fiona said. "It's a start, but we need more. Some actual receipts. We also need you to make a fuller statement. Maybe record something for social media. People need to see you, hear your voice. It makes you more relatable, more genuine. Especially when Ivy's crying all over the Internet."

Zach, finally free from on-hold limbo, moved closer to Ezra's phone. "Fiona, Zach here. What about the documentation?"

"Working on it. But right now, public opinion is turning against us by the hour." Fiona paused. "Ezra, I hesitate to say this, but we need to get Martha more involved. Her support could really turn this around."

Ezra's stomach knotted. "I... I haven't been able to reach her. She left hours ago for a meeting with her manager to work on a response. Turns out she left her phone at home."

"That's not good." Fiona's voice sharpened. "I saw the statement her team's already put out."

"What?" He sat up straighter. "What did they say?"

"It's pretty non-committal. Hang on, I'll pull it up. Here it is. 'As many of you are aware, recent allegations have been made involving Ezra Falconer and the authorship of the song "Whispers of You." Morgan is aware of these allegations and is taking them very seriously. She believes in the integrity of the creative process and hopes for a fair resolution to this situation. While these allegations are concerning, they are a matter between the parties directly involved.

"'Morgan remains dedicated to her career and to her fans, striving for excellence in her music and public engagements. It is important to separate her personal life from her professional achievements during this time.'"

"That's..." Ezra's mouth went dry. "That's all?" It was so cold. It didn't even mention that she was married to him.

"There's a bit more, but it's in the same vein," Fiona said. "I hoped that was just initial damage control from her team before she's had a chance to make a more definite statement. But if you say she's already met with them and this is what's come out... it worries me. Do you think you could talk her around? Her influence could be game-changing here. Keep trying to reach her, okay?"

Ezra stared at Martha's phone on the counter. Those couldn't be her words. She wouldn't distance herself like that. Would she? She'd left saying she wanted to release a statement supporting him, and this is what was going around in her name. Had Alex talked her into this?

His mind went back to the pale yellow dress. Martha's assurance that she would wear it because he liked it. Only for her to turn around and listen to her stylist, putting her brand ahead of his wishes.

"That statement doesn't sound like Martha," Zach said, his voice hard. "It sounds like a corporate PR team trying to play both sides. Have you tried calling Alex directly?"

Fiona cut in before Ezra could answer. "I'll leave you guys to figure that out, but there are a few more things I want to say before I go. Ezra, since we're getting nowhere with the licensing records, let's try a different angle. We need to build a timeline showing your creation of the song. Demo tapes, computer files—anything that predates your sessions with Ivy. And try to find more artists, friends, who knew you back then. Maybe someone else will back you up or have an email in their records mentioning that you wrote the song."

"Sure. Yeah." His mind kept circling back to Martha's words before she left—*I just need to tell him I support you fully and work out how to make that clear to everyone.* What had changed? What had Alex said to her?

"Ezra?" Fiona's voice grew louder. "Are you hearing me?"

"Yes." He forced himself to focus. "Yes. I'll start looking through my old files."

But even as they discussed next steps, Martha's statement haunted him. *It is important to separate her personal life from her professional achievements during this time.*

Fiona was still talking. He needed to stay on top of this.

"Okay, last matter," Fiona said. "I think it's time to bring in legal counsel. At least identify someone in case it comes to that. I've got several names—entertainment lawyers who specialize in copyright disputes."

The word "lawyers" made this horror movie real in a way nothing else had.

Ezra nodded numbly as Fiona listed credentials and specialties, the words washing over him in a blur. He couldn't process this. None of it.

Zach gripped his shoulder as Fiona ended her call. "Five hours, Ezra. Almost six. This isn't like Martha. Call Alex."

He met his mother's gaze, and she nodded. "Go on. And after that, you've got to get something to eat."

As if he could keep anything down. He headed downstairs to his studio to make the call, needing space from his brother's concerned gaze, his mother's quiet worry.

He looked around the room. He'd kicked Alex out of here, what, two days ago? The man would not be falling over himself to be helpful. But he could at least tell Ezra something about Martha's whereabouts.

He punched the call button. It rang several times before Alex answered.

"Ezra." His voice was like sharpened steel. "What can I do for you?"

"Hi. I'm trying to track Martha down. She left her phone at home when she went to see you. Is she still there? Is she okay?"

"Morgan is fine."

"Okay. If she's still with you, I'd really like to talk to her."

"Ezra, if she hasn't been in touch, it's because she doesn't want to speak with you."

"What?" The air whooshed out of his lungs as though he'd been punched.

"I said if she wants to contact you, she will."

"That's not your call to make, Alex." Ezra's jaw clenched. "She's my wife. Just tell me—is she there with you?"

"I'm not at liberty to discuss Morgan's whereabouts." Alex's tone was arctic. "All I can tell you is she's safe and well. And Ezra? If you haven't heard from her directly after all this time, I think that says everything you need to know."

The words slammed into Ezra like a poleax. He sank onto the piano bench, his free hand pressing against the smooth wood for support. "What exactly are you implying?" Was Martha choosing not to contact him?

"I'm not implying anything. But don't you have more pressing concerns right now? Your reputation is in freefall, your songs are under scrutiny... Maybe instead of trying to ride Morgan's coattails, you should focus on saving what's left of your career."

Of course, Alex was grabbing the chance to twist the knife. But that didn't matter. Not if Martha was pulling away from him again. "Just... just tell her I love her. If you see her."

"Goodbye, Ezra."

Somehow, in the space between her leaving here and releasing that cold statement, Alex had turned Martha away from him. When it came to her career, she'd chosen Alex's guidance over his wishes, time and time again, her brand always coming first.

It is important to separate her personal life from her professional achievements during this time.

As though their marriage meant nothing. As though she wasn't his wife, his partner, his heart.

He might lose everything. His reputation. His career. The life he'd built note by note, song by song. And Martha—dear God, he might lose Martha.

He clasped his hands. "Please—" he whispered, but the prayer died in his throat as tears overwhelmed him.

Chapter Thirty-Seven

"Ezra..." Martha reached across the bed. But instead of her husband's comforting warmth, her fingers met cool sheets. Where was he? Wait—this wasn't their bed. This wasn't their room.

She sat up, heart hammering, and turned toward the window. White light leaked around the edges of blackout blinds, casting unfamiliar shadows across cream and chrome furniture—Alex's guest room.

She pressed her fingers against her temples as memory came rushing back. A fog of exhaustion, Ivy's lies, Ezra fighting for his career, dozing off at the wheel, her Range Rover veering off the road. She'd come to work on a statement with Alex. She'd only meant to lie down for an hour or so. How long had she slept? Pushing back the duvet, she stumbled to the window and raised the blind.

Sunlight flooded the room, stabbing her eyes. Early afternoon light. Which meant she'd been here for—her stomach dropped as she calculated the hours. Ezra would be worried. She'd left without her phone, promising to come straight back. Pushing the door open, she walked into the hallway with quick steps.

"Alex?" Her voice echoed on the walls.

She found him in his living room, typing rapidly on his laptop.

He looked up. "You're awake. I was beginning to worry. Did you sleep well?"

"Did you call Ezra?" The words tumbled out before she could form a proper greeting. "You said you'd tell him I was okay."

"Of course I did." He closed a window on his laptop. "I spoke to him earlier. I let him know you were safe, just like you asked." He stood, stretching. "You must be starving. Let me fix you something. I've got some of those protein bowls you like from that cafe in Covent Garden."

Her stomach churned at the thought of food. "What time did you speak to him?"

"You need to eat. You've got to keep your strength up." He moved into the kitchen. "And we need to talk. The situation has escalated beyond anything we could have predicted. Will you have chicken or tofu?"

She followed him, the polished floor cool against her feet. "Chicken, please. Could I borrow your phone, though?"

"I'll get you something to eat first. While I do that, why don't you have a look at how things are unfolding?

You can use my computer. I can barely keep up with everything that's happening."

His laptop sat open on the coffee table. She leaned forward to read the headline that screamed from his browser. "Rising Star Ivy Willis Breaks Silence on 'Whispers' Controversy." What silence? She'd said plenty since last night.

How was Ezra holding up? She needed to finish this business with Alex and get back home. She'd already been here hours longer than she meant to.

Alex's voice drifted from the kitchen. "The story's gone mainstream. CNN, BBC News, major outlets have picked it up. And social media is absolutely exploding."

Martha sank onto the sofa, pulling his laptop closer. Her throat closed as she clicked through Alex's open tabs. Memes comparing Ezra to other "exposed" men in the industry. Pictures of her and Ezra on the red carpet at the Serenade launch with the question, "What Did Morgan Know?" Video compilations of Ivy's interviews set to "Whispers of You." Tweet after tweet with #JusticeForIvy, many from influential industry figures she knew. Including some she'd thought were Ezra's friends.

"Streaming numbers for 'Whispers' are through the roof," Alex said, returning with coffee and a bowl of quinoa, grilled chicken, and vegetables. He set the bowl in front of Martha. "It might even break the billion streams mark at this rate. At first, people were calling for a boycott of the song, but now there's a whole movement to blast it everywhere and redirect the royalties to Ivy. The producers of *Twice in a Lifetime* are under pressure to make a statement. Dylan Marrow has already said he's stunned, and he's urging Ezra to do the right thing. Other artists Ezra's written for are being asked to address it."

What? Martha stared at Alex. Dylan Marrow was the singer whose cover of "Whispers" was featured on the movie soundtrack. He'd lent his voice to the version of the song that had become a runaway hit. And he'd come out in Ivy's corner?

Settling into his chrome and leather armchair, Alex took a sip of his coffee. "This isn't just about one song anymore. It's becoming a conversation about power dynamics in the industry, about men taking credit for women's work. About what it takes for young women to make it in this business. And you need to be on the right side of this conversation, Morgan."

There was no way she could stomach this food. She lowered her fork. "I have to go home. Ezra needs me."

"Not yet." Alex's voice was gentle but firm. "We need to talk about how to handle this first." He leaned back. "I already drafted a statement. I ran it past the label's legal team. For now, it seems to have steadied things with your sponsors, although Libertine Lingerie is pretty antsy."

"Can I see the statement?"

"In a minute. First, you need to know—" He leaned forward. "The studio's pushing to move up the release date of your next single. They think we can leverage all this attention, especially with the demographic that's engaging with this story."

Martha stared at him. "You're discussing release dates at a time like this? I can't commit to anything while this is going on. Ezra needs me. What we should talk about is clearing my schedule. Paring it back to the things I absolutely can't delay."

"Morgan." Alex's voice softened. Setting down his mug, he stared into her eyes. "Your loyalty is truly moving. It says a lot about you and how innocent and trusting you are. I get it—your immediate impulse is to believe Ezra. But I have to be honest with you. I don't think you're going to want to hear this, but... I believe Ivy is telling the truth."

Her stomach heaved. "What?"

"She's hired Thorne and Associates. They don't take cases they can't win." He paused. "She's ready to take this as far as she needs to. And public sentiment is overwhelmingly on her side. People want to believe her. And frankly, her story adds up."

"Her story?" Martha's voice caught. "You mean her lies. There's no way what she's saying is true."

"Think about it. They spent a lot of time together. Their creative synergy was off the charts, and they wrote a lot of songs together around the time 'Whispers' came out. Their bond..."

"Stop." Martha pushed to her feet. She couldn't bear to hear her own doubts spoken out loud in Alex's voice. "I need to go home."

"And say what?" Alex's words stopped her. "That you support him unconditionally? That you don't have any doubts yourself? Any whispers in your own heart?"

She couldn't answer him.

"Your silence speaks volumes, Morgan. Deep down, you know something's not right about his story."

Martha sank back onto the sofa, her legs suddenly weak.

"That's what I thought." He leaned forward. "Look, there's something else. Ivy's on her way here."

"What?" Martha's head snapped up. "Why would you—"

"Because you need to hear what she has to say." He held up a hand. "Wait—don't freak out. Not her public story. Not what she's telling the media. The whole truth, Morgan. What really happened between her and Ezra."

"I have to go," she whispered.

"She'll be here any minute. Don't you want to know the truth? Once and for all?"

She did. She didn't. Could she cope with the truth? Would she even know it when she heard it?

The doorbell chimed.

Martha's heart lurched. She should leave now, before—

But Alex had already headed for the door.

She heard the murmur of voices in the hallway, footsteps approaching. Her chance to escape had passed.

Ivy walked in, wearing jeans and a camisole. Her face was free of makeup, her hair pulled back. Her eyes were red-rimmed, as though she'd been crying.

"Martha." Her voice wavered as she walked into the living room. "Thank you for seeing me. I know this must be awful for you."

Martha crossed her arms. "Why now? If it's true, why wait years to say anything?"

"I was scared." Ivy perched on the edge of the armchair opposite Martha. "The industry... you know how it is. One wrong move and you're blacklisted. Nobody wants to work with the woman who speaks up." She drew a shaky breath. "But seeing you, Martha, seeing how you've found your voice, how you inspire other women to be strong... it made me realize it was time to tell my truth."

"Your truth?" Martha's voice broke. "I don't believe you."

"Oh, Martha." Ivy reached for her hand. Her fingers were cold. "I never wanted to hurt you. But you deserve to know..." Her eyes filled with tears. "Your husband isn't the man you think he is."

Martha tried to pull her hand away, but Ivy held on.

"He was so frustrated back then. About everything." Ivy's voice softened. "He was making a name for himself, but things weren't happening as fast as he'd wanted. He used to talk about your background, how you didn't understand the industry. How you didn't fit in. He once told me he was... he was embarrassed to be seen with you. That the industry insiders didn't take him seriously when he brought you to those events."

Martha jerked her hand free.

Ivy said, "I told him if that's how he felt, he should teach you. Help you learn how to fit in. But he said there was no point because 'it's impossible to teach someone good taste'—his words. That's why he asked me to help decorate your home—he needed someone who understood his aesthetic, his world." She glanced down. "He told me I was his muse. That the songs came easier when we worked together."

"Stop." Martha's voice came out as a whisper. "Just stop." Ivy's words were exposing the monstrous doubts that had always skulked in the dark corners of Martha's heart, giving shape to their shadowy forms.

The nights she lay awake while Ezra was out late "working" with Ivy... the way Ivy was always the first person he called when any inspiration, any ideas, any news came about his songs. How they finished each other's sentences whenever they talked about music. Ivy decorating every inch of their home, from wall and window treatments to selecting furniture, flooring, and artwork.

"It wasn't just 'Whispers,'" Ivy continued. "There were other songs. He'd convince me to let him take lead writer credit. 'My connections will get us heard,' he'd say. 'This way the song has a real chance.'" She wrapped her arms around herself. "I was young. Naïve. I believed him."

"No." It came more of an exhalation than a word.

"I'm sorry, but it's the truth. I won't cover for him any longer." Ivy drew a shaky breath. "'Whispers of You' wasn't about you, Martha."

Reeling, Martha stared at Ivy's face.

Ivy's gaze dropped and her words were quiet, tortured. "We'd been up all night writing. The sun was just breaking through the studio windows, and I told Ezra how Nathan and I loved making love at sunrise, how it felt like the light was whispering across the sky. That's what inspired the song. It wasn't about you. He even joked that with you, it was always better in the middle of the night because he didn't have to look at your body in the dark. Later, when the movie people got interested in the song, he said it would be more marketable if people thought it was about his wife. A love song for the woman who inspired him."

Martha's vision blurred, her chest so tight she could barely breathe. Ezra joked about her most intimate inadequacies, then turned around and used their marriage as a marketing tool for the song he'd written with Ivy?

In the quiet of the morning, when the world's still asleep, I hear whispers of you in the dreams that I keep. And in the sunrise that paints the sky brand new, the light dances softly with whispers of you.

This was about Ivy and her husband? While Martha was just the butt of a crude joke from a husband who only desired her when he couldn't see her?

Her stomach churned violently, and she pressed a hand to her mouth. "I'm—I'm going to be sick," she choked out.

Alex came to her side on the sofa, his hand moving in soothing circles on her back. "It's okay, sweetheart. Just take deep breaths," he murmured. "I know the truth is brutal, but I'm here for you. You'll be okay."

He glanced up at Ivy. "Please get her some water."

Ivy filled a glass from the faucet and handed it to Martha.

Her hands shook as she took small sips, a few drops escaping and splashing onto her lap. The nausea subsided, leaving a gnawing pain in its wake.

Alex's hand continued to rub circles on her back.

Martha pressed her fingers against her temples. There was one more thing she needed to know. It couldn't be any worse than what she'd already learned. The question that had haunted her for a year pushed its way past the sickness in her throat.

"Why did you stop being friends?" Her voice came out raw. "When I was away on tour, I heard you and Ezra weren't speaking anymore, but nobody would tell me why."

Ivy's face crumpled. "I was afraid you'd ask that. And I've never told anyone before." She wrapped her arms around herself. "It was about a year ago. You were in Asia, I think. Ezra and I had been working late in his studio at your home. He said he was lonely with you gone so much. He said he had... He said he had needs." She swallowed. "The connection between us had always been intense, the atmosphere charged, but it never went beyond that. But that night... he tried to kiss me."

The floor seemed to drop away beneath Martha's feet.

"I stopped him, of course." Ivy's voice faltered. "I couldn't do that to you. But after that, I couldn't be around him anymore. I pulled away from everything—cut off contact completely. Started fresh with a different label." She looked up at Martha, eyes glistening. "I should have told you then. But you were so far away, doing so well with your tour. I thought... I thought if I just disappeared, if I kept quiet, it would protect you somehow."

Martha's body curled into itself, bile rising in her throat. All those nights she'd lain awake in hotel rooms across the world, wondering what was happening back home. All Ezra's careful deflections when she'd asked about why he and Ivy weren't friends anymore. The way he'd changed the subject whenever she mentioned Ivy's name.

"That's why I have to speak up now," Ivy continued. "About the songs, about everything. Keeping quiet... it only protected him. And I can't do that anymore."

"I know this is a lot to take in." Alex's voice was gentle, his hand still stroking Martha's back. "And with everything else going on—the media circus, your sponsors, rolling out your perfume..." He touched Martha's shoulder. "You don't have to deal with all of this right now. You can stay here as long as you need to. Take some time to process everything."

Ivy stood, tears still glistening on her cheeks. "I'm so sorry, Martha. The last thing I ever wanted was to hurt you. But secrets..." She wrapped her arms around herself. "Secrets destroy everything they touch."

"I'll walk you out. Let's give Morgan some space." Alex guided Ivy toward the door, his voice low as they disappeared down the hallway.

Martha heard the quiet murmur of their voices, the soft click of the front door.

The afternoon light slanted through the windows, catching the chrome and glass of Alex's carefully curated décor.

How could everything look so perfect, so normal, when her world had just shattered into a thousand jagged pieces? Each razor-sharp shard lacerated her to her core, shredding her heart into ribbons.

Martha drew her knees up to her chest, wrapping her arms around them as she curled into a ball. Maybe if she held herself together tightly enough, it would stop her soul from bleeding out onto Alex's pristine sofa.

The tears came then, silent and devastating, each one carrying away another certainty she'd built her life upon. Her marriage. Her husband. Their song. All of it built on lies she hadn't wanted to see.

Chapter Thirty-Eight

CAMERA FLASHES EXPLODED IN the evening air as Ezra drove toward his gate. The paparazzi pack had grown since he'd left for the lawyers' office—there were at least twenty of these vultures now, their long lenses trained on his car like weapons.

He pressed the remote and the gate slid open with a soft whir. Through his windscreen, he caught sight of Marcus at the perimeter, his Malinois standing alert, the menacing presence of dog and guard keeping the photographers at bay.

As the gate slid shut, voices called out from behind the metal bars.

"Ezra! Any comment on Ivy Willis's allegations?"

"Where's Morgan? Why isn't she supporting you?"

"Is it true other songwriters are coming forward?"

His gut twisted. Wherever Martha was, she didn't have her PPOs with her to protect her from this media frenzy. Yet again, he breathed a prayer for his wife's safety.

He pulled into his usual spot near the house. As he killed the engine, Ray approached his car, leaving Marcus to handle the gate security.

"Sir." Ray's voice was low, respectful. "Still nothing from Mrs. Falconer?"

Ezra shook his head, throat tight.

"Jane's been here since six." Ray gestured toward a silver Audi parked near the guest house. "She's not heard from Mrs. Falconer all day, either. She's worried. We all are."

Jane stepped out of her car, her usually composed face tight with anxiety. "I apologize for being here. Martha had given me today off after the launch. But when I started seeing the news..." She hesitated. "I've been trying to reach her since this afternoon. I thought perhaps I could be of assistance."

"I appreciate that. She went to meet Alex early this morning, but left her phone behind. Have you tried calling him?"

The security lights cast harsh shadows across Jane's face. "Several times. He keeps saying she's fine, that she's safe at an 'undisclosed location.' He called earlier to have me cancel all her engagements for the rest of the week. The photo shoot, the recording sessions..." She glanced at Ezra. "He said she needs time to process recent events."

Dread pulled at Ezra's gut. How long was Martha planning on staying away? His mind cycled endlessly between possibilities, each worse than the last. Was Alex deliberately keeping Martha from him? Or had she chosen this silence? What had Alex told her that made her need "time to process recent events"?

He remembered her face when she left this morning, the way she'd touched his cheek, promising to come right back. And now she needed time away from home, away from him? After everything they'd shared last night... But then again, he'd thought things were clear between them before, only to find out later that she'd been harboring doubts and hurts he'd never suspected.

Jane's phone lit up. She grabbed it, then deflated. "It's Alex again." She answered, putting it on speaker. "Hello, Alex."

Alex's voice was smooth, professional. "Evening, Jane. I trust you've handled the cancelations?"

"Yes, sir. Would it be possible to speak with Morgan? There are some personal matters that require her attention."

"I'm afraid Morgan's not available. I can relay any messages you have."

"With respect, Mr. Thompson, these are private matters that require her input. Things I'm not sure she'd want discussed through intermediaries. Could you at least let her know I need to speak with her? Even just for five minutes?"

"As I've told you, Morgan is safe at an undisclosed location—a hotel, but that's all I'll say. She's asked for privacy while—"

"Where is she?" Ezra cut in.

Alex was silent for a beat. "Ah, Ezra is there, too. I'm not at liberty to discuss Morgan's whereabouts. But I assure you, when she's ready to talk, she'll reach out."

"What have you done to her?" Ezra's voice was raw. "She wouldn't just disappear like this. She wouldn't—"

"What have I done?" Alex's tone sharpened. "I think you should ask yourself that question, Ezra. After everything that's come out today... Let's just say Morgan's had her eyes opened to quite a few things."

"What's that supposed to mean?"

"I think you know exactly what it means. Now, if you'll excuse me—"

"Alex—"

Jane stared at her phone, then at Ezra. "He ended the call."

Ezra pressed his fingers against his eyes. What had Alex told Martha? What lies had he fed her while Ezra sat in lawyers' offices, trying to prove his innocence?

"Sir, may I speak frankly?"

"Yes, of course." Ezra faced the PA.

She hesitated, as though choosing her words carefully. "I've worked with Alex long enough to understand his priorities. While I believe his concern for your wife is genuine, his focus is on Morgan the brand. Sometimes that doesn't align with what Martha the person needs." She glanced toward the gate, lowering her voice. "And right now, I think Martha needs her husband, not her manager."

The distinction between Morgan and Martha had never felt so stark. Or so devastating.

"I'll keep trying to reach her," Jane said. "When I do, you'll be the first person I call."

She straightened, her professional mask sliding back into place. "I apologize. I shouldn't have spoken so freely about Mr. Thompson. It wasn't my place."

"No, thank you." Ezra's voice was rough. "For caring about my wife. Not just the brand."

Jane's answering smile was small but genuine. He glanced at Ray, who stood a respectful distance away. These people who worked so closely with Martha—they saw past the carefully curated image of Morgan to the woman beneath. The woman he loved. The woman who, right now, was alone somewhere, believing goodness knew what lies.

It was a small comfort, knowing Martha had people like this in her corner. But it didn't stop the sick feeling in his gut as he watched Jane return to her car... as he thought of Martha in some anonymous hotel room, choosing solitude over him.

He looked at Ray again, a thought forming before he could stop it. As Martha's head of security, surely Ray could find her if Ezra asked. But no. He wouldn't violate

Martha's trust that way, wouldn't use her own security team against her. This wasn't a physical threat—it was a threat to their marriage. If she needed space, he had to respect that. Even if every instinct screamed at him to find her, to make sure she was really okay. Even if Alex's story about her needing "time to process" felt wrong on every level.

Lord, please watch over her. Bring her back home safe and well.

Ezra stepped inside his darkened house, closing the door behind himself. It felt cavernous, every empty room an accusation, a mockery.

His phone lit up with Fiona's name.

"I won't sugarcoat this," she said without preamble. "Two major labels have suspended your songwriting contracts pending investigation. They're saying they can't risk the association right now."

He sank onto the sofa. More dominoes falling. He felt numb to the news.

"But there is a bright spot," Fiona said. "*Promise Ridge* called. They're standing by you. Said they know your character and they've seen your creative process firsthand. They're putting out a statement of support tonight."

Tears rushed to his eyes. "I... That means a lot." Maybe the whole world wasn't turning on him, after all. "Please thank them for me."

"Will do. There are people in your corner, Ezra. The loudmouths always get the most attention, but a lot of people believe in you."

But Martha didn't.

"Ezra? Are you okay?"

"Yes. Was there anything else?"

"One more thing," Fiona said. "Did you get those documents from the lawyers about the cease-and-desist letters?"

"Yeah, I'll forward them now." His voice sounded distant in his own ears. "They think even just the threat of legal action might calm some of this wild speculation down. Get people to think twice before making accusations."

"Good. And with *Promise Ridge*'s support..." She paused. "Look, I know you're probably ready to drop, but tomorrow we need to focus on documenting your creative process. Early demos, writing notes, anything that shows your development of these songs. And I've got calls out to several people who were around during that period—sound engineers, studio staff. We need their statements about your writing process."

"Right." But none of it mattered. Proving his innocence to the world meant nothing if Martha believed he was guilty.

"Okay. Try to get some rest. We'll regroup in the morning—I've set up a conference call with the legal team at nine."

"Thanks, Fiona. For everything you're doing."

After ending the call, Ezra stared into the darkness. *Promise Ridge*'s support, the lawyers' strategy, even the lost contracts—it all felt hollow without Martha. He needed... he needed something solid to hold on to. Something true in a world rapidly dissolving into lies.

His fingers found his phone again, scrolling to Pastor Noah's number.

"Noah?" His voice broke. "Could you pray with me?"

Chapter Thirty-Nine

ZRA'S NECK PROTESTED AS he shifted on the sofa. Martha's absence made their bed unbearable, so he'd crashed here after Pastor Noah left, sleep coming in fitful bursts between bouts of prayer and worry.

He dragged himself up as his phone buzzed and skittered on the coffee table. Levi's name lit up the screen.

"Hey." Ezra's voice was rough with exhaustion. "How's Cedric doing?"

"The doctors are happy with his progress—thanks for asking. He's a tough old bird. But let's talk about you. How are you holding up?"

Barely. Every passing hour, not knowing where Martha was, whether she was okay...

He forced himself to focus on his brother. "I'm trying to keep my head above the water. Melody Forge and Sonic Pulse have suspended my contracts."

"Aw, man, that stinks. On the strength of what amounts to an Internet rumor?"

Ezra sighed. "Yup. But on the bright side, *Promise Ridge* is standing by me, thank God. They released a statement of support."

"Thank God, indeed. What about finding proof to shut Ivy up?"

"Fiona's trying to find documentation from when we registered 'Whispers,' but the label that released it got bought out twice. The movie studio's records are scattered too—their music supervisor retired to Florida." He rubbed his neck. "I spoke to my solicitors and they've recommended threatening defamation suits to make people think twice about shooting their mouths off."

"Sounds like a wise move."

"Yeah. But I hope it doesn't come to that."

"And what about Martha?" Levi asked. "How's she doing?"

Ezra swallowed. "She's gone."

"What do you mean, gone?"

"I... I'd rather not talk about it. But I think Alex might have got into her head. She... she didn't come home last night." His voice cracked. "She promised she'd come right back. She touched my face and promised, Levi. And now she won't even talk to me. I don't know what Alex told her." He squeezed his eyes shut. Breaking down would not help anyone.

"Aw, man." Levi's voice softened with concern. "That's... that's rough. I'm praying for both of you." He paused. "Listen, I know it might not help right now, but I remember when you talked me through my mess with Adria. You told me something I needed to hear, even though I didn't want to hear it."

"What do you mean? All I did was tell you that you were being a blockhead."

"True. And taking that advice is the reason Adria's my wife now. Although I don't know the circumstances of what's happened, I'll just say check your heart for any blockheadedness. Or your head. Or—you know what I mean. What I'm trying to say is, I know it hurts. And Alex is shady. Maybe none of this is your fault, but listen to Martha."

"Thanks. I would if she would even talk to me."

After ending the call with Levi, Ezra forced himself off the sofa. He needed to shower and change before the conference call with Fiona and the lawyers. His reflection in the bathroom mirror showed dark shadows under his eyes, his usually neat hair still rumpled from his fitful night on the sofa.

As he pulled on a shirt after his shower, his phone buzzed. Ray.

"Sir, there's a courier from Thorne and Associates requesting entrance. They have documents requiring your signature."

"Sure, let them through." Ezra was already thinking about the conference call, mentally rehearsing his timeline of events for the lawyers. Legal couriers were nothing unusual—contracts, licensing agreements, endless paperwork that came with the industry.

He headed downstairs as the doorbell chimed.

The courier handed him a thick envelope, his face professionally neutral as Ezra signed for it.

At the kitchen counter, he opened the envelope.

A wave of dizziness slammed into him as he read. The legal language was dense, but the message was clear. Ivy Willis was demanding he cease and desist from claiming sole authorship of "Whispers of You."

He had five days to formally acknowledge her as co-writer and agree to her terms for compensation, which included fifty percent of all past royalties from the song and a share in all future royalty payments.

If he failed to respond, Ivy's lawyers would file a copyright infringement lawsuit seeking both actual and punitive damages.

Five days. The words blurred before his eyes.

His phone buzzed.

Fiona was probably wondering why he wasn't on the conference call yet.

But he couldn't move, couldn't focus, couldn't—

All he could think about was Martha. Where was she right now? Was she safe? Why wasn't she coming home? What had Alex convinced her of that would make her break her promise, make her doubt him so completely?

The front door opened.

Martha walked into the living room, her eyes huge and dark.

Chapter Forty

"Martha." Ezra's voice was rough with relief.

She turned, but her eyes were glassy and unfocused, as though she were looking through him rather than at him. She still wore the white long-sleeved T-shirt and Capri pants she'd had on when she'd left yesterday morning, but her clothes were now creased and rumpled, and there was a dark stain on the front of her shirt. Her hair was gathered in a bun at the nape of her neck, with several loose strands hanging around her face.

He stepped toward her. "Thank God you're home. I've been so worried about you."

"Home." Her voice was barely above a whisper. Her gaze moved past him, roving over the lounge and the kitchen. "Our home. You let her into every corner of *our* home."

Her bag and car keys slid to the floor with a clatter as her breath quickened.

He followed her gaze. She was staring at the heavy art déco mirror above the fireplace.

Like a sleepwalker, Martha moved toward it with slow steps. "She said this would be the focal point of the lounge—pull the whole room together." She stretched a hand out, stroking the mirror with her fingertips. "Every single room in this house has her touch, her taste."

The mirror crashed to the floor as, teeth bared, Martha swept it off the wall. Glass scattered across the hardwood like diamonds.

"Martha!" Ezra hurried toward her. Something was wrong. Very wrong.

Glass crunching under her sandaled feet, she walked over to the black oak veneer bookcase. "Did you write songs together right here, Ezra? In our home?"

She grabbed the side panel and gave it a mighty heave. The bookcase toppled with a thunderous crash, missing Martha by inches and slamming into the sofa.

Dread pooled in his stomach as he stared at her wild eyes. Her fingers curled, claw-like. Dear God, what was happening to his wife?

"Or was it always at the studio?" she panted. "Late at night, when I was too fat and dowdy and embarrassing to fit into your world?"

The brittle edge in her voice sent a spear of fear jabbing into his gut. She was beyond logic or explanations—he could see it in her glazed eyes, hear it in that terrible, fractured voice. How could he reach her when she was like this?

Chest heaving, she grabbed a heavy braided porcelain and silver vase and hurled it against the wall, where it shattered the glass of a framed landscape painting. "You let her decorate our house because I had no taste. Because you were ashamed of me!"

She lifted the vase's twin, raising it high above her head, and smashed it in front of her feet. Porcelain shards exploded across the hardwood floor, skittering under furniture and catching the light.

"No!" Ezra stepped toward her. "That's not—"

"Don't lie to me!" she screamed.

She spun around to face him.

A primal roar tearing from her throat, she ran to the coffee table and flipped it over. "Not after everything else. Not after—" Her voice broke. "Not after using our marriage to sell a song you wrote about her making love at dawn!"

Ezra's heart pounded. She was delusional. Her words made no sense. Was she having some kind of breakdown?

He lunged forward as she reached for another floor-to-ceiling bookcase, catching her arms and pinning them to her sides. "Martha, stop! You'll hurt yourself!"

She had lost her mind. Who could he call? Ray was outside. They could—

"Let go of me!" She thrashed against him, her slender body shockingly strong, but he held her tighter, terrified she'd get hurt on the broken glass that covered the floor, or pull the bookcase on top of herself.

"Martha, stop. Please! Look at me."

"You made me a joke!" She sobbed, her hair slipping out of its loose bun as she struggled to pull away from him. "Making love to me with the lights off because you couldn't bear to look at me..."

"What?" Horror crashed through him. "Who told you that? Martha, that's not—"

"Everything in this house is *her*! Everything we had was a lie!" Her voice was a raw scream. "I trusted you! I loved you! And all this time, you were laughing at me. All this time you..."

Her knees buckled.

He went down with her, still holding her as they sank to the floor.

They were both on their knees. She fought his tight embrace, pushing against his chest, but there was no strength left in her blows.

He gentled his hold as she went limp, her body sagging against him.

"I believed in you." Her words, muffled against his chest, came between gasping sobs. "But you—you were laughing at me. Telling her I was too disgusting to look at."

"No." His voice cracked. "Martha, no. That isn't true."

Soul-rending sobs racked her whole body as she cried into his shirt.

He held her closer, rocking her like a child. His wife—his precious Martha—how could she believe such awful things? Who told her these sick lies? Who had done this to her?

Movement caught his eye.

Ray stood framed in the open French doors, taking in the devastation—the shattered mirror, the overturned furniture, the books and ornaments scattered across the floor, Martha weeping in Ezra's arms.

His gaze met Ezra's over her head, dark eyes widening.

Somewhere in the chaos, Ezra's phone buzzed again—he'd been vaguely aware of it ringing repeatedly but couldn't process anything beyond Martha's breakdown.

"Why don't you take her upstairs, sir?" Ray's voice was quiet as he stepped inside the room. "I'll clean this up."

Ezra lifted Martha easily, cradling her to his chest.

Her head lolled against his shoulder, her body limp even as sobs continued to wrack her frame. She felt so small, so fragile, though minutes ago she'd been strong enough to flip over furniture.

"Ray, my phone," Ezra said. "I think Fiona's trying to call. Please tell her... please tell her to cancel the meeting."

The PPO nodded, walking over to where Ezra's phone had slipped to the floor.

Martha's sobs quieted to hitching breaths as Ezra carried her up to their room.

Chapter Forty-One

ZRA SETTLED HIS WIFE on their bed and sat next to her, still holding her in his arms. "Martha, my love..." His voice was rough. "Those things you were saying... none of it is true. You have to believe me."

She remained slumped against him, unmoving. Had she even heard him? She was silent for a long, agonizing moment.

Finally, she pulled back just far enough to look at him, her face wet with tears, hair tangled and falling around her shoulders. Her voice was quiet, drained of its earlier fury. But her eyes... her eyes were dark, deep pools, filled with a pain that shook him to his core.

"Why... Why were there three people in our marriage, Ezra?"

Her question blindsided him. "Martha, I don't—"

She stiffened. "Don't tell me you don't understand."

Like a distant echo, words rang in his mind. Urged first by Pastor Noah, and then his brother. *Listen to her.*

He answered in a hoarse whisper. "I don't understand. But I'm trying. Talk to me. Please."

Long, excruciating moments passed as she stared at him, her eyes welling up. "I..." Her lips trembled, parted, closed again. "I can't... I can't get away from her." She swallowed convulsively. "Her touch is all over our home. I walk on rugs that she chose. Sit on sofas she wanted. She's everywhere. Even here. You let her choose the bed we sleep in."

"Do you mean... Ivy?"

She nodded, her breath catching.

He glanced around their bedroom. The soft gray and slate blue color palette, the furniture, the artwork—all of it chosen by Ivy. He'd asked her to decorate their new home as a favor. Her taste, her influence, was in every part of this house. But why would that suddenly upset Martha so much after all this time? Was it because of what Ivy was claiming about his song? Surely that couldn't—

"She was everywhere," she whispered. "Working out with you. Vacations. Double dates." Her words came out faster now, tumbling over each other. "At every industry party, every event. The two of you, sharing inside jokes I didn't understand. She knew your schedule better than I did. Knew about your tours before I did. And all those hours at the studio, making music..."

Understanding began to dawn, slow and terrible.

"At the Melody Awards dinner. Remember that?" Her fingers twisted in her lap. "I didn't know anyone there. You and Ivy spent the whole evening absorbed in each other, talking about things that left me out. Songs you were working on, people you knew. I just sat there, feeling more and more invisible. When I said I had a headache and wanted to go home, you put me in a cab and stayed behind all night. With her."

The memory reared up in his mind. The awards dinner was a prime networking opportunity, and he couldn't leave early. He was helping Ivy understand the terms of a confidential songwriting deal before she met with a senior executive from Coda Records. It was going to be her big break. He'd never realized how excluded Martha felt. His throat tightened. Wasn't that the last industry event she attended with him?

Martha's hands clenched into fists. "Every time the phone rang, it was Ivy. Every time you got excited about a new song, a new opportunity, a new success... you called her first." The words poured out of her now, like a dam breaking. "When you got writer's block, she was the one you went to. She became your best friend. Not me." Her voice cracked. "You used to share your music with me, even after I stopped performing. Remember how we'd sit at the piano together? But then suddenly it was all Ivy. Like my opinions didn't matter anymore." Tears spilled down her cheeks. "Do you know what that did to me? Watching my husband share the deepest part of himself with another woman?"

"Martha..." The truth of her words left him reeling. In the beginning, he'd always played his new songs for her first, valued her natural ear for music, her instinctive understanding of what worked. When had he stopped doing that? He'd been so caught up in his creative partnership with Ivy, he'd never stopped to think how it looked to his wife. How it felt. His stomach churned. "You're right. I... You're completely right."

"I used to lie awake at night when you were at the studio with her." Her voice dropped to a whisper. "Telling myself I was being paranoid. That I was imagining things. Imagining being squeezed out of my marriage. Imagining that she was the first person you told when you had any news, any joke, anything worth saying. I tried to convince myself that of course you needed someone who understood the industry, who had sophisticated taste, who wasn't an embarrassment to be seen with—"

"What?" Horror shot through him. "I was never embarrassed by you."

"She said you were." Her voice sharpened.

"That's a complete lie. I never said that. Never even felt it."

She pushed away from him. "What about 'Whispers'?"

His stomach dropped. "What do you mean?" Did she believe he'd stolen the song?

"You said you wrote it about me." She choked out a bitter laugh. "Except it wasn't about us at all, was it? It was about Ivy and Nathan making love at sunrise. You just used our marriage to market it. While joking with her about how you could only stand to make love to me with the lights off!"

He felt sick. This was the same unhinged stuff she'd been saying downstairs. Where was it coming from? "Those are complete lies, Martha. Who told you these things?"

"Ivy did." Her voice broke. "Yesterday, when I was at Alex's place. She came there and told me everything. How she was your muse. The things you said about me. And how when I was on tour, you..." She looked up at him, tears streaming down her face. "How you tried to kiss her."

Ice flooded his veins. The final piece of the bewildering puzzle clicked into place—why Martha had disappeared for so long, why she'd flipped out and trashed their living room, why she was looking at him with a soul-deep pain that seared his heart.

"Martha." His voice trembled. "She lied to you. Those are evil, wicked, hateful lies. I'll tell you what really happened that night in the studio."

She stared at him, tears still sliding down her cheeks.

"You were touring in Seoul. I was working with Ivy. Yes, it was here in my studio. Such a stupid thing to do—I can see that now." Tears stung his eyes.

"It was late, and we'd been working on different projects. Ivy was..." He drew a deep breath. "She tried to kiss me. But, Martha, I stopped her. Immediately. I told her I loved you, my wife, and she needed to leave. I made her get out. Then I blocked her number and cut off all contact. I never spoke to her again until I ran into her at that gala the other night. I've not spoken to her since then."

Martha searched his face.

"I should have told you when it happened," he said. "Now I wish so desperately that I had. But I thought—I thought if I just ended the friendship, cut her out completely, that would be the end of it. I never imagined she'd twist it around like this. Use it to hurt you. Please believe me, Martha."

"But..." Martha's voice shook. "But all those things you said about me. About being embarrassed—"

"Never." He reached for her hands. "Martha, look at me. I have never been embarrassed by you. Never. I love you. And whatever she said about me not wanting to look at your body? About me only wanting to make love to you in the dark?" His voice roughened. "That's a vicious lie. I never, ever talked to her about us. And I always loved every part of you—always desired all of you.

You were always perfectly beautiful to me. Right from the first day I met you."

Her breath hitched, and she gripped his hands tighter.

His voice thickened. "I can see what an idiot I've been. How foolish I was to get so close to Ivy in the first place. I never realized how it was hurting you. Martha, I'm so sorry."

Her eyes shimmered with even more tears. So many tears she'd cried because of him.

His own words felt hollow against the magnitude of his failure. Everything she'd endured—the loneliness, the self-doubt, feeling like an outsider in her own marriage—it all came from his choices. He'd given another woman space in their most intimate moments, their home, their creative life.

No wonder Martha had believed those cruel lies about "Whispers of You." He'd spent more time discussing that song with Ivy than he had sharing it with his own wife—the woman he'd written it for, the woman who'd inspired every word, every note.

Martha's hands trembled in his.

He said, "When I asked her to help decorate, I never thought about how it would feel for you, living in your own home surrounded by another woman's choices. Even our bed—" He broke off, the realization hitting him afresh. Their most intimate space, and he'd let Ivy design every detail. Ivy!

No wonder Martha had destroyed their living room. He'd have torn it apart himself if he'd understood what it represented—how thoroughly he'd let another woman infiltrate their marriage. What an obtuse, stupid fool!

He stood, walking to the French doors, fists clenched. "And then, when she tried to kiss me, I thought I could just cut her out and everything would be fine. I didn't want to upset you by telling you about it." He gave a hollow laugh. "As if I hadn't already hurt you in a thousand other ways. I was so blind, Martha. So stupidly, carelessly blind."

"Why didn't you tell me?" Her voice was barely above a whisper. "About the kiss?"

"I thought I was protecting you." The words sounded pathetic even to his own ears. "I didn't want you to worry about something that meant nothing. But I see now... I was really protecting myself. From having to face what I'd done. How I'd let things get so far out of hand. She would never have felt encouraged to kiss me if I hadn't given her that space."

"I kept telling myself I was being paranoid." She wrapped her arms around herself. "That it was my fault for not fitting into your world. For not being sophisticated enough, thin enough, pretty enough—"

"Stop." He came back to the bed, dropping to his knees in front of her. "Please. You were always enough. More than enough. I was the one who failed. Who let another woman make you feel second best in your own marriage. Martha... please forgive me."

He raised his hands, begging, pleading.

Her face crumpled, and she fell into his arms.

He gathered her close, one hand cradling her head against his chest, the other wrapped tight around her waist.

She clung to him, her fingers gripping his shirt.

"I'm so sorry," he whispered into her hair. "So sorry I ever made you doubt how precious you are to me."

They sat like that for a long time, her tears soaking his shirt, his own eyes burning. Each sob that shook her body was an indictment—of his blindness, his idiocy, his carelessness with her heart. But she was here, in his arms. Letting him hold her. Maybe, by God's grace, she would let him make it up to her and be the husband she deserved.

Chapter Forty-Two

SAFE. MARTHA SAT CRADLED in Ezra's arms as her sobs subsided, the disjointed rhythm of her breaths gradually syncing with the steady rise and fall of his chest. She was safe here. With him. The soul-crushing weight she'd been carrying for so many years was gone. No more wondering, no more second-guessing—she finally knew the truth. She could breathe.

Ezra didn't love Ivy. He never had.

Only... "Why didn't I just ask you sooner?"

"Hm?" He stirred, stroking her back. "Ask me what?"

"Talk to you about Ivy, I mean. As soon as I started feeling uneasy about your friendship."

His lips brushed against her hair. "I should never have let myself get that close to her in the first place. I was completely wrong, and I can't believe I didn't see it."

"But I ought to have spoken up. I was too scared to rock the boat. Afraid of looking jealous and insecure."

He pulled her closer. "No, Martha. I was the one who let the lines blur. I should have been more sensitive, more aware. I was wrong to put you in a position where you even had to question speaking up. That's on me. I'll do everything I can to make sure you never feel that way again." He kissed her forehead. "It should never have come to this."

"I won't let you take all the blame."

He chuckled. "Well, if we're splitting the blame on this, how about I carry it on every day of the week that ends in a 'Y?' You can have all the rest."

She smiled, punching him in the shoulder.

He spoke again after a moment, his voice gentle. "Martha, what happened yesterday? After you left home?"

"I almost crashed the car." She felt his body go still. "You know that straight stretch past Westcott? I dozed off and the rumble strip woke me up."

"I should never have let you drive." His arms tightened around her. "Thank God you were okay."

"I was so shaken when I got to Alex's. He saw I was in no state to drive back home and said I could rest in his guest room." She drew a shuddering breath. "It sounded like a good idea. I wanted to tell you I was going to be later than I'd said, but I realized I'd left my phone here. I asked if I could borrow his, but he said it was out of battery and he'd call as soon as he'd charged it a bit. What time did he call you?"

"He didn't."

She pulled back to look at him. "What?"

"He never called me. I called him, and he said if I hadn't heard from you, it was because you didn't want to speak to me." Ezra's jaw tightened, the muscles in his neck tensing.

"I kept telling him I wanted to speak to you. Over and over. Why would he lie like that?"

"I can think of a few reasons." His eyes darkened.

"He must have called Ivy while I was asleep. Stalled me from talking to you, from going back home. He said it would be better for my career if I—" Martha gasped as all the pieces fell into place. "He planned it all. He set the whole thing up so she'd be there when I woke up."

"What those two did to you—" Ezra's voice shook as he drew her back into his arms. His safe, warm arms.

She didn't want to think about Alex, or why he'd lied to her. She just wanted to forget everything but Ezra's embrace, Ezra's love.

His pulse raced, but he remained silent, his breathing slowly steadying again.

After a while, he pressed a kiss to her temple. "I need to go downstairs and call Fiona. She's probably wondering why I missed our meeting. Do you need anything? Maybe you should stay here and rest."

"No." She sat up, although her limbs felt weighted with fatigue. She knew he had to go, knew he had things to deal with, but she couldn't bear the thought of being away from him. "I'll come with you."

Ezra waited while she ducked into the en suite bathroom to splash cold water on her face and smooth back her tangled hair. She didn't look too closely in the mirror. Just a quick glance to make sure she didn't resemble Sasquatch's wife.

He took her hand when she emerged, and they headed for the stairs.

As they reached the bottom of the stairs, Martha drew a sharp breath, gripping the banister.

The living room lay in ruins before her—shattered glass, overturned furniture, books scattered everywhere.

Ray knelt amid the destruction, sweeping broken glass into a dustpan.

"Oh—" Her legs went weak. Had she really done all this?

Ezra's arm went around her shoulders, steadying her. "Don't look at it. Come on, let's go to the kitchen."

But she couldn't move, couldn't tear her gaze away from the wreckage she had made. Her face burned. "Ray, I'm so sorry..."

"No need to apologize, ma'am." Ray's voice was gentle as his gaze met hers. "I'm just glad you're okay. Marcus and I will take care of it."

"But I made such a huge mess. Let me help clear it up—"

"No, ma'am. We've got this."

Ezra squeezed her arm. "Ray's right. We don't want you hurting yourself." He guided her toward the kitchen, his arm firm around her shoulders. "Careful of the glass. There's a clear path this way."

She let him lead her, still staring at the devastation. That enormous mirror she'd torn off the wall, the toppled bookcase, all those broken pieces of crystal and porcelain...

"I don't know what came over me. I was out of my mind—I've never done anything like that before. I'm—"

"You were protecting our marriage." Ezra's voice was soft but firm. "In a rather spectacular way, perhaps, but I understand why you did it."

He drew her into his arms, and she leaned into him, breathing in his familiar scent.

Her phone rang from the kitchen counter, playing "Emergence—" her first hit single. She tensed, pulling back from Ezra's embrace. "It's Alex."

"You don't have to talk to him if you're not ready." His hands tightened on her shoulders as his gaze searched her face. "Not after everything."

"I'm ready. I need to do this." Stepping away from him, she walked to the counter and picked up her phone.

"Morgan?" Alex's voice oozed concern. "I swung by the hotel with breakfast, but they said you'd checked out. Do you need me to arrange something else? Another hotel, perhaps?"

"No." Her voice only wobbled a little. "I'm back home. With my husband."

He was silent for a moment. "I see. After everything we discussed, are you sure that's wise? Are you sure it's in your best interests?"

His smooth, reasonable tone—the same one he'd used yesterday—made her stomach turn. But she kept her voice calm. "We talked everything through. Ezra told me what really happened with Ivy."

"Of course he did." Alex sighed. She could almost hear the eye roll. It was amazing the volumes of meaning Alex packed into those four words. His voice took on a patient note, as though he were reasoning with a child. "Morgan, sweetheart, I know you want to believe him. That's natural. But think about what Ivy told you. The pattern of behavior—"

"You mean the lies she told me?"

"The evidence. The specific details." His voice gentled. "I know this is hard. But you need to think about your career right now. Your brand. The sponsors are already nervous about the association—"

"You were completely out of line."

A beat of silence. Then, "I'm trying to protect you. That's my job."

"Is it?" Martha felt Ezra step closer as her voice faltered, his hands coming to rest on her shoulders. "Was it your job to keep me at your house when I was too exhausted to think straight? To lie to me when Ezra tried to reach me?"

"You needed space to process—"

"I needed my husband. Instead, you orchestrated that whole scene with Ivy."

"Morgan." His tone sharpened slightly. "You're emotional right now. I understand that. But don't throw away everything we've built because of sentiment. Your career—"

"My career isn't the issue here." She leaned back against Ezra's solid presence. "This is about trust. I don't trust you after what you did yesterday. You're fired, Alex."

"What?" He laughed. "You can't be serious. After everything I've done for you? I made you who you are."

"I'm grateful for everything you've done for my career. You've been an amazing manager. You helped me find opportunities I never dreamed of. But what you did yesterday..." Her voice caught. "You abused my trust to get between me and my husband. I will not look past that."

"Morgan, I was looking out for you." His soothing, cajoling tone was back. "I was trying to protect you."

"From what? The truth?" She drew a long breath. "Even if you had the best intentions, the way you went about it—lying to me, keeping me isolated from my husband—my *husband*, Alex! I'll never feel safe around you again. I can't work with you anymore. My solicitor will contact you about ending our contract."

Alex's voice hardened. "You're making a huge mistake. One that could cost you everything you've worked for."

"I already have everything I care about. Goodbye, Alex." She ended the call, her hands shaking now that it was over.

Ezra's arms encircled her from behind. "You okay?"

She nodded, leaning back against him. "I think so."

"That couldn't have been easy. He's worked with you right from the start. Come sit down." He guided her to a stool next to the counter. "I'll make you some tea."

"I'm fine, really." But her legs felt wobbly with relief. .. or delayed shock... or exhaustion. Maybe all three.

His phone buzzed. "That'll be Fiona." He leaned down, brushing his lips against her forehead. "Hang on, I need to take this."

He moved toward the French doors, his voice low but carrying clearly enough for her to catch fragments of his side of the conversation. "I understand, but it'll have to wait... I know the deadline, but... No. My mind is made up on this."

Martha's gaze fell on a thick envelope on the counter, a legal letterhead visible through the torn opening. Thorne and Associates—the lawyers who never lost. As she reached for it, the words "CEASE AND DESIST" jumped out at her.

Ivy was taking legal action against Ezra. Her stomach dropped as she scanned the document. Five days to respond. While Ezra should have been focused on this crisis, he'd wasted precious hours dealing with her emotional breakdown instead. How much had her meltdown cost him?

Chapter Forty-Three

"EZRA, ARE YOU HEARING me?" Fiona's voice sharpened. "Our backs are against the wall here."

"I understand the urgency." Ezra paced the garden path, keeping his voice low. "But I can't focus on this right now. I need to deal with something else."

"What could be more urgent than this cease-and-desist notice? Ivy's lawyers aren't messing around. If we don't respond—"

"My wife needs me."

"Martha?" Fiona paused. "Is she okay?"

"She will be. But she isn't. Not yet. That's why I need—" He glanced toward the house.

Martha stood in the open doorway.

He lowered his voice. "Here's what I need you to do. Get in touch with our legal team immediately. I want them fully briefed on every aspect of this cease-and-desist notice. Have them start working on a detailed counter strategy. I'll check in with you at eight o'clock this evening, but until then, I'm unavailable. Thanks."

"Ezra." Martha's voice trembled. She held up the cease-and-desist letter. "You need to deal with this. I'm okay now. Really."

He ended the call and moved toward her, his heart twisting at the look on her face.

She wasn't okay. She was trying so hard to be strong, to pull herself together, but he could see how close she still was to breaking.

He wouldn't let anything distract him from her now. Not when she was still so fragile. The haunted look in her eyes, the tremor in her hand as she held up that letter—no. The legal mess could wait. His lawyers could handle Ivy's threats for now. But Martha? His Martha needed a safe healing space today. And he would give that to her.

"I'm so sorry." She looked down at the letter. "I've been such a distraction when you need to focus on fighting for your song."

"Martha." He took the letter from her fingers and stuck it inside his back pocket, then held her shoulders. "You're not a distraction. You're my priority."

"But this deadline... Let me help. I could make a statement supporting you. Or help look for documentation, proof that you wrote—"

"The thing that would help me most right now," he said, drawing her close, "is knowing that you're really okay."

"But—"

"Everything's in hand. Fiona's coordinating with the lawyers, and we've already sent out a few cease-and-desist letters of our own to the news outlets and bloggers stirring up the worst of the rumors. It's calmed down some of the speculation. Right now..." He cupped her cheek. "Right now, I just need my wife. I'm tired too, my love. And I need you."

Her eyes filled with tears. "You're sure?"

"I'm sure." He brushed away a tear as it escaped the corner of her eye. "How about we both take the day to just... breathe? Maybe order in some lunch, chill out. Deal with the rest of the world tomorrow."

She searched his face. "You really mean that?"

"I really do." He managed a small smile. "I think we've earned a day off from crisis management. Both of us."

Her shoulders relaxed. "A day off sounds wonderful."

"Good." He kissed her forehead. "Because I have big plans for us."

"Oh?"

"First, I'm ordering Thai food from that place you love. Then we're going to curl up together on the sofa and watch that ridiculous romantic comedy you like so much. The one with the wedding singer."

A wobbly smile touched her lips. "You hate that movie."

"Yeah, it's pretty dire. But I love watching you laugh at it." He stroked her cheek. "That's what I need today. Just... us. Being us again."

Her smile faded. "We haven't been 'us' for a long time."

They had a lunch of larb gai, tom yum, and steamed jasmine rice, polishing off every bite.

As they cleared away the dishes, Martha said, "You don't really want to watch that movie. How about we dust off the old Singtrix and have a karaoke battle?"

"Ooh, it's on. You have no idea what you're getting yourself in for."

Martha grinned. "You're the one going down. I'll finish up here. You go set it up."

Ezra found their old Singtrix Party Bundle system in the storage closet. When was the last time they'd used this? Probably not since they'd moved into this house. He set it up in the home cinema room, finishing up just as Martha walked in.

He tapped on the Singtrix system's touchscreen. "We need rules for this karaoke battle."

"Okay." Martha hooked her thumbs into her pants pockets. "Rule one—we have to sing whatever the other person chooses."

"No exceptions?"

"Nope. And you have to commit to it. Full performance."

His eyes narrowed. "Including dance moves?"

"It wouldn't be a full performance without dance moves." She grinned. "Your turn to make a rule."

"No singing songs from our own genres. So, no contemporary Christian for me, no pop, jazz, R&B, soul, or Broadway stuff for you."

"Deal." She held up a finger. "And no backing out once the song starts playing."

"Even if it's Tina Turner?"

"Especially if it's Tina Turner." Her eyes gleamed as he scrolled through the song library. "Ready to start?"

"You're going to regret this." Ezra chuckled. "Let's start with AC/DC for you."

"What?" Martha's eyes widened. "You're giving me hard rock? Really, Ezra?"

"'Highway to Hell.' Total commitment, remember?"

"I hate you." But she was laughing as she took the mic.

He winked at her. "Nah, you're crazy about me."

Chuckling, she rolled her shoulders and shook out her arms. "Fine. Hit play."

The opening guitar riff blasted through the speakers.

Martha closed her eyes, took a deep breath, and launched into the song, complete with head-banging and air guitar.

Ezra nearly fell off the sofa laughing as she strutted across the room, her sophisticated vocal training abandoned in favor of raw, growling notes.

She grabbed an imaginary microphone stand, channeling the energy of a rock star on a rebellious journey. As she attacked the chorus, her voice cracked spectacularly.

By the final chorus, she was fully committed—jumping around their media room, hair whipping, voice increasingly hoarse as she gave the performance her all. She finished with a dramatic power slide across the floor.

"I can't breathe!" He laughed, clutching his aching sides. "I've got to hand it to you—when you commit, you commit."

This was his Martha, the real Martha only he got to see—not afraid to look silly for him. How he'd missed moments like this.

She grinned, pushing her hair off her forehead. "It's payback time. Are you ready? I am going to make you suffer... right after I catch my breath."

She went over to the Singtrix and scrolled through the playlist, then faced him with a wicked grin. "'Proud Mary'."

"Absolutely not." Waving his hands, Ezra backed away from the mic.

"Come on! I just did 'Highway to Hell' for you."

"And it was terrifying. Okay, fine. But I'm doing the dance moves too." He grabbed the mic from her hand.

"The dance moves?" She stared at him. "You know Tina Turner's choreography?"

"Not even slightly." He struck a pose as the music started. "I'm improvising."

He massacred the song, topping off the desecration with his version of Tina's signature shimmy.

Martha doubled over laughing. "How do you even move like that?" She wiped the tears from her eyes.

"Like what? This?" He attempted another shimmy, nearly losing his balance.

"Here." Still giggling, she stood. "Let me show you how it's done. It's all in the hips."

She demonstrated the move, her body moving with fluid grace. "See?"

"I definitely do not see." Ezra attempted to copy her, with dire results. "How did you learn to move like that?"

She grinned. "Hours of dance training. The label insisted." She shimmied again with a skill that would have made Tina herself envious.

"Well, you're a much better student than I am." Watching her movements, he threw himself into the hip roll once more. "It's no good. I look like a kangaroo getting electrocuted."

"No, you're doing great!" She steadied him, laughing. "Okay, maybe not great. But you're trying. That's what matters."

"The things I do for love." He chuckled as she positioned his arms again. "Don't you dare film this now."

"No blackmail material, I promise." She laughed, then grew quiet. "You know, Keira—my opening act last year—she could really move. Natural talent. I wish I could have helped her."

His hands settled on her waist as they stopped dancing. "What happened to her?"

"Got caught up in the wrong crowd. Parties, drugs..." Martha smoothed the fabric of his T-shirt across his chest. "Her manager didn't exactly discourage it. Said it was part of the image."

"But Alex did?"

"Alex managed the image differently. More controlled. I'll give him that—he kept some of the sketchier sorts away, and I'm very grateful that he did. I was such an innocent back then, and I needed someone to run interference for me. There were still plenty of offers, though. Especially after shows, when you're running on adrenaline and everyone's celebrating."

"You never told me about that." He laced his fingers through hers. "Did you... were you ever tempted to try anything?"

"Only once. After a show in Singapore. The crowd was incredible, but afterward... I felt so alone. Everyone else was going off to party, and I just sat in my hotel room missing you. Wondering what I was doing there."

"I remember Singapore. You seemed quiet when I called."

"Someone had left something in my dressing room. Said it would help me just float away. No more loneliness." She pressed closer to him. "I actually picked it up.

Brought it back to the hotel. Turned it over in my hands. Sat there staring at it for the longest time."

"Martha." His gut twisted.

"Then you FaceTimed me. Do you remember? You started telling me about your day, about this melody you were working on that was giving you trouble. Told me what Levi and Zach were up to. About how Levi had gotten a girl into trouble. And then you asked if we could pray together before bed, like we used to."

"I didn't know..."

"I never told you. But that prayer? It was exactly what I needed. Reminded me who I was, what really mattered." She looked up at him. "You saved me from making a very poor choice that night, even if you didn't know it. Well, God used you to save me."

"That's something we haven't done in a while," he said. "Praying together before bed."

"I'd like to start doing that again."

"We can start now."

She smiled. "But it's not bedtime."

"Doesn't matter."

Hands clasped, they both prayed, thanking God for the chance to spend a quiet day together and committing the whole songwriting dispute and the surrounding crisis into His hands. Ezra asked God to strengthen them for the days ahead, and to continue to knit their hearts together.

As they said "Amen," there were tears in Martha's eyes.

Ezra wrapped his arms around her. "Promise me something, Martha."

"What?"

"That you'll let me know if anything's troubling you. Anything at all. Including if I'm being an idiot."

A watery laugh escaped her. "You're not an idiot."

"I have my moments." He caressed the nape of her neck. "I should have seen what was happening with Ivy—what I was doing. I should have noticed you pulling away. So promise me, no more suffering in silence. Even if—especially if—I'm the one causing the problem."

She took a long, shuddering breath. "I promise."

He kissed her hair. "And I promise I'll always listen. Really listen."

They stood for a long moment, holding each other, swaying gently, her head against his chest.

Ezra said, "Since we're down here, we might as well watch a movie."

"Mm. But maybe one we both like." She was silent for a moment.

"*Singin' in the Rain*," they said in chorus, both laughing.

Ezra pulled a throw blanket over their laps as they settled deeper into the sofa in front of the big screen.

Martha tucked her feet under herself, her head resting against his shoulder.

As the vibrant scenes unfolded, Ezra stole glances at his wife.

Under the glow of the screen, her face looked relaxed, a stark contrast to the strain that had etched her features earlier that day. How close had he come to losing her—if not to a car accident, then to those vultures who had done their best to break her spirit? It would take a mighty work of grace for him to forgive Alex Thompson and Ivy Willis. And himself, for creating the situation that made Martha vulnerable to their lies.

He prayed silently, thanking God for this moment of respite, for her safety, for the sound of her laughter mingling with the iconic tunes of the movie.

They chuckled through the comical "Make 'Em Laugh" and sang along to "Good Mornin'".

Then, as Gene Kelly splashed through puddles on the rain-soaked streets, Martha turned in Ezra's arms. Sliding her hand up his chest, she pressed a kiss to his jaw.

He stilled, his breath catching as her lips traced a slow, sizzling path to his mouth.

Desire exploded within him, but he fought to bank its fires. "Martha," he whispered, "are you sure? After everything you've been through today..."

She drew back to meet his gaze, her fingertips brushing over his lips. "I'm sure."

"We don't have to," he rasped.

"I want to." Another tender kiss. "I want us."

He wanted her, too—desperately—but he held back, searching her face. Was she really ready? She had been so wounded today, so fragile, so beaten down. In her eyes, he saw complete certainty and love. And a desire that matched his own.

His hand slid into her hair, now beautifully, gloriously messy after her epic karaoke performance. How he loved this woman! Her blend of vulnerability and strength, passion and sweetness, resilience and tenderness.

"My sweet, darling Martha—"

He drew her to himself, their lips brushing together. Their kiss deepened as they began a gentle, healing dance, an intricate choreography that needed no music but the rhythm of their own hearts, the cadence of their breaths. They knew the steps by instinct. It was a slow, intentional duet, a reaffirmation of trust, a piecing together of what was broken as their bodies moved in perfect sync.

The movie played on, its shifting light painting shadows across the walls as Ezra and his wife wrote their own love story in the gathering dusk.

Chapter Forty-Four

Martha watched Ezra's profile as he steered his Tesla into the parking lot of Grace Community Church. The beautiful, healing intimacy of yesterday still lingered between them. What a blessing to be truly known and fully loved, with no more secrets and shadows. Their connection felt tender and new, yet as familiar as breathing.

But reality had intruded this morning. A quick scan of social media showed that the accusations were still spreading and gaining momentum. Three artists who'd scored top ten hits with songs written by Ezra had spoken out in support of Ivy.

He did his best to hide it, but she knew how deeply the betrayal of some of his so-called friends hurt him. Her heart ached for him, for the toll this was taking.

She hoped that being here, worshiping God with their church family, would encourage and strengthen him. And she would do everything she could to protect this oasis of peace they'd found in each other, a shelter he could count on in the gathering storm.

He looked down into her face, his smile gentle. "You okay?"

She nodded, though her stomach fluttered. It had been so long since she'd come to GCC.

He glanced in the rearview mirror. "I see Ray's found a parking spot. Are you ready to go in?"

They slipped in through the side entrance hand in hand, the PPO hanging back at a discreet distance.

A soft murmur of recognition rippled through the gathering congregation. These were their people, their church family. The place where she and Ezra had first met, where they'd grown in faith together, where he still led worship. And where she wanted to belong again.

Eden appeared beside them, wrapping Martha in a quick hug. "I'm so glad you're here," she whispered.

As they settled into their seats, Martha's throat tightened. Why had she stayed away so long? She'd told herself she was too busy, that her schedule was too unpredictable. But the truth was, when she'd built walls between herself and Ezra, she'd shut herself off from everyone else, too. From Beth's motherly wisdom, from Eden's friendship, from this whole community that had loved and supported her since she was in her teens.

She'd even built a wall between herself and God.

Zach slipped into the row of seats behind them, squeezing her shoulder in greeting.

Beth arrived moments later, tears gleaming in her eyes as she hugged Martha.

"Welcome home, sweetheart," Beth whispered.

Home. The word settled in Martha's heart like a warm embrace. The familiar buzz of the sound system, the faint scent of coffee from the welcome area, the gentle chatter of voices—it all wrapped around her like a childhood blanket she'd forgotten she'd missed.

Pastor Noah caught her eye from across the sanctuary and smiled, inclining his head in welcome.

Zach stepped onto the platform, adjusting his guitar strap. The worship team settled into place behind him.

As the first chords of "In Christ Alone" filled the room, tears pricked her eyes. Her voice joined the congregation's, the words hitting her heart with fresh meaning. Her hope, her strength, was in Christ. Not in a career, no matter how successful. Not in fame. How had her success helped to heal her wounded heart or restore her marriage? Not one bit. What had her fame done to give her hope? Sitting alone in that hotel room after a sell-out concert, she'd felt so lonely and empty that she'd considered escaping into the oblivion that a pill could bring.

Her hope wasn't even in Ezra, no matter how breathtakingly amazing he was. He was only human. God alone was her hope—their hope—the only one strong enough, faithful enough, wise enough to never fail.

She'd lost her moorings when she'd forgotten where her hope truly lay.

She glanced at Ezra beside her. His eyes were closed as he sang, tears glistening on his dark eyelashes. His voice carried the harmony as naturally as breathing. "Firm through the fiercest drought and storm." She prayed he would draw strength and hope despite the dark, frightening storm that threatened his reputation and livelihood.

The service enveloped her in warmth, making her feel safe and comforted. Joining the rest of the church in prayer for other people's needs, listening to Pastor Noah's sermon about how Joseph handled himself when mistreated and falsely accused, lifting her heart and her voice in worship—all of it poured comfort and strength into her spirit.

She caught Ezra looking at her, and she smiled at him, squeezing his hand. They had so much to be thankful for.

When the final song ended, she expected to feel that familiar urge to slip away quickly. Instead, she lingered, drawn into conversations she'd missed more than she'd realized.

Susan, who ran the church book stall, wanted to hear about her travels.

James and Rachel's children, so young when she'd last seen them, were now gangly teenagers who shyly asked for selfies.

And Mrs. Cutler, still a force to be reckoned with at ninety-five, came to hug her. "I saw your beautiful video post on Instagram last night, saying how you believe in your husband. Brought tears to my eyes. Such a terrible business. But we're praying for you both, my dear."

Martha's own eyes were moist when Eden came up to her seconds later.

"Could the two of you come into Noah's office for a little while?" Eden said. "We're having a short meeting."

In the pastor's office, Martha looked around at the small group that had gathered. Besides Noah and Eden, Zach and Beth were also here.

Martha settled onto the sofa between Ezra and Beth, lacing her fingers with his.

"Before we start," Zach said, "I just want to say how good it is to have you back with us, Martha. All of us have really missed you."

Beth squeezed her knee.

Zach went on. "Now, for those who don't know the latest—Ivy Willis's lawyers have given us five days to respond to their demands."

"It's four days now," Ezra said. "The letter came yesterday."

"Right. Four days. They're demanding that Ezra acknowledge her as co-writer of 'Whispers of You' and pay her fifty percent of all past and future royalties. We have four days to respond before they file a copyright infringement suit. The media's running wild with it. Everyone and their mother appear to be talking about it on social media, including some other artists who are also jumping on the bandwagon."

He leaned forward, elbows on his knees. "But we're making progress. The legal team's working on our response, and *Promise Ridge*'s support has given some weight to our side. Not to mention your social media reel, Martha, countering Alex's earlier statement. Lots of views on that. Of course, Levi and I have also made statements."

Zach looked around the room. "What we need now is wisdom about how to handle the next few days. And we need prayer. Lots of prayer. And in more practical terms, while the legal team works, we need to build a stronger timeline of the song's development."

"How can Eden and I help?" Noah asked.

"Pray for us." Ezra's voice was quiet, his grip tightening around Martha's fingers. "I hope Martha doesn't mind me telling you that this whole thing wasn't just about my career. It's been an attack on us at every level." He glanced at her.

She squeezed his hand and nodded. She didn't mind him sharing this with their family.

He went on. "God is healing us, but please pray that we'll be able to stand strong, no matter what happens."

Noah nodded. "Of course."

"And, of course, pray that we'll find the evidence we need. Mum's coming this afternoon to help Martha look through my old notebooks and any other records in the storage shed. I'll go through my digital records, and Zach is following up on people I was working with back then."

They formed a circle to pray, hands linked. As their voices rose together, Martha felt something settle in her spirit. This was what they'd been missing in their struggle—not just each other, but their family, their community, their foundation of faith. They weren't meant to face this alone. God had given them a network of support.

When the prayer session was over and everyone got up from their seats, Eden touched Martha's arm. "Walk with me?"

They drifted toward the window, creating a small bubble of privacy. "You look different," Eden said. "More peaceful. Radiant, even. Have you worked on some of the things we talked about earlier?"

"Ezra and I talked." Martha's voice caught. "About everything. All the things I was afraid to say. About Ivy, about feeling invisible..." She glanced at Ezra, who was deep in conversation with Noah. "He listened. Really listened."

"And?"

"He admitted he'd been completely blind about Ivy. He never saw how inappropriate their friendship was, how he let her come between us." Martha drew a shaky breath. "And Eden... you were right. She did manipulate everything. When he finally ended their friendship—it was because she tried to kiss him. He stopped her immediately, cut off all contact. But she twisted that around too, telling me he was the one who tried to kiss her."

"I knew she was trouble," Eden said. "But what matters is that you and Ezra are finding your way back to each other."

"We are." She glanced over at him as he stood talking with Pastor Noah. "He's promised things will be different. No more blurred lines, no more letting other people into spaces that should be just ours. I realized I was doing some things that hurt him, too. Things about my image. And I promised I wouldn't keep things bottled up— that I'll talk to him." A sudden rush of emotions brought tears to her eyes. "I don't know why I stayed away so long."

"Because sometimes when we're hurting, we run from the very people who could help us heal." Eden's voice was gentle. "The enemy loves to isolate us, make us think we have to handle everything alone. But you're back now. That's what matters."

Eden was quiet for a moment. "Martha... you may not want to hear this right now, but you need to forgive Ivy."

"What?" Martha stiffened. "After what she's doing to Ezra? To us?"

She lowered her voice as Ezra and Noah glanced their way. "You have no idea what she tried to do to us, how deep her sick behavior is."

"Not to excuse it. What she did—what she's still doing—is wrong." Eden's voice was gentle but firm. "But bitterness will poison your heart if you let it take root. And you've come too far, healed too much, to let that happen."

Martha wrapped her arms around herself. "I hear what you're saying. I do. And I know—intellectually—that forgiveness is important." Her voice dropped. "But Eden, this isn't just about me. She's trying to destroy Ezra's career, his reputation. Everything he's worked for."

"I know."

"She tried to destroy our marriage." The words caught in her throat. "Used my deepest fears against me. Made me doubt everything."

"That's exactly why you need to forgive her." Eden touched her arm. "Not for her sake. For yours. For your peace. And because God requires us to forgive those who've wronged us."

Martha stared out the window. She'd been a Christian long enough to know Eden was right. She'd heard countless sermons about forgiveness, had even counseled others about it. But this... this felt different. Raw. Personal.

"I don't know if I can," she whispered. "Not yet."

"I'm not saying it will be easy. Or quick." Eden's voice was soft. "But pray about it. Ask God to help you get there. Because if you don't..."

"The bitterness will eat me alive." Martha closed her eyes. "I know."

Noah appeared beside them. "Eden, we need to get going. That meeting with the youth leaders?"

"Right." Eden hugged Martha. "Think about what I said?"

Martha nodded. "You have an annoying track record of being right about things like this."

Smiling, Eden squeezed her hand.

Ezra came up beside Martha. "Ready?"

She turned into his arms. "Yes."

The warmth of their church family's support still wrapped around Martha as she and Ezra walked to their car. The summer sunshine bathed the churchyard in a soft, golden glow, filtering through the leaves of the old oak trees that lined the path. After so long away, coming back felt like finding solid ground again.

Her phone buzzed. Jane.

"I'm sorry to call on a Sunday," Jane said, her voice tight. "But I thought you should know—Libertine Lingerie has just terminated your contract. Effective immediately."

"What?" Martha stopped walking.

"They're citing breach of brand values. They say they can't be associated with someone supporting..." Jane hesitated. "Well, you know."

A startled laugh escaped Martha.

Ezra glanced at her, frowning.

"That's not all," Jane continued. "Maison Duval also called. They're deeply concerned about the optics of your Instagram post last night. Your perfume launch was built around female empowerment, and they're saying your support of..." Another careful pause. "They're worried about the message it sends."

The laugh died in Martha's throat. Maison Duval was different. That was serious money, serious prestige. Everything they'd invested in the launch of Serenade...

"Have they made a decision?" Her voice sounded strange in her ears.

"Not yet. But Martha—they're talking about pulling the perfume. And the other sponsors are getting nervous too. They're waiting to see how this plays out, but..."

"Thanks for letting me know." Martha ended the call, her hand trembling slightly.

Ezra touched her arm. "What's wrong?"

"Libertine Lingerie dropped me." A smile tugged at her lips. "Apparently I'm in breach of their brand values because I love and stand by my husband."

"Martha, I'm so sorry. This is my fault—"

"No." She stopped him. "I'm actually relieved."

He blinked at her. "You are?"

"After seeing those little girls at the perfume launch, trying to be sexy, knowing how you feel about it, God's conviction in my own heart... To be honest, I was wondering how to get out of my contract with them. They've saved me the trouble." She hesitated. "But Maison Duval—that's different. They're talking about pulling my perfume."

His face went still. "Because you're supporting me."

"They say it undermines the 'empowerment message'." She made air quotes, tried to keep her voice steady. "Having their face of female empowerment stand by a man accused of stealing a woman's work."

She would take a big financial hit. Her projected earnings from Serenade were well into eight figures over the next five years. But more than that—she'd lose credibility in the luxury market. The kind of damage that could take years to repair.

But looking at Ezra's face—the guilt in his eyes, the way he was already pulling back to protect her—she knew with absolute certainty that she did not care.

"Losing Serenade would hurt. A lot," she said softly, slipping her arms around his waist. "But you matter more. I'll never regret standing by you. And I won't let anyone intimidate me into backing down. In fact..." She grinned, raising her chin. "I think I'll post another reel tonight to say I stand by you even harder."

His hands came up to cradle her face. "Martha..."

"I've been praying about changing my image, anyway. About truly living out my values, even through my work. Maybe this is God's way of making it happen. And Maison Duval—if they're going to work with me, they need to know that you matter more to me than any corporate buzzword they're trying to peddle. I'll show them 'female empowerment' if they try to bully me into shutting up."

His hands slid to her shoulders. "Martha, wait. Think about what you're risking. You've worked so hard with this contract with Maison Duval. You don't have to—"

"I have thought about it," she cut him off. "And I don't care. I won't be silenced. No one will stop me from standing up for you."

He studied her face, his eyes glistening. "You'd really risk all of it? For me?"

She thought of those little girls again, of being back in church today, of finally feeling like herself again. Of him, and how she wanted the world to know she believed in his integrity with all her heart. No matter what it cost her. "Yes. For you. For us. It's not even a hard choice."

He pulled her close, and she leaned into him, knowing that whatever came next, this was where she belonged.

Chapter Forty-Five

"LIONEL? THANK GOD I finally reached you." Martha paced Ezra's studio in the Wednesday afternoon light, her phone against her ear.

The last three days of leaving messages had finally paid off, and she had the ex-Silvertone sound engineer on the line.

"This is Martha Falconer, but you might know me better as Morgan—the one behind 'Resonance'?"

"Morgan! What an incredible honor." His voice was warm. "'Resonance' is absolutely sick. How can I help you?"

"I hope you don't mind me calling out of the blue, but I'm reaching out on behalf of my husband, Ezra Falconer." She perched on the edge of Ezra's desk.

"Oh, yeah, yeah. Been following all this mess in the news. Awful business."

"Yes, it is," Martha said. "I'll get straight to the point. We're trying to find people who remember when Ezra was writing 'Whispers of You.' I know you were there for a lot of his early sessions."

"I do remember something about that song." He sounded enthusiastic. "Late night at Silvertone Studios, must've been... what, 2019? Ezra was always there late, writing."

Martha's heart leaped. Finally! "Yes, exactly. Do you remember anything specific about when he was working on the early demos?"

"Let me think..." A thoughtful pause. "Yeah, there was definitely a night when he was really excited about a new melody. Had us all come listen."

"That would be so helpful if you could confirm—"

"Of course, memory's a bit fuzzy after all this time." Lionel's tone shifted. "Though it might get clearer if it were helped along a little."

"Helped along?"

"Yeah, you know. The right incentive might help me recall the relevant details."

The hope in Martha's chest turned to ice. "What exactly are you saying?"

"Look, Morgan, everyone knows Ezra Falconer's desperate for witnesses. I'm sure we could come to an arrangement about what I remember."

"I see." She spoke through gritted teeth. "Goodbye, Lionel." She punched the end call button. What an utter lowlife. How could someone try to profit from Ezra's desperation?

"Any luck?" Ezra looked up from his stack of papers.

"Lionel Davis from Silvertone. Remember him?" Her voice trembled with anger. "He said he remembered you writing 'Whispers'. Started talking about late nights at the studio, how excited you were about the melody..."

He sat up straighter. "Yeah?"

"He offered to remember whatever we wanted. For a price."

Ezra's laugh was bitter. "Guess we know how Ivy found her witnesses." He slumped in his chair. "Who else has she paid to lie about me?"

"I'm sorry. I thought—when he started talking about remembering those sessions..." She pressed her fingers against her eyes. "I should've known it was too good to be true. I hung up on him."

"You did the right thing." But his voice was hollow as he turned back to the endless papers. "Two days left, and all we've got are people willing to sell their souls. Unless this old backup drive holds something."

Martha watched him connect yet another external hard drive to his laptop. The screen flickered to life, showing hundreds of folders.

"This was from my old setup. Before the studio upgrade." His fingers flew over the keyboard. "There has to be something. Early demos, work files, anything."

They had scoured every box, trunk, and container in their storage rooms, seeking any piece of evidence that could prove he wrote "Whispers of You"—old hard drives and any other storage media, journals, sheet music. They were running out of places to check.

Martha moved behind him, hands settling on his shoulders as he began yet another digital search, clicking through folder after folder. Sound files, half-finished songs, email archives—nothing was from the right time period.

He groaned in frustration. "I remember every detail—the sun coming up, that melody just flowing..." He slammed the laptop shut. "But without proof, who's going to believe me?"

He pushed his hands through his hair. "You know what people used to call me when I signed with Silvertone? The next Chris Tomlin. I wrote my first real song at six, scored it for guitar and piano. I was a genuine child prodigy. I was going to change the world with my music." His laugh was bitter. "Such promise, right? And look at me now. Can't even sell my own albums. Silvertone drops me, and now..."

He spun his chair around, gesturing at the chaos surrounding them. "I can't prove I wrote my own songs. The only genuine success I've had in years is writing for other people, and now that's gone too." His voice dropped. "Maybe everyone was right. Maybe I peaked at nineteen."

Her heart broke to hear him talking like this. "Ezra—"

"Without my music..." his voice faltered. "I don't know who I am anymore."

"Stop." Martha gripped his shoulders, turning his chair to face her. "Your music is a gift, but it's not your identity. You're a man of integrity. A faithful, wonderful husband. A brother, a son, a friend. Most importantly, you're a child of God. Nothing Ivy does can touch that."

"A child of God." His eyes glistened. "Who can't even feel Him right now. I've been praying, Martha. Begging Him to help us find something, anything. But it feels like He's silent."

"I know that feeling." She took his hands. "Remember what you told me that night in Singapore? When I felt so alone?"

"That was different—"

"Was it?" Her thumbs traced circles on the back of his hands. "You reminded me who I was. That God was with me even when I couldn't feel Him. That His silence doesn't mean His absence."

"I just... I thought I was doing what He wanted. Using my gift to glorify Him. But what if I got it all wrong?" His voice caught. "This music, these songs—they just flow through me. Like breathing. Like prayer." His eyes glistened. "It's the one thing that's always made sense."

"Your gift is a beautiful, amazing part of you," Martha said. "But you know what's really incredible? There are things about you that are even more precious, more mind-blowing to me than your music. Like your heart. Your spirit. The man inside—that's who I love so desperately. And that's just me. What about your Father in heaven? He treasures you, whether you never write another song or write a thousand more. Your identity in Christ isn't something so fragile that Ivy can steal it. That doesn't change. Trust His heart."

Moving onto his lap, she wrapped her arms around him. The lyrics of his song rose naturally to her lips as she sang it softly to him in the quiet studio. "When the melody is silent, when I've lost my song, I hear whispers of you telling me to be strong. When I've lost all hope, can't find a way through, the promise of tomorrow, it whispers of you."

His arms tightened around her and she sensed the tremor in his shoulders, heard his shaky breath, felt his tears dampen her neck.

"You wrote that," she whispered against his ear. "And no one can take that truth from you."

Chapter Forty-Six

EZRA SAT IN HIS darkened studio staring at the cease-and-desist letter. The paper had grown soft at the edges from his constant handling, but the words remained stark and immutable. Under twelve hours left until Ivy's deadline.

Upstairs, Martha slept—finally. She'd fought exhaustion all week, determined to keep searching for evidence to clear his name. Despite their combined efforts, along with hours of work by Fiona, Mum, Zach, and Jane, they had managed to compile only a disjointed collection of early song sketches, partial email threads, and second-hand testimonials.

Each piece, while hinting at Ezra's deep involvement in creating "Whispers of You," lacked the concrete proof he needed to deliver a knock-out punch to Ivy's claims. The evidence was there, scattered and suggestive, but it didn't add up to a strong defense against the looming legal challenge. And time was running out.

His phone lit up. It was Jeremy Walsh, his lawyer.

"Sorry to call so late." Jeremy's voice was grim. "But Ivy's legal team just sent through some documents you need to see."

"More demands?"

"Worse. They're threatening to name your wife as either a party to the suit or a material witness."

Ezra's heart froze. "They can't do that. Martha has nothing to do with this."

"They're arguing that, as your wife, she has direct knowledge of your songwriting process during that period. They want to depose her about your relationship with Ivy, your work habits, the state of your marriage—"

"No." The word came out sharp. "Absolutely not. Are they even allowed to do that? I thought you couldn't be forced to testify against your spouse."

"That's a common misconception," Jeremy said. "You're thinking of criminal cases. This is different. In UK civil cases, spousal privilege is limited to communications that are explicitly meant to be private."

Ezra shook his head. "I don't understand. Surely what my wife and I talk about in the privacy of our home is private?"

"It's not that simple," Jeremy said. "Anything Martha observed about your work habits, your creative process, your friendship with Ivy—none of that would be considered privileged communication. The court would likely view those as observable facts, not private marital communications. We could fight any attempt to join Martha as a party to the lawsuit, and I think we would probably win. But it's much harder to prevent them from subpoenaing her as a material witness. In civil cases such as this, the law does not provide a broad shield against a spouse testifying on any matter."

"But that can't be right," Ezra said. "They can't force her to testify about our private life, our marriage—"

"I've seen it happen before." Jeremy's voice was grim. "Particularly in entertainment industry cases. When there's public interest involved, the courts tend to favor transparency. Just last year, I watched a record label force a producer's wife to testify about his work habits in a contract dispute. It wasn't pretty."

Ezra's grip tightened on the phone. "But Martha wasn't even there when I wrote the song."

"The court might still see her testimony as relevant—about your work habits, the studio environment, your interactions with Ivy during that period. A judge might agree to her being made to testify. The threat is very real, Ezra." Jeremy paused. "And frankly, that's exactly what Ivy's team is counting on."

"What do you mean?"

"They know forcing Martha to testify would put enormous pressure on you. Even if she doesn't have relevant information, the process alone would be brutal. She'd face depositions where they'd question her about every aspect of your relationship with Ivy, about your marriage, about—"

Ezra had heard enough. "I won't let them do that to her. Not after everything she's been through."

"I understand. But you need to be prepared. Their lawyers could make this extremely uncomfortable for Martha, probing into sensitive areas and looking for anything to support their narrative. And if my read on this is correct, I'm pretty sure they'd be happy to let the press see those depositions. If they push for it, I may not be able to prevent that access. As I already said, the high public interest in this case might influence the court toward transparency."

"No. Find another way." Ezra's jaw clenched. "Whatever it takes. I don't care what they do to me, but they are not dragging my wife into this."

Martha was just starting to heal. They were finally finding their way back to each other. There was no way he would let Ivy destroy that.

Silence stretched between them. Finally, Jeremy spoke. "We'll explore every possible avenue to protect her. But you need to understand what we're up against. These lawyers are masters at applying pressure where it hurts most. And they've identified your weakness."

"Martha is not my weakness." He snapped out the words. "She's my strength. And I will not let them use her to get to me."

"Then we need to move fast," Jeremy said. "We have until noon tomorrow to respond to their original demands. If we're going to find another way, we're running out of time."

After ending the call, Ezra sat motionless in the darkness, Jeremy's words echoing in his mind. The full weight of Ivy's diabolical threat crashed over him like a tidal wave.

Martha would have to relive everything—every painful memory, every lonely night, every moment she'd felt invisible in her own marriage. She'd be forced to describe watching him grow closer to Ivy, to tell hostile strangers how it felt being slowly pushed out of his life. All the raw, devastating hurt she'd finally trusted him enough to share would be picked apart by cold-eyed lawyers in sterile conference rooms.

His chest tightened as he remembered her breakdown just days ago—the violence of her pain as she'd torn apart their living room, screaming about how he'd let Ivy into every corner of their home. The agony in her voice when she'd accused him of being ashamed of her. She'd been so wounded, so devastated by Ivy's lies, it had taken everything in him to help her find solid ground again.

And now Ivy wanted to force Martha to relive all of it under oath. To have her most intimate pain splashed across entertainment news sites, dissected on social media. "Morgan's Marriage Crisis!" He could already see the headlines, imagine the gleeful speculation as every detail was twisted into clickbait.

His hands shook with fury. This wasn't just about his career anymore. This was Ivy's ultimate act of manipulation—using the legal system to torture Martha, to destroy what they'd rebuilt together.

He wouldn't let it happen. He couldn't.

But what choice did he have? Eleven hours until the deadline. And no proof.

"Lord, what can I do?" he prayed. "How can I keep Martha safe?"

Ezra stared at his phone for a long moment, then hit the callback button.

"Jeremy? I've made a decision." His voice was steady despite the sick feeling in his gut. "Contact Ivy's team. Tell them I'll concede. Tell them... I'm willing to discuss settlement terms."

"Are you sure? This morning you were adamant—"

"On one condition." Ezra's voice hardened. "Martha stays completely out of this. No depositions, no testimony, nothing. They don't come near her."

"Ezra, think about what you're saying. This would mean—"

"I know exactly what it means." He swallowed. "But I won't let Martha suffer anymore because of my poor judgment. I let Ivy get too close once before. I won't let my mistakes hurt my wife again."

Silence stretched across the line. Finally, Jeremy spoke. "You understand this will likely mean acknowledging her as co-writer? Paying back royalties? Giving up half future earnings on the song?"

"Whatever it takes." Ezra closed his eyes, fighting down the bile rising in his throat. "Just... make it clear. This offer is contingent on Martha being left completely out of it. If they try to involve her in any way, the deal's off."

"I'll reach out to their team immediately." Jeremy paused. "Have you discussed this with Martha?"

"No." The word came out rough. "And I need you to move fast. Before she finds out what they're threatening. Please."

"I'll call you as soon as I hear anything."

Ezra ended the call, his heart heavy. The thought of giving Ivy credit for his song—for the honest cry of his heart about his marriage—made him physically ill. But the thought of Martha being forced to relive her pain, to have their private struggles turned into a public spectacle...

He couldn't do that to her. He wouldn't.

"Lord," he whispered into the darkness, "give me strength to do the right thing. To see it through. Even if it costs me everything else."

The soft creak of the bedroom door woke Martha. As she opened her eyes, Ezra's silhouette moved across the darkened room.

"Ezra? You're up late."

He turned and came toward her, settling on the bedside next to her.

"I didn't know you were awake. Since you are, I'd better tell you this now."

She pushed herself up on one elbow, suddenly alert. Something had happened. "What is it?"

His voice caught. "Jeremy called. Ivy's lawyers... they're threatening to subpoena you as a witness."

"What? Why would they do that?"

"Jeremy says it's a high-pressure tactic. They want to force you into depositions—hours of hostile questions from Ivy's lawyers about everything. About my friendship with Ivy. About our marriage." He sucked in a breath. "All the stupid things I did that hurt you. The long hours in the studio, the time spent socializing with Ivy at industry events. They want you to relive all of that, to tell it to strangers. And because of the public interest in the case, everything you say would become entertainment news. They'd take all our private pain and turn it into headlines."

Martha swallowed. "I still don't understand why."

"Because it will hurt and humiliate you." He spoke through gritted teeth. "They're pretending you have information about how I wrote 'Whispers,' but Ivy knows you don't. This is all about hurting you. Jeremy says he might not be able to prevent it because the courts usually allow this kind of testimony in high-profile cases. I won't take that risk. I'm going to settle."

A chill washed over her. "Ezra, no, you can't do that!" He couldn't seriously be thinking of giving in to Ivy.

"I have to." His hand found hers in the darkness. "Don't you understand? They'd make you relive all of it, Martha. Every painful moment you suffered. I won't let that happen."

"But the song—"

"Isn't worth watching you hurt like that again." His fingers tightened around hers. "I almost lost you once because I was blind about Ivy. I won't risk that again. I've already told Jeremy to start settlement talks. On the condition that they leave you completely out of it."

She sat up fully now, her heart pounding. "No. I won't let you do this. I'll face whatever questions they throw at me. I'll testify about everything—about how you poured your heart into that song, about how I heard you working on it late into the night." She laid her hand on his chest, her words coming faster. "We haven't looked everywhere yet. There must be something we've missed—old emails, earlier drafts—"

"Martha." He put his hand over hers, and his voice was gentle but firm.

She caught the sheen of moisture in his eyes.

"It's done. I've made my decision. I won't give Ivy the power to hurt you again. I won't let her use the legal system to tear open wounds we've only just begun to heal."

"But don't you see what this will do to your career?" Her throat ached. "If you settle, if you give her credit... other artists will think twice about working with you. Everyone will believe you stole her song. They'll think you lied when you denied it."

"I know." His words, though quiet, throbbed with pain. "But even if this kills my career, Ivy can't take away my music. It's part of who I am. The songs will still come, whether anyone hears them or not."

"I'm part of you too," she whispered. "And she can't destroy that either."

He gathered her into his arms, holding her against his chest. "I'm so sorry," he whispered. "You've lost so much already, standing by me. Your perfume contract, your sponsors... you were so brave, so public in your support. And now I'm going to make you look foolish for believing in me. Everyone who dropped you will feel vindicated."

"Don't even think about that," she said fiercely against his chest. "I'll never regret standing by you. I don't care what anyone says or does."

She nestled closer as a tear rolled down her cheek. "Only... it means Ivy's won."

"No," he murmured into her hair, tightening his embrace. "We're together. Stronger than ever. We've already won."

Chapter Forty-Seven

TWO POINT SEVEN MILLION pounds. Ezra stared at the numbers on the whiteboard in Jeremy Walsh's office, his eyes gritty from lack of sleep. After his decision last night to concede to Ivy's demands, he'd barely rested, lying awake and listening to Martha's steady breathing beside him. Now, in the harsh morning light, the cost of his surrender was spelled out in stark black and white.

He sat motionless as Jeremy broke down the figures.

Martha's hand was warm in his, her thumb moving in small, soothing circles against his skin.

On the large screen mounted on the wall, Fiona watched from her LA office, her brows drawn sharply downward. She was not pleased about Ezra's decision to concede to Ivy.

"These are worst-case numbers," Jeremy said, capping his marker. "Based on estimated earnings from streaming, radio play, sync licensing, cover versions, and other revenue streams. We'll negotiate hard for a lower percentage on the back royalties—argue that any collaboration was more limited in the early stages. But you need to be prepared that they might push for the full fifty percent." He tapped his pen on the obscene figure.

"The industry implications are significant, Ezra." Fiona added. "We need to discuss the announcement. How we frame this will be crucial. The wrong wording could affect negotiations with other artists, future contracts—"

"I want control of the announcement," Ezra cut in.

"We can negotiate that," Jeremy said carefully. "Though they'll want input. What are you thinking?"

"Something simple. Professional." Ezra's voice was steady. "No accusations, no details about the writing process. Just a straightforward acknowledgment that resolves the dispute."

Fiona nodded. "That would be ideal. Keep it dignified and minimize speculation. We could draft something now."

"Yes, and include it in our initial proposal," Jeremy said. "Along with the twenty-five percent figure for back royalties. But be prepared—they might try to use this as a bargaining chip."

"Then make it clear it's non-negotiable," Ezra said. "I'll concede on the royalties if I have to. But I want control of how this is announced."

Martha squeezed his hand, and he knew she understood. This wasn't about pride. It was about maintaining some small measure of control over how their story was told.

"I can cover the back royalties," Martha said. "All of it. I have more than enough—"

"No." He turned to face her. "This is my mistake to fix. It's my poor judgment that let things get this far."

"But Ezra—"

"No, my love. Ivy's not getting a penny from you." He held her gaze for a moment. He added, his voice lower, "She's already cost you too much."

Jeremy cleared his throat. "There are several ways we could structure the payments. Future royalties could offset some of the back payments. We might be able to negotiate a payment plan."

"What about the meeting they're asking for?" Martha's voice was tight. "You said they insisted on face-to-face negotiations?"

"Yes." Jeremy settled behind his desk. "They're making it a condition of settlement. They want certain assurances directly from Ezra." He fixed them both with a steady gaze. "I need to be clear—this will not be pleasant. It's a power play, pure and simple. Ivy wants to see Ezra concede in person."

Of course she did. She was probably grinning from ear to ear right now, ready to rub her victory in his face.

"She's already positioning herself as the wronged party in the press," Fiona added. "This meeting is probably just another part of that narrative."

Ezra's jaw tightened. "I don't care about her games. Let's just get it done."

"There are rules we need to discuss first." Jeremy leaned forward. "Martha, while you're welcome to attend, you cannot speak."

Ezra turned to her. "You don't have to be there. I understand if you'd rather not be in the same room with her."

"I want to come." She pressed his hand. "You're not facing her alone. And I want her to know that I believe in you."

His throat tightened. Even now, at the moment of Ivy's triumph, Martha would stand with him to the bitter end.

"All right," Jeremy said. "As I said, Martha, you cannot speak during the negotiations. Not one word. Ezra, you say as little as possible. Let me do the talking." He paused. "They will try to provoke you. Both of you. You cannot react. Especially you, Ezra. Anything you say could affect our negotiating position."

"And could be leaked to the press," Fiona warned. "Every word in that room should be treated as potentially public."

Martha's fingers tightened around Ezra's.

Jeremy shuffled through some papers. "We'll start by offering twenty-five percent of back royalties, fifty percent going forward. They'll likely counter. We'll negotiate. But Ezra—" He met Ezra's eyes. "Once we're in that room, you cannot show any hesitation about acknowledging her contribution. Any hint of reluctance will weaken our position on the percentages."

"I understand."

"One more thing," Jeremy said. "There will probably be a non-disparagement clause. You won't be able to publicly dispute her claims about the song's creation."

"Which means that her version becomes the accepted narrative," Fiona said. "Are you prepared for that, Ezra?"

Nausea churned in Ezra's gut as the implications sank in. He would have to live with Ivy's lies. Stand by with his mouth shut and watch them become accepted as the truth.

Martha's other hand came up to cover their joined fingers. He drew strength from her touch, from her quiet presence beside him. "I'll just have to live with it. What time is the meeting?"

"Ten-thirty. Her solicitor's offices." Jeremy glanced at his watch. "Which gives us about two hours to draft the announcement and go over exactly what you should and shouldn't say."

"I'll stay on the line," Fiona said. "We need to coordinate every aspect of this."

Ezra nodded, squaring his shoulders. This was a bitter pill to swallow. But he could do this. He would do this. For Martha.

Chapter Forty-Eight

S O, THIS WAS IT. This was where he'd wave the white flag of surrender to a gloating Ivy.

A bitter taste sat on Ezra's tongue as he sat in the glass-walled corner conference room of Thorne and Associates, staring out at the panoramic view of London's financial district.

The glare of the morning sun caught the windows of nearby skyscrapers. Martha's small, warm hand clasped his beneath the polished mahogany table.

Across from them, Ivy sat perfectly at ease in a cream silk suit, flanked by her legal team. Every hair was in place, her makeup perfect, her porcelain doll lips curved in a slight smile. She probably had the champagne on ice nearby, ready to break out as soon as her victory was sealed in black and white.

He hoped she'd have the decency to wait until he and Martha were out of the room, but he wasn't holding his breath.

Her lead counsel, Richard Thorne, spoke first. "Good morning, gentlemen, ladies. We appreciate you coming in today." His cultured voice matched his silver hair and bespoke suit.

"Before we begin," he said, "I want to make it clear that we're here in good faith. My client has no desire to see this matter drag through the courts, causing damage to all parties' reputations."

Ezra clenched his jaw. Good faith? When they had threatened to brutalize his wife in order to bludgeon through this legalized theft of his song?

Thorne continued. "However, we're also prepared to pursue this to its full conclusion if necessary. I trust we all understand what that would mean." His gaze lingered on Martha.

Ezra's hand balled into a fist. *Lord, give me strength not to cross this conference table and throttle this sanctimonious bully.*

Thorne cleared his throat. "Given the tight deadline, we're prepared to move quickly. Our position is straightforward—fifty percent of all royalties, past and future, plus co-writing credit."

In the reflection of the glass wall, Ezra caught Ivy's satisfied smile.

"Twenty-five percent of back royalties," Jeremy countered. "No writing credit."

"Unacceptable." Thorne's response was immediate. "Ms. Willis's contribution to 'Whispers of You' was substantial. We have multiple witnesses prepared to testify—"

"Thirty-five percent," Jeremy cut in. "But no credit."

"Fifty percent and full co-writing acknowledgment," Thorne said. "Or we proceed with the lawsuit. Including Mrs. Falconer's testimony."

Martha's fingers tightened around Ezra's.

He fought to keep his breathing steady, to maintain the mask of calm Jeremy had drilled into him. This wasn't a negotiation. Ivy was conceding nothing.

She glanced at Martha, a smirk on her face.

That gloating, triumphant, serpent-like smile at his wife—forget cool legal strategy. Ezra couldn't let such malice go unchallenged. "Why are you doing this, Ivy?"

"Ezra." Jeremy's warning was sharp.

But Ivy was already answering, her voice honey-sweet. "You know why. I want what's owed to me. What I earned." Her gaze slid back to Martha. "What was taken from me."

Martha went still beside Ezra. His free hand curled into a fist under the table.

"Taken?" The quiet intensity in Ezra's voice silenced the room. "The woman who inspired 'Whispers of You'—which I wrote alone—is sitting right here next to me. The woman who's lived every line of that song with me. You can take half the royalties, Ivy, but you'll never measure up to my wife. And we both know it."

"Ezra," Jeremy barked.

Ivy's perfect composure cracked, her features contorting as she hissed, "You didn't seem to think that when—"

"That's enough," Thorne cut in. "Let's keep this professional."

"Yes, let's stay focused on the terms," Jeremy said quickly. He pulled out a document. "We're prepared to include a comprehensive confidentiality agreement. No parties discuss the settlement details or make any public statements except through approved channels."

"Acceptable," Thorne said, glancing at the document Jeremy slid over. "Provided the fifty percent royalties and co-writing credit remain."

"With one condition." Jeremy's voice was steady. "Mr. Falconer retains control over the wording of the public announcement."

A frown crossed Ivy's face. Good. She shouldn't have this all her way.

"That's not—" she began, but Thorne held up a hand.

"We'll need to review the announcement before it goes out."

"Of course," Jeremy said. "But final approval rests with my client."

Thorne conferred quietly with Ivy.

The junior lawyer's fingers flew over his laptop keyboard, updating the agreement in real time.

"Agreed," Thorne said finally. "Fifty percent past and future royalties, co-writing credit, mutual confidentiality, and coordinated announcement. Do we have a deal?"

Jeremy looked at Ezra, who gave a curt nod. What choice did he have?

"We have a deal."

The next few minutes passed in a blur of efficient activity as Ezra and Martha sat quietly. The junior lawyer made final adjustments to the document. A printer hummed in the corner. Thorne reviewed the pages on screen and suggested two minor changes.

Through it all, Ivy kept her eyes on Ezra's face, her smile growing with each passing moment. Despite his outburst, he could tell that she knew what this was costing him. And it wasn't just two point seven million pounds.

The final copy emerged from the printer.

Thorne gave it a last look, then slid it across the table. "Once you sign here, Mr. Falconer, we can all put this unfortunate business behind us."

Hardly unfortunate for Ivy. Or Thorne. What would the lawyer get, thirty-three percent of Ivy's fat payout?

Ivy leaned back in her chair, fingers steepled beneath her chin, that same slight smile still playing on her lips.

Martha's hand trembled in his as Ezra reached for the pen.

The conference room door burst open.

"Wait!" Zach's voice filled the room. "Don't sign anything!"

Chapter Forty-Nine

OR A MOMENT, EVERYONE in the conference room froze. Zach stood in the doorway, out of breath, clutching an ancient MacBook. A sheen of sweat covered his forehead.

Ezra dropped the pen, heart thundering.

Thorne was first to speak. "This is completely irregular," he spluttered. "You can't just burst in—"

"I need to speak to my brother." Zach's voice was firm. "Now."

"We're in the middle of—"

"A brief recess," Jeremy said, rising from his chair. "Ten minutes." He nodded to his junior associate. "Thomas, please stay and keep our friends company."

Ezra got to his feet, his hand still firmly around Martha's.

"This way." Jeremy gestured toward another conference room down the hall. Were they allowed to use it? Who cared?

Ezra, Martha, Zach, and Jeremy walked inside, and Jeremy pushed the door closed behind himself.

Zach placed the laptop on the table. "Remember this, Ez?"

Ezra stared at the scratched case, the worn Apple logo. "That's my old MacBook. From before the studio upgrade—" His voice caught as the implications hit him.

"Wait..." Zach was already pulling a charger from his bag. He plugged it in where Jeremy indicated a floor outlet. "I got Martha's text this morning," he continued as the laptop powered up. "About you conceding to Ivy. I was gutted—could not believe this was happening. Then as I turned on my laptop—you know, the one you gave me a couple of weeks ago—I remembered it was yours. And how many others you had given me over the years."

Ezra stared at the computer, his mouth dry.

Zach said, "I tried calling you both, but your phones were off. Probably already in with Jeremy." He grinned. "I'm expecting a couple of speeding tickets from the cameras I passed getting here. Worth every penny."

The ancient machine wheezed to life. Zach's fingers flew over the keyboard.

Martha squeezed Ezra's arm as Zach navigated through folders.

"Here." Zach turned the screen toward them. "Look at this."

Ezra's breath caught. There in the Finder window was a GarageBand icon next to a file named 'Whispers_draft1.band', dated March 15, 2019.

"I can't believe I forgot about this," Ezra muttered. "When I switched from GarageBand to Logic Pro, I didn't bother transferring my old projects."

"That's not all." Zach clicked through to another folder labeled 'Pidgin Logs.' "These are from your old Pidgin account—the one you used back then."

Chat logs filled the screen. Ezra's eyes caught fragments of a conversation with Ivy from spring 2019:

IvyLyricVine: wow just heard ur new song rough cut! what's that 1st verse about??

EzTunes_Falconer: martha at dawn. thx! not feeling the bridge rn tho

IvyLyricVine: yeahhh i get that... but that melody is beautiful

EzTunes_Falconer: still working on it tbh. gonna fix up the arrangement more in studio

IvyLyricVine: cant wait to hear the final!

Next to him, Ezra heard Martha gasp, "Thank You, Jesus!"

"There's more." Zach scrolled down. "Pages of her acknowledging it was your song. Asking about your inspiration. Even offering suggestions for the bridge—as a friend, not a co-writer."

Ezra's legs went weak. He sank into a chair, pulling Martha down beside him.

"Jeremy?" His voice was hoarse. "Is this enough?"

His lawyer studied the screen, expression sharpening. "Time stamps, metadata, contemporary messages showing her clear acknowledgment of your sole authorship?" A smile spread across his face. "This doesn't just prove your case, Ezra. This blows hers out of the water. She can't claim you stole a song she clearly knew you wrote."

"Thank God," Ezra said, his throat tightening.

"And there's more," Zach said. "Demo recordings. Early drafts. All with clear creation dates that predate any studio sessions."

Martha's fingers trembled against Ezra's. "He did it," she whispered. "God helped us find proof. Zach... I don't know what to say."

Ezra stared at his brother. All those laptops he'd handed down over the years, teasing Zach about his inability to keep up with technology. And now...

"I can't believe you found this."

Zach grinned. "Neither could I, Mr. EzTunes Falconer. The moment I saw those messages, I drove straight here. Not bad for a guy who can't find the 'on' switch, right?" He sobered. "I'm just glad I made it in time."

Ezra's head felt light. If Zach had arrived a minute later—

He stood, pulling his brother into a fierce hug.

"More than in time." Jeremy was already typing on his phone. "Thomas confirms they're still in the conference room. Ivy's getting impatient, but they haven't left." He looked up at Ezra. "Ready to go back in there and show them what we've found?"

Ezra took a deep breath, then blew it out. This time, when he walked into that conference room, he wouldn't be surrendering anything.

He stepped forward, reaching for Martha's hand. "Let's do it. I want to see Ivy's face when she realizes her lie has fallen apart."

Chapter Fifty

ZRA WORKED HARD TO contain the face-splitting grin that wanted to burst out, keeping his features carefully neutral as they filed back into the conference room.

Martha's hand was steady in his now, and Zach followed with the laptop. The morning sun still blazed through the glass walls, but everything else had changed.

Ivy stared at him through narrowed eyes.

He held her gaze for a moment, then turned toward Martha, pulling her seat out for her and making sure she was settled.

They linked hands again, this time on top of the conference table.

"My apologies for the interruption." Jeremy's voice was smooth as he resumed his seat. "But some pertinent evidence has just come to light. Evidence that rather changes the situation."

Thorne's gaze sharpened. "We were about to complete the signing of our agreement. Our client is prepared to continue, despite this highly irregular interruption."

"Quite. I believe you'll want to see this first." Jeremy gestured to Zach, who set up the laptop where both legal teams could view it. "This is Mr. Falconer's old MacBook from 2019. The one he used before upgrading his studio setup."

Ivy's lips tightened, and Ezra allowed himself a small smile.

"If you'll note the creation date on this GarageBand file..." Jeremy turned the screen slightly. "March 15, 2019. Some months before any studio sessions began."

"That proves nothing," Ivy said quickly. "I was already collaborating with—"

"I'm not finished." Jeremy's tone remained pleasant but firm. He navigated to the chat logs. "These are contemporary messages between Ms. Willis and Mr. Falconer. I draw your attention particularly to this exchange."

Ezra watched as Ivy's perfectly maintained composure began to slip. Her face went pale as she read her own words from five years ago, acknowledging his sole authorship of the song.

"This could be fabricated," Thorne cut in. "Files can be altered."

"The metadata is intact," Jeremy said. "But more importantly, these messages come from an account Mr. Falconer hasn't used in years. The time stamps, the conversation threads, the context—all consistent with

2019. Your own digital forensics team is welcome to verify."

Martha's thumb brushed across Ezra's knuckles. He fought to keep his breathing steady, to not show the fierce satisfaction rising in his chest as Ivy's lawyers huddled together, speaking in urgent whispers.

"There are pages more," Jeremy continued. "All showing Ms. Willis's clear understanding that this was Mr. Falconer's original composition. Not to mention the early demos, the rough drafts—all with verifiable creation dates."

Ivy's fingers were white where they gripped the edge of the table. "I don't—that is—" She stopped short. For once, she seemed to have no words.

"I suggest," Jeremy said, "that we take a short break. Give everyone time to... reassess their position." He smiled. "Unless you'd prefer we proceed with a countersuit for defamation?"

Thorne straightened his tie. "A brief recess would be appropriate." His cultured voice had lost some of its polish. "Thirty minutes?"

"Of course." Jeremy gathered his papers unhurriedly. "When we return, we'll be discussing the wording of Ms. Willis's retraction. Including a full admission that she knowingly made false claims about the song's authorship."

Ivy's head snapped up.

"Now see here—" Thorne began.

"The alternative," Jeremy said, still pleasant but firm, "is that we release these chat logs to the media. Let them see exactly how long Ms. Willis has known the truth about 'Whispers of You.'" He stood. "Shall we reconvene at noon?"

Ezra felt Martha's slight tremor of suppressed emotion beside him. Or maybe it was his own hands shaking. He didn't dare look at her. Not yet. Not until they were safely out of the room.

"Noon." Thorne's voice was tight. "We'll need to discuss this with our client."

Ezra waited until they were well down the hallway before pulling Martha into his arms.

"Thank God," she whispered against his chest.

Zach grinned. "I thought her head was going to explode when Jeremy mentioned the retraction. And did you see her face? When she read her own words on that screen?"

Ezra just held onto his wife, still processing how completely the situation had turned around. Ten minutes ago, he'd been about to sign away his song, his earnings, and his reputation in order to protect her—a choice he would easily make a million times over again if he had to. But now it was all over. Martha was safe and he still had everything else. With this sweet vindication, God had done the impossible.

"Well done, everyone." Jeremy was already on his phone. "I'm updating Fiona. She'll want to coordinate the media response once we have Ivy's retraction in hand." He looked up. "I don't anticipate much resistance. Those messages are incriminating, and Thorne knows it. He'll advise her to cut her losses."

"What do you think they're discussing in there?" Martha asked, wiping tears from her eyes.

"Damage control," Jeremy said. "Scrambling over how to salvage what's left of her reputation. Whether she has any legal recourse against us for threatening to release the chat logs." He smiled slightly. "She doesn't, by the way. Truth is an absolute defense."

Ezra finally found his voice. "I still can't believe..." He turned to his brother. "Zach, I don't even know how to thank you."

Zach grinned. "Paying off my speeding tickets would be nice. And hand-me-down laptops for life."

Ezra laughed, clapping his brother on the shoulder. "You've got yourself a deal. Speeding tickets, parking tickets, road tolls, impound fees, and all the old Apple tech you can handle."

Chapter Fifty-One

ARTHA SAT BESIDE EZRA as Ivy's trembling hand moved across the document. The woman who'd swept into the conference room three hours ago radiating triumph was gone. Her cream silk suit was slightly crumpled now and her lips trembled as she brushed a strand of hair off her face.

"Initial here as well." Jeremy pointed at another spot on the sheet of paper.

Martha studied Ivy's downturned face. The mask of sophisticated confidence had cracked, revealing something raw and desperate beneath. Something familiar. Martha remembered that feeling—of being not quite enough, of watching someone else inhabit a world you desperately wanted to belong to.

Ivy's hand shook so badly she had to start her signature over.

"And here." Jeremy turned another page.

A complete retraction. An admission that she'd knowingly made false claims. An apology for any damage to Ezra's reputation. The words were Jeremy's, but they'd be released under Ivy's name. Her career in the industry was probably over.

Martha's hand found Ezra's under the table. They'd won. More than won—they'd been completely vindicated. Everything Ivy had tried to do—destroy their marriage, wreck Ezra's reputation, financially cripple him—all of it had failed.

But watching Ivy's humiliation brought her no satisfaction.

Lord, help me forgive her. The prayer rose unbidden in Martha's heart. *You were able to forgive Your enemies while they were in the very act of crucifying You. Please help me let go of any bitterness against Ivy.*

"That's everything," Jeremy said, gathering the papers.

Ivy finally looked up. Her gaze met Martha's across the table and for a moment, Martha glimpsed such emptiness there that her chest ached.

All that plotting, all those lies, all that manipulation—and for what? In the end, Ivy sat here alone. No husband by her side. No true friends to support her. Just expensive lawyers who were already edging away from their toxic client.

"I think we're done here," Thorne said, pushing his chair back, looking anywhere but at Ivy.

Jeremy exchanged a whisper with Ezra before standing up straight.

"Just to be clear," the lawyer said, gathering his papers, "Mr. Falconer has decided not to pursue damages, despite having grounds for a substantial defamation claim."

Martha squeezed Ezra's hand. Despite all she had done, he didn't want to kick Ivy when she was down.

Something flickered in Ivy's eyes—surprise, maybe relief. She glanced at Ezra, who looked back at her, his gaze steady but not unkind.

As everyone stood to leave, Martha felt a sudden urge to say something. Not to gloat or condemn, but... what? She wasn't sure.

But before she could form the words, Ivy turned abruptly and walked out, Thorne and his associates following close behind.

In the hallway, Martha caught a last glimpse of Ivy's rigid back as she disappeared into the elevator. All that carefully constructed poise couldn't quite hide her defeat.

The events of the past hours—the past days—slammed into Martha like a tidal wave. The fear, the fury, the despair, Ezra's selfless sacrifice, the unexpected and overwhelming relief. Her fingers trembled in Ezra's hand, and the fluorescent lights suddenly seemed too bright.

"You okay?" Ezra's voice was soft beside her.

"Yes. I just..." She hesitated. "Your reputation, your career, all that money—you were a heartbeat away from giving it all up rather than see me hurt." Her throat tightened as she looked up into his eyes. "It just—it takes my breath away. I love you so much, Ezra." Tears welled up as she buried her face in his chest.

Ezra rubbed small circles on her back. "Everything I have—my music, my career, all of it—it means nothing compared to you. I'd make that choice a million times over. You're my song, Martha. My inspiration. My heart. The rest is just... details."

He held her for a long moment, allowing her the release she needed as her tears flowed.

When she had herself under control again, she pulled back slightly. "Thank you. I pity Ivy, though. Isn't that strange? I think I'm ready to let it go. All of it."

His eyes searched her face. "Eden talked to you about forgiveness, didn't she?"

"How did you know?"

"Because I had a similar conversation with Noah." He drew her closer. "He reminded me that bitterness only hurts the person holding onto it."

Martha leaned into him, grateful for his strength, his wisdom, his love. They'd walked through fire together and come out stronger. While Ivy...

"Let's go home," she said softly.

Chapter Fifty-Two

HE LATE EVENING SUNLIGHT streamed through the floor-to-ceiling windows of London's Westminster Park Hotel's conference room, casting its glow over the hive of activity and bathing Ezra in warmth.

Fiona had done well to pull together this press conference so quickly, just hours after Ivy dropped her co-writing claims. Ezra and Martha had just enough time to go home, shower, and change—Martha into a purple silk blouse and tailored gray pants, Ezra into a charcoal suit.

He stood at the podium in front of a line of microphones. Martha's presence grounded him, the subtle scent of lavender teasing his senses. She radiated calm, which amazed him, given the rollercoaster events of the day.

The room buzzed with journalists and photographers. What were they expecting to hear? Denials? News of a court case? His capitulation to Ivy's demands? It was time to finally let the world know.

"Thank you all for coming out today," Ezra began, his amplified voice clear and steady. "I want to share some good news. The claims about who really wrote 'Whispers of You' are now cleared up." He paused, letting the room absorb the moment as cameras clicked. "While I can't dive into the specifics, I'm pleased to say it's been confirmed beyond doubt that I am the sole writer of the song."

Questions burst from the crowd. Ezra caught fragments. "Ms. Willis—" "—any comment on—" "—legal action—"

He held up a hand. "I won't be discussing details about how the matter was resolved except to say it's completely and emphatically settled. My focus now is on moving forward with my music. I'm happy to take a few questions."

"Mr. Falconer!" A woman near the front raised her hand. "Jessica Lane, *The Guardian*. It sounds like Ms. Willis's claims were disproved, but she has been very vocal about them for several days. Will you be pursuing damages against her?"

"No, I will not be pursuing damages against Ms. Willis. As a follower of Christ, I've received grace myself and choose to extend it."

"Paul Thompson, *Rolling Stone*. Congratulations on this outcome. How do you feel about so many of your industry colleagues taking Ms. Willis's side?"

How should he answer this one? How did he feel about most of his colleagues, including people he had considered friends, turning on him? His unvarnished thoughts would not be printable.

He spoke slowly, feeling out his words. "I think it shows something positive about our industry—that people are willing to support someone they believe has been wronged. That readiness to listen to grievances is important and, I believe, healthy. It keeps us all accountable. Though perhaps the lesson here is that we should strive to hear both sides of any story before rushing to judgment."

"I have a question for Morgan," someone called out. "Laura Kim, *Billboard*. Morgan, do you have any response to the sponsors who dropped you—particularly Maison Duval pulling Serenade—over your support for your husband?"

Ezra moved aside to allow Martha space in front of the microphones.

"Not really," she said. "Standing by my husband was the easiest decision I've ever made. He's one of the most honest and principled people I know, and supporting him through this was a privilege. I have no regrets."

"My wife has sacrificed a great deal to stand by me," Ezra added, leaning toward the mics over Martha's shoulder. His throat tightened, roughening his voice. "She chose truth over profit, integrity over image. I'm incredibly blessed, and I couldn't be more proud of her."

An avalanche of camera clicks and flashes followed as Ezra blinked away the rush of moisture in his eyes.

Jeremy stepped forward. "We'll take one more question. Only one question."

"Mr. Falconer, Tony Clark, *Music Weekly*. What's next for you? Do you have any upcoming projects?"

"Actually, yes." Ezra smiled. "I'm excited to announce a collaboration with my wife and my brothers Levi and Zach on a charity album. The proceeds will support New Beginnings Outreach, which provides housing and support for young people aging out of the care system." He paused, then continued, "And as part of this project, Martha—um, Morgan—and I will be recording our own version of 'Whispers of You.'"

Murmurs rippled through the room.

Ezra said, "It feels right, especially now that this song, which was always about our journey together, should finally be performed by us both in a way that gives back to a community we want to support."

Martha's fingers tightened around his, and he could feel her quick intake of breath. They hadn't discussed this—the idea had just popped into his head this very second—but from the way she squeezed his hand, he knew she approved.

"Thank you, everyone," Jeremy said as the room erupted with questions. "That's all for today."

As they left the podium, Ezra's hand settled on the small of Martha's back, cameras still flashing behind them. Just days ago, he'd been about to sign away his song. Now, walking tall with his wife beside him, he felt nothing but gratitude.

The door closed behind them, shutting out the clamor of the journalists and their questions. In the quiet of the hotel corridor, Martha turned to face him.

"You handled that perfectly," she said. "And I love that we'll finally record 'Whispers' together. And it'll bless Adria's charity project. That was absolutely inspired."

He squeezed her hand. "Ready to start working on that charity album?"

"More than ready." Her smile was bright. "Let's make some music worth hearing."

He cupped her face in his hands and kissed her tenderly.

Martha's arms slid around his waist as she kissed him back. Every time she melted into him like this, he fell in love all over again.

Later that evening, scrolling through entertainment news sites, they discovered that the dominant image wasn't from the press conference at all. Instead, every outlet ran with a hastily snapped photo of their hallway kiss—Morgan and Ezra Falconer, lost in their own world, clearly very much in love.

The kiss had gone viral on social media, with body language experts weighing in on what it said about the couple.

"I guess someone left a door open," Martha said, laughing.

"Good." Ezra pulled her closer on the sofa. "Let them see the truth."

Chapter Fifty-Three

ARTHA SAT STRAIGHT-BACKED in Harmony Records' glass-walled conference room, grateful for Jeremy's steady presence beside her. Because they were severely outnumbered.

Across the polished table, the label's CEO Cameron Griffith and three other executives watched her with carefully neutral expressions. Their lawyers flanked them like a row of expensive suits.

Martha took a deep breath, steadying herself. She and Ezra had prayed about her proposal, discussing it at length with input from Jeremy and Fiona following the events with Ivy. All she needed to do was keep her cool and remember her talking points.

"I'm very grateful for everything the label's done for my career," Martha began. "We've had incredible success together. But I need to grow as an artist. I want to focus more on the actual music—my voice, the songwriting, creating something that sticks around."

Cameron sat back, steepling his fingers. "But your current direction works perfectly right now. 'Resonance' is smashing streaming records. Your tour numbers are off the charts. Why fix what isn't broken?"

Claire Peterson, Head of A&R, nodded. "Our research backs this up. You're connecting with every audience we want to reach."

"I hear you," Martha said. "But we can keep that success going with a more mature sound. My voice has always been my biggest strength. I want to lean into that."

"Feels like going backwards," Cameron said, crossing his arms. "We've put a lot into building the Morgan brand. The tours, the sponsorships, the whole package—it's gold."

Jeremy spoke up. "Speaking of that winning formula, I need to bring up a serious issue about Ivy Willis—the songwriter you brought in for Mrs. Falconer's next project. Without Mrs. Falconer's input, I might add."

Cameron's frown deepened. "Ivy Willis has written hits for some of our biggest artists. She has a solid track record."

"Had," Jeremy cut in smoothly. "Until she tried to steal credit for a song she didn't write and caused problems for my client's family. Ms. Willis provoked a very public legal mess involving my client's husband, which, may I remind you, led to significant financial losses for my client. Given these facts, I have to ask what kind of screening process Harmony Records has for its creative partnerships."

"That whole situation was... messy." Claire shifted in her seat.

Jeremy nodded. "More than messy. It shows what can go wrong when a label doesn't line up creative partnerships with what their artists want and believe in. Martha needs to think about how Harmony Records can help her grow as an artist who stands for something real. Trying to keep her in a box that doesn't fit anymore isn't just bad business—it could really hurt her career."

Good old Jeremy. Martha watched the executives exchange glances.

She kept her voice steady. "I trusted you all with the creative decisions. But now I need more say in those choices. I want to work on material that really shows what my voice can do, that connects with people on a deeper level."

"People are connecting just fine now," Cameron said, but he sounded less sure. "The numbers—"

"The numbers are great, and I'm proud of what we've achieved," Martha said, gesturing with her hands. "But we're missing out here. There's an entire audience out there looking for something more meaningful. This isn't about changing just for the sake of it—it's about growing with our fans and picking up new ones as their taste in music gets more sophisticated."

Claire nodded. "You know, I have to say the news about you recording 'Whispers of You' with Ezra has gotten people talking. The press is eating it up."

Martha nodded. "Exactly! Going deeper with my music isn't just following my heart. It's smart business too. We could reach people we're not even counting right now. We're not just talking about making music—we're talking about making an impact and keeping my brand strong down the line. This is about making music that lasts."

Cameron tapped his chin with a pen. "The duet version of 'Whispers'—that could be interesting. We'd want to be involved in that release."

Martha frowned. "But it's going on my family's charity album."

"Which could go through Harmony," Claire jumped in, leaning forward. "We've got the marketing muscle, the distribution channels—"

"That's something we can talk to Zach Falconer about," Jeremy said. "He's handling the contracts for the album's production and distribution. I think he might be open to discussing it. Harmony's distribution network could really boost what we raise for New Beginnings."

Martha nodded. "And it's perfect timing to introduce my new sound and brand. People's reaction to the announcement shows they're ready for something different from me. Something more real."

"What about your current commitments?" Cameron asked. "The tour schedule, the sponsors—it's all built around your current image."

"We can work out how to transition," Martha said. "I'm not saying we throw everything out overnight. But going forward, I need more say in my image and creative direction."

Cameron drummed his fingers on the table. "A gradual transition might work. We could test the waters with the charity album." He glanced at Claire.

"We'll need to iron out the details," Jeremy said. "Both for the charity album and Martha's upcoming projects."

"Of course." Claire was already making notes. "We could set it up so you get more creative control as we hit certain goals. How does that sound?"

As they worked through the details, Martha felt a deep sense of peace. This was right. This was the direction she needed to take. She could align her music and her image with her values and no longer feel like her career was pulling her away from what really mattered. She breathed a prayer of thanks.

"I think we're done here," Jeremy said finally, gathering his papers.

Martha stood, shaking hands with the executives. She'd walked into this room expecting a fight. Instead, she'd found a way forward. Only by God's grace.

Chapter Fifty-Four

ARTHA'S EXHAUSTION AFTER HER long meeting at Harmony Records lifted as soon as she found Ezra in his studio, his face lit by his monitor's glow.

"You're not going to believe how well the meeting went," she said, perching on the edge of his desk.

"Tell me everything." He pushed back from his keyboard.

"They've agreed to my changing direction—not just my sound, but the whole image." She let out a breath. "No more provocative performances or suggestive marketing. I can just focus on the music."

His eyes softened. "That's wonderful news."

"I know!" She squeezed his hand. "I think Jeremy mentioning Ivy might have helped them see reason. He brought her up just when they were getting difficult."

He raised his eyebrows. "Using the whole Ivy situation as leverage? Smart thinking."

"And there's more. They want in on the charity album, thanks to all the buzz around us recording 'Whispers of You' together. We told them they'll need to talk to Zach, but I think it might be really helpful for the project. What do you think?"

"That sounds wonderful. I'm sure Zach and Levi will be very interested. Sounds like you've had a super productive day." He pulled her onto his knee. "I've had some good news, too. Remember Dan, the music supervisor from *Promise Ridge*?"

"Of course."

"He's moved to StreamVista. They're developing this huge period drama—think *Downton Abbey* meets *North and South*. He wants me to score the whole first season."

"Ezra! That's wonderful!"

"And even better, I just got off a video call with Levi." He linked his hands around her waist. "Cedric's doing much better. They're talking about coming home in a couple of weeks."

"Thank God." Martha relaxed against him, soaking in all the good news. After everything they'd been through, it felt like all the wayward pieces were finally falling into place.

"Actually..." Ezra's voice softened. "I've been waiting for the right moment." He reached past her to open his desk drawer. "This felt like it."

Her breath caught as he pulled out a small velvet box.

"I know nothing can replace the original," he said, opening the box. "But I hoped..."

Inside lay a flat court platinum wedding band, identical to his own. The metal caught the soft studio lighting, glowing warm against the dark velvet.

"It's perfect," she whispered, touching it gently.

"There's an engraving." He slipped the ring from its cushion and held it where she could see.

She tilted it to catch the light, squinting at the tiny text.

"The jeweler tried to talk me into something shorter," he admitted with a sheepish smile, "but I wanted every word."

She finally made out the words carved in elegant script inside the band—*Martha, my heart whispers of you.*

Tears sprang to her eyes.

He took her hand. "It's always been you, Martha. Only you."

She nodded, unable to speak as he slipped the ring onto her finger. It fit perfectly, the weight of it familiar and right. When she finally found her voice, she said, "I love you."

He brushed away her tears with his thumb. "I love you too. Always have. Always will."

Chapter Fifty-Five

EZRA STOOD IN THE wings of Grace Community Church on a crisp September evening, peering through a gap in the curtains at the packed sanctuary.

Perhaps it was an unusual choice for such a high-profile launch concert. But Ezra, his brothers, and Martha agreed it made sense to launch "Sheltered Hearts" from here. GCC was their spiritual home, and closely affiliated with Adria's New Beginnings Outreach charity.

The atmosphere was electric. Industry executives filled several rows, their designer suits a sharp contrast to the casual wear of the GCC regulars.

Above them, a projection screen displayed streaming numbers, which climbed steadily as viewers from around the world tuned in.

The audience was still buzzing from Levi's performance of "Hometown Melody," his one songwriting credit on the album. A deeply personal piece inspired by his and Adria's love story, it had already become a fan favorite during pre-release streaming.

But the surprise highlight of Ezra's evening so far was his performance of "Shelter," featuring a fresh arrangement by the young producer Jim Chen. Jim had found a way to make it contemporary without losing its heart. The positive response proved Martha had been right about building bridges between generations.

The best was yet to come, though. His gaze returned to Martha. She sat in the front row between Beth and Adria, radiant in that flowing yellow dress he'd picked out months ago for her perfume launch. The one she'd originally set aside in favor of Kelsey's golden sequins.

Now she wore it with such natural grace—elegant, dignified, and somehow more radiant than ever. Such a contrast to the Morgan who'd performed "Resonance" at the perfume launch. This was Martha as she truly was.

"Before our final performances tonight," Zach announced, his voice filling the sanctuary, "I have some amazing news to share." He gestured to the projection screen, where streaming numbers were vividly displayed. "Every stream of 'Sheltered Hearts' directly contributes to the New Beginnings Outreach housing project. Combined with album pre-orders and tonight's live stream revenue, we've not only met our funding goal—we've exceeded it by fifty percent."

The sanctuary erupted in cheers. On the screen, the numbers kept climbing as more viewers tuned into the live stream.

"That's over one point five million pounds raised so far," Zach continued, his voice thick with emotion as he grinned at Levi and Adria. "Construction begins next month and proceeds from ongoing album sales will fund the next phase of the project. These young people will have a real chance at a fresh start."

In the front row, Adria pressed her hands to her mouth as Levi wrapped his arms around her.

"Friends, we've done it!" Zach held a lengthy pause, letting anticipation build. "And the evening's not over yet."

The audience, sensing there was more to come, leaned in eagerly.

Ezra grinned. His brother knew how to milk the moment.

Zach's smile broadened. "And now, the moment you've all been waiting for. Because I know you're not here to see me talk. Please welcome—the incredible, the incomparable Ezra and Martha—Morgan—Falconer, performing 'Whispers of You.'"

Thunderous applause resonated off the church's high ceilings as Martha rose and walked onto the stage. The applause didn't stop until she stood in front of the microphone.

Ezra walked out to join her, cradling his Martin D-28. Everyone here had heard the song countless times before as the polished pop hit that had broken streaming records. But now, he would perform it the way he always intended it to be—an intimate, heartfelt ode to the love of his life.

His fingers danced over the strings in the gentle intro. Gazing at Martha, he began to sing. "In the quiet of the morning when the world's still asleep, I hear whispers of you in the dreams that I keep. And in the sunrise that paints the sky brand new, the light dances softly with whispers of you."

She joined him in the chorus, their voices blending like two hearts united in love. "Whispers of you, in the breeze that flows through the fields where the wildflower grows. In every shadow, in every hue, my heart softly whispers, it whispers of you."

Strings lifted up the song, and Martha took the second verse solo. The sanctuary held its breath, and Ezra's heart swelled at the heartbreaking beauty of her gift. Phone lights swayed gently in the darkness as her rich, warm voice filled every corner of the space.

"When the melody is silent, when I've lost my song, I hear whispers of you telling me to be strong. When I've lost all hope, can't find a way through, the promise of tomorrow, it whispers of you."

Their final chorus together brought tears to his eyes. No auto-tune, no overwhelming production. Just their voices, guitars, and gentle strings, telling their story through his words and her soul.

The audience erupted, rising to their feet in a thunderous ovation. As the applause filled the church,

Martha turned to Ezra with a warm smile, extending her hands toward him in a gesture that said, "This is all yours."

She joined in the applause, and the sound rose to deafening heights.

His heart thrummed with such overwhelming joy, it felt like it would burst right out of his chest.

Claire Peterson and Cameron Griffin were on their feet, beaming. The streaming numbers kept climbing. It looked like Harmony Records approved.

The last song of the night was a new one, which Ezra had written as he and Martha emerged from the nightmare of Ivy's accusations.

Martha moved over to the piano and touched the keys. It began simply—just Martha's exquisite voice rising above gentle piano chords, raw and honest. "We've walked through fire, felt the cold bite of doubt. Silent hours, where words just wouldn't come out. But every storm that raged somehow made us new, learning pieces of us we never knew."

Her voice soared into the chorus, so powerful that Ezra couldn't breathe. "Through it all we've found a way, turning darkest night to day. Hand in hand, stronger we stand, love's true colors vivid and grand. Through it all, through every fall, we rise above, we conquer all. With every tear that made us raw, we built a love that will endure."

The rest of the band entered seamlessly as Martha rose from the piano and walked to center stage, letting the full instrumental arrangement take flight. Her body moved with the music as she channeled all her being through her glorious voice, each note carrying the weight of lived experience—heartbreak, despair, hope, joy, triumph.

This wasn't just a song—it was their testimony of God's grace, their journey from darkness to light, their declaration that the love they had been gifted could withstand any storm.

As she hit the song's final note, Ezra set his guitar aside and pulled her into his arms. The crowd went wild—cheering, whistling, threatening to bring the roof down.

While the waves of ear-shattering applause crashed around them, Martha clung to him, her body shaking with what might have been laughter or tears or both. He wasn't sure whether he was laughing or crying, either. But it didn't matter. This was who she was meant to be. Who they were meant to be.

Together.

Epilogue

DECEMBER SUNLIGHT SLANTED THROUGH the uncurtained windows of Martha and Ezra's empty living room. She knelt with the interior decorator amidst a sea of fabric swatches and paint samples, their voices echoing off walls stripped clean of Ivy's carefully curated vision.

Ezra and Zach leaned on the kitchen counter nearby with laptops open, reviewing the renovation timeline.

"I love the warmth of this," Martha said, touching a swatch of rich copper velvet. "Could we use it for the accent chairs?"

Emma, the decorator, nodded. "You've got a real eye for this! That will be perfect with the wall color you've chosen. And look at these prints for the cushions."

"The timeline looks good," Zach said. "Everything should be ready by the time you lovebirds are back from Thailand." He grinned at Martha. "Assuming you can trust my taste enough to liaise with Emma while you're away."

"After finding that laptop? I trust you with any-thing." She smiled at her brother-in-law. "Besides, you've done an amazing job managing the charity album release."

"Which has officially gone platinum," Ezra added. "The label just confirmed it."

"Who would have thought a charity album could do so well?" Zach shook his head. "Though I suppose having Morgan and Ezra Falconer performing together helped. The two of you are the real dynamic duo."

He chuckled. "Even Maison Duval figured that out—crawling back with that his-and-hers fragrance deal. 'Harmony by Morgan and Ezra Falconer.' Pretty clever marketing, I'll give them that." His voice faltered. "You're an exception to the rule when it comes to celebrity couples."

Martha looked up sharply, but he was already gathering his things. "I should go. Got a meeting about the next phase of funding."

"I'll walk you out." Ezra squeezed Martha's shoulder as he went past.

After Emma packed up her samples, Martha stood alone in the empty room. Just months ago, she'd torn this room apart in a frenzy of pain and betrayal. Now she could hardly believe she'd been that person—so wounded, so desperate.

They could have redecorated sooner—Ezra had been happy to gut the house straight after Ivy conceded. But after working with the counselor Eden recommended, they'd agreed to take some time to heal so they could reclaim their home thoughtfully rather than reactively.

Her gaze traveled to where the mirror had hung, where the bookcase had stood. All gone now, along with every trace of Ivy's influence. The bare walls waited for fresh paint, for new memories, for the home she and Ezra would create together.

Warm arms slid around her waist. "Penny for your thoughts?"

She leaned back against Ezra's chest. "Just thinking about how far we've come."

"Mm." His chin rested on her shoulder. "Four weeks in Thailand. No phones, no cameras. Just us."

"Perfect." She turned in his arms. "We're not doing that again, you know. Being apart for months at a time."

"Never." He pulled her closer. "I don't care how successful either of us becomes—we learned that lesson the hard way."

"So, no solo tours for a while?"

"Of course we can do solo tours. As long as we do them together." He grinned and brushed a kiss against her temple. "The label will just have to work around that."

"You know, Ezra," she said against his chest, "all that Thai food..."

"Mm hm." He kissed the top of her head.

"So..." She bit her lip. "What if I get heavy again?"

"Ooh, more of you to love? I'm here for it, baby," he growled, tightening his hold on her.

Her heart swelled. "You mean that, don't you?"

He pulled back for a moment, gazing into her eyes, her cheek cupped in his hand. "Yes. Your body has always been beautiful to me."

Her eyes filled with tears, which he gently kissed away. What had she done to deserve this man? God was so, so good.

Martha smiled, breathing in the familiar scent of him. Her new wedding band caught the winter sunlight as she lifted her hand to his face. "Ready to go? We've got a flight to catch."

"In a minute." He drew her closer. "Let's just stand here a moment longer. Right here where you knocked over that horrible bookcase."

She laughed against his chest. "You hated that bookcase, too?"

"Loathed it. But I love you."

"I love you too." She closed her eyes, soaking in the quiet joy of being in his arms. Their whispers had become a rich harmony, and from now on, they'd sing it together.

The End

But Wait! There's More!

Thank you for sharing Ezra and Martha's journey back to each other. If you're not quite ready to say goodbye to their world, I have something special waiting for you.

Would you like to hear the actual songs from the story? Yes—"Whispers of You" and the other songs mentioned in the book really exist! In fact, these melodies were playing in my head long before I wrote the first word of the book. They helped shape the story and brought Ezra and Martha's hearts to life.

And, because I wanted to peek a few years down the road and see how Ezra and Martha are getting on, I wrote an extra epilogue showing how the seeds of healing planted in *Small Town Harmony* have blossomed into something beautiful.

I've created an exclusive bonus content portal where you can:

- Listen to "Whispers of You" and five other songs from the story
- Access a special bonus epilogue that peeks into Ezra and Martha's future.

Want in? To access these exclusive extras, visit https://millaholt.com/smalltownharmonybonus/

Zach Has a Story, Too!

Big brother Zach Falconer's journey to his own happily ever after unfolds in *Old Town Symphony*, the final book in the *Rhapsody of Grace* trilogy. And this time, he's not just stepping in to solve someone else's crisis—he's facing his own heart's deepest questions.

Here's more about *Old Town Symphony*:

He knows fame and love don't mix. She never wanted either—until now.

Kezia Blair has always believed that true talent doesn't need shortcuts. But after years of performing to half-empty venues, her dreams of a musical career are fading fast. Now, as a reluctant contestant on the reality TV show *Starbound*, Kezia is forced to make a painful choice: chase stardom at the risk of losing her artistic soul, or stay true to herself and let her shot at success slip away.

Zach Falconer didn't just create *Starbound*—he staked his reputation and future on it. After being burned by an ambitious ex who used him to climb the ladder to fame, Zach is determined to keep his reality show untainted by scandal and his heart safe from pain. The last thing he needs is to fall for a contestant. But Kezia's raw passion and skepticism about the industry challenge everything he thought he knew—awakening feelings he knows he must ignore.

As the competition intensifies, Kezia finds herself drawn to the very man whose vision could make or break her career. Meanwhile, Zach faces an impossible choice: protect the show he's built or risk everything for a love that could destroy them both professionally. In an industry where authenticity rarely survives the spotlight, how will they find the courage to choose love when it might cost them everything?

Order *Old Town Symphony* on my online shop at **https://shop.millaholt.com** or wherever good books are sold online.

About the Author

I write fiction that reflects my Christian faith. I love happy endings, heroes and heroines who discover sometimes hard but always vital truths, and stories that uplift and encourage.

My family and I live in the east of England where we enjoy rambling in the countryside, reading good books, and making up silly lyrics to our favorite songs.

To learn about my other books, visit my website at https://shop.millaholt.com.